KEEPERS

The journey of Stefan Kumansky draws to its conclusion in the city of Altdorf. With the Storm of Chaos – the largest ever invasion from the evil gods and their followers – rising and threatening to break over the civilised lands, Stefan's previous battles will be nothing compared to the one he now faces. The secret society 'The Keepers of the Flame' have uncovered a Chaos plot to strike at the very heart of the Empire. Stefan must free a Chaos cultist from the authorities in order to get vital information on the coming attack. Surrounded by a hand-picked team of adventurers, Stefan must descend into the darkness. But is this cultist all that he seems? With the fickle powers of Chaos, nothing is ever what it first appears and Stefan may have only one chance to stop the hordes of darkness.

Intrigue, danger and excitement abound in the final Stefan Kumansky novel. The Storm of Chaos erupts into the Empire and one man must sacrifice all to hold back the night.

Also by Neil McIntosh

· **THE STEFAN KUMANSKY NOVELS** ·
STAR OF ERENGRAD
TAINT OF EVIL

More Warhammer from the Black Library

· **WARHAMMER NOVELS** ·
RIDERS OF THE DEAD by Dan Abnett
BLOOD MONEY by C. L. Werner
BLOOD & STEEL by C. L. Werner
BLOOD OF THE DRAGON by C. L. Werner
WITCH HUNTER by C. L. Werner
WITCH FINDER by C. L. Werner
VALNIR'S BANE by Nathan Long
HONOUR OF THE GRAVE by Robin D. Laws
SACRED FLESH by Robin D. Laws
DEATH'S MESSENGER by Sandy Mitchell
THE DEAD AND THE DAMNED by Jonathan Green
FORGED IN BATTLE by Justin Hunter
THE MARK OF DAMNATION by James Wallis
ZAVANT by Gordon Rennie

GOTREK & FELIX by William King
TROLLSLAYER • SKAVENSLAYER
DAEMONSLAYER • DRAGONSLAYER • BEASTSLAYER
VAMPIRESLAYER • GIANTSLAYER

A WARHAMMER NOVEL

KEEPERS OF THE FLAME

Neil McIntosh

For Sian, and for Mary

A BLACK LIBRARY PUBLICATION

First published in Great Britain in 2005 by
BL Publishing,
Games Workshop Ltd.,
Willow Road, Nottingham,
NG7 2WS, UK

10 9 8 7 6 5 4 3 2 1

Cover illustration by Geoff Taylor.
Map by Nuala Kennedy.

A CIP record for this book is available from the British Library.

ISBN 13: 978 1 84416 186 7
ISBN 10: 1 84416 186 2

Distributed in the US by Simon & Schuster
1230 Avenue of the Americas, New York, NY 10020.

Printed and bound in Great Britain by
Bookmarque, Surrey, UK.

See the Black Library on the Internet at
www.blacklibrary.com

Find out more about Games Workshop
and the world of Warhammer at
www.games-workshop.com

THIS IS A DARK age, a bloody age, an age of daemons and of sorcery. It is an age of battle and death, and of the world's ending. Amidst all of the fire, flame and fury it is a time, too, of mighty heroes, of bold deeds and great courage.

AT THE HEART of the Old World sprawls the Empire, the largest and most powerful of the human realms. Known for its engineers, sorcerers, traders and soldiers, it is a land of great mountains, mighty rivers, dark forests and vast cities. And from his throne in Altdorf reigns the Emperor Karl-Franz, sacred descendant of the founder of these lands, Sigmar, and wielder of his magical warhammer.

BUT THESE ARE far from civilised times. Across the length and breadth of the Old World, from the knightly palaces of Bretonnia to ice-bound Kislev in the far north, come rumblings of war. In the towering World's Edge Mountains, the orc tribes are gathering for another assault. Bandits and renegades harry the wild southern lands of the Border Princes. There are rumours of rat-things, the skaven, emerging from the sewers and swamps across the land. And from the northern wildernesses there is the ever-present threat of Chaos, of daemons and beastmen corrupted by the foul powers of the Dark Gods. As the time of battle draws ever nearer, the Empire needs heroes like never before.

Claws

North of Here Lie The
Dreaded Chaos Wastes.

Grengrad.

Here Be Trolls...

Praag.

...heim.

middle mountains.

Kislev

Kislev.

Wolfenburg.

Talabheim

The Empire

...dorf.

Karak Kad...

Nuln.

The
Moot.

Sylvania.

Dracken
-hof.

Zhufbar

Averheim.

Black
Water.

Black fire Pass.

...ak
Norn.

CHAPTER ONE
First Came the Rains

IT WAS NEARING midnight, in the last, fading hour of Hexentag when Peter Selendorf realised he was about to die. An hour before, he had made his excuses and left the throng of wealthy diners crowded about their table, to seek solitude in one of the private chambers on the far wing of Gustav Ehrhart's mansion. For a while Selendorf sat looking out into the night, watching the rain tumble in a ceaseless curtain upon the glimmering lights of Altdorf. Rain had been falling, hard and unrelenting, for a day and a night. It fell with such gusto that already the people of the city were wondering whether it would ever stop. Now, seated alone after the banquet, Peter Selendorf realised that, for him, it never would.

He had got close to his enemies. Close enough, almost, to reveal the serpent they had hidden in their midst. So close to tearing away the mask of the traitor. Tonight, he felt sure those same enemies would come to silence him. They'd tried to kill him before, as Sigmar was his witness they had tried. Now, the insistent premonition and a heavy silence in his soul told Peter Selendorf that, tonight, they might finally succeed.

He did not fear death. He did not even especially begrudge the claim that Morr, sombre god of death, would soon lay upon his soul. His had been a life poised on the very edge of chance, balanced between triumph and peril. A secret life shared with only a few loyal comrades who, like him, were committed to one cause above all others. For more than ten years, he had lived his life within the shadows, far from the gaze of the everyday world, battling the dark forces that schemed to enslave the Empire, his cherished land.

Those who toiled in the service of Tzeentch, the dark Lord of Change, were old adversaries. He had grown wise to their ways, always staying one step and one thought ahead. Selendorf had spent long years chasing their shadows, and the game of cat and mouse had grown more perilous with each successive encounter. Now instinct told him they had reached the endgame. The final trap was about to spring shut, and he would be snared within its jaws.

'Peter!'

Selendorf was tugged from his sombre thoughts. He looked up, momentarily distracted from his lonely rumination on death. The familiar figure of his friend and comrade, Gustav Ehrhart, loomed into view. He held an elaborate iron candelabrum aloft in one meaty hand.

'Mercy of Ulric, Peter! Is our company that bad? You've been gone over an hour.'

Ehrhart set the light down carefully on the table and eased his considerable frame into the low chair at Selendorf's side. For a moment they watched the rain beat down upon the labyrinth of streets that stretched out beyond the walls of the house.

'To tell the truth,' Ehrhart said at last, 'their company was pretty poor, even for a host to stomach.' He reached for a flask that sat untouched at his colleague's side, and poured himself some wine.

'Merchants are fools one and all,' he reflected. 'How it irks me that politics dictates that I share my table with their kind. War rages on their very doorstep, and all they care is whether the prices on the Reikmarkt will go up or down.' He sipped at his wine, and sighed. 'If only they knew, eh?'

Peter Selendorf smiled weakly. Ehrhart let the silence sit between them for a few moments then went to the rain-spattered window.

'Do you know what they're saying in the city?' he asked. 'That on a clear night you can see the fires burning around the walls of Middenheim. Would you credit it?'

'Utter nonsense,' Selendorf responded crisply, prompted by the absurdity of the idea. 'By my guess Middenheim is more than five hundred miles distant. The fires of Chaos could burn on the tallest building in all the Old World, and you'd still not see a flicker at that distance.'

'Careful, my friend,' Ehrhart cautioned. 'Our enemies have keen ears, even in Altdorf. Whisper the names of the dark ones softly.' He returned his gaze to the window. The black sheets of rain now obliterated everything, even the baleful glare of the twin moons that usually cast an eerie light upon the witching night of Hexentag.

Ehrhart settled back in the chair. 'But the story shows how the people have become fixed on war in the north. A month ago, few had given so much as a thought to

Middenheim. Now–' he drank deep from his glass. 'Now, they talk of little else.'

Selendorf did not reply. His gaze was fixed upon the rain-swept night, as if momentarily diverted by the idea that he might actually see some echo of the distant fires of war. At last he turned back, favouring his friend with a wan smile.

'Actually,' he said at last, 'I've found my attention drawn closer to home recently.'

Ehrhart frowned. He lifted a ruddy hand to his cheek. 'I knew as much. There's something you're keeping from me.'

Selendorf shook his head in an unconvincing show of denial.

'Come,' Ehrhart persisted. 'We've shared more secrets in these few dark years than those fools at the trough would know in a lifetime. Something's wrong. Tell me. What is it?'

Peter Selendorf let out a short and self-conscious laugh.

'I've just realised,' he said, turning back once more to face his companion, 'that I'm about to die.'

FAR BELOW THE rain-glossed streets of Altdorf, deep within the belly of the ancient city, figures toiled in the subterranean gloom. Some were human. Others were nothing but a cruel mockery of the human form, their bodies and faces disfigured with the first buds of mutation: the stigmata of the Dark Gods. Peter Selendorf would have known every one of them, man or mutant, as his bitter enemy. His enemy and the enemy of everything that stood for hope and light, upon the face of the world. But they toiled, unseen by Selendorf and unseen by the thousands of souls living their lives above.

There were a dozen or more of them, steadily and stealthily excavating a channel through the narrow tunnel that threaded a forgotten path beneath the Imperial city. The tunnel was old: so old it had been forgotten by most who lived their lives in the city above. The creatures that had first built it were long gone. The tunnel had been abandoned, the passageways silted up, barricaded by falls of earth and stone. But, step by slow step, the way was being re-opened, ready for a dark purpose yet to be fulfilled.

Heavy picks and staves cut away at the cloying lime and clay. Words rang out, some in the common language of the man, others in an older, darker tongue. The sound came in waves, each ebb and flow reaching a crescendo until a single voice barked a command that cut off the babble in mid-flow.

'Stop your foul mouths!'

Light flared briefly in the gloom. The speaker tugged a cowl from his face, and glared at the handful figures standing round. It was recognisably a man, though the skin of its face was leeched of all colour, and the flesh was pinched tight against the bone. The eyes that scanned the workers had dulled to an opaque, milky glaze.

'What is it?' the creature hissed. 'Would you wake the sleeping babes of Altdorf? Do you want the watch to cut out your guts before we're even halfway to our destination?'

Muffled curses rang out in response; the voices were quieter now.

'We're half a mile below the stinking ground,' one muttered. 'No one hears us.'

The gaunt-faced man drew out a rapier-thin sword and touched the tip of the blade against the man's throat.

'You'll curb your tongue or I'll cut it loose with this.' He gestured to the mutant figures shuffling through the darkness. 'That goes for the rest of you, too. We're right beneath the city. You'll make as little noise as possible.' His lidless eyes scanned the tunnel, before coming to rest upon one figure that stood apart from the group. The creature stood upon two legs, but something in its reared-up posture marked it as something other than human.

'You,' the leader called. 'How much further now?'

The creature inclined its head, exposing a tapered profile and a jaw matted with a scabrous, grey fur. It looked up at the leader with a black, jewel-like eye. 'Our sacred writings say–' it began.

'I don't give a daemon's spit what your cursed writings say. I want to know how much further we have to crawl through this filthy tomb.'

The rodent creature emitted a low sound, half way between a purr and a growl.

'You must work hard,' the creature replied at last. 'You work hard, we break through before dawn.'

The leader nodded. 'Very well,' he concluded. 'You others heard our friend. Put your backs into it, and hold your tongues. Our god will reward our success. And he won't forgive failure. Whatever the reason.'

He sheathed his blade with a half-muttered curse, and turned back towards the mouth of the tunnel. One by one his servants took up their tools, and followed him into the darkness.

PETER SELENDORF SAT with his host until the first hour of the new day chimed on distant bell-towers. They had not conversed much, but what little Peter had said was of great, perhaps unimaginable, significance. He still wasn't sure whether he should have shared the secret with his friend. But he knew that if he hadn't, there might not come another chance.

Gustav Ehrhart poured more wine from the flagon, and insisted that Peter drink. Selendorf sipped at it, then pushed the glass away.

'I think sober reflection would serve me better,' he commented.

'You are not going to die,' his friend remonstrated, a note of steel creeping into his voice. 'Not if we set our will against it. We've fought them too long to surrender now.'

'Yes,' Peter agreed. 'We have fought them long. Too long, and I am weary. But I fear I shall die tonight, whatever my endeavour.' He smiled, ruefully, and took up the wine. 'Perhaps this is best after all.'

Gustav Ehrhart drew his chair up close. 'Listen to me,' he said, gravely. 'You did the right thing just now. Sharing what you have learned. It's a secret that no man should carry alone.' He glanced about; more from habit than from necessity, for the two were still quite alone. 'If anything were to happen to you, then I would know—'

His voice trailed off. Then his hand slapped down upon the arm of the chair. 'But Taal's breath,' he exclaimed, 'nothing is going to happen. Why should it?' He glanced over his shoulder towards the corridor that led back to the salon where the other guests were dining. The sound of conversation had steadily diminished, until only the occasional crackle of laughter, or hearty exchange of farewells now broke the silence.

'Our friends are fat and feasted,' Ehrhart concluded. 'They're all on their way home to their beds, to dream their dreams of golden fountains and silver streams.'

Selendorf laughed softly, forgetting himself for a moment. 'Let them dream while they may,' he said.

'Stay here,' Ehrhart urged. 'Send your driver home, or let him bed here if he will. In the morning the streets will be safer. Whatever danger you fear lies in wait will surely have passed by then. What do you say?'

Selendorf considered the proposition. Perhaps he should accept the offer. After a good night's sleep, and in the light of a new day, his fears might have receded. All he need do was nod his head, or hold out his glass for it to be replenished, and it would be done. The choice would have been made.

But the Chaos gods and he were old adversaries. Over years of struggle they had come to know each other well, had they not? The ways of the changer were subtle and devious. Perhaps this was the very choice that would lead him to his doom, here in the very heart of his friend's house? Perhaps it was here that he was destined to die.

He looked up at Ehrhart. 'What awaits me, awaits me,' he said. 'And I have taken up far too much of your hospitality already.' He smiled. 'Forgive me, old friend, but I must go.'

He set down his glass. 'Promise me this,' he said. 'That the knowledge I've shared with you this evening will be used wisely if anything happens to me. Promise me you will use it well.'

Ehrhart took both his friend's hands in his own. 'I shall,' he said. 'I promise you, I shall.'

Peter Selendorf turned away from his companion and walked through the now deserted corridors towards the courtyard of the house. There his coachman waited, seated alone upon a narrow bench by the heavy oak doors. His peers had long since departed into the night with their masters.

He favoured his servant with a thin, sorrowful smile. 'I'm sorry, Matthieu. I've been too long,' he said, briskly.

'Come. Fetch the horses. I'll meet you by the gates. We're going home.'

PROGRESS HAD BEEN good, better than expected. Denied their chatter, the gang had put their energy into their work to slowly but surely cut a path through the mud and stone blocking the tunnel. Now the mutant at their head called a halt, and they were utterly still in the half-light. The passageways had been long forsaken; it was many years since any living thing had come this way. The carcasses of dead animals lay amongst the pools of stagnant water, their bleached bones protruding like the masts of sunken ships from the mounds of debris. The place stank of things long dead, of damp and foetid air. For the mutants it reeked too, of the thousand human souls who lay in their beds up above, oblivious to the invaders below, oblivious to the fate about to overwhelm them.

The pale mutant raised his eyes. He could smell their warm, nauseous human stench; their rich blood that was ripe and ready to spill.

'How much further?' he demanded of the skaven.

The rodent creature exhaled; its rancid breath mixed with the foul air of the tunnel.

'Slowly, we come to it,' it said. 'Slow, hard work it is. But not so far now. Soon we come to heart of the city of men. Stinking heart,' it smiled, exposing a row of yellowed teeth, ground to stumps along the line of its jaw. 'City of men forget,' it went on, 'forget about old ones here before. But we do not.'

The mutant surveyed the shadowed, grimy faces of the figures standing in the shadows behind him. His labourers were silent now, not so much as a single word passing between them.

'Soon you will have your chance for commotion,' he assured them. 'Soon there will be a commotion so great, and so loud, it will raise the very dead from their slumbers.'

He gazed into the darkness above, turning his lidless eyes towards the unseen, unknowing multitudes, towards the distant drumming of the rain upon the streets above. The mutant mouthed a silent tribute to his dark master.

'Soon, very soon,' he said.

As THE COACH sped away, and the lights of the house disappeared into the rain-swept night, Peter Selendorf sensed a burden being lifted from his shoulders, quite at odds with the growing anxiety he had felt as he sat in the snug warmth of the house. It was a feeling akin almost to relief, and it took him completely by surprise. Perhaps it was because his destiny was once again in his own hands. In his hands and in the hands of the gods who dealt the fates, whether for good or for ill.

The rain had not relented. Still it battered like a thousand tiny hammers upon the thin roof of the carriage. The coach wheels slithered and spun upon the waterlogged carriageway.

Selendorf drew back the curtain from the window and peered out. He could see nothing, no light or landmark to guide him, but judged that they must be yet some four of five miles from the safety of home – perhaps less if they took the shorter route through the quiet streets of the merchant quarter. He was about to rap on the connecting pane and give Matthieu the command, when another thought came to him. No, they would take another, quite different route. Gustav had been right. There would be no tame surrender to death's embrace. He was not ready for that, not yet. His struggle with the changer had not yet run its course.

He slid back the pane. A gust of wind blew into the cabin, spraying icy rain about him. If Sigmar chose to spare him, he would reward Matthieu well for this journey, so late on this miserable night. He leaned forward as far as he could and yelled a greeting to the figure seated up high behind the horses.

'Not our usual route, Matthieu,' he shouted. 'Steer right up ahead, into Jaegerstrasse, then listen for my command.'

The figure of the driver, swaddled up against the rain in oilskins and a thick leather cape, inclined towards him briefly and seemed to nod his head. Selendorf sank back against the bench seat, chilled through from the sudden exposure to the night air. He rubbed his hands together vigorously, and stamped his feet on the floor of the cabin. He felt a better humour, absent for too long, starting to return.

A few moments later the cabin tilted and the coach started to swing off the main carriageway. But it was turning to the left, down the narrow streets that snaked towards the Altmarkt, not through the brightly lit avenues of the Jaegerstrasse. Selendorf supposed his instruction had been misunderstood, though that seemed unlikely, despite the rain and the howling of the wind. Irritated, he stretched forward again and pulled back the communicating pane a second time.

'Matthieu!' he exclaimed, raising his voice still louder. 'You've gone left at the fork, instead of right. We must go back. Turn around.'

This time the driver made no acknowledgement, but stayed staring ahead. The pace of the coach slowed, but there was no attempt to turn. Selendorf began to think Matthieu was toying with him, punishing him for keeping them so late at the house. Selendorf was just resolving how to punish his insolence, when something caught his attention. It was a hammering of horse hooves, ringing out above the thunder of the rain. The unmistakable sound of urgent pursuit.

Selendorf turned around. Where before there had been only an empty road, now there were at least three riders bearing down upon the solitary carriage like emissaries from Morr.

Had he been a nobleman, or one of the self-obsessed gluttons dining at Ehrhart's table, he would have thought it was a robbery. Consoled, perhaps, that a few coins and a little jewellery were always replaceable, he might have resigned himself to that fate. These things happened, even in Altdorf. But Peter Selendorf did not for one moment mistake the shadowy figures for simple robbers. They may well strip every ounce of silver and gold from his body, but they wanted more than that. It was just as he had foreseen. This was death; the three riders his escorts to the gates of Morr. But he had not come unprepared. Peter Selendorf reached beneath his cloak and fastened his hand tight around the hilt of his sword. By all the gods, they would not earn their prize cheaply.

'Matthieu, take care–'

It was meant as a warning, to tell his driver to stand ready to fight for his very life. But the words had barely left his lips when he realised his single, perhaps fatal, mistake. There was something in that profile, the posture, and the angle of the face… Selendorf did not know what it was. But he knew the figure steering the carriage was not Matthieu. He realised at that moment that his driver was probably dead, and that he was set to join him.

The first of the three pursuers drew level with the coach. Selendorf caught a glimpse of the horse, a sleek beast of monstrous proportions. The rider was clad in robes like a priest. The horseman swung his mount into the side of the carriage, as if intent on driving it off the road.

The coach slowed as it lost momentum. Without waiting for it to stop, Peter pushed open the door of the cabin, and threw himself clear. The ground was hard and soaking wet. Shards of flint raked at his flesh through the thick folds of his clothes. For the briefest of moments Peter Selendorf lay, fighting for breath. Then he was up, running for his very life.

He looked around, ready to confront his attackers. The years had taken a predictable toll on his frame, but he was still a fighter at heart. He drew out his sword with a flourish. Raw anger surged where fear might flow through lesser men.

A horseman materialised out of the darkness, and bore down on him at speed. Selendorf flinched away, narrowly avoiding being trampled into the earth. His sword tracked after his opponent, but it cut only through thin air. More horses, two of them this time: one to his left and one to his right. Selendorf held back until they were all but upon him then he feinted to one side, so close to one of the horses that its flank brushed against his face. As the second horse raced past Selendorf thrust out his blade, lancing the thigh of the rider with surgical precision. A cry of agony from his tormentor gave him hope, as well as satisfaction. Whatever these creatures were, they still bled like mortal men.

But the rational part of his mind told him that this was an unequal struggle. He had to get away from this exposed space, and find a place where he could try to fight on his own terms. He looked around desperately. He was half-blinded by the still driving rain and struggling to make sense of his surroundings. To his left the coach, all its lights extinguished, one of its wheels stuck fast in the ditch. Directly ahead, the three riders turned in formation to attack again. Out of the corner of his eye, he saw a single, narrow alleyway that led off the main highway, too narrow for any horse to pass through. It was a faint hope, but it was the only one he had.

Selendorf ran as hard as he could for the alley. The horses thundered down on him, their hooves drawing up great waves of water in their wake. Somehow, he avoided the rushing beasts again. But this time he could not avoid the riders' swords. He parried one with his own blade; steel rang on steel. A second dealt him a bruising blow to the shoulder, the flat of the blade knocking him off balance. The third found a deeper mark, and cut through the back of his cloak into the flesh between his ribs. He felt a sudden flaring pain then a cold numbness spreading through his shoulder.

The black strip of the alley was just twenty yards away, the sort of distance a gentleman might stroll in the matter of a few moments. But it might as well have been twenty miles. He knew he wouldn't make it. A searing pain replaced the numbness in his shoulder. Still he ran on. There was nothing left to do but run.

He was perhaps less than ten yards from the alley when his attackers caught him. The horseman cut him down casually, knocking him off his feet with a single swipe of his blade then pinned him where he lay with a second, driving blow.

Peter Selendorf lay face down upon the sodden ground for the second time that night. This time he knew he would not rise again. His instincts had proved unerring, but that was of little consolation now.

He lay there for what seemed like an age, before he felt the skewering blade being pulled from out of his leg, and hands grasping hold of his body to flip him over onto his back. Up above, the sibling moons of Morrslieb and Mannslieb glowed, sickly pale through the rain-streaked sky. He gazed up, knowing he would never look upon them again.

They were all standing over him. The three riders and the man – if man he was – who had been driving the coach. The coachman stepped forward and pulled loose the cloths wrapped about his face. He bent down towards his victim.

Selendorf could not make out his face. It was half in shadow, and in any case, his eyes were failing him. The rain blurred his vision and there was blood running from a gouge on his face. But he could smell the stench of the man: it was putrid and foul. He stank of the place that Selendorf would soon be taken to.

Peter opened his mouth. His tongue felt dry and swollen, but he was determined that he would speak before he died.

'Kill me if you must,' he said. 'But know that this is no victory. It isn't over.'

The creature above him tilted its head to one side. Selendorf glimpsed him now: the pale, pockmarked face; the cruel, beaded gleam in his eyes. The man began to laugh, softly at first, then steadily louder. It was an odd, humourless giggling, like a lunatic child's. He pulled out a knife and held it over Peter Selendorf's throat.

'Of course it's not over, not at all,' the man whispered. He raised the knife higher.

'It has only just begun.'

CHAPTER TWO
The Long March to War

THE LINES OF soldiers stretched almost as far as the eye
could see. The massed ranks marched in step along the
Sigmarsallee, towards Altdorf's northern gate. Rows of
wagons drawn by teams of four horses rolled in their
wake, each laden with stores and armaments. The faces
of the men marching, as well as those pressed tight
inside the wagons, were gaunt, tense with fear and anticipation. The Empire was expecting a long campaign. So
far, the great city of Middenheim had held out, but the
war against the dark armies of Chaos was only just
beginning.

Tucked anonymously amongst the crowds of sight-
seers Stefan Kumansky and his comrade Bruno
Haussman stood watching the procession. Every so
often Bruno would use his stocky frame to muscle
through the crush, envying the view afforded by his
comrade's extra height. His efforts were rewarded with

the sight of another five battalions: more than five hundred men advancing along the road to war, rain spattering their newly-minted armour.

'What a sight,' Bruno muttered. 'Surely nothing could stand against such a force?'

'Maybe not,' Stefan agreed. 'But there'll be scarcely a man remaining to defend Altdorf,'

'The war is far away,' Bruno reasoned. 'It'll never touch us here, not while Middenheim holds.'

'Perhaps,' Stefan agreed. 'And perhaps we should be going with them. Offering our swords to the defence of the Empire.'

Bruno laid a hand on his friend's shoulder. 'Let me remind you, we've been on the road for a long year,' he said. 'Giving our all in battle, against those self-same enemies. Ulric's flame, Stefan, we've barely been home a month.'

'True,' Stefan conceded. 'But still it galls me to stand by watching them march to war.'

'Who knows, the tide of war may be turning? They may be back before long. Besides,' Bruno added, more sombrely. 'We have business to attend to here, remember?'

Stefan did remember. The meeting that lay ahead with his brother was very much in his mind. And there was more. He touched the outline of the wafer of paper that lay inside his breast pocket, checking that it was still safe. Business to attend to indeed.

Just at that moment a carriage flanked by liveried outriders pulled into view on the main thoroughfare, travelling in the opposite direction to the soldiers marching to the north gate. As the carriage gathered speed along the Sigmarsallee, people in the crowds lining the street called out, some prostrating themselves upon the ground. A pale face looked out briefly from the carriage window then turned away, before drawing down the window blind. It was Johann Esmer, Grand Theogonist of all Altdorf.

'Well,' Bruno said. 'Not for him the fires of Middenheim.'

'It seems not,' Stefan agreed. 'The Grand Theogonist sacrifices glory to remain at home.'

'To protect our souls,' Bruno added, dryly.

Stefan cast a final glance toward the retreating carriage, then steered his friend away. 'Come on. We've seen enough of this. Time to meet Mikhal.'

The two friends picked their way through the crowd, seeking out the quieter streets on the far side of the Sigmarsallee. Bruno muttered a curse, and tugged his cape up to cover as much of his shock of copper hair as possible.

'Sigmar preserve us from this damned weather,' he said. 'Raining hard enough to douse the fires of Morr. When will it ever end?'

'No sign of it since we've been back in Altdorf,' Stefan replied. 'Not much of a homecoming, eh?'

The two swordsmen crossed Konigsplazt and made their way into the warren of alleyways that wound south across the city towards the docks. On their way they passed taverns, shops and street vendors selling cakes and ale by the pot, the people and places they had known for years. All of it familiar, and yet somehow altered. Altdorf was not the city they had bid farewell to almost a year before. Stefan walked in silence for several minutes before commenting upon the change.

'Seems like every other window has bars across it now,' he said. 'And there's something else you wouldn't have seen a year ago.' He pointed towards the wall that ran the length of an ostler's yard. The whitewashed façade had been freshly daubed with crude but deliberate insignia: linked circles and crossed staves.

'Warding signs,' Bruno said. 'People are frightened, Stefan. Middenheim may be far away, but people feel the breath of war upon their necks.'

'If the Dark Ones ever got this far, it would take more than iron bars and a few runes to keep them at bay,' Stefan replied, grimly. He picked his way across a heavily pot-holed section of the street, cursing as water splashed up over his shoes and breeches.

'I suppose we should be glad that the rain has washed away some of the stench of the place,' he said. 'If for nothing else.'

'I'm not sure I like the smell of what's left behind much better,' Bruno retorted. 'Up ahead, for instance.' He pointed down the alley towards a small group of figures that was crossing the street ahead of them. Each was weighted down with circlets of heavy chains, like garlands about their necks, and each carried some kind of wooden flail or switch, some adorned with nails. As they walked they chanted, accentuating the rhythm of their chanting by beating at their own bodies. The contorted faces of the men wore an empty, feral look, and their eyes blazed with the raw anger of religious fervour. Blood dripped from open sores on their emaciated bodies, and spotted the flagstones where they walked.

'Flagellants,' Bruno said, sourly. 'Perhaps the war is already here. The war that eats at the soul.'

Stefan shook his head in disbelief at the savage procession. 'Truly not the homecoming I was expecting.' Seeing the flagellants had immediately made him think of his brother. It was not an association he found comfortable to make.

He paused then picked up the pace once again. 'Come on. We'll feel better after a pot of ale or two.'

'How's Mikhal faring?' Bruno asked, as though reading his friend's train of thought. 'Taal's breath, he had a melancholy air about him last we met.'

'Business is better,' Stefan replied. That was true enough. The war had ruined many of the smaller merchants, but Mikhal had traded wisely. He had learned to diversify, to match supply with demand, and to make up in volume what he could not earn through price alone. He was a good businessman, and plied his trade as skilfully as Stefan wielded his sword. But the other news of Mikhal had been less encouraging.

'He looked troubled last I saw him,' Bruno went on, keeping up a steady pace at Stefan's side. 'As if some great unhappiness had fallen on him in the months we were gone.' He met Stefan's eye. The expression he saw there was all the answer he needed. 'Well,' he concluded. 'Let's hope we find him in better spirits.'

'Aye to that,' Stefan agreed. 'And to some good beer to fortify us into the bargain.'

THE BAR OF the Helmsman was a crush of bodies: steaming huddles of drinkers were taking refuge from the weather and whatever other ills the day might bring. Stefan and Bruno were greeted warmly by many of the drinkers. Stefan made polite refusal of several pots of proffered beer as he fought his way to the corner table where Mikhal sat waiting. He was younger than Stefan by a full two years, of a similar height but more slightly built. Ever since Stefan had saved his brother from death as a child, he had felt in some way responsible for him, as though the act of childish heroism had marked a commitment that would last for life.

He embraced his brother before settling himself on the bench at Mikhal's side. Bruno took the empty chair

on the other side of the table, and poured out a pot of
beer for himself and his friend.

Stefan drank deeply then fixed his brother with a
searching look.

'Well?' he asked of Mikhal. 'How do things go with
you, brother?'

Mikhal's face brightened, though Stefan sensed it was
more through effort than disposition. 'They go well,' he
answered. 'Trade's been brisk, brisk enough at least. And
I've been feeling…' His voice trailed away for a second
or so. 'More at peace, I suppose.'

'That's good,' Stefan said, quietly.

'How about your new venture?' Bruno enquired.
Mikhal looked at him suspiciously. 'What venture?'

'Shipping!' Bruno replied. 'Your new investment.'

'Ah, you mean the boat,' he said, relief in his voice.
'The *Karla*. It's going… well, I suppose. Manifests are
full, there's not often space in the hold. It's going well
enough.'

'You don't sound very enthusiastic,' Stefan commented. 'It sounds as though things are going very well
indeed.'

'Well, it never pays to be over optimistic,' Mikhal
responded. 'Especially in these times.' He broke off, and
gazed about the tavern. 'Anyway,' he said at last, 'why are
we still talking about me? There's much more you've yet
to tell about your adventures to the east.'

'That there is,' Bruno agreed. 'More than I could ever
do justice to.'

Stefan shrugged. He could see he was not going to get
far with Mikhal in this guarded mood. 'All right,' he said.
'Where had we got to?'

'Erengrad,' Mikhal told him. 'You described how the
siege was broken. But what happened afterwards? What
kept you from coming straight back to Altdorf?'

Stefan supped his beer, contemplating events still fresh enough to be raw in his memory. 'Unfinished business,' he said. 'Bad business.'

'We had to look for Alexei,' Bruno explained. 'Track him down, and, in the end, kill him.'

Mikhal's eyes widened. He looked perplexed. 'Alexei?' he asked. 'Alexei Zucharov? But you were comrades. Didn't you ride together to Kislev?'

'Aye,' Stefan confirmed. 'And he fought with us at Erengrad. But he took something more than plunder from the battlefield.'

'The taint of evil,' said Bruno, then lowered his voice, 'The taint of Chaos.'

Mikhal looked shocked. 'So you tracked him down… and then…' His voice tailed off again. 'Where did all this take place?' he asked.

'Beyond the plains of Ostermark,' Stefan replied. 'In a place called Sigmarsgeist. It is a place that does no honour to its sacred name.'

He broke off. Weeks had passed, but memories of Alexei Zucharov's death sat no easier with him.

'Let's save that story for another time,' he said.

An awkward silence fell upon the group, which Bruno eventually chose to break.

'I'm glad you're feeling more yourself,' he said to Mikhal. 'Taal knows, these rains are enough to dampen the heartiest of souls!'

'The rains will stop, soon enough' Mikhal told him, matter-of-factly. His face crumpled and fell, like a mask being lowered. 'First will come rain, then will come fire.'

Stefan looked up, startled out of his own thoughts by the odd remark. Before he could ask Mikhal what he meant, the door to the tavern swung open, and a group of penitents dressed in cleric's garb entered.

'Sigmar save us,' Bruno groaned. 'More merchants of misery.'

The hooded figures began chanting. The sound could be heard over the hum of conversation around the inn. It was a prayer, or some kind of invocation, a call to repentance. The unpleasant, keening wail echoed around the busy room. The newcomers hadn't come to eat or drink. They were interested only in one thing, and went about that business single-mindedly. Each of them carried a vessel of some kind: a pail, or battered cup. They moved singly or in pairs between the groups of drinkers, seeking out contributions for their cause.

Most of the crowd ignored them, or dismissed them without ceremony. A few dropped odd coins, coppers mostly, into the pails so they could quickly be left in peace. Eventually two of the penitents came to the table where Stefan and his companions were seated. The two men stood before the table, and one stretched out his hand in supplication.

'Bloodsuckers,' Bruno muttered under his breath. Then, when it became clear that they would not move on, he added, 'You're in my light. And I don't much care for the shadow you're casting.'

One of the men spoke. His voice was surprisingly soft and measured. 'Penance for your souls, brothers. Purge the sin within you.'

With a sudden jolt, Stefan realised that the words were addressed specifically towards Mikhal. He was about to add to Bruno's advice when his brother abruptly stood up, and began fumbling in the pockets of his breeches and jerkin.

'Mikhal,' Stefan remonstrated. 'There's no need. They'll soon… '

But Mikhal was not listening. He had found some money – loose change lying in his pocket – and was dropping it into the collecting vessel. The penitents gave no signs of moving off. The man kept his hand outstretched, waiting for more.

'For your soul,' he repeated, gently. 'For your eternal soul.'

Mikhal nodded, and searched again. This time he produced a leather pouch that was tied tightly around his neck. Without examining the contents, he placed it into the hand of the man in front of him. The man nodded appreciatively, then after a pause, he and his companion turned and walked away.

As the door of the tavern closed behind the last of the penitents, a collective sigh of relief passed around the room. Conversation picked up again, and the hooded figures were soon forgotten. But Stefan had not forgotten. Something in the transaction he'd just witnessed disturbed him deeply.

'How much was in the purse?' he demanded of Mikhal. 'How much did you give them?'

Mikhal flushed slightly – whether from shame or anger was not clear. 'I don't know,' he replied, tersely. 'I didn't count it. Thirty, maybe forty crowns. What does it matter?'

Bruno let out a low whistle of astonishment.

'Forty *crowns*?' Stefan was aghast. 'That's the better part of a week's work for someone like you. What in Taal's name were you thinking?'

'You heard them,' Mikhal shot back, a tremor in his voice. 'There's not much time left. We all must purge the sin from our souls. Me more than most.'

'By all that's merciful, Mikhal, what are you talking about?'

'You know,' Mikhal muttered. 'You've seen the coming of the Dark Ones. You've fought them. You know there's no holding them. Even Middenheim won't hold them.'

Stefan exchanged glances with his friend. Bruno raised his eyebrows in disbelief.

'Listen to me Mikhal,' Stefan said. 'I don't know what's got into you since I've been away, but you've got things wrong. If the Dark Forces ever breach the walls of Altdorf, all the flagellants and doomsayers in the world aren't going to save us. We'll stand or fall by the deeds of our swords alone, you can be sure of that.'

'*If* the war ever comes to Altdorf,' Bruno emphasized. 'And there's no saying it will.'

Mikhal shook his head, emphatically. 'You're the one who's got it wrong,' he said. 'You don't understand. Not at all.'

'No,' Stefan agreed, wearily now. 'I don't understand.'

'I told you I'd found peace,' Mikhal went on. 'The followers of the True Path have shown me the way.'

'True Path?'

Bruno inclined his head toward the door of the inn. 'Our pious friends.'

'They have shown me my sins, and the poison inside me,' Mikhal proclaimed.

Stefan started to laugh, but the sound caught in his throat. 'What poison?' he demanded, incredulously. By way of answer, his brother held out his arm, and pulled back his sleeve to expose his wrist.

'Remember Odensk?' he asked. Now Stefan did indeed laugh, but it was laughter devoid of warmth or humour.

'Remember it? Remember the place where our father died and our homes were destroyed? I'm hardly likely to forget.'

'The Norscans,' Mikhal continued. 'The raiders who tried to kill us. They left me with this,' he indicated the line of a scar that was faded but still distinct, where a Norse blade had found its mark. 'It is the mark of damnation,' he concluded, soberly.

'It's nothing of the sort,' Stefan retorted, struggling to check his anger. He held out his own arm to reveal a similar, but deeper scar. 'The same blade was responsible for this,' Mikhal said. 'Are you telling me I'm marked by Chaos too?'

'You've had the chance to purge the poison through your deeds,' he said. 'I have not. Now the age of darkness is all but upon us. I must find atonement, before it's too late.'

Stefan took a deep breath, forcing himself to think before he spoke. He wanted to shake this madness out of Mikhal.

'Listen,' he said, as calmly and reasonably as he could manage. 'That day in Odensk changed our lives. But as for being tainted… tainted by…' his voice trailed off as he struggled for words. 'Believe me, I know what that looks like. I saw what the poisons of Chaos did to Alexei Zucharov. I saw him transformed from a man into a monster. Mikhal—' he took his brother's hand and clasped it in his own. 'Mikhal, there's nothing wrong with you.'

'Then why does my soul feel weighed down with chains?' his brother demanded. 'Such a terrible, unshakeable sense of dread.'

'The whole city is sick,' Stefan replied, 'but not in the way you mean. Fear has taken hold where hope and cheer once held sway. People like those ghouls who would rob you blind, do nothing but stir the unrest. Altdorf would be well rid of them.'

Mikhal made no reply, but Stefan could see by his face that his argument had made little impact. It was Bruno who finally broke the awkward silence.

'Come on,' he cajoled. 'This dismal talk won't do. Let's have another round of beer, what do you say?' Mikhal nodded, acquiescing in an absent-minded fashion. Stefan held his mug out to be refilled. As he did so, a distant clock chimed, the first single bell of the afternoon. Stefan looked up in surprise, shocked that it was already so late.

'Beer,' Bruno repeated. 'The blessed barrel will sour if you don't get a move on!'

Stefan reached into his pocket and drew out a folded envelope. He held it below the table and opened it out. It was not addressed. The only mark on its face was a symbol in the shape of a star. Inside, a single sheet of paper bore an address, a date and a time. Today. Only an hour from now.

He got up hurriedly and pushed the table back.

'We're not done,' he turned to Mikhal. 'We'll talk of this again.' Then he said to Bruno, 'The beer will have to wait, old friend. There's an appointment I need to keep.'

CHAPTER THREE
The Dark Future

THE NOTE HAD been passed to Stefan by a figure hurrying through a busy alley the day before. The messenger was gone in an instant, but the symbol imprinted on the envelope told its own story. The Star of Erengrad. For Stefan, there was no mistaking its meaning, or its significance.

The address scrawled on the note took him to a large rundown building amongst the tangle of streets that wound through the merchant quarter down towards the docks. Water spilled from ledges and rooftops, soaking through every layer of his clothing. From the outside the house appeared deserted, even derelict. He checked the note a second time to make sure this was the right address. There was no mistake, this was the place.

He was trying to decide whether he should knock, or simply wait, when the door in front of him was opened. A young, slightly built man dressed in green looked Stefan up and down, and offered him a fleeting smile.

'Good. You're alone,' he commented. 'Come inside.'

Stefan stepped across the threshold into the dank interior of the building. Having come this far, it would be senseless to turn back now. The building smelled damp and unlived-in. The air smelled dead, as if it had been freshly exhumed. The place was cavernous and gloomy; gravity hung heavy upon the still, cool air.

The green-clad figure walked on ahead of Stefan.

'They're waiting for you upstairs,' he said casually. 'Follow me.'

Stefan hesitated, part of him still wondering if this could be some kind of trap.

'Who are *they*?' he asked.

The young man turned and looked at him, quizzically. 'Who do you imagine?'

Stefan held out the envelope. 'I imagine the Keepers of the Flame.' His companion nodded briefly, as though confirming an evident fact. 'Follow me,' he repeated.

'And your name,' Stefan said. 'May I know that?'

The other man paused on the stair. 'I am known by a number of names,' he smiled. 'But you may know me as Nikolas Kranzen, who serves that same order.'

Nikolas walked on, a lantern held aloft above his head. At the head of the stairs he stopped, and waited in front of a set of heavy oak doors. He bowed his head and murmured something, the words inaudible to Stefan. The heavy doors opened inwards in a slow, stately movement. Nikolas beckoned to Stefan, and nodded his head slightly, as if to offer re-assurance.

'Who am I meeting?' Stefan asked.

'A man,' Nikolas replied simply. 'He has a name, but no rank or title. Or none that matters. He will explain our purpose to you.'

The door led into a corridor that stretched for thirty or forty feet, perhaps the entire length of the building. It was lit by a series of candles that flickered at intervals along the walls. There were no decorations, no features at all save for a line of plain doors that ran along either side. This might once have been a merchant house, where commodities were bought and sold, and deals struck and contracts signed. And now – now it was a place of ghosts, ghosts that passed unnoticed amidst the bustle of Altdorf. Ghosts known to a few as the Keepers of the Flame.

Halfway along the length of the corridor Nikolas stopped by a door on his left. He knocked on it twice then, without waiting for an answer, pushed the door open and motioned for Stefan to step inside.

Beyond the door was a tall room that was empty save for a featureless round wooden table and a row of por-traits on the walls. Sitting on one side of the table, facing Stefan and Nikolas were not one, but two men. Niko-las's face registered a momentary flicker of surprise then he bowed and turned back to Stefan. 'This is it,' he whis-pered. 'Good luck.'

Stefan had a hundred questions spilling into his head but his guide had gone, and the door was closed behind him. Stefan fixed his attention on his new companions. One was a stockily built man with a trimmed mane of silver-steel hair and a distinct, military bearing. The other man was smaller and bookish by comparison, with clear blue eyes that offset his otherwise bland fea-tures. Stefan didn't immediately recognise either man, but both seemed to know exactly who he was.

'Welcome back to Altdorf, Stefan,' the smaller man began. He indicated the chair. 'Please sit.'

Stefan took the offered chair, and looked about. The room was featureless and anonymous, empty but for the three of them. Stefan had the distinct impression that the house had been commissioned specifically for their meeting.

'My name is Marcus Albrecht,' the man continued. He did not introduce his companion. 'I serve an order known to you as the Keepers of the Flame.'

Stefan nodded. 'Then you'll know I've spent much of the last year in their service. But my work is now done.'

Albrecht bowed his head in a gesture of humility. 'We are heartened to have you safely returned from Erengrad,' he said. 'We owe it to you that the dark tide was stemmed in the east. At least for a while.'

Stefan picked up on the words. 'For a while? We broke the Chaos siege. Erengrad was reclaimed by the people.'

Albrecht glanced at the other man. 'What I am about to tell you is not widely known,' he said, gravely. 'But the conflict around Middenheim is only part of a larger war, a campaign waged by the Dark Armies against all the Old World. Six months ago, while their forces were massing to the west, they fell upon Kislev again, and besieged its cities and ports. '

'What of Erengrad?' Stefan interjected urgently.

'Burning,' the silver-haired man offered, breaking the hovering silence with a terse, single word.

'The city has not fallen.' Albrecht added hastily. 'Not totally. The fighting continues. Forces loyal to the Old World continue to fight on.'

Stefan sat in stunned silence. This was news indeed, and unwelcome news at that. For him, Erengrad was far more than a name given to a far-distant place.

'What of Elena?' he demanded, abruptly. 'Elena Yevschenko. What about her?'

'Like all the rulers, she is alive,' Albrecht said firmly. 'At least when last we heard.'

Stefan expelled a breath, quietly shocked to find the emotion was still so raw inside him.

'Elena *Kuryagin* is alive,' Albrecht continued. 'She and her husband are leading the resistance against the invading forces.'

Stefan felt his face flush. 'Sigmar be praised for that,' he said. 'We endured untold hardships together, so that Elena could return safely to Erengrad. For her to have perished would have been unbearable.'

For a moment he was lost in his own private thoughts. Memories flooded back. Memories of the journey east, and of the young noblewoman who had briefly become his lover. Memories, too, of Kuryagin, the Kislevite lord who waited in Erengrad for the bride he had never met. The marriage had been forged at a terrible cost, but it had re-united a troubled city, and, seemingly, turned the tide against the forces of Chaos. He could not bear to think it had been all for nothing.

'Is that what you want of me, then?' Stefan asked. 'To return to fight for Kislev a second time?' His heart was heavy at such a prospect, but if that was what it would take, then he knew what his answer must be. But Albrecht shook his head.

'No,' he said, quietly. 'There is nothing more you can do for Kislev, or for the city of Erengrad, Stefan. It is all part of a larger war now.'

Stefan was struggling to marshal his thoughts. He was still shocked by the news. 'What of Gastez Castelguerre?' he asked. 'He led the army that broke the assault on Erengrad. Wasn't he one of your own people? One of the Keepers? What of him?'

'Castelguerre is alive and well,' Albrecht confirmed. 'But he is no longer at Erengrad. He had pulled his troops back to the west, to try and fortify the line holding Middenheim.'

'Is it to be the city of the White Wolf, then?' Stefan asked. 'You want to send me to Middenheim?'

'No,' Albrecht said again. 'What we ask of you will not take you to the east, nor to Middenheim in the north. There is a threat much nearer to home. You must help us save Altdorf, Stefan.'

Stefan stood up, impatience mixing with his feelings of confusion. He drew out his sword and slammed the flat of the blade hard upon the table, sending shivers through the wooden frame. 'I came here in good faith,' he said. 'But it seems that faith was misplaced. Murderous war is being raged on two fronts, yet you tell me you would have me stay here, in Altdorf, where there is no war? What kind of sense is that?' he demanded.

'Altdorf is in peril, I assure you,' Albrecht answered. His voice was measured and calm. 'We will need everything you can offer, and perhaps more.'

'If Altdorf falls, then all the Empire will surely fall with it.' His companion spoke up for the first time.

Stefan focused his attention on the second man. 'We haven't been introduced.'

The man smiled. 'You won't know me,' he said. 'My name is Gustav Ehrhart. I am a commander of the Altdorf watch.'

Stefan did recognise the name, vaguely. 'Then the Keepers of the Flame are already well represented here in Altdorf.'

'Gustav is not of our order,' Albrecht said. 'But he is a good and trusted friend.' He paused. 'He has brought us news which has convinced us that we must act before it is too late.'

Stefan shook his head. The riddle was getting no clearer. 'This makes no sense,' he said. 'If the city is under threat, then the army, or... ' he glanced at Ehrhart. 'Or the watch will deal with it. Why come to me?'

'Because the threat is intangible, invisible,' Albrecht told him. 'By the time it becomes visible, it may be too late.'

Stefan put away his sword. He was of a mind to leave. Once he had set his affairs in order here, he would return to the war. Whether to the east or to the west barely mattered, but he could not sit idle.

'I see no reason to stay here, and every reason to head to Middenheim,' he said. 'Or back to Erengrad. At least I could be of some use there.'

'You could indeed,' Ehrhart agreed. 'But you would be of more use to us in the service of Altdorf. It's here that the greatest peril lies.'

Stefan shook his head. 'I'm sorry. I don't believe that. A few idiots and madmen spreading woe and damnation round the streets doesn't add up to danger.' He looked to Ehrhart. 'Your men are quite capable of mopping up that sort of threat. You don't need me.'

'That isn't the threat we had in mind,' Albrecht replied, stonily.

'Then what?' Stefan demanded. 'Tell me.'

Ehrhart nodded. 'Tell him.'

Albrecht sighed, resigned to giving up his secrets one by one. 'We've recently gained information of a Chaos plot against Altdorf. I'm not talking about a few cultists to be flushed out. I'm talking about a plan that would threaten the very existence of the city. If we don't move against them soon, it may well be too late.'

Stefan looked at Albrecht. The other man's face was steeped a fiery red, and his eyes burned with a passion that Stefan sensed was sincere. But he still didn't think this was any business of his.

'I'm a swordsman,' he said. 'Not a strategist, or a breaker of secret codes.'

He started to get up, but Ehrhart bid him stay seated.

'Wait,' he said. 'If we could prove the gravity of the danger, would it change your mind?'

'It might,' Stefan conceded. 'How do you propose to do that?'

Ehrhart exchanged glances with Albrecht. Albrecht shrugged. 'Very well,' he muttered. 'If we must.'

'We'll show you the city,' Albrecht said.

'I've seen enough of the city already,' Stefan said. 'Seen enough of the scaremongers who are beating up a frenzy of fear amongst good, level-headed people.'

'I wasn't proposing to show you the city as it is now,' Albrecht murmured. 'But as it will be if we do not act.'

The door behind Stefan opened. Nikolas re-entered the room. There was something unsettling about having the man present behind him, something that sent the faintest of shivers down the length of Stefan's spine.

'Nikolas will lead you on a journey,' Albrecht continued. 'A journey to an Altdorf which, great Sigmar willing, will never come to be.'

Stefan stared at the other man, blankly. 'Where would this place be precisely?'

'This is an inner journey, Stefan,' Ehrhart told him. 'A journey of the soul.'

'A journey into time,' Albrecht added.

'You can show me the future?' Stefan was both alarmed and awe-struck by such a prospect.

'I can show you one possible future,' Nikolas replied. 'We can touch those other worlds that have not yet come to pass. There are infinite futures, Stefan, untold possibilities. The choices we make today will shape the world that dawns tomorrow.'

'You answered our call,' Albrecht reminded him. 'You must at least be curious. Will you allow Nikolas to show you a glimpse of that future, before you make any decision?'

'And if that decision is still "no"?'

Ehrhart bowed his head, then looked up to meet Stefan's eye. 'Then our business is ended. This meeting will never have taken place.'

'You won't say no,' Albrecht said, firmly. 'Not if you are half the man we know you to be.'

Stefan pondered for a moment. This could surely do no harm. There was nothing to be lost. He looked around at the three men, and nodded his head.

'Good,' Ehrhart said. 'You have made the right choice.'

'We shall leave you with Nikolas,' Albrecht said. 'But be warned. Whatever happens, whatever you see, you must stay with your guide. Do not lose contact with Nikolas, whatever you do.'

'Whatever you say,' Stefan agreed. At that moment, any risk seemed largely imaginary.

Ehrhart smiled. 'Good luck, Stefan. We shall return to speak again shortly.'

NIKOLAS REACHED FOR one of the empty chairs and sat down. He beckoned Stefan to draw closer.

'What happens now?' Stefan asked. At heart he was deeply sceptical, but his curiosity had led him this far, and would not let him go now.

'All you need do is let me guide you,' Nikolas said. 'Empty your mind of all feeling and thought.'

That was impossible. Stefan's mind was racing, filled with all the tangled clutter of the day, from his conversation in the tavern with Mikhal, to the events that had led him to this strange encounter. But he let Nikolas place his hands on either side of his face. He held them there whilst he sat in silence, head inclined.

Stefan felt nothing beyond a slight weariness. Just for a moment, he may have allowed his eyes to fall closed. When he snapped to again, nothing had changed.

Nikolas was still sitting as before, with his eyes firmly shut, and his hands held gently against Stefan's face. Stefan could see little sense in prolonging the charade. He waited a few moments – more out of politeness than anything else – then gently broke contact with the other man. Nikolas looked up at Stefan. His eyes were bright and questioning.

'I think we should go,' Stefan suggested. Somewhat unexpectedly, Nikolas agreed. 'Yes,' he said. 'Let us go, now.'

Stefan stood up quickly, too quickly, because a wave of giddiness rushed over him. Instinctively, he reached out a hand for Nikolas to steady him.

'Over here,' Nikolas said. 'Only a short way.'

Nikolas held open the door, and stood back to allow Stefan to pass. 'Careful,' he urged. 'Whatever should come to pass and whatever you may think you have seen, stay close to me at all times.'

Stefan stepped out to where the candle-lit corridor had been, only to find he had somehow emerged onto the street outside. He looked around in confusion. He could make out no door, only the grey, featureless exterior of the building.

The rain had stopped. There was no trace of the endless deluge now. Even the ground beneath his feet felt dry, almost parched. Even less explicable was the light, or lack of it. When he had arrived at the house it had been early afternoon, and broad daylight. Now the sky above his head was pitch black. Only the faint sickly glimmer from the moon, Morrslieb, cast light upon the streets.

He had no memory of any journey. No recollection of any vision of Altdorf, past or future. All sense of time had gone. His headed pounded with a vague, insistent ache.

'It is so dark,' he muttered.

'Here it is always dark,' Nikolas told him. 'Stay close by me, Stefan.'

Stefan fell in step behind the man who had now taken on the role of guide. Somewhere inside his mind, a voice nagged at him. This was a dream; he could wake from it whenever he wanted. But it felt so real. He could touch the rough cast of the wall at his side. He could feel the cobblestones, dry and flint-strewn beneath his feet. No dream could take on such solid form.

Nikolas beckoned and Stefan followed.

At first the only sound was their feet upon the road. Everything else was silent, thick and heavy as the dark curtain of night that had fallen so suddenly across the city. Then Stefan heard them. The voices. Only one or two at first, but others gradually added to their number. They were the voices of men, women and children. All different, yet all united by a single theme. It was the sound of a people, of a city in unending, unutterable pain. The sound of the cries and screams grew in intensity until Stefan had to clamp his hands over his ears to shut them out.

'Merciful Sigmar,' he exclaimed to Nikolas. 'What monstrosity is this?'

Nikolas turned to him and said, 'It's the sound of dead souls, Stefan.'

At the top of the street the road opened out onto a broad thoroughfare. Now the sounds of human suffering were joined by a distant thunder, the thunder of marching men. Hundreds, or even thousands of soldiers on the move, and coming their way. Seconds passed. The thunder grew louder. Then, in an instant, the enveloping darkness was transformed, set alight by the glare of a thousand torches held aloft against the tar-black sky.

Nikolas seized hold of Stefan, and pulled him back towards the shadows. They took shelter in the recess of a doorway. Before their eyes, the armies of the night advanced, unchallenged, along the broad avenue, towards the heart of Altdorf.

Stefan looked on in stunned silence as the monstrous army poured into the city. First came the footmen, a hideous infantry clad in blackened steel, row upon row of hulking figures, metal-shod feet grinding down upon the cobblestones. Then came the knights astride their monstrous steeds: cruel champions bearing shields anointed with the stain of innocent blood. As they rode, the horned-helmed riders lashed the crowds with their swords, cutting down anyone who fell within their path. Finally, in their wake, came legions of mutants, creatures so far deformed by their malignant masters as to be all but unrecognisable from the mortal men they had once been. The light of a thousand torches shone down on their skeletal bloodless faces, on flesh that glittered like reptile scales. The creatures lifted their faces to the skies and wailed a guttural, cacophonous tribute to the Dark Gods.

Stefan was transfixed by the scene. His instincts had already guided his hand to his sword, but common sense told him that this was no battle he could ever hope to win. There were too many, far, far too many. If he were to cut one monster down, a dozen would rise up to take its place. This was not some bloody tableau of war, hundreds of miles removed. This was Altdorf, the very heart of the old city.

Evil had conquered the Empire, his beloved homeland. How long had he been standing there watching them march past? Five minutes? Ten? Yet still they came, these cadaver-soldiers in a sea of skull-faces and mutant bodies. They marched to the unending beat of drums, their foul breath frosting the chill air with sulphurous clouds. Stefan tore his gaze from the black tide to the streets beyond, then realised the horror was only just beginning.

At that moment he saw the bodies. Bloodied, blackened and broken; the remains of ordinary people who had been slaughtered or maimed then hung like bunting from windows and doors, and left to rot. It was a savage, chilling warning to any who dared oppose the new masters of Altdorf.

Stefan retched. Thin bile spilled into his throat. 'By all that's holy,' he swore, 'they'll pay a fearful price for this.'

'How will that help these people?' Nikolas asked. 'It's already too late for them.' He took Stefan's arm. 'Look,' he said. 'There's more.'

The main body of the army had passed. In their wake came the prisoners. Stefan saw soldiers of the Empire, officers and men of the watch, and swordsmen, young and old, who had given their all in a vain attempt to stem the flood. Now they were paying the price for their bravery. There were hundreds of them, line upon endless line of men, tethered by tightly fastened ropes around their wrists, or their ankles. They were being drawn face down through the filthy streets. Their bodies, already bruised and beaten, were chafed by the raw, freezing stones. Those who still had strength screamed out in agony. But scream or stay silent, it made no difference to the monsters that dragged them, like dead meat, towards their fate.

The men stared out blindly, all hope abandoned. Stefan looked on in horror at their bloodied faces and mutilated bodies. Then, by the orange torchlight, came a sight that chilled him to the very bone.

'Bruno!' The cry was out before Nikolas could stop him. Stefan looked again. The once stocky frame had grown pitifully thin, but there was no mistake. His comrade stared back without recognition, as his broken body was hauled through the streets.

Nikolas shouted a warning, and tried to hold Stefan back, but he was gone, driven on by an instinct of loyalty that no amount of warnings could subdue. Sword in hand, Stefan was already in the thick of the crowd, desperately trying to beat a path to his friend. A slender figure with its back towards Stefan turned to face him as he approached. Stefan stared at the woman. They had never met, he was certain of that, yet something about her was hauntingly familiar. The expression on the young woman's face was beaten and cowed, but her eyes struck an eerily familiar chord with Stefan. They were the colour of deep, icy seas, the colour of winter storms. The look in those eyes was of reproach, a long, unforgiving stare of undiluted hatred.

Stefan reached out to her, but as quickly as she had appeared the young woman was gone, swallowed up in the mass. The faces milling around him were changing. They were no longer men, they were monsters, the spawn of Chaos. Stefan tried to force a way through their ranks. When the weight of his body yielded him nothing, he used his sword to hack a path of blood through the mutant horde. Silver-skinned mutants, men with misshapen heads and the horns of beasts, turned to block his path. Razor-edged talons clawed his face, and tore at his flesh. Stefan tasted the salty tang of blood flowing into his mouth. This was no dream. His sword reaped a harvest of death, but still they came, swarming towards him, roused to a frenzy by the scent of blood.

Stefan redoubled his efforts. He was fighting now for his very life, but it was hopeless. He could never kill enough of them. The mutants fell upon him in a poisonous swarm. Stefan looked around, seeking any ally amongst the crowd, but Bruno and the rest of the prisoners had gone. There was nothing left for him, but to fight and kill until he himself was killed. He raised his sword high, and was preparing to strike, when he felt a hand settle upon his shoulder.

He spun round, expecting to see Nikolas. Instead there was a line of figures, dressed in priest's robes, heavy and all enveloping. The men – or creatures – stank with the ripe, sickly sweet odour of death. If they were priests, they worshipped no god that Stefan could recognise as his own.

Stefan shook himself free and swung his sword. Before it reached its target, the first of the figures tilted back the heavy black cowl covering its head. Stefan's blade hung, frozen, in mid-air.

His brother was recognisable, just about. The skin on Mikhal's face had turned waxy and translucent, like a parchment steeped in oil. In places, where the paper-thin flesh had ruptured, gangrenous pus leaked out from the wounds to run, like acid tears, down his cheeks. Only his eyes, pure, uncorrupted cornflower blue, reminded Stefan of the brother he had known. Stefan's mouth opened in an involuntary scream. He was only dimly aware of the scrabbling, claw-like hands that fastened onto him, to hold him captive. He barely heard the voice, or voices, distantly calling his name. All he was aware of was Mikhal's cold, unseeing stare, and the blade of the dagger moving towards his heart. Stefan closed his eyes, and uttered a last desperate prayer.

Somewhere in the distance he heard a voice that he dimly recognised as Nikolas's. From the corner of his eye he saw a blur of green, moving through the crowds. But it would be too late; it was all too late. He looked up one final time into the face of the creature he had once known as his brother, and bid a silent farewell.

HE FELT A jolt, a small death deep inside of him. Stefan opened his eyes. The street, and all its scenes of death and devastation, had gone. The solid walls of the chamber took shape once again around him. Stefan looked up to find Marcus Albrecht and his companion Ehrhart staring down at him.

Stefan examined his hands. For a moment, he swore, he could see the scarlet wounds where the mutant claws had torn at his flesh. The image faded, like the vision that had gone before it. He opened his mouth to speak, but his tongue had been stilled by what he had seen. His body was shaking; it was soaked with sweat, and there was a sickness buried deep in the pit of his stomach.

'Don't try to speak,' Albrecht advised. 'Here.' He handed Stefan a beaker of cool water. 'Drink this first.'

Stefan drank. Gradually, his shivering subsided. 'Whatever you did to fill my being with such imaginings,' he whispered. 'I beg you, never do it again.'

'That was no mere imagining,' Albrecht replied. 'Your soul was in real, mortal peril. You may thank Nikolas for your safe return.'

'That future can still be prevented.' Ehrhart told him. 'There is still time.'

'But we must act,' Albrecht interjected. 'We must act now.'

'What must be done?' Stefan asked. 'I swear, I'd move the very heavens to make sure the things saw never come to pass.'

The two men exchanged glances then Ehrhart went on, 'Just over two weeks ago, a man was murdered here in Altdorf.'

'His name,' Albrecht added, 'was Peter Selendorf. He was a member of our order.'

'And a friend of mine,' Ehrhart said. 'He was returning home from my house when his carriage was attacked, and he was killed.'

'We believe he was killed not only for who he was, but also for what he knew.' Albrecht added.

'Peter Selendorf knew of the peril facing Altdorf,' Ehrhart said. 'The night of his death he shared important news with me. The same news that brings us together now.'

Albrecht opened a drawer in front of him and removed a scroll of parchment, which he opened out onto the flat surface of the desk. Stefan looked down at a likeness of a man, drawn in charcoal upon fine white parchment. The face was lean, with a close-cropped beard and eyes that stared out from the picture with an uncanny intensity. Something about the face was both familiar, and unsettling.

'His name,' Albrecht told Stefan, 'is Heinrich von Diehl.'

'His family have a reputation for evil that stretches back for generations,' Ehrhart added. 'Now, Sigmar be thanked, he is the last of an infamous line.'

Stefan nodded. He knew the name well enough to know that it represented everything he opposed. 'You want me to find this von Diehl? And kill him?'

'Find him, yes, although that won't be difficult,' Ehrhart replied. 'Kill him, no. Heinrich von Diehl is securely under lock and key, in an Imperial prison.'

'Well, that at least is good news,' Stefan ventured, puzzled.

'On the contrary,' Albrecht said. 'It is not good news. As far as his gaolers are concerned, von Diehl is a just another cultist. Evil undoubtedly, but of no particular consequence. They consider him to be little different to hundreds of his kind, who plot and scheme against mankind in the service of their Dark Masters.'

'Von Diehl is a servant of Tzeentch,' Ehrhart explained. 'But an exceptional one.' He put a finger to his forehead. 'The knowledge he holds up here sets him apart.'

'Von Diehl has knowledge of every Chaos cult in Altdorf seeded somewhere in his mind,' Albrecht said. 'He knows the name of every acolyte, every human soul that has been turned from the path of righteousness. And there's more. Inside his head is the whole plan, every detail of the devastation that Chaos will unleash within the walls of this city. From start, Sigmar forbid, to finish.'

'But if he's in prison, it's only a matter of time before that information is prised out of him,' Stefan observed.

Ehrhart laughed, dismissively. 'The Imperial gaolers are men of limited imagination, and crude but limited means,' he said. 'They have tortured our friend, and learned nothing. Maybe,' he added, 'they even believe there is nothing to be learned.'

'Our best information is that Heinrich von Diehl will be executed in a matter of weeks,' Albrecht said. 'And if he dies, then what he knows dies with him. We need von Diehl alive.' He paused, holding Stefan's gaze. 'And we need him here.'

'Selendorf discovered the value that von Diehl could be to us,' Ehrhart said. 'No doubt that knowledge cost him his life.'

Stefan sat, gradually absorbing the significance of what was about to be asked of him. There was, he imagined, still the option to turn his back on Albrecht and his co-conspirator once and for all. Or perhaps he was already in too deep for that.

'Let's be clear about this,' he began. 'You are asking me to risk my life by breaking into an Imperial prison, and helping an known creature of Chaos escape?'

'Hardly break in,' Ehrhart replied, almost nonchalantly. 'We will have prepared a route into the prison. We hope that force will not be necessary.'

'And hardly "escape" either,' Albrecht added, his tone contrastingly harsh. 'Once with the Keepers, von Diehl will face an ordeal far harsher than anything he has faced in prison.'

'What makes you think you'll fare any better than his gaolers?'

'I shall summon a gathering of the Keepers of the Flame,' Albrecht replied. 'I will gather together our brothers from across the Empire. Together we have access to powers – powers of persuasion greater than anything the Imperial gaolers can muster. Whatever von Diehl knows, the Keepers shall know.'

'Nonetheless,' Stefan insisted. 'What you are asking breaks every natural law of man or gods.'

'Of course,' Albrecht concurred. 'That is why we're asking *you*, Stefan. Few men would be capable of leading a mission such as this. Even fewer would understand why it must be done. But you truly understand the forces of Chaos, and the sacrifices that must be made if we are to prevail.

'But can von Diehl truly hold the key to...' Stefan forced himself to recall the images. 'To the future that I witnessed?'

'With the knowledge that he holds, we could make sure that future never happens,' Ehrhart assured him, gravely.

'You wouldn't be working alone,' Albrecht went on. 'You'll lead of group of men, loyal to our aims. Men you can trust with your life. All we need is your assent. We'll arrange the rest.'

'You understand,' Ehrhart said. 'There are details which we cannot divulge to anyone, until the eve of the mission itself. Take all the time you need to come to your decision. But once you have decided, then, my friend, you are committed.'

'We will pay you well for your work,' Albrecht added for good measure. 'But you must be ready to leave Altdorf at a few hours' notice.'

For a moment Stefan thought he had misheard. 'Leave Altdorf?' he said. 'But I thought you said…'

'Von Diehl isn't in Altdorf,' Ehrhart explained. 'He's being held somewhere far away from here. A place you may never have heard of. A place most men would hope never to know.'

Stefan sat silently contemplating his options. The proposal that was being put to him was insane. But he couldn't shake the image of the two men. Bruno, his all but lifeless body being hauled through the streets of Altdorf like the carcass of an animal and Mikhal, his own brother, his flesh and soul corrupted beyond all redemption. Surely he would never know evil greater than that. He remembered the accusation written on the face of the anonymous woman; her face tugged at some distant memory. He shuddered at each recollection. Then he looked up at Albrecht and his companion.

'Make the arrangements,' he said. 'If von Diehl can be taken alive, I will deliver him to you.'

Albrecht clasped Stefan by the hand, clearly relieved. Ehrhart merely nodded.

'Nikolas will find you when we are ready,' Albrecht said.

'Enough explanations,' Ehrhart declared. 'We have told you all we can for now. You are with us, Stefan Kumansky?'

Stefan nodded his head once, a simple motion, which signalled an irrevocable choice.

'Then our business here is done,' Ehrhart concluded. 'You will hear from us again soon.'

Stefan forced a smile, even though at that moment he felt anything but encouraged. 'I thought perhaps you were going to tell me I wouldn't regret my decision.'

Albrecht inclined his head slightly. A shadow of sadness passed across his features.

'Alas, nothing in this life is ever so certain, Stefan.'

CHAPTER FOUR
Beyond Redemption

ANOTHER MESSAGE WAS delivered into Stefan's hands before the week was out. On the face of the letter was the same star symbol. Inside was another address – a place somewhere in the university quarter – as well as a cryptic note.

Stefan crossed the city from the south, and passed over the mighty Sigmarsbrucke Bridge that spanned the river towards the north of Altdorf. Nothing he saw along the way gave him much cause for cheer. More doors than ever were closed and bolted, and more windows barred. It was true that the shops and market stalls that were open for business were doing a brisk trade. Any food that could be salted down or stored was being snapped up, and Stefan witnessed more than one fistfight between townsfolk anxious to gather in stocks against the prospect of hardship ahead. At least they were still buying food, not looting it. So far.

Along the way he passed zealots, pilgrims and doom-sayers, as well as the flagellants that scoured their bodies as they proceeded mournfully through the streets. The whole city seemed to be gripped by a fearful anticipation of events to come, and an equally frenzied quest for redemption. Everywhere there was talk of a great ceremony, some weeks distant – the Blessing of the Souls. The Grand Theogonist himself, Johann Esmer, would preside over prayers for the soul of the city.

Stefan was a pious man when the occasion demanded, but he had always believed that deeds spoke louder than words. He had little time for false prophets, or for those who spread their words. He wondered whether the Blessing of the Souls would truly unite the city, or whether it might simply provide an opportunity for those who sought profit from fear. He pushed on, through the crowds on the Taalbrucke, past the beggars and the trinket merchants who sheltered in the hollowed alcoves on either side of the bridge. Still the rain fell on Altdorf; a veil of endless tears. The river below was brown and swollen, and churned uneasily beneath his feet. Stefan hurried on, eager to get out of the rain, and set the next great journey in motion.

He stopped on his way only once, his attention drawn to a rain-washed poster on a wall. It was a wanted notice offering money for information on the whereabouts of a hunted man. Stefan read the name – Karl Hoche – and looked at his face. It was the face of a man about his own age, staring out with a baleful gaze. The artist's likeness did Hoche no favours, but to Stefan he seemed to be a man much like himself. A fighter, a warrior, a man who lived by his wits and by his sword. How narrow was the line, Stefan wondered, between those who served the light, and those who fell into darkness? He glanced once more at the poster, and hurried on.

He found the rendezvous easily enough, it was a nondescript shopfront tucked amongst cramped, run-down dwellings barely five minutes from the Koenigsplatz. There was nothing about the place to suggest that any business transacted there would be anything other than routine – victualling maybe, or even whoring or petty gambling. But Stefan had already come to understand one truth about his employers. The Keepers of the Flame were everywhere in Altdorf, and they were nowhere. They would gather where and when the occasion demanded, and disappear just as quickly, melting away like smoke on the air.

He pushed open the green-painted door. Inside it was gloomy and quiet, the only sound the drumming of the rain against the cracked windowpane. The shop was stocked with trinkets: worthless ornaments and cheap icons fashioned from brass or tin. Two customers browsed idly amongst the piles of objects. Behind the single counter, a stooped, bald-headed man in an apron was busy entering figures into a notebook.

The old man looked up and smiled vaguely at Stefan, a tiny magnifying lens clamped against one eye. 'May I help you?' he enquired, mildly.

'I was given your name by a friend,' Stefan began, tentatively. 'He said you might have something of interest to me. A statue of Taal.'

The old man nodded, absent-mindedly. 'Ah, yes. Our little alabaster god. Quite a fine effigy. Would you step this way?'

The man ducked behind a curtain to one side of the counter. Stefan followed, to find himself standing facing a blank wall. The shopkeeper looked him carefully up and down.

'What did you say your friend's name was?'

'Nikolas,' Stefan said. The man nodded, and turned a key in a lock hidden within a recess in the wall. He set his weight against the panel and it began to revolve upon an axis to reveal a passageway beyond.

'Up the stairs,' he said. 'They're waiting.'

Stefan climbed the narrow flight of steps to the room on the upper floor. There, at a table by the window, two men sat nursing cups of wine or ale, staring out into the pewter grey afternoon. Neither of them was Nikolas.

Stefan was about to introduce himself, but found he had no need. As the man to the left turned his angular face toward the door, Stefan realised that he recognised him. In fact he knew him quite well.

'Stefan Kumansky, welcome.' Karl Maier stuck out a hand and Stefan shook it in greeting. Maier was a mercenary, a sword for hire, and a good one at that. Stefan knew enough of his reputation to hold him in some esteem. There were rumours that Maier had once escaped, single-handed, from an Imperial prison near Nuln. The story had served him well over the years. He and Stefan weren't exactly friends, but the two men regarded each other with a mutual respect.

'So what's your reason,' Maier asked Stefan, 'for risking your neck on this?'

'Belief,' Stefan said simply. 'Belief in what needs to be done. Yours?'

Karl Maier laughed, and turned out an empty pocket for Stefan to inspect. 'Money,' he replied. 'Any risk is worthwhile if it pays well enough.'

'Which it does,' Stefan added.

'Which it does,' Maier agreed. 'At any rate, we're in it together. Beyond redemption now, eh?'

He turned back towards his companion, a surly look-ing man a head shorter and probably five or so years older than him. The other man regarded Stefan with a wary stare.

'Forgive me!' Maier exclaimed. 'Such ill manners. Stefan Kumansky – Ernst Nagel.'

Stefan greeted the other man formally. 'I don't believe we've met.'

'I don't suppose we have,' Nagel agreed. 'I'm only wanted for my particular experience.'

'Which is?'

Nagel's eyes narrowed. 'Four years working as a guard inside Stahlfort.' He smiled a thin, bitter smile. 'Didn't part on the best of terms.'

Stahlfort. It was the first time Stefan had heard the name of the prison openly mentioned.

'It's a charming little place on the river, north of Carroburg,' Maier said, answering the question in Stefan's mind. 'You won't have heard of it, in all probability.'

Nagel nodded. 'Few have, until they're on their way there. Believe you me, it's a one-way trip in most cases.'

Stefan believed it. 'Let's hope we prove exceptions to the rule.'

Maier lifted his cup, and drained it in a single gulp before reaching for the flask to replenish it. 'Aye to that,' he said. 'Let's hope the magician can do his bit.'

'The magician?'

'Keppel,' Nagel said, delivering the word as though it was somehow toxic. Maier laughed again. 'Our friend here doesn't exactly hold with the magic arts,' he explained. 'But Horst Keppel is one of the best in all Altdorf. He's worked for the Keepers before. If anyone can get us in and out of that Morr-hole, Keppel can. Right, Nagel?'

'We'll see,' Nagel replied.

'Nikolas must be bringing him,' Maier paused. 'They should be here by now.' He filled another cup and held it out toward Stefan. 'Whilst we're waiting,' he said.

Stefan took the wine and joined the other two men at the table. None of the three had much inclination to talk, or at least, not about anything of any significance. Their trade had taught them all the habit of secrecy. They bided their time, and waited. Eventually there were sounds of movement from the floor below. Voices – two or perhaps three – could be heard conferring quietly. Then a single set of footsteps ascended the stairs.

The door opened and Nikolas entered. His expression was blank, but Stefan sensed he was ill at ease. Nikolas nodded to each of them in turn.

'Sorry to have kept you waiting. There had to be a change of plan.'

'Where's Keppel?' Maier demanded, his tone less nonchalant now.

Nikolas hesitated. His face looked pale by the light of the lamp.

'Keppel's not coming,' he said. 'He's dead.' He sat down. 'They fished his body from the Hallansee Canal this morning. He'd been stabbed at least a dozen times.'

Maier held his cup poised between the table and his mouth. 'I thought he had no enemies,' he said at last.

'Well, it seems he has,' Nagel commented, sourly.

Maier shook his head. 'Then the deal's off,' he said. 'No spellbinder, no bargain. That was what we agreed.'

'You shall have your spellbinder,' Nikolas responded, 'as soon as you are ready to leave.'

Nagel looked up. 'Who?' He demanded. 'You expect me to put my life into the hands of just anyone?'

'Not anyone. Keppel's replacement is equally gifted. This one has the potential to be as great a magician as any other in Altdorf.'

'Gifted?' Nagel spat. 'And do they have a name, this *gifted* trickster?'

For Stefan, the next few moments passed as a blur. Later, he recalled that Nikolas paused momentarily to glance briefly in his direction before he spoke. He then turned towards the door and issued an instruction to the servant waiting outside.

'Zucharov,' he said. 'The magician's name is Zucharov.'

A maze of possibilities opened out in Stefan's mind in that instant. Among them, the most bizarre, the most horrifying possibility of all: that the man that Stefan had left for dead beneath the waters of the lake at Sigmarsgeist had risen again. That the man he had once called his friend, the man whom Chaos had transformed into a monster, was about to walk through the open door.

His hand tightened on the hilt of his sword when a shadow fell across the threshold, before the newcomer had even stepped inside the room. As the figure moveded into the light, Stefan saw that it was not Alexei. It was not, in fact, a man at all.

It was the eyes that held Stefan first, held him, and would not let him go. They scanned him with an intense, probing curiosity. Stefan gazed back at the fine, chiselled features of a dark-haired young woman, no more than nineteen or twenty years old. A flickering memory told Stefan that this was the woman he had seen in the vision. And now, as he looked again into those ice-blue eyes, Stefan realised what it was that seemed hauntingly familiar.

'Natalia Zucharov,' Nikolas announced, quietly. 'A student of the celestial college of magic.'

By now, Stefan had made the connection. Alexei Zucharov had had a sister, some ten years younger than himself. Hadn't she been a student somewhere in Altdorf? This was surely she. If so, the coincidence was bizarre, rather than alarming. He stood up and bowed to the young woman.

'Stefan Kumansky,'

Natalia's tone was formal, neutral. 'I know.'

She sat down opposite Stefan. Her eyes didn't leave him. Did she know him? And if she did, what did she know about the aftermath of Erengrad? For a moment, he saw her again in the dark streets of that other Altdorf. He remembered the unspoken accusation in that Natalia Zucharov's eyes. What was the meaning behind the accusation? Was it something he had done? Or something he had *not* done? Could that be what the vision had been telling him? That he must act to save Altdorf, or else the blood spilt at Sigmarsgeist would have been for nothing?

Natalia gave a brief, tense smile, before looking away. The answer would not be revealed just yet.

'To business.' Nikolas produced a sheaf of papers from the lining of his cloak and spread a scroll of parchment across the table.

'The mighty Reik,' he explained, indicating the course of the river that was drawn in a rich, winding line across the parchment. 'To the north, the river divides. Your destination lies that way, towards the Midden Moors, and to this island on the river spur. There lies the garrison of Stahlfort.'

'Why hold von Diehl there, rather than in Altdorf?' Stefan asked.

'Since the start of the war prisoners have been moved out of the cities,' Nikolas replied. 'The more dangerous of them, at least. Stahlfort is one of the most secure prisons in the Empire. It was built to ensure that no one unwelcome gets in – or out.'

'That doesn't sound promising.'

'If all goes well, you will walk in and out through the main gate,' Nikolas said.

'You will present yourselves at the gate as envoys of the witch hunters, come to collect a man by the name of Koch for interrogation.'

'Is there such a man?' Maier asked.

'Oh yes,' Nikolas affirmed. 'He's a common criminal, a lesser light. In truth someone made a mistake in his judgement; the man barely warrants being in Stahlfort. They should be happy to let you take him off their hands.'

'So we arrive with a warrant for Koch,' Stefan said, 'and we leave with–'

'Von Diehl,' Nikolas affirmed. 'Exactly so. But I'm afraid that getting to him won't be quite as easy as that.'

Maier grimaced. 'I thought we'd have to earn our money somehow.'

'That's where I come in,' Natalia Zucharov said, softly.

'Correct,' Nikolas replied.

'They won't let a woman just walk into the place,' Nagel growled. 'I should know. I've worked there.'

'The papers you present at the prison will introduce Natalia as a steward of the witch hunters, like the rest of you.' Nikolas said, simply. 'They'll have no option but to admit her – to admit all of you.'

Nagel muttered to himself, unconvinced. Maier slapped a hand on his shoulder. 'Cheer up, Ernst,' he said. 'The chances were never going to be better than remote anyway!'

Nikolas flashed Maier a brief smile, but there was no humour in his voice. 'My friends, the time for second thoughts is past.'

'There'll be no second thoughts,' Stefan assured him. 'We're all committed to this.' Committed indeed. Maier was right: they had passed beyond the point of all redemption.

IN THE SUBTERRANEAN world below the streets of Altdorf there was no dawn, no dusk. Here was only an eternal twilight, created by the spluttering glimmer of the tallow-fat lamps that stank in the sweltering darkness.

For weeks the mutant gang and their skaven guide had continued to excavate the passageways beneath the city with staves, with picks, and even bare hands. Often they found themselves knee-deep in cloying filth. But still they worked on, unseen and oblivious to the world above, driven by the cruel lash of their master.

At least three had died in earth-falls or sudden floods, but it did not matter. They were fodder: dispensable tools whose only destiny was death. So long as they reached their destination, it did not matter how many of the scum died in the process. And they were very close to that destination now, within touching distance of their enemies. Here, in the musty tunnels near the heart of the city, the creatures of man dwelled below the surface as well as above.

They had encountered the first of them earlier that day, as the mutant excavators toiled in the perpetual twilight of the underworld. A wall of rock and mud had given way under the sustained assault from their picks to reveal a cavernous chamber beyond. The gang master had barely taken a step inside the cavern when he saw the eyes, glittering like beads in the guttering light of the lamps. There were half a dozen or so of them, barely human, but human nonetheless.

The gang master was momentarily surprised. He was unprepared for combat. The tunnels were supposed to be long-abandoned; there should have been no patrols, no soldiers of Altdorf down here. Then he realised. These were not soldiers, and their purpose in the tunnels was not to patrol or guard; it was to survive. These pallid wraiths had not seen the light of day for weeks or months. They and their kind were troglodytes, subterranean dwellers who passed their worthless lives in the labyrinth of old passages beneath the city.

Pale faces stared back at him, frozen by shock and terror. The human creatures had nowhere to run. Instead they shrank back against the walls of their hovel, as if hoping to vanish from beneath the withering gaze of the intruders. The gang master surveyed their emaciated bodies and shrunken, translucent faces. These were the very dregs of humankind, pitiful scum barely deserving even of his hatred. An impulse struck him. He would waste no more time on these starving bundles of rags. They would leave them shivering in their filth. He must press on. Time was of the essence now, and killing these wretches would only delay them.

But where there was even one human soul, might there not come others? Theirs was a battle that could not be considered won until all of the cursed humans had been slaughtered, and the streets of their cities ran red with their blood. They had not come this far to risk being discovered now. They were not ready. Not yet.

He felt breath, hot and sour, against the pitted skin of his face. The skaven had risen up on its muscular hind legs. It slavered hungrily, spittle dripping from its parted jaws. The gang master looked from the skaven to the tunnel-dwellers, paralysed with fear at the sight of the monster. He nodded once towards the men at his side. Without a word, two of the acolytes darted towards the tunnel-dwellers.

Realising what was about to happen, the humans turned to flee, seeking refuge in the darkness. But the mutants caught them and held them fast, stifling their futile screams.

The gang master lifted his lamp and called for one of the filthy wretches to be brought forward. The creature squirmed and writhed with surprising determination; it was a desperate, but futile struggle for survival. The leader gripped hold of the human, and ignoring his

pitiful pleas, propelled the man into the embrace of the
waiting ratman.

'A small reward,' the gang master murmured, 'for your
efforts so far.'

The skaven flexed and cracked open his mouth. Its
jaws parted in a languid yawn. Rows of yellowed fangs
gleamed in the lamplight. The tunnel-dweller screamed
and put up his arms to shield his face, but there was no
escape.

The skaven fastened its rodent jaws, almost tenderly,
around the man's neck. For a moment it did nothing
more than hold its struggling prey secure in its ven-
omous grip. Then came a sound like the breaking of
bone-dry tinder. Blood gushed from the open wound,
flowing down into the sodden mass of mud below. The
skaven twisted its head, and tossed the tunnel-dweller
from side to side. Strips of flesh ripped from the dead
man's face and neck.

When it had done, the creature dropped the body into
the blood-soaked filth at its feet, and cast its gaze
around, eager for another offering

The gang master nodded his quiet approval. The first
blood had been shed, the first drops of what would
soon be a river.

'SOUNDS LIKE QUITE an adventure,' Bruno commented.
He expelled a deep breath. 'And secret indeed if you
can't even name the destination. But there's one question you must answer – when do we go?'

'Wait a minute,' Stefan urged him. Although they
were alone in Bruno's rooms, he still found himself
looking around to check for eavesdroppers. 'There's
more,' he said. 'I will give you one other name. The
woman that I talked about. The magician. It's Alexei
Zucharov's sister.'

Bruno's eyes widened. 'His sister? Sigmar's glory, Stefan, that's a twist in the tale we could have done without!'

'I know. The fates have played a strange hand.'

'How did this come about?' Bruno asked, still shaking his head. 'Did the Keepers know what happened with Alexei?'

'Well,' Stefan replied, 'they certainly do now. I made sure of that. But it seems there's nothing to be done. The original spellbinder meant for the mission was found murdered.'

Bruno whistled. 'Bad timing.'

'Indeed,' Stefan agreed. 'It seems Natalia Zucharov is the understudy. She's clever, gifted, and dedicated to the cause. The perfect choice, except–'

'Except for the fact that you killed her brother,' Bruno offered. 'Taal's breath! How much does she know?'

'I'm not sure,' Stefan replied. 'The Keepers have told her nothing, but she probably knows that Alexei rode with us to Erengrad.'

'And that he didn't ride back,' Bruno added. His voice trailed off, and he sat lost in his thoughts for a few moments. At length he looked up, and held Stefan's gaze. 'What are you going to tell her?' he asked.

'I don't know,' Stefan admitted. 'The truth – or perhaps part of the truth,' he said at last. 'I might mention that Alexei rode into battle at Erengrad. That he fought like a lion, and that he died because he was prepared to surrender his life and soul for the causes that he believed in.'

'But what about the rest?' Bruno asked, quietly.

Stefan turned away. For a moment he was looking again at Natalia Zucharov, or perhaps it was the other Natalia, the half-formed face of the woman from his darkest imaginings. The look of accusation in her eyes was still vivid in his memory.

'What can I tell her?' he asked. 'Would *you* want to know that your brother died as a mutant, as a monster poisoned by the taint of Chaos? Is that what you would want your final memory of him to be?'

'I haven't got a brother,' Bruno responded. 'But I do take your point.' He sighed, and ran his fingers through his tangled shock of hair. 'Anyway, it's just one more thing that we will have to deal with along the way.'

Stefan hesitated. This was going to be the hardest part of all. 'Bruno,' he said, tentatively, 'there isn't going to be a "we" this time. I have to do this alone.'

Bruno frowned in disbelief. 'What are you saying? Are the Keepers refusing to have me join their mission? Why? It wasn't a problem for them when I risked my life for them in Kislev.'

Stefan shook his head, slowly. 'No, no, that's not it,' he insisted. He forced himself to meet his friend's eye. 'It's not the Keepers that don't want you to go, Bruno. It's me. I need you to stay here in Altdorf.'

Bruno was stunned by what he had just heard. 'So that's it,' he said at last. 'Is my sword grown too blunt for your liking, or am I simply no longer to be trusted with such important work?'

Stefan jumped to his feet. Bruno drew back, but Stefan seized hold of his friend's shoulders and forced him to look at him. 'Bruno!' he said. 'You are my oldest, my dearest friend. There is no man alive I would trust more with my life. And no blade I would rather have at my side in battle than yours.'

'So it was in Kislev, and in the Ostermark,' Bruno agreed, grudgingly. 'So why not now?'

'Because,' Stefan began, struggling for the words, 'because this is different. When we set off for Erengrad our goals were clear. We were taking Elena home to claim her birthright. We were going to heal the wounds that had broken the city. Our goals were clear, and they were… pure.' He sat down, slowly. Bruno joined him. The look on his face was quizzical; the first flush of anger had passed.

'This time I've crossed a line, a line that – well, I don't know I should have crossed. I can't ask you to do the same. Ulric's toil, Bruno, I shouldn't even be telling you all of this!'

'Nothing you share with me will ever go further,' Bruno retorted, hotly.

'I know that. By all that's holy, there's no one more trustworthy than you,' Stefan assured him. 'Please. Don't make this any harder for me. I've taken a decision to walk a dangerous path. I'm putting my soul in peril, Bruno. I don't want you to do the same. Besides,' he added, 'there's something else. Something I need you to do.'

'Name it,' said Bruno, brightening a little. 'We're comrades, Stefan, remember. There's no burden we can't share.'

Stefan nodded, encouraged. 'I'm worried about Mikhal,' he said. 'He hasn't been himself since we returned to Altdorf. I'm worried about what may be happening to him.'

'Do you think he's sick?'

'In body he's as strong as a horse,' Stefan replied. 'But his soul seems troubled. All this talk of purging fire, and the idea that he's been somehow tainted by evil – I don't like the sound of it.'

Bruno shrugged. 'What would you like me to do?'

'Watch over him,' Stefan replied. 'Follow him, if necessary. Find out what he's getting into. If you can, keep him out of harm's way.'

Bruno mulled it over for a few moments. 'I'd rather be going with you,' he said at last.

'I know you would. That's the sacrifice I'm asking you to make.'

Bruno stood up and took a few paces around the room. 'Very well,' he said. 'Don't worry about Mikhal. I'm watching over him.'

Stefan took Bruno's hand. 'This means a lot to me.'

'So,' Bruno concluded. 'When do you… go?'

Stefan smiled at his old friend. 'Soon,' he said, quietly. 'We ride tonight.'

CHAPTER FIVE
Secret War

MARCUS ALBRECHT SAT alone in the sanctum, the single room that had been set aside for the times when the ghosts would meet; those few occasions when the Keepers of the Flame would gather together from across the far corners of the Empire. It was a secret place, a room seldom if ever visited by any outside that most secret order. It was their temple, the holiest of places: a chamber locked within a chamber, sealed and hidden from the outer world.

Albrecht pondered the row of portraits that hung above his head. The pictures depicted the men who had served that secret order. They had never been many, but now their numbers were diminishing as each month passed. Every year saw more of his brothers carried to the gates of Morr, swept away before their time by the dark tide, invisible casualties of an unending war. This was not the war that raged on the fields of Middenheim, nor at the gates of Kislev and the cities of the east. It was a war unseen and unheard amidst the commotion of everyday life. But for all that, it was a war that cut to the very heart of the Old World. Its outcome would determine the fate of each and every soul that walked the land. It was a war that might well never be won. But, Albrecht knew, it must never be lost.

Albrecht considered the faces of the dead. There was Otto Brandauer, who had first recruited Stefan Kumansky for the mission to Erengrad. He had been murdered by Chaos in the very heart of Altdorf. Andreas Leichtmann, noble priest of Middenheim, slain by Chaos on the hallowed ground of the Morrspark that he tended.

Peter Selendorf was the latest of his brothers to die. How many more would there be? How long now before he, Albrecht, would surrender his mortal soul?

The order would need fresh blood before too long. There would be no shortage of men and women ready to pledge themselves to the eternal struggle, but very few would be truly fit to carry the burden. Might Stefan Kumansky be one of those? Or even the Zucharov girl, a raw spirit, but not without promise. Both of them were so young, so very, very young. But the time for old men was drawing to a close. Soon, one way or another, he and his kind would be dust. Their time was almost over.

But as long as he lived, Marcus Albrecht was determined to make his mark. He looked at the nine empty seats arranged around him. Soon, Sigmar willing, those chairs would again be occupied. He, Marcus Albrecht, would have summoned them. He had set in motion a chain of events which all the Old World would have cause to remember, and give thanks for. He would wield the knife that cut the Dark Ones to the core, to the very core of their evil hearts. *That* would be his mark, and though his body would surely fall to dust, that mark would never fade.

A door opened. Someone entered the chamber. Albrecht did not need to look round to know that it was Nikolas. Here, in this secret place, it could be no one else.

'What news?' he asked, softly.

Nikolas came and stood at his master's shoulder. 'They should be on their way by now. At the city gates, if not beyond.'

'The first test,' Albrecht mused. 'The first hurdle.'

'Their papers will bear scrutiny, I would vouch for that,' Nikolas said. 'Besides, Ehrhart's influence will smooth their path out of the city. The watch won't trouble them.'

'Probably not,' Albrecht concurred. 'But getting back in will be quite another matter.'

'There is other business we need to discuss,' Nikolas reminded him. 'There is the summoning of the ten. What news of the brothers?'

Albrecht sized up his lieutenant. Faithful Nikolas, always dependable, always on hand. Companion, inspiration, sometimes even his conscience. By rights, Nikolas should be his true inheritor when the time came.

'I've sent word to Talabheim and to Nuln,' Albrecht replied. 'And to Castelguerre, at Middenheim, if the war can spare him.'

'Then you think all ten can be gathered?' Nikolas asked.

Albrecht rubbed his fingers against the polished grain of the table. 'Great Sigmar willing, they can.' He hesitated, as though distracted, then abruptly changed the subject. 'What of the other matter?' he asked of Nikolas. 'What of the enemy within?'

'The eyes are continuing to watch those zealots who are at large inside the city,' he said. 'As expected, they grow more numerous and more active by the day. Several of the larger sects are starting to test their strength in earnest.'

'Which ones?' Albrecht asked.

'The Apostles of Morr, the Black Confessors and the True Path. There are others, but those have been the most prominent.'

'Some may be harmless enough, I suppose?'

'Almost certainly. But it looks increasingly as though the Dark Ones have infiltrated the ranks of at least one of them. There's no conclusive proof as yet, and we do not know what their intentions may be.'

Albrecht nodded, abstractedly. 'We're treading a narrow path,' he murmured. 'You must be careful, Nikolas. We must all be careful. The Grand Theogonist himself has spoken out in praise of religious zeal. The power of prayer, Nikolas, in this, our time of need.'

'The Grand Theogonist knows he must cultivate the pious,' Nikolas commented. 'Whether they be priests of the temple who quietly serve, or those whose piety takes a more strident form. But his first loyalty will be to Altdorf.'

'That may well be so,' Albrecht concurred. 'But we cannot afford to move openly against the zealots until we have absolute proof of their intent.'

Nikolas waited a few moments. 'Did you talk to Kumansky?' he enquired, tentatively. Albrecht shuffled the papers on the desk in front of him, and avoided eye contact.

'About his brother?' he said at last. 'About Mikhal's involvement with the zealots?' He cleared his throat, self-consciously. 'No. I did not.'

'We agreed it might be better if he were told,' Nikolas said.

Albrecht frowned, clearly uncomfortable with the line of questioning. 'I consulted Ehrhart,' he responded, crisply. 'His counsel was that it was better to say nothing that might weaken Kumansky's resolve for the mission.'

'Gustav Ehrhart is not of our order,' Nikolas reminded him.

'Indeed not,' Albrecht snapped back. 'But he was a good friend to Peter Selendorf, and he has proved a useful ally of the Keepers of the Flame.'

'All I meant,' Nikolas rejoined, mildly, 'was that it is possible to rely too much on the counsel of one man. Particularly an outsider.'

Marcus Albrecht looked up and smiled; it was a thin, terse smile. 'We are treading on dangerous ground,' he said softly. 'Soon enough, we may need all the help we can get.'

FROM THE MOMENT of Stefan's departure, Bruno had been feeling restless. Doubtless his friend had told him all he could about the mission he was embarking on, but the details were still sketchy. In truth, Bruno had little idea of where Stefan was headed, nor when – or if – he would be back. Altogether it was very unsettling. Despite all the reasoning and argument, a part of him knew he should have been with Stefan; they'd been through so much together. But now Bruno had to sit and wait, whilst the great acts that would shape the course of war were played out on another stage.

The night Stefan rode from the city, Bruno had taken a little supper at the Black Goat. Then he spent an hour or so walking through the darkening streets, finding some pleasure in the respite from the rain. But he was killing time, and he knew it. On impulse, he turned about, and headed back in towards the waterfront.

Lights still burned in the front bar of the Helmsman, it would be an hour or two yet before the last drinkers were ready to surrender the day. Bruno hesitated, then pushed open the door. After all, he had a duty to perform, and it occurred to him that Mikhal might be there. If so, then they would talk. About what, exactly, Bruno wasn't quite sure. But they would talk.

The bar was swaddled in a fog of smoke and addled conversation, the floor sticky wet from a night of spilled beer. It was a comfortable, familiar sight, almost guaranteed to put Bruno in better spirits. He peered across towards where Mikhal habitually sat, but the corner table was empty. That was no surprise; Mikhal Kumansky was a man of few friends, and he often kept late hours at his office or warehouse. The odds of finding him enjoying a pint even at this time of evening were probably no better than even.

Bruno looked about the rest of the bar. There were a few faces that he recognised. There was Franz Sterkel, sitting amongst a group of hangers-on; Bruno surmised he was probably planning some petty thievery or other. Sterkel had a reputation as something of a rogue, but there wasn't a lot that passed him by.

'Hey there,' Bruno called out. 'Any of you seen Mikhal?' Sterkel broke off from his debate and looked over. He winked, knowingly.

'Stefan's brother? You missed him. He was here, earlier. Went off with his friends.'

'Friends?' Bruno asked. 'What friends?'

Sterkel leant forward, and pressed his hands together tightly in a parody of religious supplication. The men standing around burst out laughing.

'Here,' Sterkel said to Bruno. 'Come and have a drink.' He kicked out a chair from beneath the table and held it out.

'No thanks,' Bruno replied, his good humour suddenly quite evaporated. 'I've lost my thirst.'

He turned and walked out of the tavern, filled with a new urgency to track down Mikhal. But, once back out on the street, he pulled himself up short, and looked around in frustration. He realised that he had no idea where to start.

ABOUT THE TIME Bruno Hausmann was leaving the Helmsman, the mutants burrowing deep beneath the fabric of the city were nearing the end of their journey. The gang master paused to sniff the air. Not far from these stale, foetid tunnels, thousands of human souls waited like fruit upon a branch. Ripe, ready for the harvest.

The mutant raised a skeletal arm, lifting the flickering lamp above his hooded head. Light flared briefly in the narrow confines of the tunnel. Tongues of shadow licked the walls inscribed with the runes and symbols of a long-forgotten age. The creature at his side panted and scrambled ahead, scuttling through the tunnel like a huge, silver-furred rat.

The skaven peered at the runes and emitted a low growl of satisfaction. Its belly was full, sated with the blood and flesh of mortal men. Those it had not fully devoured it had ripped apart in its razored jaws, sundering flesh from bone for sport alone. It had been meagre fare: sour, diseased meat. But soon there would be more, much, much more. Soon the skaven and its kin would have the run of Altdorf, and they would feast on as many carcasses as they wished.

The rodent face scanned the daubings on the walls, picking out familiar shapes amongst the faded lettering. The time was coming for old scores to be settled. The sons of man would have cause to remember they had built their city on plundered land. A reckoning was due, and they would pay a heavy price.

'Cease tunnelling.'

The words rang out crisply in the gloom. The tunnellers set down their tools. The gang master turned to the skaven; they were so close they were almost touching. The creature's mouth was thickly crusted with a dark, glutinous gore, and its breath carried the stench of decaying flesh. The gang master suppressed a shudder of disgust. Even amongst his kind, the rodent creatures were loathed and despised. Once the bidding of the great Lord of Change had been done there would be no need to tolerate their presence any further. The skaven would be exterminated, and the pits of the dead would be home to man and rodent alike. But for now…

'Are we here?' he demanded. 'Be precise. There is no room for even the smallest of errors. We must be in the exact place.'

The skaven fixed the gang master with a beady stare, and flexed its blood-spattered features into a grotesque approximation of a grin. It, too, drew in the scent of the air, seeming to orientate itself by smell and sound alone. At length it nodded, apparently satisfied.

'This is place,' it replied. It raised its eyes towards the tunnel roof. 'Up there,' it grunted. 'Up, straight. This is place.'

'Are you sure?' the gang master demanded. 'How can you be sure?'

For a moment the skaven's eyes flashed in anger. A muted, savage roar rattled in its throat. 'You forget,' it told the mutant. 'You know nothing about this place. Less even than the human scum who took our home. This not their land. Neither is it yours. It is ours. Ours for long past. Ours for long time coming.' A dribble of blood-flecked spittle fell from the creature's jaws. The skaven coughed, and ejected a greasy nugget of half-digested flesh onto the sodden ground at the gang master's feet.

'This is our ancient home,' it growled. 'I know, as you never will.' It glared back at the mutant. 'This is the place,' it repeated. 'No mistake.'

The gang master flexed his long, clawed hands. Talons expanded and contracted in a slow rhythm. How dearly he would love to tear this vermin limb from limb, and let the lesser rats grow fat on its corpse. But not yet. He must wait, and maintain the pretence of alliance yet awhile. The gang master forced a smile, his face gaunt and sepulchral by the light of the lamp.

'You are our honoured guide,' he said, his tone more placatory. 'Naturally I defer to your ancient knowledge. I just wanted to be sure. None of us wants to make a mistake, not now that we are so close.'

A shuffling and a clatter of metal on stone in the tunnel behind him drew his attention back to the figures standing in line in the gloom. The other mutants stood silently awaiting developments. Their dull, milky eyes were fixed on their master and the skaven. Finally one of them summoned the courage to speak.

'What is your will, master?'

The gang master pointed to the roof just above his head. 'Now we dig,' he said, softly, 'straight up towards the surface.' He paused, trying for a moment to imagine the size and shape of the chamber that lay above.

'Then, when our lord has made ready, we shall deliver our gift to mankind.'

THE LIGHTS OF Altdorf had faded with the passing miles. After an hour of steady riding the city was a flickering of stars on the horizon. After two it was gone, lost beyond the cradle of dark hills that rose up around the riders.

Now the only light came from above. The clouds had been banished and the moons were full; the silver orb of Mannslieb was set like a newly minted coin against the western sky. To the north, its sickly brother, Morrslieb, shone a baleful bronze against the velvet shadow of the hills. The rain had ceased and the winds had fallen. It was as good a start as they could have hoped for, yet Stefan was unable to quite shake off a feeling of trepidation and unease. The signs everywhere told him that the world was becoming a far more dangerous place.

At first, mindful of the sentries and possible spies that the watch may have set along the way, the four riders had followed the way-marked road that constituted the main causeway out of Altdorf. It wound steadily westwards towards the distant city of Marienburg. Their exit papers had named that distant city as their destination, and for as long as possible, they would stay true to their declared course.

Finally, as the lights of Altdorf vanished into the night, they turned off the Marienburg road, plotting a new course toward the bleak landscape of the Midden Moors, where the Reik fractured into a web of arterial waterways. Somewhere in the midst of that barren, inhospitable maze, lay the island garrison of Stahlfort. Inside that fortress, amongst the countless thieves, murderers and monsters held captive, was the single reason for their journey: Heinrich von Diehl.

All along the Marienburg road, they had other travellers for company. It was a major trading route, and for the first hour or so the main concern for Stefan and his companions was to avoid the lumbering wagons that crawled, often unlit, along the pot-holed carriageway.

But as soon as they turned to the north, the part-paved roadway disappeared, and with it most other human company. The majority of the villages now were abandoned, the inhabitants having long since fled to seek sanctuary inside the city. Those few souls brave or foolish enough to stay on did so behind locked doors and barred windows. Only the occasional glimmer of candlelight through shutters betrayed their presence. It would be a week before the riders reached another town of any size, and two weeks or more before they reached the cluster of lakes and waterways that enclosed Stahlfort.

Even though they had not passed another traveller in more than an hour, Stefan knew that they were far from alone. Unseen, silent for much of the time, someone or something had started shadowing them, and was following in their wake. Stefan slowed the pace of his horse to a steady trot and waited for Maier to come alongside.

'Looks as though we have company,' he said, quietly. 'Now we start to earn our purse.'

CHAPTER SIX
The Road to the Island

MAIER TOOK THE news calmly and nodded as he might in response to a greeting.

'Are you sure?'

'Positive,' Stefan replied. 'Someone or something's been watching us ever since we turned off the Marienburg road.'

'Hostile?'

Stefan nodded. 'Could be. Just keep riding, for the moment.'

He made a careful check of his surroundings. To all intents and purposes the four riders were alone, with only the glowering hills and a scattering of derelict farm buildings for company. If they were being observed, then the observers were too wary – or too clever – to make themselves known.

He looked over his shoulder at Nagel. The former prison guard was riding some way back from the rest of the group, lazily steering his horse with just his left hand on the reins. He made brief eye contact with Stefan and acknowledged him with a nod. At the same time, his right hand moved to his sword. Stefan hadn't taken much to the grizzled, dour Nagel, but he was no fool.

That left Natalia, Alexei Zucharov's sister. The past year had taught Stefan all he needed to know about her fearsome brother, and the greed for adventure that had cost him his mortal soul. But what of the young magician who now rode with them? Stefan knew little of Natalia beyond what Nikolas had told him. He had no doubt that her magic skills would prove their worth in Stahlfort. But what about out here, in the wilderness, where craft of a cruder kind would often be needed? Would Natalia prove an asset or a liability?

From the look on the girl's face as she rode, Stefan guessed that she had rarely ventured beyond the city. That wouldn't be unusual, or surprising. Few sane people travelled far into the wilderness unless they had to. It was too dangerous, even at the best of times. And these were not the best of times.

He overtook Maier and signalled him to slow down. The horses ambled slowly through the ruins of another village. The empty shells of the houses were silhouetted against the moonlight like a row of blackened, broken teeth.

'Whoever they are, they aren't showing themselves,' he said in a low voice. 'Perhaps our friends have decided we aren't worth the effort?'

'I doubt that,' Maier replied. 'I think they're still with us.' His casual tone belied the effort he was putting into concentrating all of his senses on the world around them. Stefan knew Maier's strengths. He could smell trouble long before it could be seen or heard. His judgement was rarely wrong.

Stefan took stock of the derelict buildings. 'Maybe we should pull up here a while,' he said. 'If we're going to have to fight, then any shelter may be better than none.'

'Keep moving!' Nagel's clipped intervention came as a reminder to Stefan that his hearing, at least, was good. He would have to remember that. The former guard steered his horse to the front of the pack. 'They'll pick us off here. Keep moving.'

Stefan looked to Maier. Maier nodded. 'Probably best.'

Natalia rode up and laid a hand on Stefan's arm. 'What's the matter?' she asked. 'Trouble?'

'Maybe,' Stefan replied. 'We need to stay alert.'

Natalia looked around. 'I can't see anything.'

'That's why it may be trouble.'

He wanted to tell her that she had entered a different world now, a world where even the limited certainties of life in the city count for nothing. Where nothing was as it first seemed, and nothing could be taken for granted. Natalia was looking directly at him, seemingly hanging on Stefan's every word. *She trusts me* Stefan realised, *trusts me without question.* He was both reassured, and yet somehow troubled, by the realisation.

Moments later, something emerged at speed from a building at the side of the road. Stefan heard a cry, and a horse whinnying. There was a sudden blur of motion, and he felt something coarse and hard brush against his leg. Instinctively he reached for his sword, drawing it left-handed to fend off the attack. Moonlight glinted on the silvered steel. Stefan swung the blade in an arc, and swept the ground beside him, but his blade failed to find any mark. The next thing he heard was Nagel laughing.

Stefan pulled his horse about. Maier, like Stefan, had drawn his sword, but Nagel hadn't even got as far as lifting his weapon from its harness. He leaned back in the saddle, still laughing; a dry, oddly humourless sound.

'Boar,' he called out. 'It was a boar. Snuffling around for scraps in the house. That's all it was.'

Stefan exchanged a terse smile with Maier. Natalia just looked relieved.

'Come on,' Stefan called. 'There's a way to go before we can bed down for the night. Ride on. Stay alert.'

Just outside the village, the path forked. Either of the ways looked possible, but only one could be right.

'Which way?' Maier asked, directing his question at Stefan. Stefan had no idea. The maps and directions – such as they had been given – had been far from detailed; they had only been shown a single, little-used path bisecting the land between the Marienburg road and the moors. But what Stefan did know was that the land that ran to the moors, and beyond to the islands, was treacherous. Away from the beaten paths it was a quagmire of deep, stagnant pools and hidden marshes, death traps for the unwary, especially at night. Whatever path they chose, they had to be sure it was the right one. He looked to Nagel.

'Well? You must know the road.'

Nagel shook his head. The supercilious expression had faded. 'I don't remember anything like this,' he said. 'It wasn't like this before. Must have changed.'

'It wasn't like this, or you just can't remember?' Maier demanded. He tapped his finger against his forehead. 'This is what they're paying you for, remember? What you've got up here.'

Nagel snarled, but didn't rise to Maier's taunt. 'I don't remember it being like this,' he said again. He spread his hands, half apologetic, half indignant. 'Sorry, but I don't know.'

Stefan swore under his breath. 'Which looks the more likely?' he asked Nagel.

Nagel shrugged, and pondered each path in turn. One was clearly the wider of the two, but snaked away from the village then bore off to the right. The other path, though narrower, drove straight ahead. 'To the right, maybe,' Nagel muttered. 'I'm not sure.'

'It looks like the main path,' Natalia offered.

'Wait a minute.' Maier nudged his horse forward to inspect the trail at closer quarters. After a few moments he turned back towards the others. 'It looks a while since this one was used,' he said, indicating the path to the right. 'There's brush strewn across the way, and plants growing up along the path. The track leading straight ahead is clearer, and there's hoof prints, too.'

Stefan joined him. The prints in the wet, loamy soil were reasonably distinct, and so probably relatively fresh. That could be good news, or bad. But Maier was right: the second path didn't look as though it had been used for some time.

'We'll go straight on,' he told the others. 'Go slowly.'

They had gone barely twenty paces along the track when they heard sounds ahead. This time, Stefan could tell that this creature travelled on two legs. This was no boar.

A figure materialised out of the darkness. A man was running directly for them, his face bleached white in the wash of light from the moons above. As one, Stefan and Maier drew swords. The man took a while to see Stefan and the others, but when he did, he held his hands up above his head and kept on running, regardless of the glint of the steel that waited for him.

'Halt,' Stefan commanded, extending his blade to make clear his intent.

The man slithered to a halt in front of Stefan's horse, and fell to his knees, hands clasped together in supplication.

'Save me!' he implored. 'I beg of you, take me with you.'

He was a short, stocky man in his middle years. From the look of his rounded face and marble-smooth skin he was no farmer or hermit, and not, Stefan guessed, from these parts. He was wearing a simple hooded smock, a featureless robe of the kind favoured by travellers when they wanted to avoid attention. Whoever he was, he was no immediate threat. Slowly, Stefan sheathed his sword, though motioned to Maier to keep his drawn.

'What are you doing here?' he demanded of the man. 'What are you running from?'

The man in the trailing robes gazed up at Stefan, the fear in his eyes matching the trembling in his body. 'Hurry!' he said. 'We must get away from here.'

'We're not moving an inch until you answer our questions,' Maier said, coolly. He moved his horse around to block off any potential escape.

The man looked beseechingly at Stefan.

'I beg you,' he said. 'My party was ambushed along the road. We were trying to get across the moors. They disguised the paths and lured us into an ambush. Please,' he implored. 'We have to get away.'

Stefan peered into the darkness along the way the man had just come. He could see nothing. 'Who ambushed you?' he demanded.

'Bandits,' the man replied, breathlessly. 'At least a dozen. They murdered my comrades, and took everything we had. The horses, too.'

Stefan looked at the man again. His robes had been shredded, perhaps by a blade. Blood was oozing from cuts visible on his upper arms. He looked ready to weep. 'Please,' he implored again. 'I have nothing left here to offer you, but if you get me safely to the nearest village you can name your price and I'll see it's met.'

'We don't want your money,' Stefan muttered. In truth, he was more concerned about having an unwanted addition to their party. Sigmar only knew how long it would be before they came to the next inhabited place.

'Let him ride with us,' Natalia urged. 'At least until we get to safety. He can ride with me if need be.'

'No,' Stefan replied. He looked down again at the man kneeling before his horse. Bent down and shivering, he made a pathetic sight. 'Get up behind me,' Stefan said at last. 'Then we'll see how far we can take you.'

Gasping his thanks, the stocky figure clambered up in the saddle behind Stefan, hauling himself up with an agility quite at odds with his appearance.

Stefan pulled on the reins and brought the horse about, nudging it on towards the twisting path that lay to the right.

'Thank you,' his passenger exclaimed again. 'You won't regret this.'

'I'm regretting it already,' Stefan said, flatly.

The four riders moved off, leaving the village behind. The road climbed steeply for a short distance, and twisted through narrow turns before levelling out. Stefan's passenger was an appreciable burden, perched like a weighty sack behind him, his arms wrapped about Stefan's midriff to keep his balance. All the while the man kept up a muttered monologue, offering thanks to Stefan, thanks to the greater gods, all interspersed with low moans of pain.

Stefan was wondering whether it might after all be better to share this new burden between them when he saw Maier's horse appear to dip and stumble in front of him.

'What's the trouble?' he called out. 'What's happening?'

Maier turned in the saddle to reply, but Stefan already had his answer. His own mount had begun to falter, and was sagging beneath him as though drugged. A tug on the reins met with no response. Stefan glanced down at the ground. A heavy, black slurry had bubbled up over the horse's legs, dragging the animal down. He shouted a warning back to the others.

'Hold up! Don't come any further. We're running into the marsh!' He hauled back on the reins, desperately trying to steer his horse clear of the danger. He looked ahead, and saw Maier trying to do exactly the same. Then he saw that their troubles were only just beginning.

From above the ridge of either side of them, and across the crest of the hill at their backs, lights suddenly appeared. Any fleeting hope that this might be some kind of rescue dissipated as flaming torches came into view. Some of the riders looked like men, others like nightmarish fusions of man and beast. All of them were armed to the teeth, and they were bearing down on Stefan and his comrades at speed. Stefan counted six of them, maybe seven, closing in from three directions. With the way ahead impassable, they had ridden into the neatest of traps.

Stefan went for his sword, but found he could not move. The fleshy arms of his passenger around his waist had turned to bands of steel, seizing him in a vice-like grip. The mumblings had ceased as well. Now, when the man spoke in Stefan's ear, it was with quite a different voice.

'Be good,' it rasped. 'And maybe we'll let you die easy.'

Stefan flexed his muscles, desperately trying to free himself from the man's grip, but his captor had him secure. The flabby, babbling merchant of a few moments before had been transformed into a deadly assassin.

Directly ahead, Maier was fighting a battle on two fronts, struggling to drag his horse from the quagmire whilst fending off an attack from a brace of mutated riders, creatures with twisted canine heads atop thickly muscled bodies. Somewhere behind him, out of his line of sight, he heard Nagel call out and Natalia respond, as steel met with steel.

Stefan swore an oath and doubled his efforts to break free. Pinioned on his own horse he wasn't in the fight at all; he couldn't even spit in the face of his assailant. There was no doubting that the man holding him – if man he was – was his equal in strength. Or even his better. Stefan's attempts to wrestle out of his grip only caused him to lock down ever harder in response.

A rider was closing in hard on him from the left flank, clutching a glittering sabre in one hand. Stefan was defenceless, held out like a target waiting to be skewered on the blade. He had a view of the incoming rider as the horse bore down on him: a glimpse of yellowed bones protruding through putrid, rotting flesh, and dead-fish eyes that glittered in the moonlight. The reins hung tantalisingly out of reach; try as he might, Stefan could not reach them.

At the last possible moment he jabbed his spurs sharp and fast into the flanks of his horse. As if it could smell the urgency, the horse leapt forward, pitting all its strength against the sucking, cloying mud. The horse staggered forward a few steps. Not much, but enough for the incoming rider to streak clear past, the sabre-blade scything the air inches from Stefan's face.

Stefan forced one elbow free then brought it sharply back. He jabbed as hard as he could into the other's ribs. The stocky man grunted, from surprise as much as pain. At last, Stefan had worked himself a little space. He rocked back, then forward in the saddle, jabbing out with his elbows where he could. The stocky man slithered backwards and momentarily lost his grip. Stefan threw all his weight forwards, hauling the bulk of the man over his shoulders and throwing him from the horse.

The man landed with a muffled thud in the cloying mud. He rolled over then looked up, aghast, at Stefan. Stefan could have finished him then, but first he had other calls on his attention. The mutant with the face like an open wound was closing in again, the air ringing with its inhuman screams. The manoeuvre mirrored the mutant's first attack, but this time Stefan had his sword. He held back until the last possible moment, drawing the raider on. The mutant had grown too confident; it had committed itself too soon. Just before the two horses crossed, Stefan saw the look in the glass-bead eyes change from indifference to alarm. The mutant lashed out, but Stefan had read the attack. With the mutant's guard exposed, he struck a reply. His blade passed through the other's tattered tunic, cleaving rotten meat from the bone. The mutant's screams intensified as it tried to break free. Stefan pulled back his sword and struck again. His second blow cut deep into his opponent's shoulder. The third all but slashed its head from its shoulders. The mutant slid from its horse into the deadly embrace of the marsh.

Stefan circled, trying to gain a sense of what was happening around him. Maier had felled one of his opponents, and was getting the better of the second. Nagel had forced another rider from its horse, and was setting about the downed mutant with a vengeance. That left two more raiders, and Natalia. They were harrying her relentlessly, pushing her further and further back towards the swampland. Natalia was driving her horse first one way and then the other, riding at speed and with astonishing skill to shake off her attackers. But, little by little, her avenue of escape was being whittled away. Stefan raced forward, hoping he could get to her before they did. The first of the attackers had drawn a blade, and was closing for the kill. Natalia parried the attack, but she was tiring, her defence growing slower, wearier.

Stefan shouted out, but he had no idea whether she heard him. He saw the first raider position itself for the decisive attack. Natalia had her sword in her left hand; the raider was closing from her right. She would stand no chance. Stefan wrenched every last ounce of speed from his mount, but knew he could not make up the ground in time. He saw the raider lift an arm, and take time to place a blow, emboldened by what now looked an easy kill.

Natalia stood her ground, but continued to hold her sword down at her side, making no show of any defence. The mutant uttered a scream and charged down on its defenceless prey. Then, only feet away, its horse appeared to stumble. The creature bucked, and reared up, throwing the raider from the saddle. Natalia took a step back, and coolly drove the blade home, stabbing it with force into the chest of the prostrate rider.

The second raider spun round, either unwilling to take on Natalia, or sensing Stefan speeding in from behind. This one was a mutant, too, with parched, leathery folds of what might have once been human skin stretched across the contours of an eerily grinning skull. Whether the creature with its flesh mask had even known mortal life Stefan did not know, but he was determined to despatch it to the halls of Morr with as much speed as he could muster.

The mutant must have known that the odds of battle had turned against it, and that it was now outnumbered. But if it had any fear of the annihilation that awaited it, it did not show. Instead the creature drew a second sword from the harness hanging at its side, so that it now had two heavy blades, one in each stump-handed grip. Each was fashioned in the curved shape of a crescent and honed to a murderous sharpness. The creature locked its gaze on Stefan, its ghastly grin widening, then it charged.

Stefan met the charge, driving his own horse to the left of the mutant. Sparks crackled in the air as the blades clashed. The mutated steed flashed past Stefan, towards the road that led back up towards the village. Now it was up to Nagel and Maier to block off the route of escape. The mutant wheeled around, seeking out another possible avenue of flight, then charged a second time towards Stefan. This time, Stefan knew, the creature would throw all caution to the winds.

He pulled a short knife from his belt, and clenched it tightly in his left hand. Once again, he positioned himself to the left of the oncoming rider. Once again, steel bit hard against steel, momentarily locking the two sword-bearers together. The mutant lashed out at Stefan with the second sword, aiming for the base of Stefan's neck. Stefan flung himself flat against his horse, narrowly avoiding decapitation, and plunged the knife deep into the mutant's flank with all the strength he could muster. He was rewarded with a scream of pain, and a gout of blood that spread in a dark stain across the mutant's filth encrusted tunic.

The creature dropped the sword from its left hand and tried to staunch the flow of gore from the wound. He whipped his blade across the leathery flesh, gouging an incision across the width of the mutant's lower body. The creature expelled a gasp, a sharp cry, and tumbled from the saddle.

Stefan slumped back on his horse, exhausted. He only vaguely heard the sound of the others approaching, and their words of congratulation.

'It's over,' he heard Natalia say at last. 'We finished them.'

No, Stefan thought. It wasn't over, not quite. He pulled his horse around, and retraced his steps to the beginnings of the battle. At first he could see nothing, then, against the dark contour of the land in front of him, something stirred.

The fat man who had led them into the ambush was still alive. But the marshlands had him firmly in their grip, and only his head and upper shoulders, coated in glutinous grime, were still clear of the surface. Stefan dismounted, and moved as close as he could without sinking back into the mire.

Somehow, the man managed to pull one arm free of the swamp, and reach out towards Stefan.

'For pity's sake,'

The others gathered around. There was little pity to be shared amongst them.

'Kill him,' Nagel said flatly. 'Kill him and be done with it.'

'Why waste the effort?' Maier said. 'Let nature do it for us.'

Stefan looked at Natalia, but she looked away. Perhaps she was battling with a natural compassion that no longer had a place in this barren land. Stefan raised his sword, and wiped the blade carefully along his sleeve. He looked at the fat man who was still staring up pathetically from the slowly stirring blackness.

'No,' Stefan said at last, and to no one in particular, 'I won't let nature rob me of what I'm owed.'

He lifted the blade high, and took careful aim.

IT WAS LATE, and the last embers of the campfire were starting to die. Nagel had taken first watch, and had moved off to position himself on a rock overlooking the camp. Maier had already wrapped himself in a blanket to seek some sleep. Natalia finished what was left of her food, then picked up her blanket and moved closer by Stefan's side. Stefan acknowledged her with a single nod.

'Not a very hospitable place, is it?' Natalia began, drawing the blanket around her shoulders for warmth.

'It's not,' Stefan agreed. 'But I've known worse. And doubtless we'll all know worse before this business is done.'

Natalia sat quietly for a moment, watching her breath condense into frosted wisps of cloud on the night air. 'There were humans out there – ordinary men, I mean – amongst the mutants who attacked us. What fortune could bring about such a terrible alliance?'

'Misfortune, mostly,' Stefan replied. 'Opportunity and dire necessity. Good and evil don't always align themselves in the ways we expect.'

There was a longer silence then Natalia said, 'You were with him, weren't you?'

It was the moment Stefan had been dreading, and yet now that it was upon him, he felt relieved. He didn't need to ask her who 'he' was. He turned to the young woman in the fading orange glow of the fire. 'With Alexei? Yes, I was with him, at Erengrad.'

Natalia nodded, as though, for the moment, that was all she needed to know.

'Why have you waited so long to ask me about your brother?' Stefan asked. 'You must have known that we rode together from Altdorf.'

She nodded again. 'I never heard from him again, you know, once he left Altdorf. I kept hoping for something, maybe even a letter, but nothing ever came.'

She sighed, a small, lost sound. 'But, all the time that he was gone, and with no word, I could hold onto the hope that my brother was still alive. Somewhere, out there, he was still alive.' Her eyes were moist, and rimmed with red. 'I knew when I sat down to talk with you, I'd have to face my worst fears. Everything I have dreaded this last long year.'

Stefan sat staring at the fire, waiting for what was to come. When she finally spoke again, it was though a blade had pierced him.

'He's dead, isn't he?'

Stefan drew down a deep breath. 'Yes,' he said, quietly. 'I'm sorry.'

Natalia didn't respond at first. She poked at the embers of the fire, as though distracted by some distant memory. 'You were there?' she asked at last.

'There?' the words felt awkward on Stefan's tongue. 'You mean, there when he–'

'Died, yes.' She looked directly at him now, staring at Stefan with the storm-blue eyes so reminiscent of her brother. 'Were you there?'

'Yes,' Stefan said, softly. 'I was there.'

'Well then,' she went on, her voice betraying no emotion. 'That's some comfort at least.' She turned away. 'How did he – how did he die?'

'Are you sure you want to talk about this?'

Natalia suddenly kicked out at the fire, scattering the coals across the ground. 'Yes, Sigmar take you, I'm sure!' she shouted at him. 'I need to know.'

Stefan reached out an arm towards her, then drew back. This wasn't the time. Nothing felt right. He waited for a moment, trying to find the words that he had rehearsed a thousand times. 'He died fighting. Carrying the fight against the darkness to his very last breath,' Stefan told her.

He braced himself. Did she want more?

There was a pause. Then Natalia sighed. 'That's about all I can bear to hear for now.'

'Conviction and courage took your brother to Kislev,' Stefan said. 'Neither virtue failed him.'

Natalia brushed a hand across her face. 'That's true enough. The Alexei of our memory will never fade or die.' She reached out and touched Stefan, just once, lightly upon the hand. 'Thank you,' she said.

Stefan let a lengthy pause lie between them before he spoke again. 'You did honour to his memory today,' he said at last. 'You fought well. Very well indeed.'

She smiled, fleetingly. 'I had a good apprenticeship,' she said. 'I'll never be a warrior like my brother was. But he did teach me how to handle a sword.'

'That was more than handling a sword,' Stefan said. 'Standing your ground with that mutant thundering towards you. That took some courage. How did you know–'

'That the horse would throw its rider?' Natalia laughed, a brittle, child-like sound. 'I gave myself a little help.'

'Magic, you mean?'

'Of a sort. Scaring a horse – even a mutant horse – takes no great art.' She glanced up at him, almost shyly. 'You know, for the most part magic, and the power of illusion, is simple, Stefan. It's just understanding it which is so hard.'

Stefan looked to the fire. Most of the embers had been brushed away. All that remained was a feeble glow. 'I'd get some sleep if I were you,' he said. 'I'm due to take over the watch from Maier soon.'

Natalia stood up, and drew her blanket around her. 'Just one more thing,' she said. 'You killed the man trapped in the marsh, even though he was no longer a danger to us.'

Stefan looked up at her. Was this disapproval, or shock? It was impossible to tell from her voice. 'What would you have done?' he asked.

Natalia gave a slight shrug of her shoulders. 'Truly, I can't say,' she said. 'I don't know if I could have killed a man in cold blood, that's all.'

'We never know what we are capable of doing, until we need to,' Stefan replied. 'But evil is evil, regardless of the shape or circumstance it takes.' He poked at what was left of the fire, and drew the embers together into a small pile by his feet.

'Now get some sleep. Our journey has barely started.'

CHAPTER SEVEN
We are all Born to Pain

Bruno had to do something about Mikhal. The easiest thing would have been to go to his house, and confront him. At heart, Bruno was a straightforward man, not given to secrecy or subterfuge but on this occasion he was not at all sure that the simple approach was best. What he had heard about Mikhal in the tavern that evening had worried him, and he was fairly sure it would have worried Stefan as well. There was no good reason for Mikhal to be hanging around with zealots or penitents, or whatever they might be. That wasn't the Mikhal he knew. In fact, Stefan's brother had become a different man; utterly altered. And not, Bruno would have to say, for the better.

Rather than confront Mikhal, for the time being at least, Bruno decided that he would follow him, to see if he could find out what he was getting himself mixed up in. Perhaps there would be a perfectly reasonable explanation. So far, Bruno had been wracking his brains in vain to think what that explanation might be, but he was as fair-minded as he was honest, and resolved to give Mikhal the benefit of any doubt.

That market day morning found Bruno tucked out of sight in a doorway across the street from Mikhal's rooms on Reikstrasse. The house he had chosen as his vantage point was unoccupied, that much Bruno knew. Beyond that, he hadn't much of a story to account for his being there if anyone challenged him. This was a part of the city favoured by traders who were moving up in the world. Strangers loitering aimlessly on doorsteps were not a welcome sight around here.

Fortunately for Bruno, no one had troubled him so far. But this was the third day he'd been keeping his watch, and so far his observations had yielded nothing. On both previous days, Mikhal had left the house soon after eight bells, and had gone directly to his warehouse alongside the city's harbour wharf. There he had stayed – bar the odd errand – until returning home at dusk. He hadn't ventured out beyond that, neither to the Helmsman, nor anywhere else. Bruno was beginning to think he was wasting his time. This morning more than ever, he was wishing he were on the journey with Stefan – wherever he might be.

Stefan's younger brother appeared, punctual as ever, just as the nearby chapel bell struck eight. Bruno sighed and folded away the pamphlet that he'd been pretending to read. He stepped out into the street, taking care to put just enough space between himself and his quarry. Bruno yawned, and rubbed his stomach. Once again, he had neglected to eat a proper breakfast, a situation he vowed to remedy tomorrow… if there was a tomorrow. Perhaps the time had come to abandon the whole, futile exercise.

Mikhal walked smartly to the end of the street, turned left and then first right. Bruno followed at a distance behind. So mechanical was Bruno's progress that he almost missed Mikhal when, instead of following the next street to the end, he turned off into a narrow side alley. Suddenly Bruno was alert, his complaining belly forgotten. This was not Mikhal's normal route, nor was it a route that would lead him to the waterfront. He was heading in a wholly different direction, away from the docks towards the no-man's land that straddled the Konigsplatz and the university. Bruno tugged his hat down over his face and followed, hoping to keep Mikhal in sight.

Mikhal strode on, purposefully, his shadow twenty feet or so behind. More than once, Bruno feared that Stefan's brother would turn around and discover him. The streets here were narrow and quiet, and there was every chance that he would be seen. But Mikhal appeared wholly absorbed in his journey. After about twenty minutes of walking they entered the edge of the merchants' quarter, an area known locally as Leder-garten. Once it had been a flourishing market for skins and hides, but for the last few years, business had run down until the sector was largely deserted. Once bustling warehouses and shop-fronts now lay empty, crumbling wrecks awaiting demolition. Bruno could think of no reason why Mikhal might have business here, at this or any other hour of day.

Now, for the first time, Mikhal looked round. Bruno shrank back against the wall, grateful at that moment for an alcove that neatly accommodated his sturdy frame. Mikhal checked the street in both directions before hur-rying on. A few steps further down he turned another corner, into a street or alley hidden from immediate view. Bruno gave him a few moments then followed, cautiously. He had a troubling image of Mikhal waiting to spring out on him at the top of the alley. He would demand to know what he was doing. What indeed, Bruno wondered. What was he – or Mikhal – doing?

He reached the corner of the street and peered round. The alley was poorly lit, still dark in the early morning. Just in time, Bruno caught a glimpse of Mikhal at the far end, turning into a door or gateway. There was somebody else nearby – two people, in fact. Mikhal disappeared from view. The two others stood stock still, like sentries.

Bruno waited a few moments and then set off along the alley. He kept up the steady pace of a casual but confident passer-by. As he approached, the two men turned in unison towards him. Both were dressed in knee-length jerkins of the sort worn by labourers, with grey cloth cowls pulled up over their heads. They were standing in front of a pair of rusted iron gates, leading off the alley. Bruno had no idea what to do next. Try and bluff his way in, and find Mikhal? Keep walking past, marking the place for a later visit? He wasn't sure.

The two men stirred as he approached. They were still watching him, albeit without much apparent interest. Bruno could now see where the gates led: it was the entrance to an old warehouse or factory. Like most of the area, it had long since been abandoned. Bruno checked his pace, and raised a hand in greeting.

'Good morning both,' he said, cheerily. 'Looks a better day.'

Pairs of eyes peered out at him from beneath the cowls. Neither man spoke.

'I'm supposed–' Bruno grappled for inspiration. 'I'm supposed to meet some associates here,' he said. 'Take a look over the old building.' He took a tentative step forward. 'I'm rather late,'

The two men moved closer together, barring the way through the gates.

'There's no meeting here,' said one. 'We're here to keep people out,' the other said. 'Not show them in.'

Bruno nodded, trying to seem as friendly as possible. Perhaps there might be a back entrance into the building. He fumbled in his pocket for a scrap of paper, which he pretended to read. 'Ach, Taal's breath,' he exclaimed. 'Wrong address. All these old places look alike, don't they?' He raised his hand to his brow. 'I'll wish you gentlemen a good morning. Sorry to have troubled you.'

As he turned to move off, Bruno was conscious that one of the two men was following. He turned around smartly, ready to offer more pleasantries. But any conversation vanished from his head the moment he saw the knife.

The hooded figure lunged at Bruno, grabbing him and shoving him back against the wall. Bruno was caught off-guard; the jagged bricks cut into his flesh. For a moment, his head was spinning. But what he lacked in speed he more than made up for in strength. As the man thrust the knife again, Bruno parried the blow with his fist, powerfully enough to knock the weapon out of the man's grip.

Something rammed into his face. Momentarily, Bruno was blinded. The man had punched him hard, but not as hard as Bruno punched back. His fist smacked into his opponent's jaw, and knocked him into the wall on the far side of the alley. The man staggered forward, and grabbed for the knife, but Bruno had seen the attack coming. He kicked the man's legs away from beneath him, and seized him around the throat as he fell. The hooded figure struggled for all he was worth, clawing and biting at any part of Bruno he could find. But Bruno didn't slacken his grip around the other man's windpipe until his struggling had subsided. He dropped the lifeless body to the ground.

That still left one of them. The other had a knife too, but he was hesitating, unsure whether to attack or retreat back inside the building. If he runs inside now, Bruno said to himself, then it's all up. He saw the man glance at the second knife lying on the ground, well out of Bruno's reach. Bruno locked eyes with his assailant and took a step forward, daring his opponent to come on to him. The hooded figure looked up, then ran full tilt at Bruno.

Bruno swerved to one side to avoid the blow, but the blade still grazed the side of his face, drawing blood. Bruno swore and lashed out in a fury at his attacker. But this one was stronger and smarter than his comrade. Before Bruno could get in a clear aim he was struck again, this time with a boot or fist. Before he knew it he was down, and the filth of the street was filling his mouth and nostrils.

Instinctively, he rolled to one side, to avoid another blow. He looked up, desperately trying to make sense of the situation. He was aware of his attacker closing upon him again, a blur of movement above him. From the corner of his eye, he saw the knife, lying just out of reach on the far side of the street. He had to get the blade, or he was dead.

His attacker read his intentions, and in so doing made his first mistake. Before Bruno could reach the knife, the hooded man had recklessly plunged for the blade. The movement was ill-timed. Bruno caught hold of his leg and brought him down. His assailant had his fingers around the hilt of the knife, but Bruno was onto him before he could use either weapon again. He smashed his fist down hard on the other man's hand, forcing the blade out of his grip. Bruno grabbed at it as it slithered across the cobblestones, clamping the hilt of the knife in his hand before it slipped out of reach.

For a few moments the two men were locked together in a deadly embrace, a struggle from which only one could emerge with his life. The hooded man cursed and spat at Bruno, trying desperately to break away. But it was Bruno who landed the decisive blow. His assailant finally worked one arm free. As he pulled back to stab with the knife, Bruno jabbed his own weapon home, ramming the blade into the other's throat. The man's eyes widened, and a pearl of foamy blood spilled from his mouth. Gradually his grip on Bruno slackened, and he slumped back, his head cracking hard upon the ground.

Bruno made a rapid check of the two bodies. There was nothing on them or about them that gave any clue as to who they were, or what they were about. The answer clearly lay on the other side of the rusted gates. He scanned the alley in both directions – there was still no one else in sight.

He took stock of the damage he'd sustained. His upper body was drenched in blood, but to his relief, it wasn't his. His only wounds were a cut along one cheek, and some grazing to his upper arms. Bruno patted his face to satisfy himself it wasn't bleeding badly then set about finding somewhere where he wouldn't be disturbed.

Like most of the buildings in the street, the one across the way looked long disused. Either way, he had little time or opportunity to knock and enquire. Bruno aimed a hefty kick at the door. The rotting timbers were compliant, and gave way immediately. Bruno hauled the bodies of the two men off the street. Once inside, he went through their pockets more carefully, but found nothing to identify them. Bruno looked at the two men.

The larger one was near enough his size. His clothes were the worse for wear in places but otherwise intact, with no obvious bloodstains on them.

Bruno took a deep breath, and started unbuttoning his own, blood-soaked tunic. 'In for a penny,' he muttered to himself.

WHEN HE EMERGED a few minutes later, the street was still quiet with was no one in sight. But the silence was not total, not quite. Somewhere, not far away, he could hear voices, coming from inside the warehouse the men had been guarding.

Bruno pulled the hood of the borrowed jerkin as far forward as it would go, but there was no masking the fresh cut to his face. He would just have to hope he passed muster. He eased open the creaking gates and walked steadily towards the sound of voices.

A covered path led directly to a further set of doors. The voices were coming from a room somewhere on the other side. Bruno reached the doors and paused. This was his last chance to turn back. He had no idea what he would face on the other side; no idea how many men there were, or whether they were armed. He wondered whether Mikhal would recognise him, and what would happen if he did. He took a deep breath and stepped inside.

His first impression was of a vast, dimly lit auditorium. The place might once have been a warehouse, but it had long since been stripped of the stocks of its trade. But it was far from empty. In fact, it was practically full. The chill air outside was quickly replaced by the warm fug of human bodies. There must have been a hundred there, maybe more. A few were dressed more or less like Bruno; the rest in long grey robes that covered them from head to foot. Bruno remembered those robes from the Helmsman. Then he recalled the change that had come, instantaneously, over Mikhal. Ready or not, this was what he'd been searching for.

He looked around, trying to locate Mikhal. That was going to prove impossible. If he had entered the place wearing his everyday clothes, he was not wearing them now. He was lost, faceless and anonymous amidst the sea of grey. Bruno looked around for others dressed like him, in hide jerkins. There were probably a dozen in all, and most had taken up a position around the edge of the hall, like guards. From recent experience, it was safe to assume that all were armed.

Heads turned, then turned away, as Bruno entered the hall. Almost everyone was gazing towards an elevated rostrum set at the front. A tangible sense of anticipation hung in the air. Bruno could feel it, an edgy, cold tension in his gut. The pressure inside the hall continued to build for a few minutes longer, then, without warning, it was released. A collective cry, something between a cheer and a wail of anguish, went up around the hall as a robed figure, flanked by two guards, climbed the rostrum.

Bruno stared up at the figure, and wondered if, by some bizarre circumstance, this could be Mikhal. But even though the hood and folds of the robes carefully hid the face, Bruno knew it was not Mikhal. This man was fuller in figure, and shorter. Bruno had the impression it was an older man; a man accustomed to leading. He stood behind the rostrum, allowing the sound around the hall to rise, and then extended both hands towards the crowd, abruptly silencing them.

Bruno had the eerie sense of being in the presence of an unyielding, omnipotent power. The figure on the stage had not yet spoken a single word, yet he had the crowd mesmerised, held in thrall to his power. When at last he spoke, it was in a voice that was at once rich and deep, yet utterly cold and devoid of hope.

'Suffering,' the man bellowed. 'Suffering must be your penance, if you are to earn salvation. For only through suffering will you purge your sins, and find redemption.'

Something inside Bruno relaxed a little. He even had to suppress the urge for a wry smile. This was nothing special. Hadn't he heard this miserable claptrap a hundred times before? By all the gods, when he got hold of Mikhal, he'd march him to the Helmsman and shake this nonsense out of him over a few quarts of ale…

'Suffering must be your testament, and it will be the gospel that you shall spread through all the temples of sin, through all this wanton place.'

A finger of ice touched Bruno. His lighter spirits vanished as quickly as they had come. The atmosphere around him changed, abruptly. A darker, more threatening mood began to take hold.

'It is not enough that we suffer, each within ourselves,' the preacher continued. 'If Altdorf is to be saved, if the Empire is to be saved–' The heavy figure pressed forward against the rostrum. 'If the Old World and all its peoples are to be saved, then all must be cleansed. Cleansed and made pure through suffering.'

Somewhere amidst the crowd a voice cried out: 'Only through suffering will they be made whole!'

And another: 'First comes the rain; then will come fire!'

Bruno's mood was less easy now. He looked at the faces of those standing around him: they were utterly in thrall to the figure at the rostrum. Whatever he told them, they would believe. Whatever he told them to do, they would do. Hundreds of otherwise ordinary people packed inside the cavernous space stood ready and willing to do the preacher's bidding.

Bruno's instinct was to get out, but he could not simply turn and run. There was a menace in the words he was hearing, a threat in the stifling air that was sounding a warning to him. He did not yet fully comprehend what that threat might be, but he knew it could not be ignored.

The preacher struck out a hand to silence the crowd. 'Without doubt, there are some who are not ready,' he said. 'Not ready to suffer, not ready to be made whole once more.' The hooded head scanned the hall from one side to the other. 'Perhaps there are even some amongst *you* who are not ready.'

Bruno tensed, feeling a hundred pairs of eyes boring into his very soul. Surely his disguise would be exposed. Any moment now there would be a shout, and a tangle of arms would grab out at him, pinning him to the ground. But the gaze of every person inside the four walls remained fixed, spellbound, on the rostrum.

'Those that are not ready we must carry with us,' the preacher warned. 'There is no time left to prevaricate. They who shun suffering now will surrender their souls to eternity!'

The preacher's gaze swept the crowd, his hooded eyes scanning the gathering, sifting the strong from the weak; the believers from those still clinging to their doubts.

'Who amongst you is ready to pledge their soul to the struggle?' he demanded. 'Who amongst you is ready for the sacrifice the great gods command?'

All across the room, hands were raised up into the air. Voices rang out, clamouring to be chosen. Bruno looked around. He was the only one he could see who had not raised his hand. Slowly, he lifted one arm tentatively into the air, praying to almighty Sigmar that the preacher would not choose him.

He was not chosen. As he looked up, Bruno saw the preacher point towards the back of the hall, and beckon a disciple forward. Gradually the hands were lowered, and an expectant silence fell upon the gathering. A zealot, dressed like most of the others in an all-enveloping robe, made his way towards the rostrum. As he mounted the podium, the preacher lay a hand on his disciple's head.

'The gods smile upon your devotion,' he said, quietly. He turned back towards the crowd. 'We are all born to struggle,' he proclaimed. 'We are all born to pain.'

A cry, raw and angry, rose up from the gathering. The preacher called for silence, and turned to the figure beside him.

'Are you ready to embrace sacrifice, brother? Are you ready to embrace pain?'

The disciple was shaking, visibly trembling. He nodded his head, just once. 'I am, master,' he said, his voice hoarse and unsteady. 'I am ready for whatever you command.'

Bruno felt a chill like ice in his gut. The words meant nothing at all to him, but he recognised the voice at once. The man standing on the stage was Mikhal.

'TWELVE BANDITS,' NATALIA insisted. 'At least three beastmen, and I swear, an orc.'

'I'm not sure about the orc,' Maier countered. 'It ran before any of us could finish it, remember?'

Nagel grunted. 'Orcs never run. They stand and fight until you've ripped the very life from their ugly ape bodies.'

Stefan laughed. 'Let's call it an orc, if it makes Natalia happy.' He took a pull on his beer then turned his attention to the bread and cheese on the plate in front of him. His belly was comfortably full, and he was feeling content. Progress had been good over the first week, in more ways than one. They had reached Balzen, a sizeable village more than halfway to Stahlfort. They had made the journey in good time, and without casualty. Natalia's tally of opponents might have been inexact – Stefan wasn't convinced about the orc – but it wasn't far off.

They had been attacked again, and more than once, since that first ambush on the marshes. But they had weathered each assault with the lightest of consequences – a few cuts and bruises, which time and a judicious use of herbs would heal. They had all acquitted themselves well.

That included Natalia. If Stefan still had concerns about Alexei Zucharov's sister, then it wasn't on account of her courage, or even her fighting skills. She might not be a swordsman, but she was more than capable of defending herself. She had dealt with at least two of the bandits who had been unwise enough to try their luck. Maier, and Nagel too, had done everything that had been asked of them. Money might well have been their driving motive, but they were both prepared to earn it. Stefan was growing increasingly confident about them reaching their destination. What happened when they got there was another matter.

Natalia stretched and yawned. 'Sweet Shallya, I'm looking forward to a good soft bed,' she said. 'I could sleep for a week.'

'Well, you can't,' Nagel muttered, literal as ever.

'I don't remember any promises about the beds being soft, or even good for that matter,' Maier remarked, 'but right now any bed sounds good.'

Stefan agreed with them. It had been a long, arduous journey, and they had earned a brief respite. Balzen was the only habited village of any size on their route, and stopping there was more a matter of necessity than choice. But so far they'd been made tolerably welcome, as welcome as strangers ever are in a village as remote as this. Money always helped, and Albrecht had seen to it that they were well provided for. They'd managed to buy all the supplies they needed for the rest of their journey, and they had found an inn that provided food and a bed for the night. In the morning they would rise early and be on the road by dawn. Even the warmest of welcomes could be outstayed.

For all her protestations of exhaustion, Natalia seemed in no hurry to leave the table. Maier went first, taking Nagel, who had steadily drunk himself to a standstill, with him. That left Stefan at the corner table with Natalia. There were a handful of others still in the bar, but like so many travellers they preferred to mind their own business and keep out of others'. To all intents and purposes, the two of them were alone.

Inevitably, they would talk of Alexei again. Since that first night, she had made the most of opportunities that came her way to prise more out of Stefan. He, in turn, had grown accustomed to talking about her brother; indeed, in many ways, he welcomed it. She had never returned to the moment of her brother's death, preferring instead to draw on Stefan's memories of Alexei during that last fateful journey to the east. He was able to tell her about the man he had respected, not the monster he later became.

'He never wrote, you know,' she began. 'Never wrote to me. Did I mention that?'

'You did,' Stefan affirmed. He delved deep into his memories. After a while, an image came to mind. A late night, deep in the forest. Alexei, sitting by the fire, some paper in his hands. Stefan remembered him looking secretive, almost shy for once. What had he been doing?

'I think,' he said at last, 'I think he may have written. Written to you, I mean. But I don't suppose he ever got the chance to send the letter. We were a long way from home.'

Natalia nodded. The expression on her face grew unusually sad. Whether it was the thought of her brother, or just the fatigue, Stefan couldn't tell.

'You were very close,' Stefan ventured. 'You and Alexei, weren't you?'

'Yes, we were,' she whispered, almost inaudibly. Then she brightened a little. 'But for Alexei, our father would have had me married off by now to some imbecile count, some lord of nowhere. In fact,' she reflected, 'but for Alexei, I wouldn't be here at all. He saved me from drowning when I was a child.' She laughed, briefly. 'Back then I was invincible, or so I thought. A lake of melting ice and a very angry brother taught me otherwise.'

She went to drink from her mug then pushed the rest of the beer away, untouched. 'Alexei made me the person I am now. I owe him everything.'

'I'm sorry he's dead,' Stefan said. 'Truly, I am.'

A silence fell between them that neither appeared ready or able to break. Finally Natalia said, 'What do you think he'll be like?'

'What do you mean?' Stefan asked, a little confused.

'Von Diehl,' Natalia said, keeping her voice low. 'He's the reason we've come all this way.'

Stefan thought for a moment. He remembered the likeness that Albrecht had shown him. The narrow, pinched face, the coldness in the distant gaze. But a likeness was all it was; nothing more than an image. That was not Heinrich von Diehl.

'I think he will be much like evil has always been, wherever I have encountered it,' he said at last. 'I think he will be the shadow to my light. He will be the living embodiment of the cause against which I lift my sword. And he will be the reason I cannot rest, so long as he and his kind draw breath upon this world.'

Natalia sat back, and mulled over Stefan's words. 'For most of my life, I never had any idea that such evil existed,' she said.

'It exists, believe me,' Stefan told her. 'Nor are we ever very far from it.'

She looked around, to be sure that they could not be overheard. 'And yet this is the man that we are to free from captivity? Truly, we are living through strange and troubled times.'

'We are,' Stefan agreed, sombrely. 'Troubled times indeed.'

CHAPTER EIGHT
The Single Thread

MARCUS ALBRECHT WATCHED the carriage and its outriders disappear along the length of the boulevard then turned back from the window in disdain.

'Morr take that wretched man,' he declared. 'He struts about Altdorf like a golden pheasant. Or perhaps that should be a prophet, a prophet without testament.'

Nikolas was contrastingly sober in his assessment. 'Indeed, but a prophet with a host of followers,' he pointed out.

He steered his mentor back to his chair. 'And heresy is still heresy,' he said. 'Even when spoken by men of high standing.'

Albrecht peered at the younger man, unsure whether Nikolas was entirely serious. The look on his face suggested that he was.

'Heresy?' Albrecht snapped. 'Because I speak a few uncomfortable words of truth about our noble Grand Theogonist?'

'Well, yes,' Nikolas replied, ever the pragmatist. 'Exactly that. And you're not being entirely fair, either. Esmer may have his own reasons for remaining in Altdorf. But there's no arguing that he has rallied the people. He's an inspiration to many.'

'Exactly my point,' Albrecht muttered, irritably. He caught the look of mild reproach in Nikolas's eyes, and his tone softened. 'Ah, Nikolas. Thanks be to Sigmar that you're here to curb my tongue,' he chuckled. 'Your advice is sound currency, as ever.'

Nikolas bowed discreetly. 'It's a shame you don't always heed it,' he chided, mildly. 'But you too have a point. Altdorf could do with a little less religious fervour at the moment.'

He looked around at the book-lined walls of his mentor's study. How many students of the university had passed through this room, oblivious to the secret life of their eminent professor of philosophy? He exchanged a brief glance with Albrecht. Time to get to business.

'They should be well on their way by now,' he observed, quietly.

'Indeed,' Albrecht agreed. 'Whatever happens to Stefan and the others is now beyond our control. We must turn to matters closer to home.'

Nikolas reached down and set a leather bag on the table. He removed a sheaf of papers, each inscribed with cryptic notes in a neat hand. Nikolas frowned as he studied each of the sheets in turn.

Albrecht leaned closer, and nodded approvingly. 'Our observers have been diligent.'

The frown on Nikolas's brow deepened. 'Yes. Plenty of incidents reported, all across the city. But not much linking them together.'

'Something is coming,' Albrecht insisted. 'I can feel it.' He drummed his fingers on the table. 'Start with the zealots,' he said at last. 'What news since last you reported?'

Nikolas took up three or four wafers of parchment and studied them carefully. 'More meetings,' he said. 'More converts and more evangelical preachings. It may indicate a wider plan. But then again, it may not.'

'The Black Confessors have caused trouble before,' Albrecht remarked. 'I'll warrant they will again.'

Nikolas shrugged, doubtfully. 'Perhaps. But perhaps not. The True Path are now the single largest zealot group.'

'But a few weeks ago they were nothing. Almost unheard of.'

'That's what gives cause for concern. Suddenly they're everywhere, yet we still know little about their leaders, and even less of their motives.' He paused. 'Of course, we could take a more... direct approach. We could either buy the confidence of one of their disciples, or simply interrogate them.' He waited a moment. 'Stefan's brother, for example.'

'Mikhal Kumansky? He's a peripheral figure. I doubt he'd know much,' Albrecht said. 'No, whatever plans the True Path may have, we need to smoke them out carefully. At this stage I won't risk anything that might alert them to our interest. Keep watching, Nikolas. Nothing more.'

He leafed through the papers on the desk. 'What else do the eyes tell us?'

'Murders, disappearances, robberies,' Nikolas told him. 'Nothing out of the ordinary for a week in Altdorf. Except–'

'Except?'

'Some human remains that were washed out of the sewers beneath the Sigmarsbrucke. The bodies looked like they'd been crudely butchered, or else torn apart by a particularly violent assailant.'

Albrecht winced. 'Butchered, then the corpses hidden in the sewers, you think?'

'Possibly. But reports all remark upon the pallid look of them. Almost as though they'd been some while without daylight. Before they died, I mean.'

Albrecht pondered on the significance of Nikolas's words for a few moments. 'All right,' he said at last. 'Anything more?'

'The usual concoction of rumours and stories.'

'For example?'

Nikolas scanned the papers again. 'Let's see… a costermonger, Ferdinand Schiller was overheard in a tavern talking about seeing a daemon enter the city through a gap in the north wall…'

Albrecht raised an eyebrow. 'Actually,' Nikolas continued, 'that's the same costermonger that saw the same daemon come through the east wall just a month ago… Wait, though,' he said. 'Here's something.' He lifted two separate sheets of script and compared them. 'This is interesting,' he said.

'Go on,' Albrecht commanded.

'Two separate reports, tavern talk once again,' Nikolas said. 'Neither particularly credible on their own, but both with a similar tale.'

'Which is?'

'Two men, one a market porter, the other a tailor, overheard talking about hearing sounds below ground on separate occasions.'

'Sounds?'

'One described some kind a tremor within the earth. A portent of doom, he would have it. The tailor was more restrained in his telling. What he described was the sound of men labouring below ground, or perhaps

trapped, and trying to get out.' He shrugged, apologeti-
cally. 'Again, it could be nothing.'

'Find these two men, Nikolas,' Albrecht urged. 'Talk to
them. Try and find out more. I'll have a discreet word
with Ehrhart, and see if his men have heard anything
similar.' A troubled expression crossed his face. 'These
fragments,' he said. 'These pieces of stories. Somehow
they are linked together by a single thread. We must
trace the path of that thread, Nikolas. We must find
where it leads.'

BRUNO'S FIRST INSTINCT had been to go to the watch. He
had escaped from the warehouse undetected. His gut
feeling was that it was time to extricate himself from an
increasingly dangerous situation. He felt he should go to
the watch and tell them everything. Dealing with cultists
was their business, not his.

But as time passed he began to have second thoughts.
Go to the watch, and tell them what, exactly? That he
had been to a meeting where a preacher was prophesy-
ing doom and damnation? Hardly anything new in that,
particularly in these uncertain times. The more he
thought about it, the less his story seemed to have any
substance. What he had heard inside the warehouse had
convinced him that the city itself was in peril. But now,
in the cold broad light of day, it didn't seem quite like
that. He imagined the questions the watch sergeant
might put to him:

What were the threats he had heard made against the
people of Altdorf? None. The menace lay in the chill
that he had felt along the length of his spine, in the rising hysteria of the disciples around him. But no sedition
had been spoken, no plot raised against the city or its
inhabitants. The threat had been in what he had felt, not
what he had heard.

What forbidden rituals had he seen performed? None. In truth, Bruno had little knowledge of such things, but nothing he had seen looked that much out of the ordinary. All he had seen was a single man addressing a crowd, a crowd gathered there of its own free will. And these days there was nothing so unusual about that.

What were the names of those there? The only name he knew was the one he would be most reluctant to divulge – Mikhal Kumansky. And that was the irony of it all. If, as he suspected, the meeting had been part of something altogether more sinister, then it was all the more important to extricate Mikhal before things went too far. Until then, it would be better not to involve the watch, not to mention the matter of the two dead bodies that he might be called upon to explain. No, he would stay clear of the watch for a while.

What would Stefan have done? What would Stefan have wanted *him* to do? He would want him to protect Mikhal, in any way that he could. That was the answer. He would talk to Mikhal, and get to the truth of things. If there was a harmless explanation for the ravings of the hooded preacher, well and good. He'd be content not to trouble himself with Mikhal's business any further. If not – well, Bruno hadn't yet managed to think his way through that. But, somehow, he would rescue Mikhal. Rescue him, if necessary, from himself. He would waste no more time. He would go to Mikhal's warehouse on the docks, and confront him.

It was a dank, dull day, and even at noon lights were still lit in the windows of the taverns and workshops. The harbour wharf was the hub of the city, the artery through which the life-blood of trade flowed in and out of Altdorf. The waterfront was crammed with warehouses, silos and merchants' chambers of every conceivable shape and size. The lights along the wharf twinkled like a thousand stars in the murky noon twilight.

Around the wharf, the bustle and shouted conversations of the stevedores tried to tell Bruno all was well with the world; that life continued, vibrant and robust. It was a strangely comforting scene, quite at odds with the unease that gnawed at him. About a dozen vessels lay at rest on the glassy water of the harbour, but Mikhal's freshly painted ship, the two-masted *Karla*, was not amongst them.

He picked out Mikhal's offices, a brightly painted cluster of buildings half way along the quay. Stevedores hauled sacks of grain in and out of the warehouse doors. Any that recognised Bruno hailed him with a cheerful greeting. There was nothing to suggest that but the day was not continuing as normal.

Stefan's younger brother looked up from his papers as Bruno entered his office. The expression on Mikhal's face was first of surprise, quickly followed by alarm.

'Bruno! What brings you here at this hour of day? It's – it's not Stefan, is it? Not bad news?'

'No, no, nothing like that,' Bruno assured him. 'No word of Stefan, but then I was expecting none. I'm sure all's going to plan.'

'He was utterly secretive about the whole thing with me,' Mikhal said. 'Wouldn't say a word about where he was going, or what he had to do when he got there.' He pointed to a chair, inviting Mikhal to sit. 'I daresay he told you a deal more, though?'

Bruno shrugged, and took a seat. This wasn't going at all as he thought it would. He had thought he might find Mikhal drawn and distraught, ready to take him into his confidence. Instead, Mikhal sat there, every inch the successful man of commerce, confident and in command. Rather than being about Mikhal, the conversation had immediately steered towards Stefan, and what Bruno might or might not know. This wasn't what he had planned.

He was struggling to find a way of bringing the talk back to matters at hand, when Mikhal helped him out.

'You'll forgive me, Bruno. But I'm damnably busy at the moment. If not about Stefan, then why, exactly, are you here?'

Bruno took a deep breath. There was no way of dressing up what he had to say. He might as well get straight to the point. 'In a way this is about Stefan,' he began. 'He asked me to – to look out for you.'

Mikhal stared at Bruno, clearly incredulous. 'Look out for me? Staff of Ulric, Bruno, I'm twenty-two summers grown. I'm not a boy any more!'

'He's worried about what you're getting yourself into,' Bruno blurted out. The words just spilled from his tongue. 'And, for what it's worth, so am I.'

Mikhal continued to stare at Bruno. The incredulous expression hardened to something colder. 'You'd better say precisely what you mean.'

'I think you know what I mean,' Bruno replied, doggedly. 'The business with the zealots. The One Path, or whatever they call themselves.'

Mikhal sighed, wearily. 'So that's it. Look, I gave them money in the tavern. Maybe it was a lot of money. What of it? Look around you, Bruno. Business is flourishing. And it's *my* business what I do with my money,' he added, peevishly. 'My business, not yours.'

'I thought you said your mortal soul was in peril,' Bruno persisted. 'The scar on your wrist, remember. Didn't you call it the mark of damnation?'

Mikhal rotated his arm and glanced at the faded remnant of the old wound, rather as he might look at something which had long since lost all significance. 'I was under a lot of pressure,' he told Bruno. 'I hadn't been well for a few days. It was probably the beer talking.'

It was on the tip of Bruno's tongue to say it. That was what he had really come here to talk about. Just say it: *That morning. At the Ledermarkt. I was there. I heard everything.*

But, before he could say another word, Mikhal said, 'Anyway, I haven't seen or heard from those people, whoever they are, since that day in the tavern. And there's no reason why I should.' He looked up at Bruno, and offered him a brisk, businesslike smile. 'Was that it?'

Bruno couldn't fathom why Mikhal was lying to him. But he knew for sure was that he was lying. There would be no talking Mikhal around; no amicable chat over a pot of ale in the Helmsman. Things, clearly, had gone too far for that. He stood up and put on his coat.

'Sorry, Mikhal,' he muttered. 'My misunderstanding. Sorry to have troubled you.'

Mikhal stood and offered his hand. 'No trouble, old friend,' he said. 'It's reassuring to know Stefan still looks out for his little brother.'

Bruno's eyes searched for clues amongst the papers and records lying about the room. But there was nothing, just the clutter of everyday commerce. 'I'm glad trade is good,' he said, light-heartedly. 'By the way, where's the *Karla*? I didn't see her on the jetty.'

'The *Karla*?' Mikhal's tone grew noticeably edgy. 'She's not in port.'

'That's a pity,' Bruno commented. 'I was looking forward to taking a proper look at her.' He had an odd feeling that the balance of the conversation had shifted, yet couldn't pinpoint why. 'Where was she bound?'

'North,' Mikhal replied, vaguely. 'Talabheim.'

'Talabheim? Won't that take her close to the fighting?' When Mikhal didn't respond, Bruno continued. 'What's she carrying?'

'Nothing,' Mikhal shot back, irritably. 'She's running out empty and bringing back a cargo of cornmeal. What's it to you, anyway?'

'Nothing,' Bruno said quietly. 'It's nothing to me at all.' He took up his hat and made for the door. 'I'll bid you a good day,' he said.

TWO DAYS OUT from Balzen, and the landscape had become more desolate than ever. Now there were no villages and no travellers at all venturing out upon the road. Even the raiders that had so plagued their progress on the first leg of the journey west had disappeared.

'Nothing between here and Stahlfort but wilderness and water,' Nagel had promised, and so it was. Slowly but surely, the landscape had transformed. First the towering hills and thick pine forests had been supplanted by marshlands. Now the marshes themselves were gone, replaced with undulating swathes of open grassland, vast, dazzling fields of bright, emerald green. Then came the lakes, empty expanses of water often several miles across.

Not for the first time, Stefan marvelled at the majesty of the Empire, and all its bewildering complexities. Wilderness it might be, bleak and unforgiving. But it was also a place of stark, cruel beauty; a huge sapphire vista that mocked the puny ambitions of the mortals cast briefly upon its face. Stefan felt awed and diminished to think of himself, so tiny a piece in the greater picture.

Mere days ago, Stahlfort and Heinrich von Diehl had been just names: imaginary places, imaginary people on a journey without end. But as each day and each step brought them closer to their destination, the names had started to assume more solid forms in Stefan's mind. Soon the travelling would be over, and then the real journey would begin.

At first light they buried a bundle of documents wrapped tightly inside an oilskin pouch. Inside were the identity papers of four merchants returning home to Altdorf. And there was a fifth: Mannfred Dursten, a silversmith by trade. A fictional identity for a man soon to become all too real. Stefan swept the freshly turned earth with his foot and smoothed the level ground. He looked up, fixing in his memory the two, forked trees that stood guard above. 'Remember this place,' he told Natalia. 'We'll need to find it again if we're to get safely back into Altdorf.'

Until they returned to this place they were merchants no longer. Now they would have only one identity, their mission and letters of instruction vouchsafed by no less an authority than the Imperial witch hunters of Altdorf. The papers, Nikolas had assured him, were excellent forgeries. Soon they would put that confidence to the test.

Over the last few days, Natalia had been a talkative, and inquisitive companion. But now, as the riders set off on the final few miles towards their destination, she grew very quiet, trying to imagine, perhaps, what awaited them on the far side of the water on the island. Stefan had no answer, except perhaps, that she should be prepared for almost anything.

Nagel, too, was quiet, even by his own taciturn standards. Perhaps he had started to wonder what sort of reception he would receive on his return to the prison he had served as a guard. He'd left on less than amicable terms, that much Stefan knew. Nagel's knowledge of Stahlfort might well prove invaluable, but, in other ways, Stefan couldn't help thinking he could just as easily prove a liability.

That morning only Maier seemed unaffected by what lay ahead. This came as no surprise to Stefan. He had recognised the easygoing bluster for what it surely was: a mask that Karl Maier rarely, if ever, let slip. But so long as Maier's sword earned him his pay that was fine with Stefan. These were his fellow journeymen, not his friends, and not for a moment did he forget it.

As the hours rolled past towards noon, the green panorama ahead steadily changed. There was less land now and more water. The path they had been following became little more than a raised strip, one of a series of narrow ridges that marked a web of paths across a drowned land. Soon the paths would end, and there would be no more land. Water swirled around the horses' hooves as they pressed on to the north and west in single file.

The landscape had remained almost totally flat, nothing between the riders and the far horizon. Then at last a dark bruise appeared against the pale blue of the sky, a compact spur of rock that jutted like a clenched fist above the waters. Stefan slowed down and shaded his eyes to get a better view. From a distance, it was difficult to gauge its size, or tell how far away it was. Unlike the greenery all around, the rock, or island, was a smear of grey, devoid of trees and shrubs. In fact it was quite featureless, aside from the skirt of cliffs surrounding it, and the faint outline of some buildings that nestled towards the centre.

'Is that it?' Stefan asked. Nagel nodded. 'That's it. Stahlfort.'

'There's no road across to the island?'

'No road. They'll send a ferry for us.'

'A ferry?' Natalia queried.

'A one-way service,' Nagel muttered, 'taking prisoners to the island.'

They pushed on cautiously, working their way along the promontory that jutted out towards the island. Conversation was muted. The mission was about to enter a quite separate, and far more dangerous phase.

Stefan turned his thoughts to the man whose name was inscribed in the warrant papers in his pocket. Until now, his focus had been firmly on Heinrich von Diehl. He had all but forgotten the other man, the ghost whose identity would grant them entry to the stronghold and, Sigmar willing, would get them out again. Walter Koch was a criminal, but a petty one by Stahlfort's standards. He was held in the main block, well away from von Diehl and the other Chaos prisoners. If the witch hunters wanted Koch, then Stahlfort would doubtless let them have him. It would be one less mouth to feed, and ultimately, one less corpse to dispose of.

They would arrive with a warrant to transport Walter Koch back to Altdorf for questioning. They would leave with a prisoner in their custody. Again, Nikolas had assured Stefan, the paperwork was near perfect, the forgery all but impossible to detect.

Koch was the ideal decoy. His criminal career was long enough to make him of possible interest to the witch hunters, but his crimes were minor enough to make the gaolers of Stahlfort happy to see the back of him.

If all went to plan, then Walter Koch would become the unwitting hero of the story. To the end, he would never know what contribution his sacrifice would have made to the salvation of Altdorf. For all their sakes, Stefan prayed that it would be worthwhile.

Closer up, Stahlfort began to reveal its ugly secrets. Jagged cliffs surrounded the island on all sides, the only way in or out was a single narrow fissure in the rockface. There was no greenery, not so much as a single blade of grass to relieve the leaden grey. The garrison stood above the cliffs, a slate grey monolith forged from the same dark rock that formed the island.

If escape from the island itself had not already been improbable, it was rendered impossible by the construction of Stahlfort. The face it presented to the outside world was one of sheer, impenetrable walls, with guard towers that reached to the sky at each corner. What few windows there were on outer walls were nothing but narrow cracks, good for only a trickle of air or light to pass through.

The island looked quiet, almost peaceful. There was no visible sign of any life, human or otherwise. But Stefan knew the other side of those forbidding walls was teeming with life… if existence in such a place could be called life. He imagined approaching the island as a prisoner. How might it feel, as you crossed the water, knowing that this would be your last sight of open skies? Knowing that life, as you understood it was at an end? Not yet knowing what purgatory lay ahead.

'Does anyone ever get out?' Stefan wondered aloud.

'Not alive they don't,' Nagel replied.

The narrow track dwindled away to nothing as it met the water's edge. There was nothing but open water ahead. The riders dismounted and stood looking out towards the island.

'Do we just wait?' Natalia asked. 'We could be here for an eternity. How are we supposed to signal that we want to get across?'

'No need for signals,' Nagel replied, tersely. 'They'll know we're here.'

'He's right,' Maier said. 'Look over there.'

Stefan looked towards the island. Something was moving in the water just ahead of the rock, a small boat ploughing a steady course towards the shore.

'Our own private carriage,' Maier murmured. 'How charming.'

The boat sat low in the water, four or five men rowed on either side. A further two sat in the prow, with shields and weapons prominently displayed. This was no welcoming party.

'How deep is the water?' Stefan asked.

'Deep enough,' Nagel assured him. 'You wouldn't want to swim across, believe me.'

With the boat still some twenty feet from shore, one of the men in the prow stood up. His uniform and livery was similar to that of an Imperial Guardsman, but instead of the cross of Sigmar, he wore the emblem of a prisoner fastened in chains emblazoned in white upon his black tunic.

'What is your business?' he called out. 'You're trespassing on the Emperor's land.'

'We're here on the Emperor's business,' Stefan replied firmly. 'Here by appointment and invitation.' As he spoke, he prayed that their mission was not about to founder on the first outright lie.

'I know nothing of that,' the man replied, equally firmly. 'There are no visitors expected.'

'It's not my fault if your records aren't in order,' Stefan shouted back. He removed the bundle of papers from his pocket and brandished them above his head. 'I have sealed copies of our orders here. We have come to claim back a prisoner for the witch hunters.'

The boat had drifted closer into shore. Stefan snatched a good look at his interrogator. The man was older than he had first thought. Silver streaked his hair and beard; his age was belied by his ramrod posture and muscular build. Not a man to cross lightly. The man stared directly at Stefan through a single, unblinking eye. Where the other eye should have been, the flesh closed over an empty socket.

'Examine the papers for yourself,' Stefan continued, 'if you care to break the Imperial seal.'

The boat ran aground, the prow nuzzling into the mud at Stefan's feet. Four guardsmen sprang out to surround Stefan's party, followed by their one-eyed captain. He snatched the papers from Stefan's hand without ceremony. If he wasn't satisfied, Stefan realised, his men would probably butcher them where they stood.

'This is the first I've seen or heard of this,' he remarked. He looked up at Stefan, the single eye appraising him with a probing intensity. 'And you say you have ridden from Altdorf?'

'That's right,' Stefan affirmed. 'Our masters would be gravely disappointed if we returned empty handed.'

'I'll wager they would,' the man agreed, a veiled sarcasm in his voice. He read through the documents a second time. 'Very well,' he said at last. 'We'll see what they make of this at the gate. Step up to the boat and hand over your weapons as you board.'

'What about our horses?' Natalia asked. The one-eyed man shifted his gaze towards Nagel and Maier, each holding two of the horses by the reins. Stefan thought he saw Nagel avert his face, as though unwilling to be caught by the stare. But the warder was only interested in the horses. Clearly, there would be no space for the beasts on the ferry.

'They stay here,' he said. 'My men will take them to the stable house.' Stefan followed his gaze. Along the shore, almost hidden behind the tall reeds growing up around the water's edge, was a low wooden building surrounded by a stockade. He was reluctant for them to be parted from their only means of escape, but it seemed there was little choice.

'Hurry up,' the one-eyed man commanded. 'We must catch the tide.'

Stefan stepped onto the prow and into the body of the boat.

Maier scrambled aboard, followed by Nagel, each relinquishing their weapons as they had been instructed. As the boat cast off, Nagel made his way to the stern and sat down between Stefan and Natalia. He looked anything but happy.

'Whatever they're paying me, it isn't enough,' he muttered, under his breath.

Natalia took his hand. 'It's going to be all right,' she said, encouragingly. 'Have faith.'

Nagel glowered at her, and pulled his hand free. 'Save your faith for the journey back,' he said. 'If we ever get that far.'

CHAPTER NINE
Among the Dead

As THE PRISON boat slipped between the towering cliffs of the island, the shadows closed in and the last glimmerings of light were sucked from the sky. Prisoners arriving here must have felt they were passing through the very gates of Morr, thought Stefan.

The channel cut through the cliff before opening out to reveal a horseshoe-shaped harbour, with a wooden jetty where the boats disembarked. From the jetty, a flight of steps hewn from the rock led to the cliff-top. The grey outline of Stahlfort stood in the distance, a dark fortress of high towers and heavy walls, waiting to fold them into its unyielding embrace.

More armed guards waited on the jetty. As Stefan and his companions stepped ashore they were searched and a slender dagger Maier was carrying was seized.

'This is it,' Nagel said to Stefan. 'Most climbing these steps know that their life is as good as over. We're amongst the dead men now.'

'Let's try and be the exceptions to that rule,' Stefan muttered. He looked back to find Natalia a few paces behind, just ahead of Maier.

The one-eyed man was last off the boat. Only when the jetty was clear did he start to climb the steps. Stefan caught Nagel looking away, trying to avoid the myopic stare.

'You know him,' he said. 'There's something about him that frightens you.'

Nagel muttered an oath beneath his breath. 'His name is Friedrich Krieger. He was here in my time at Stahlfort. There's good enough cause to fear him.'

'Who is he?'

'Head of the Sekurheitszicke – the chief officer of security. A cold, ruthless bastard.'

'How did he lose the eye?' Stefan asked.

'Prisoner trying to escape,' Nagel said. 'Put Krieger's eye out with a metal bar ripped from a cell window.'

Stefan pictured the image, briefly. 'Did they… escape?'

Nagel gave a hollow laugh. 'What do you think?'

Beyond the steps was a wall easily thirty feet high. The only way in was through an enormous set of gates, fashioned from heavy iron. The two main prison blocks lay on the other side, desolate and austere, like massive grey stone tombs.

Krieger strode ahead – not towards the gates – but to a single storey building off to one side.

'The guardhouse,' Nagel explained. 'Any visitors have to be checked in there first. We're not in yet.'

Inside the guardhouse, their papers were scrutinised again by a guard commander. The commander looked each of the new arrivals up and down and then scanned the warrants. His face was devoid of expression.

'Why is it that we weren't given prior notice of your arrival?' the commander wanted to know. Stefan gave much the same answer he had offered Krieger.

'I can't answer for your record keeping,' he said. 'But, as you see, our papers are perfectly in order.' When the commander hesitated, he added, 'We've come a long distance to collect this man. There'll be questions if we return empty-handed.'

The commander eyed Stefan, and exchanged glances with Krieger. 'You don't look much like witch hunters,' he said, eying Natalia in particular.

'With respect,' Stefan replied, crisply. 'We have just journeyed two weeks through lands forsaken by man and god. How do you expect us to look?'

The commander shrugged. 'What's so special about Walter Koch?'

'That's a matter for our masters to know,' Stefan replied. 'Not my business.'

'But it is *my* business,' the commander retorted. 'What do the witch hunters want with him?'

Stefan sensed Krieger standing at his back. He imagined the intensity of the single eye burning into him.

'Koch may not have any particular connection to the Dark Powers,' he replied. 'But we have him responsible for a string of thefts and robberies across Altdorf. The witch hunters believe the proceeds of those crimes may have found their way into the hands of cultists.'

The commander looked to Krieger. 'I wouldn't have thought Koch was bright enough to mastermind anything,' he commented, sourly. 'It's true: the villain was picked up in a sweep of cultists, but that was more by coincidence than design.' He hesitated again, drawing the silence out. 'We were only going to have him hung. If you want him, you can take him, I suppose.'

Stefan bowed, deferentially. The commander wasn't done yet.

'Why are you here?' he demanded of Natalia.

'It's in the papers,' Natalia replied, meeting his gaze directly.

The commander stared back at her, unmoved. 'I don't care what's in the papers. I want to hear it from you.'

'I am an appointed steward of the witch hunters,' Natalia said, curtly. 'If you have any problem with that, I suggest you take it up with them.'

The commander thrust his face towards Natalia. 'This is no place for a woman.'

Natalia's gaze didn't waver. 'If I still had my knife, we could argue that point. Just you and I.'

The commander looked away, and grunted in disgust. 'Who are we to argue the will of our Imperial masters?' he said to Krieger. 'Or the wisdom of the glorious witch hunters?' His eye fell upon Nagel. 'You. You served here as an officer, isn't that so?'

'That's right,' Nagel replied, tersely.

'And you were dismissed, isn't that right?'

'No, that is not right,' Nagel retorted. 'I resigned my commission. To take up another position.'

'So I see,' the commander replied, dryly. He looked to Krieger. 'I take it this one has been searched thoroughly?'

Krieger nodded. 'With particular care.'

'Make sure you do the same on the way out,' the commander said. 'Very well.' He signalled to the guards. 'Take them through to the gates.'

At the wall they were searched again, then led in single file through iron doors secured by means of a series of locks, each requiring its own separate key. The gates were so heavy it took two men just to haul them apart.

This was the entrance to the main part of the prison. The lesser criminals like Koch were kept here. Von Diehl and the rest of the Chaos prisoners were confined separately, in a second, even more secure part of the fortress. Getting access to the cultist was going to be difficult.

They were met inside the main block by a new contingent of guards. Stefan presented the papers yet again, and waited while they were checked.

'You've come for Walter Koch?'

Stefan nodded. 'Good riddance to the useless scum,' the guard commented. 'You're welcome to him.'

Now they were inside the prison proper, Stefan began to appreciate its sheer scale. Stahlfort was a human warehouse; its rows of cells arranged in layers, floor upon floor. Each had its own guardhouse, a squat, heavily fortified cage from where the warders kept watch over the prisoners in their charge.

The first thing that hit them was the smell. The warm stench of bodies, ripe and rancid; a mixture of sweat, blood, and human ordure. To exist in such conditions, even for a few hours, seemed beyond all endurance. Natalia clamped a hand across her face to shut out the all-pervading smell. A guard grinned, sardonically.

'It's a prison, not a lodging house,' he commented. 'Life is hard here.'

'But mercifully short,' his comrade added. Both men laughed.

There had to be hundreds of prisoners, jammed inside the close confines of the cells. They were starved of air and light, with only the rats for company. Stefan tried to visualise a lifetime – or what remained of a lifetime – spent in such conditions. It was unimaginable.

Natalia gazed around with a look of ill-disguised horror. 'When are they allowed time out of the cells?' she asked.

The guard looked at her as though she were mad. 'Out? These bastards only get out when it's time to stretch their necks.'

'They're dangerous vermin,' the other added. 'They leave their pits when their time's up, or when we need them moved. That's often enough.'

The prisoners couldn't be seen, but by now they could mostly certainly be heard. A background hum like the drowsy buzzing of a swarm of insects quickly grew to a crescendo, pitiful voices calling out as the visitors crossed the first walkway. Amid the cacophony, they could detect cries for help, pleas for mercy, and the pure babbling of the insane. Stefan had seen his share of prisons before, but nothing like this. The barrage of sound welled up around them, drowning their thoughts.

'The goddess Shallya would weep to see this,' Natalia said aloud. 'It's an abomination.'

'These are the enemies of the Empire,' Stefan reminded her. 'Men who have committed abominable crimes.'

'Visitors always excite them,' the guard commented, nonchalantly. 'It'll die down again in a bit. This is nothing. You should see what it's like over the other side.'

'The other side?' Stefan asked, latching on to the words. 'You mean the Chaos prisoners?'

'Aye,' the first man said. 'Them and the others too bad or mad to be allowed on this side. But you've just come for Koch, right?'

'That's right,' Maier affirmed.

The two guards shared a look of weary resignation. 'Miles away,' one complained. 'Ach, Morr's blood,' the other said. 'I'll take them. Let's be quick about it.'

The guard marched them quickly towards the far end of the prison block, making it clear he wanted this lapse in their routine over and done with as quickly as possible. They passed row after row of featureless cells before the guard stopped, removed a set of keys from the belt around his waist, and unlocked one of the doors.

'Walter Friedrich Koch,' he announced. 'And you're welcome to him.'

The cell was cramped and squalid; the shortest of confinements would seem like a lifetime in such a place. What little light there was leaked in through a tiny slit high up on one wall. If the stench outside the cells had been bad, the stink inside was overpowering. The floor was strewn with a covering of straw in the manner of an animal's stall. It was clear it hadn't been changed for several days, or even weeks. Stefan took a sharp intake of breath and immediately wished he hadn't.

'Where is he?' he asked, fighting the urge to retch.

The guard indicated a pile of rags stuffed against one corner of the cell. 'That's Koch,' he replied. 'You can chat to him until Geheimnistag for all I care. But if you want to get out of this hole then I suggest you hurry up about it.'

Stefan peered into the gloom. Slowly, almost imperceptibly at first, the pile of rags stirred. The prisoner opened one yellow eye and stared, uncomprehending, at the visitors. After the briefest of moments the eye flickered shut again. Koch slumped back against the wall, defeated. The guard picked up the water pail from beside the cell door and threw the contents over the prisoner.

'Wake up, you filthy pig,' he yelled. 'It's your lucky day. You're going on a little outing.'

Stefan felt a momentary stab of pity. He knew very little of Koch's actual crimes, but at that moment it seemed hard to reconcile his guilt, or the guilt of any mortal man, with the filth and abject misery that Stahlfort meted out. Worse, they would be doing nothing to relieve that misery. Koch would be going on a journey. But it would be short, and his end would be no different.

'We'll just check a few details,' Stefan said. 'We need to be sure we have the right man.' He caught Natalia's eye, and nodded. Natalia turned towards the guard. 'He will ask the prisoner a few questions,' she said, speaking slowly and deliberately. 'Others may also have questions. We might be here for an hour or so.'

'Don't treat me like an idiot,' the guard snapped, and shoved Natalia aside, out of his line of sight. Natalia grabbed his hand, and stood her ground. With her free hand, she drew a circle in the air. As her hand moved, she spoke a scattering of words. Their meaning was unintelligible to Stefan, but he quickly felt their force. There was a moment of absolute stillness. Then the air filled with a crackling sound, and Stefan felt something shoot through him: a sharp, stinging pain that ran down the length of his body. The guard felt it too. Stefan saw his eyes widen in shock and disbelief then grow dull and lifeless. It was over in an instant. The guard had become utterly subdued.

'He's asking the prisoner some questions,' Natalia repeated, slowly. 'We are all here, in the cell. We may be here for an hour, maybe more.' She held eye contact with the guard. The guard's face was glazed and blank.

'I can see that,' the guard said, slurring his words. 'No need to tell me what I can see with my own eyes.'

'What do you see?' Natalia demanded.

The guard shuffled his feet, and rubbed sleepily at his eyes. 'He's asking the prisoner a few questions,' he said. 'Could be an hour or more.'

'That's right,' Natalia affirmed. 'All you need do is stand and watch, while we ask the questions.'

Tentatively, she let go her grip, and stood back, appraising the effects of her spell as though it were some fragile, newly minted creation. She passed a hand in front of the man's face. No reaction.

'Is that it?' Stefan asked, keeping his voice low.

The guard stared blankly ahead. Natalia bit her lip. 'That's it,' she said.

'Get his keys,' Stefan instructed Nagel. Nagel stepped forward apprehensively. 'Safer to have knifed him in the back,' he muttered.

'These are not our enemies,' Stefan retorted, sharply. 'There'll be no murder done here by us.' He looked closely at the guard. The man hadn't moved a muscle. He was breathing regularly, and had both his eyes open, but otherwise he might have been transported to a different world. The guard didn't flinch when Nagel deftly removed the belt with the heavy set of keys from around his waist.

'Good work,' Stefan said to Natalia. 'How long can we expect this to last?'

'I tried to fix an hour into his mind,' she said. 'But it could be a lot less than that.'

'All right. We'll move as quickly as we can.'

Walter Koch sat slumped on the floor of the cell. The months of captivity had taken a toll on his mind as well as his body. He seemed to regard the newcomers without either hope or trepidation, but now the time had come for him to play his part.

Stefan went to pull the dumbstruck prisoner to his feet.

'Get up,' he commanded. Koch struggled feebly, but offered little resistance. His desiccated body was a bag of bones, and his clothes, what was left of them, were tattered and crawling with lice. The man was crusted with filth from head to toe, and he smelt every bit as bad as his surroundings.

'Among the dead indeed,' Maier observed.

Working as quickly as he dared, Nagel peeled the tunic and insignia from the frozen figure of the guard. Stefan's eyes lighted upon a tin canteen clipped to the man's belt.

'Throw that over here,' he said. He drew the cork from the canteen and sniffed its contents. A strong smell of liquor hit him: gin, or brandtwein, providing a momentary relief from the foul air permeating the cell. He replaced the stopper. 'We'll take this,' he told Nagel.

Nagel pulled on the guard's tunic and tightened the belt around his waist. He clipped the canteen back in place next to the keys. 'Now,' Stefan said to Koch. 'Let's take a walk.' Koch fixed him with a bleary stare. A dribble of spittle escaped his lips and fell into the matted mess of his beard.

'You're about to make a great contribution to the Empire,' Stefan muttered, 'though you'll never know it.' He checked outside the cell, and signalled for the others to follow. He cast one final glance in the direction of the half-naked guard, who was keeping his statue-like vigil over the now vacant cell.

'Don't go away,' Stefan whispered, and eased the cell door shut.

THEY FOLLOWED THE stairs to the bottom level of the main block. Stefan and Karl Maier carried Koch between them. The sight of a prisoner taking his last walk to the rope or the executioner's blade earned no more than a passing glance from the guards. Nagel was a different matter. A burly warder heading in the opposite direction took a double-glance at Nagel as their paths crossed. The warder held out one beefy arm, to block the way

'Hang about,' he said. 'I know you. What are you doing back here?'

'What do you think I'm doing?' Nagel retorted, bluntly. The warder looked at him again, and sized up the uniform. Then he took in Stefan, Koch and the others. A look, part puzzlement, part suspicion, passed across his face. 'You were kicked out, I heard.'

'You heard wrong,' Nagel snapped back. 'I got another offer elsewhere, that's all.'

'What are you doing back here, then?'

'Made a mistake,' Nagel said, tersely. 'Everyone's allowed one.'

Stefan could see the man turning the questions over in his mind. He was torn between moving on and raising the alarm. Unsure of which way he might go, Stefan stepped in between them. 'Excuse me,' he said. 'But we're in a hurry here. Unless you're going to check our warrants yet again, I'd ask you to let us pass.'

The warder eyed the sheaf of warrants, warily. 'So you came back then, did you?' Nagel grasped the bunch of keys hanging at his side, and shook it forcefully. 'Looks that way, doesn't it,' he said, his voice heavy with sarcasm.

The warder muttered something inaudible, then hurried on his way. Nagel breathed a sigh. It was the first time Stefan had seen him genuinely worried. 'He's not the sharpest. He can barely read,' he said by way of explanation to Stefan. 'We won't be so lucky next time.'

'We'll handle it,' Stefan assured him. 'Just get moving.'

The area holding the Chaos prisoners was joined to the main block by a tunnel of steel, a metal cage with locked gates at either end. It was in effect, a prison within a prison. Stefan approached the checkpoint, and held out the warrants for inspection.

'Prisoner Koch, in the custody of the witch hunters,' he announced. 'We're taking him to Altdorf for interrogation.'

Koch moaned and started to struggle, ineffectually. The guards paid him no attention. One opened the warrants and began to read through. No one was in any hurry to unlock the doors.

'Altdorf's not this way,' another guard observed, dryly.

'We want him to identify one of the mutants you've got locked up,' Stefan explained. 'Koch was involved with Chaos cultists. We want to see who he knows.'

The guard looked unimpressed. 'Doesn't say that in here,' he said, holding up the warrant.

'Yes, it does,' Natalia insisted. 'Let me show you.' She reached out, and deftly removed the warrant from the guard's grip. 'Here,' she said, helpfully. She guided his hand to a line on the page. 'It's there in the warrant, as plain as day.'

The guard looked, and rubbed his eyes. 'Where?' He demanded, irritably.

'There,' Natalia repeated, looking from the page directly into the guard's eyes. 'As plain as the light of day.'

Koch mumbled something inaudible. The guard peered again at the warrant, then flung it back at Natalia; his concentration had been broken by Koch's interruption. 'You're going to the pits of Morr, where you belong,' he blazed at the prisoner. He gestured to the men on the gate. 'Open up,' he commanded.

He looked at Nagel. A momentary, passing flicker of recognition. 'Keep a close eye on them,' he said. 'Watch them like a hawk.'

'I will,' Nagel promised.

They stepped through the first set of gates, down the corridor of steel that led to the second gate, and the entrance to the Chaos cells.

'That was close,' Natalia whispered to Stefan. 'I had trouble fixing belief in his mind. I can't be sure how long it's going to hold. We must hurry.'

The gate at the far end of the steel passage opened. They were nearing the dark heart of Stahlfort.

'What sort of beasts are caged here?' Stefan wondered aloud.

'Everything that you might have seen in this life,' Nagel answered. 'And more. Things you've only imagined in your worst nightmares.'

Stefan's pulse was racing; blood pumping hard through his body. There was no turning back now.

'Let's get this done,' he muttered. 'And get out of here.'

A swirl of sound, an insane, inhuman wailing, had been growing steadily louder and more persistent. Now, as Stefan followed Nagel through the second gate into the dark space in the belly of the prison, the sound stopped abruptly. Do they sense us amongst them, Stefan wondered, even through the solid walls of their windowless cells? His gaze darted from one side to the other, half-expecting the caged monsters to break loose from captivity and fall upon them.

This part of the prison was different. Stefan could smell it, feel it in the ice had entered his bones. Here was true evil; evil beyond all bounds of the collection of thieves and murderers they had been amongst a few moments earlier. Stefan felt the presence of the Dark Powers like a physical force reaching out toward him. He felt it like an ache, a black, brooding energy probing for any opportunity, any weakness. He sensed the evil, and knew it had sensed him too. They were old adversaries, avatars of an ancient enmity.

He shook himself free of disturbing thoughts. 'Which cell?' he asked Nagel. 'Let's get this over with.'

'I'm not sure,' Nagel responded. He saluted a guard, patrolling the length of the cells in the opposite direction. 'Where's von Diehl being kept?'

'Von Diehl?' the man thought about it for a moment. 'He's down for extermination. Moved down to the condemned cells. Here, I may as well take you.'

The guard raised his lantern and led the way through the foetid gloom. Initially, the only sound was the echo of their footsteps. Then the voices started. Softly at first, but with a growing intensity. Voices whispering, cajoling, coaxing, calling out. Stefan heard them calling to him; they were getting inside him. Inside his head, inside his soul. But these were not the coarse, guttural voices of mutants and monsters. These were the sweet, imploring voices of friends and loved ones. They were the voices of the lost, the voices of the dead. Voices Stefan had never expected to hear again.

He heard the voice of his father, long laid to rest in the cold Kislev soil. 'They have left me here to rot in chains,' he whispered. 'For the love of Sigmar, Stefan, set me free of this torment!'

'Stefan,' the voice of his lover Elena called out. 'I'm dying, Stefan. The flames of Morr are consuming my soul. Don't let them murder me, Stefan, don't let them!'

He heard a scream, human and very real, behind him. He turned to see Natalia, her hands pressed hard against her ears, trying to block out the sound. Tears were running down her face. No need for him to guess the voice that she heard.

'You get used to it, eventually,' the guard commented. 'You learn to shut it out. This is the cell. Need me in there?'

'No,' Nagel told him. 'I can handle this.'

'All right,' the guard agreed. 'I'll be waiting outside.'

As the door to the cell swung open, Stefan retrieved an image of Heinrich von Diehl from memory. A narrow face, with a dark, close-cropped beard. The unmistakable cruelty lurking behind the placid, bland expression. It was the face of a man used to power, and unafraid of using it.

Stefan took a step forward into a cell that was very similar to the one that had held Koch – the same dimensions, the same soaking, stinking straw wadding on the floor. And, at first glance, the same pathetic figure huddled in a heap in one corner of the cell. Heinrich von Diehl might have been a very different proposition to the likes of Walter Koch when he came to the prison, but Stahlfort, it seemed was a great leveller.

Maier took the lantern from Nagel and held it up. The cropped dark hair and beard had grown straggled and wild, and his skin hung down in pale, loose folds around the sunken bones of his cheeks. But when Heinrich von Diehl turned his face towards the light, the eyes that settled upon Stefan and his comrades were quite different. Where Koch had looked through them with dull incomprehension, Heinrich von Diehl was instantly alert, flicking a measured gaze across each of the newcomers. For a moment, Stefan had the strange sense that von Diehl had even been expecting them.

The prisoner took a sip from the bowl of water by his side. Stefan noticed how his hands shook when he lifted the bowl to his lips. Physically this creature was not a threat to anyone, surely? Heinrich von Diehl rinsed the filthy water around his mouth then returned every last drop to the bowl. He eased himself into a sitting position in the corner of the cell.

'Well now,' he said. 'Visitors. What a welcome diversion.' The voice had grown reedy and thin, but a vestige of defiance still remained.

'So who are you? My executioners, or my salvation?'

'Neither,' Stefan replied. He had expected his hatred of von Diehl to be instant and visceral. Expected and wanted it to be. But hatred was hard to reconcile with the beaten down creature in chains before him.

'Co-operate with us and you'll have a chance to leave this place,' Stefan said.

Von Diehl smiled, weakly. 'How so?'

'You have information that could be of use to our masters,' Maier cut in.

'Really?' Von Diehl smiled again. '*My* masters have abandoned me. And, as for my present hosts…' He turned his face to look around the cell. 'It seems I've outlived my usefulness.' His eyes locked on Stefan, and the tone in his voice hardened. 'But who are your masters?'

'We're not here to treat with you,' Stefan said. 'Do as you're told, and you have a chance of getting out.'

Von Diehl stared back at Stefan. A knowing look settled over his face.

'The gaolers don't know about this, do they?' He paused. 'A word from me now, and you and your friends would rot in here with the rest of us.'

Stefan seized the dishevelled figure and dragged him up onto his feet. The stench of sweat and filth coming off von Diehl was overpowering. Stefan would gladly have wrung the man's neck there and then, and be done with it. Only the stark, nightmare vision of a defeated Altdorf stayed his hand, and kept him in mind of their greater purpose.

'Let's understand each other,' he told von Diehl. 'As far as I'm concerned, you're the living spawn of evil, no different to any other Chaos scum in here. But we're offering you a way out, and I'm guessing you won't pass up the chance to save your verminous skin.'

Heinrich von Diehl raised a bony hand to his chest, and prised himself out of Stefan's grip. 'We understand each other very well,' he said, mildly. 'You're right. I'd gladly exchange this glade of Morr for any other place.' He looked around the cell, at Natalia, Maier and Nagel, and at the sorry figure of Koch. 'I'll save my verminous skin by any means I can.'

Stefan nodded to Nagel. 'Unchain him. And be careful.' Then to Maier, 'Get our friend Koch settled in.'

At that moment Walter Koch understood his fate. He began whimpering, pitifully. Stefan grabbed the canteen of gin from Nagel and thrust it into his hands. 'Here,' he said. 'Drink your fill of this.'

Koch eyed the canteen suspiciously then raised it tentatively to his lips. He took two quick sips, then tipped the flask back, pouring a long draught of the fiery spirit into his throat. After the second draught, he began to stumble. He offered no resistance when Maier led him to the wall of the cell. Standing next to von Diehl, the two wretches looked remarkably alike: they were similar in height, and of much the same, scrawny build. Close examination would undoubtedly tell them apart, but, at a cursory glance, the resemblance was more than superficial. Enough to give them a chance.

Nagel unlocked the door. Maier and Natalia stepped out, followed by Stefan, who kept a tight grip on the length of chain securing von Diehl. He had a last glimpse of Walter Koch. He was slumped against the wall with the canteen still pressed tight against his mouth. He didn't want to think too much about what would happen to Koch when the guards finally discovered him there. But he consoled himself with the knowledge that it could hardly be any worse than the fate that already awaited him.

Stefan closed the door to the cell and locked it. 'Your liberty comes at a heavy price,' he told von Diehl. 'By the holy might of Sigmar, I'm going to make sure you earn it.'

CHAPTER TEN
No Way Back

FINALLY, BRUNO FOUND the *Karla*. Weeks after sailing from Altdorf, Mikhal's ship returned to port, slipping past the harbour walls like a thief in the night. It had moored up on the far side of the wharf, as far from view as it was possible to be. It was largely down to luck that Bruno tracked her down at all… luck and a small sum of money paid to one of the harbour boys to watch for the return of the newly painted two-master. With the ship finally located, Bruno bided his time until nightfall, and then set off to discover what secrets the *Karla* might hold.

In the dark she would have passed for a ghost ship. Not a light was showing, above deck or below. There was no sign of crew aboard, or of watchers posted on shore. There was no sign of life at all, just the dark shadow of the hull slowly lifting and falling on the water.

Bruno leapt from the quay onto the deck of the ship. He fell heavily, but came to no harm as a pile of ropes and empty sacking broke his fall. He lay perfectly still for a moment feeling the boat lurch beneath him. If there were a soul aboard, then his landing would surely have alerted them. Seconds passed. He got to his feet and dusted himself off. Convinced that he was alone, he took a candle stub from his pocket and touched a spark to the wick. The flame shuddered in the breeze that blew off the harbour, creating shadows that danced amongst the dark recesses on the prow. Bruno found the hatch that led to the lower deck, and tugged it firmly. The hatch opened, smoothly and without a sound. He held the light out in front of him, and climbed down into the belly of the ship.

The master's quarters were shuttered and locked. Bruno set his weight against the door and heaved, forcing it open. The cramped, pitch-black cabin smelled of wax and newly seasoned wood. A sudden draft of air blew the candle out. Bruno fumbled in the dark until he found a locked desk that was positioned below the single window. He put the candle down and re-lit it, this time sheltering the flame with his hand. Once the candle had settled, he set about the desk lock with his knife. The mechanism offered little resistance, and before long, Bruno had the slim drawer open.

Again he paused, listening out for any movement aboard the boat. The decking stretched and groaned around him, and up above deck the wind whistled incessantly about the rigging. But Bruno was alone. That was all he needed to be sure of. He removed some papers from the drawer and spread them out on the desktop, under the light of the candle.

The results were disappointing, or reassuring – he wasn't quite sure which. There was nothing in the papers to link either Mikhal or the *Karla* with the zealots. The only references to cargo were to wheat and cornmeal, the most mundane of commodities. But then, just as Bruno was beginning to wonder if he was wasting his time, he found something odd. One of the manifests was sealed, and covered in stamps like those issued by the port watch when granting ships permission to enter the harbour. Bruno broke it open. The dates inscribed in smudged ink tallied roughly with the *Karla*'s dates of sailing. But the destination didn't. The berthing warrants weren't for Talabheim. They were for Nuln, a city hundreds of miles in the opposite direction. Why had Mikhal lied? And why did his ship sail all that way just to pick up a cargo of grain? It made no sense.

Bruno replaced the papers and locked the drawer. If the answer was aboard, then his guess was that he would find it in the ship's hold. He took up the candle and threaded his way through the narrow galley. He climbed carefully down the hold ladder. Each step echoed through the empty ship. The hold was a dark, empty pit. The ghosts of other voyages hung on the still air – the tang of spices, the sweet perfume of new-seasoned timber. But there was another, more alien, scent as well. The cargo she had been carrying was gone, but a residue had been left behind. Bruno detected the sharp, sulphurous odour immediately. It carried memories of – what? Something bad. Instinctively Bruno pinched the wick of the candle to snuff out the flame.

Now he was in utter blackness. He turned around slowly, trying to regain his bearings. He could feel something underfoot: it was a loose dusting of powder, like coarse sand. He bent down, and scooped a little into his hand. It had the consistency of grain, but, when he put it to his lips, it didn't taste like it. Bruno swore softly, and spat the bitter substance from his mouth.

It was time to get out. He'd seen enough. Bruno climbed back out of the hold and tracked back through the galley to the main stair. He was almost level with the deck when he thought he saw something move above. It was gone in a second. A shadow had stirred in the darkness, then pulled back out of his view. There was someone up there, behind the wheelhouse. Someone waiting for him. Bruno felt his muscles tense. His hand went to his sword. Steadily, stealthily, he edged up the step.

He climbed out onto the deck, whistling softly, trying to sound casual and unconcerned. Despite the darkness he thought he could make out the outline of a man, crouched and ready to pounce. Bruno took a few steps towards the near side of the boat. The timbers bowed and creaked under his feet. One more step, then another, and he was level with the wheelhouse. Bruno stretched, as if reaching for the ship's rail, then spun round. His hands fastened on cloth and flesh as he hauled the crouching figure from its hiding place.

He had a brief glimpse of a tall, lightly built man, his head covered by a darkish hood. As he went for his sword, he was hit, hard. A fist connected smartly with his jaw. The blow nearly knocked Bruno off his feet. He stumbled backwards, and clattered into the superstructure of the wheelhouse. Bruno cursed, and reached for his sword again. This time he succeeded, but his adversary knocked the weapon away. Bruno watched in horror as the sword flew from his hand and vanished over the side of the ship.

The other man hadn't drawn a weapon. He seemed intent on beating Bruno to the ground with his fists. Bruno deflected a punch then hit back, aiming for the man's face. His opponent ducked the blow easily, and landed another of his own. This time he struck Bruno in the gut. Bruno doubled up, gasping for breath. He straightened up, before diving to one side to avoid another punch. At last, he managed to get his retaliation in; a swinging blow, which struck his hooded attacker on the side of the face. Bruno was rewarded with a groan of pain from the other man.

He pressed home his advantage, hurling his adversary against the side of the boat. Wood cracked and splintered as the *Karla* shuddered under the impact. Bruno had a glimpse of the other man's face as he turned. There was blood running from a cut above one eye.

Whoever or whatever you are, Bruno thought, you still bleed like one of us. He struck out again, but this time he wasn't so lucky. His opponent intercepted the blow and grabbed hold of his fist. Bruno lost his balance, only his opponent and the side of the ship breaking his fall. He felt a jab to his ribs, then another. For a moment he was powerless, and prayed it wasn't a knife. The two men rolled along the length of the boat, locked together in combat.

Bruno was tiring. The thought flashed into his mind that he might have met his match. Then, just as he was steeling himself for one last, sustained assault, the gods intervened. His opponent broke free and stepped back, tripping across the coils of rope lying upon the deck. It gave Bruno a moment – all the time he needed. He struck his opponent with all the strength he could muster. The blow sent him reeling, defenceless, against the side of the boat. Before he could regain his senses, Bruno seized hold of the man's waist, and heaved his bulk up to the side rail.

His opponent fought like a man possessed, but Bruno was in no mood to let up. He gave one final heave, and let go. The man clawed frantically at the side of the ship, but it was too late. Bruno had once last glimpse of his face before he tumbled down into the harbour below. He watched the body hit the water, then made good his escape.

THE WALK FROM the screaming bedlam of the Chaos cells to the gates dividing the prison seemed to have taken an eternity. Each step of the way, Stefan prayed. Prayed to the gods Taal and Ulric, prayed to the mercy of the goddess Shallya, and prayed to almighty Sigmar himself. He prayed that somehow, against all odds, they would pass through these gates of damnation, and see again the light of the world beyond. Would the gods listen? Would they understand what he had done? However weak, however wasted, Heinrich von Diehl still embodied evil. He was the cruel machination of the Dark Gods made flesh and blood. He, Stefan, had released von Diehl from deserved captivity. Would the gods ever forgive him for that?

So far, the signs were that they would. Each step they took brought them closer to the first gate, to the iron-caged passageway that led back to the main prison. No one had challenged them. No one had so much as looked at them. Four of them had come in, with one prisoner. Now four of them with their prisoner were going out. They were going to make it. It was going to be all right. The creatures of Chaos bayed from their cells, threatening, pleading, cajoling. Stefan blanked them all from his mind. He blanked everything, except the prospect of escape that grew closer with each passing moment.

He handed the warrants back to the guard at the gate. The warden scanned them and cast an eye over Stefan's party. Natalia stood ready to fix the illusion in the guard's mind. But no magic was needed. Heinrich von Diehl's physical appearance was enough to convince the guards that this was the same verminous wretch who had entered the compound in Stefan's custody.

'Where are you taking him now?' the guard asked, only half interested.

'Altdorf,' Stefan said. 'For interrogation.'

Von Diehl stood with his head bowed; a curtain of greying, greasy hair obscuring half his face. At that moment, the idea that he could be any threat, or of any use to anyone seemed far-fetched in the extreme. The guard extended a hand toward the prisoner then drew back in disgust.

'Poisonous wretch,' he grunted. 'Rather you than me. Filthy bastard.' Von Diehl whimpered; an uncannily facsimile of Walter Koch's reedy voice.

'Shut up, you craven scum,' Maier admonished him. He jerked the prisoner's chains, and tugged him forward. He nodded to the guard.

'When you're ready.' The guard gave von Diehl another cursory glance then turned the lock in the first gate.

'Pass through.'

A few more steps. A few more steps and they would be at the companion gate on the far side – the gate that led back to the main prison. All that remained then would be to present themselves at the outer wall, and they would be clear. A matter of minutes, that was all. Stefan felt a thrill of anticipation rise up in him. Against the odds, it was all coming together.

He held the warder's gaze, as he waited for the second set of gates to be unlocked. The guards had seen enough; no one was interested in looking at the warrants again. 'Five in, five out,' one muttered. The gate closed behind them with a heavy crash. The key turned in the lock. Then, at the last moment, a voice called out.

'Wait a minute!'

Stefan turned, trying to look unconcerned. 'What now?'

A guard was checking the shackles fastened about von Diehl's wrists. 'He hasn't been searched,' he said.

'Searched?'

'Any prisoner moving between the two blocks has to be searched.' The guard nodded in the direction of the Chaos cells. 'That lot didn't bother. They've left it to me again.'

Stefan relaxed a little. So long as von Diehl had nothing on him that could identify him… The guard seemed eager to get the unpleasant job over as quickly as possible. Von Diehl stood, passive and compliant, whilst the guard satisfied himself that the prisoner had nothing that resembled a weapon. When he had done, he grabbed hold of von Diehl by the lank mane of hair and pulled his face p towards the light. He peered at the pale, grime-encrusted face for what seemed an age. Something was troubling him.

'What's the name again?' he asked. Natalia stepped forward, between the guard and von Diehl. 'His name's Koch,' she said. 'Walter Koch. We have a warrant to take him back to Altdorf. You remember that.'

The guard brushed her to one side, and shoved von Diehl back towards Nagel and Maier. 'Can't expect me to remember every one of them. On your way.'

Stefan passed through the gate with Natalia.

'Well done,' he murmured. Natalia wore an expression of cool detachment, but beneath the mask Stefan could see anxiety eating away at her.

'In the name of Taal, let's get moving,' she hissed at him. 'I don't know how much longer any of this will hold.'

'We can't be in too much of a hurry,' Stefan told her. He checked his pace, and paused to look around at the grim rows of windowless cells. 'Go steady. We mustn't give ourselves away now.'

He walked on, resisting the urge to run for all his worth until they were far from this ungodly place. Now, above all, they had to hold their nerve. Time peeled away. The gatehouse came in view ahead; the final barrier separating them from the world beyond. The duty guards looked up as they approached. One went towards the gates, keys in hand, ready to let them through. They were going to make it. Stefan kept repeating the words to himself. He had to keep believing. He raised a hand in salute, and prepared to call out a greeting.

The words, if they ever passed his lips, were never heard. All conversation was drowned out in the sudden commotion that broke out around them. A deafening crescendo of bells rang out, angry and insistent. It was a sound fit to waken the dead.

The gate was already half open. Now, as the deafening clamour filled the prison, the guard pushed it back. The air rang with the sound of bells and the slamming of doors. Guards spilled out onto landings. In a matter of moments they were everywhere, filling the stairways like scrabbling insects. Stahlfort was closing in around them, a steel trap springing shut. Freedom was slipping from their grasp. Stefan shot a glance back at his comrades. They must move quickly.

He grabbed hold of Natalia, and shouted a command to Nagel and Maier, and ran. Von Diehl moaned in protest, but his body responded. Somehow he summoned the strength to match his captors' pace. Everything was utter confusion. There was a clatter of men and steel, and voices struggling to be heard above the din. Stefan didn't even know for sure that the alarm was anything to do with them. But one thing he did know. In a matter of moments Stahlfort would be locked down, and then there would no escape.

'Hold the gates!' he yelled out. 'Let us pass.' For a moment the guards reacted instinctively to the tone of authority in Stefan's voice. Then, as the alarm bells pealed, they drew their swords and blocked the way.

'Stay where you are!' one called out. 'No one's going anywhere!'

Stefan turned to Natalia. 'If ever we needed your magic, we need it now,' he shouted to her.

'There's something–' she began. 'But I'm not sure I can–'

'Just try,' Stefan demanded. 'Try anything!'

The gate slammed shut. Natalia closed her eyes, and ran forward. The warder on the gate paid no heed to the slender woman. With the gates locked shut, there would be no way out for any of them.

Natalia spread her arms wide and fell upon her knees before the armed men. The guards looked on in astonishment as the words of the spell tumbled from her lips. Stefan gleaned no meaning from the invocation, but the impact was immediate and unmistakable. Everything inside the prison grew dim, as though a mighty shadow had fallen on its already dark heart. The moment's darkness was followed by an intense, blinding light. The air around Stefan's head crackled and flamed. Then the light was gone, sucked away as quickly as it had appeared.

The guards looked momentarily stunned. The first to recover made a grab for Natalia. The young magician evaded the clumsy challenge, and turned face on before the two guards. She raised her hand, palm extended, and drew their gaze like a snake fixing its prey.

'Your keys,' she called to them. 'The metal is burning, red-hot to touch. You can't bear to touch them. The keys are burning through your very flesh.'

At first the guards simply stared, as though Natalia had lost her mind. Then the warder nearest the gate cried out, in astonishment as much as pain. He dropped the keys, and clutched his hand to his chest. The skin was charred and blistered, as though scalded by a hot iron.

The other guards raised their swords, but before they could get near Natalia, they began screaming in agony and threw their weapons to the ground.

Stefan ignored what instinct was telling him. He reached down and took a firm grip on the keys. The metal was cold to his touch. The guards made no attempt to stop him. Temporarily, they were powerless, oblivious to everything except their torment. The burns might have been illusory, but the pain they were experiencing was real enough.

Stefan and Nagel pushed past the helpless guards, and hauled open the gates.

'Get their swords too,' Stefan yelled. Behind them, a storm was breaking loose. But they were through the gates now, and on the other side of the great wall. Nagel jammed the key back into the lock and forced the mechanism home until the head of the key sheared away from the steel shaft.

'That should hold them for a while.'

They broke out into the courtyard, Maier and Nagel propelling their prisoner ahead of them. Natalia began to laugh; it was the sudden, almost hysterical laughter of unexpected release.

'Ulric's toil!' she exclaimed. 'I've never managed anything like that before!'

'Congratulations,' Stefan shot back. 'Now, run for your life.'

The jetty steps loomed into view beyond the wall of the prison. They had to pass over thirty or forty yards of open space, then down the steps to where the boat lay at anchor. Forty yards was all that lay between them and flight from Stahlfort. Stefan had covered almost half the distance when he realised that Natalia was not keeping pace. He spun round in alarm, and saw her languishing some distance behind. Her face was gaunt, almost white, her body wet with perspiration. Her limbs seemed to have turned to lead.

'What's wrong?' Stefan shouted. 'Are you hurt?'

Natalia staggered forward, struggling to make up ground. 'The spells,' she gasped. 'Magic drains all energy from the soul. It's not usually this bad. It's not–' She toppled forward, and would have fallen if Stefan had not caught her. He seized her hand and ran on, willing her to somehow stay with him. Maier and Nagel were a few paces further back, propelling von Diehl between them. All they could do now was keep going, and hope.

From the corner of his eye, Stefan saw the low, slate-grey building tucked close against the far wall of the prison. A door at the far end of the barrack room flew open, and soldiers in the black livery of Stahlfort spilled out. The prison bells continued to ring, but the soldiers weren't going into the prison. They were coming after them. Stefan glanced back across his shoulder. A dozen armed men, maybe more, were rushing towards them. Somewhere above the tolling bells, Stefan thought he heard Krieger barking out commands.

The soldiers sprinted from the shadow of the barracks, trying to cut them off before the jetty. But they had a head start over their pursuers; there was still a chance. They had come so far. Stefan couldn't fail now. If they could just keep up the pace, they would reach the boat.

They were almost at the jetty steps. Stefan let go of Natalia's arm.

'Go on ahead,' he gasped. 'Find the boat and get ready to cast off.' He looked round. The guards were closing on them, but not fast enough. Surely, they could not catch them now? Stefan allowed himself one moment of triumph. Then he heard Natalia cry out. He looked up just in time to see the blur of movement. A figure clad in light armour had risen up above the cliff-top.

The soldier seemed to have come from nowhere, but of course he had not. He had come from the jetty. The man had been guarding the boat, Stefan realised, when the alarm sounded. The soldier drew a sword, and lunged at Natalia. Stefan's response was instinctive; the reaction of a warrior.

He threw himself forward and launched out with his sword. The first sweep of the blade parried the soldier's aim, and deflected the blow away from Natalia. If his aim had been to draw the soldier's attention, he had succeeded. Stefan met a second heavy blow from the soldier's sword, and then a third. He dropped back, feinted to the left then got in a retaliatory strike, lashing his sword in beneath the soldier's guard.

He only meant to strike the man with the flat of his blade, to stun him, or, at worst, knock him unconscious. But as he struck out, the blade swerved and twisted in his hand. His unintended aim was inch-perfect, fatally and lethally perfect. The sword slid home beneath the soldier's breastplate, deep into his belly. Stefan didn't need to hear the man cry out, or watch his body crumple to the ground. As soon as he landed the blow, he knew the other man was dead.

He stood back, aghast at what he had done. He felt someone tug at his sleeve. He heard Nagel's voice, urging him down the steps. He looked around, and saw Maier with von Diehl, both staring at Stefan. Just for a moment he thought he detected a knowing smile cross von Diehl's face. Then Maier seized hold of his arm, and Stefan was all but flying down the jetty steps towards the expanse of blue-green water below. The voices of the other soldiers thundered in his ears, the roar of vengeful murder.

The boat lurched under him as he jumped aboard. Nagel pushed off strongly. The boat rolled drunkenly, and eased away from the jetty's edge.

Stefan collapsed in the stern, and cradled his head in his hands. Maier clapped a hand on his shoulder, but Stefan paid no heed. He was only vaguely aware of what was happening around him. The shouts of the pursuing guards. The missiles – spears and arrows – flying in, but falling harmlessly wide or short. They had done it. They had taken von Diehl and had escaped the clutches of Stahlfort. But Stefan wasn't celebrating. In his mind, all he could see was the face of the fallen guard. His life had been the price of von Diehl's freedom. A loyal servant of Sigmar was dead, and he, Stefan, had been his executioner. He had crossed a line he never thought he would cross. Now, there might be no way back.

CHAPTER ELEVEN
Hunter and Hunted

BRUNO HAD SPENT a troubled night wrestling with the decision he had to make. But when he finally awoke, in the grey light of dawn, his mind was made up. He could delay no longer. He would go to the watch, and unburden himself of some troubling knowledge.

Just before noon, he presented himself at the anonymous, grey tower annexed to the courts of justice, the forbidding buildings known across all Altdorf as the Palace of Retribution. Unsure who he should ask for, Bruno simply gave his name and stated his business. He had information that might be vital to the safekeeping of the city. He was shown up to a featureless room with a table and a single, barred window. He was told to wait. By the time an hour had passed, he was feeling more like a prisoner than the saviour of the city, but there could be no backing out now.

At last the door opened again, and a man wearing the insignia of a watch commander entered. Bruno bowed, deferentially. The commander gave him a courteous nod and settled himself across the table from Bruno. Unlike the bored, surly guardsmen who'd barely given him the time of day, this man had a quiet attentiveness about him that Bruno found immediately reassuring. Now, at last they were going to get somewhere.

'Bruno Hausmann,' Bruno said, reckoning that was as good a place as anywhere to begin. The man smiled and nodded then offered Bruno his hand. His handshake was as firm and solid as his outward appearance.

'Gustav Ehrhart,' he replied. 'Have we met before?'

'No,' Bruno said. 'Not to my knowledge.' He hesitated. All the doubts that had previously beset him suddenly bubbled up once more. 'I'm sorry to be taking up your time, but–'

'But nothing,' Ehrhart retorted. 'Let's hear what you have to say. By Sigmar – haven't they so much as offered you a cup of wine while you've been waiting?' Bruno shook his head. Ehrhart opened the door and barked a command into the corridor outside.

'Now,' he continued. 'What is it you have to tell me?'

Bruno took a deep breath then told his story. He had resolved to play down Mikhal's involvement as much as he could, but that wasn't going to be easy, since he was a key part of the tale. He tried to portray Mikhal's role as sympathetically as possible, suggesting that he had become the unwitting victim of forces he did not properly comprehend. He explained why he had decided to start following Mikhal, and what he had seen and heard. He began with the meeting at the warehouse, and ended with his nocturnal visit to the *Karla*.

He had feared that the watch might laugh at his story or even that they would lock him up as a nuisance or a

madman. To his relief, Ehrhart listened intently to everything he had to say, nodding and scribbling at intervals
in a book. Bruno reached his escape from the boat, and
then paused. He could think of nothing more to add.
Ehrhart stopped writing and looked up.

'The man who attacked you on the boat. You've no
idea who it was?'

Bruno shook his head. 'I hope I haven't wasted your
time.'

Ehrhart made a final note in the margin and closed
the book. 'On the contrary,' he replied. 'I take what
you've just told me very seriously indeed.'

Bruno felt encouraged, but also a little anxious. 'Do
you think there may be some kind of trouble being
planned by the zealots?' he said. 'Some greater plot
against the city itself?'

'What do you think?' Ehrhart asked. Bruno remembered the pinch of powder he had taken from the hold
of the Karla; it was the only tangible evidence of his
story that he could produce. He took a twist of paper
from out of his pocket and unfolded it upon the table.
The sprinkling of pepper-grey dust looked innocuous
enough in the dim light of the interrogation cell.

'That's not grain flour, not from Talabheim nor anywhere else,' he said. Ehrhart reached out and brought the
paper to his nose, before sniffing carefully.

'Indeed it isn't,' he concurred. He closed up the paper
and placed it in a drawer with the notebook. 'You did
the right thing, coming here,' he said. 'You've done well.'

'What will happen to Mikhal?' Bruno asked. 'At heart
he's a good man. I swear that he is. He's been duped,
misled – these people are using him.'

Ehrhart shrugged. 'What can I say? His involvement
seems beyond dispute, even if we don't yet know the full
extent of what he has got himself involved in.' He

paused, and folded his arms across his chest, deep in thought. 'But, you know, I believe you're right. I think Mikhal Kumansky has been foolish, to say the least. But he's no ringleader. More likely he has found himself pressured into doing something against his will.'

Bruno nodded, emphatically. 'That's exactly how I see it.'

'Then, with your testimony, and my influence, there may be hope for him yet.'

Bruno breathed a sigh of relief. The greater part of the burden felt like it had been lifted from his shoulders. 'So what happens now?'

'Now,' Ehrhart said, 'you leave everything to me. I'll find you again when you are needed.'

The commander smiled, then sat back. Bruno suddenly realised that the interview was at an end. He hesitated for a moment then stood up.

'You know,' he said. 'When I came here I was worried that you weren't going to take me seriously. That you'd hear what I had to say, but do nothing.'

Ehrhart shook him by the hand again. 'Don't worry,' he assured him. 'I'm going to take what you have just told me very seriously indeed. And I'm going to act upon it without delay.' He opened the door for Bruno. Two men of the watch were waiting outside. 'My men will escort you out,' Ehrhart said. 'You'll be hearing from me again before long, I promise you that.'

THE PRISON BOAT slid through the waters, away from the island and out towards the mouth of the bay. The pursuing guards had reached the jetty and were giving chase from the shallows. Baying cries of bloody vengeance echoed across the bay.

Stefan kept his eyes fixed on the shore, as his arms relentlessly worked the oars. Every sinew in his body was screaming out for rest, but the sight of the guards falling steadily into the distance gave him cause for hope, and the determination to carry on. Then, inexplicably, the guards seemed to give up their pursuit, and fall back towards the jetty steps. Was it over? Stefan allowed himself the luxury of the thought for just a few moments. Then he saw the others arriving to form a line along the edge of the jagged cliffs far above, twenty or so men, each carrying a weapon on their shoulder – bowmen.

The marksmen on the cliff slotted home their arrows and took a careful, deliberate aim. Stefan looked around desperately. The narrow boat offered virtually no shelter. They were drifting in the open water, just waiting to be picked off.

Natalia watched the marksmen take aim with a horrified fascination. 'What do we do?' she shouted at Stefan.

'Pray,' Nagel answered, grimly. Stefan heaved back on the oars, digging ever deeper into his reserves of strength. 'Keep going,' he told them. 'Our only hope is to get beyond their reach.'

The boat ploughed into the waves. Above the sound of the oars churning the water, they heard the sigh of the bowstrings as the arrows were launched. Stefan watched the lethal darts fly loose, piercing the sky and vanishing into the grey haze of the clouds. There was a moment's respite before the first wave fell, like sudden rain, into the water near the stern of the boat.

Natalia heaved an audible sigh of relief. 'Praise Taal.'

'Keep rowing hard!' Maier yelled at her. 'They're only finding their range.'

Stefan knew that Maier was right. The archers reloaded their weapons and took careful aim. When the second flight of arrows drove into the water some ten or fifteen feet ahead, Stefan knew what would come next.

And there was only one thing in the boat that could conceivably offer them any cover.

'Put up the oars,' he shouted back. 'Draw them up over the boat!' He pulled his oar from the water and held it out crossways above his body to indicate to the others that they should use the oars for shelter. It would be poor protection from the arrows, but better than nothing. The four of them huddled together beneath the makeshift canopy, leaving von Diehl alone. He was shackled in the prow of the boat, totally exposed. Von Diehl stared at Stefan. His expression was one of – what? Contempt? Amusement? Stefan would gladly have left him to perish, but he knew that wasn't possible. He swore and grasped hold of the prisoner, hauling von Diehl towards him and under the crossed oars.

'Gods alive,' Nagel snarled, 'Are you putting his miserable life before ours?'

'No,' Stefan shot back. 'I'm putting Altdorf first, and so should you.'

The boat drifted on for a few seconds. Then they heard the sigh of the arrows being loosed, and the deadly rain began to fall. Arrow shafts thudded into the boat, striking home with a juddering force. The crossed oars deflected some of the missiles, but still more got through. Natalia screamed as a shaft tore through her tunic, missing her flesh by a hair's breadth. The boat shuddered and rolled in the water as it was struck over and over again. An arrow ricocheted off the oar above Stefan's head. The impact knocked him sideways, but also saved his life. As he fell back, a second shaft dropped from the skies into the boat, plunging between Stefan and von Diehl. For one brief instant the two enemies faced death as equals.

The torrent of arrows relented. Stefan sat up, and swung his oar over the side of the boat.

'Now row,' he shouted. 'Row with every last ounce of your strength.'

One of the arrows had wedged deep into the side of the boat below the waterline. Natalia reached down to pull the shaft free. Quite without warning, von Diehl suddenly stirred to life, and sprang forward as far as the limit of his chains would allow. Before Stefan could intervene, he'd caught hold of Natalia's wrist.

'Don't do that,' von Diehl cautioned. They were the first proper words he'd spoken since leaving his cell. Stefan, Nagel and Maier all turned.

'Don't touch the arrow,' von Diehl said, his tone calm, matter-of-fact. 'It's through the hull. If you wrench it out, chances are you'll flood the boat, and drown us into the bargain.'

He let go of Natalia's arm. Natalia looked vaguely stunned. She glanced first at Stefan, then at Nagel. Nagel shook his head slowly, and grunted. 'He's right. Leave it where it is.'

A rushing through the air above their heads signalled another assault. Stefan's body tensed. If he had miscalculated, they were all dead. Then he heard the arrows spattering the water in their wake. All had fallen short. They had got beyond the archers' range. Stefan tugged harder on the oar. Slowly but surely, the boat gathered momentum.

'Praise Sigmar,' a relieved Natalia exclaimed. 'We're clear.'

'We're clear of the arrows,' Stefan said. 'But the rest of the sport may only just be beginning.'

AN HOUR AFTER leaving Ehrhart, Bruno found himself in the taproom of the Black Goat. He was feeling restless, troubled by something he couldn't quite put his finger upon. Part of him wanted to seek out Mikhal and warn him. But he knew that would be wrong. He had seen enough in the last few days to know that warning Mikhal might well amount to warning the zealots, and that must not happen. He had to take a back seat now, and wait for events – and the investigations of the watch in particular – to take their course. So the Black Goat seemed like a ready diversion, and a mug of beer a good antidote to his cares. He was already on his second.

The chill afternoon had gathered the usual suspects to the place. Chief amongst them was the old rogue Sterkel who was holding court again with a gaggle of fellow travellers. For once, Bruno accepted Sterkel's offer of a drink, and eased himself into their company. It was undemanding, just what he needed. Bruno knew the routine. He would stand his round and pick the right moments to join in the laughter. Nothing more would be asked of him.

Time slipped by. Before he knew it Bruno was staring at the bottom of his sixth or seventh pint. The shadows in the street outside had grown long. Bruno knew he should be heading home, but the nagging at the back of his mind just wouldn't relent. It didn't seem to matter how much he tried to lose himself in beer and idle chat. Gradually the buzz of conversation dropped away. Either that, or he was tuning it out. Bruno's mouth was making all the right responses, but his mind had drifted elsewhere.

He went back over the events of the last days, particularly his visit to the watch. Ehrhart had promised that Mikhal would be treated sympathetically. Or had he? Had he actually said that, or was that just what Bruno hoped to hear? Even though the damning, soothing, numbing blanket of alcohol was dimming his memory, Bruno took another swig of beer. He started thinking about Ehrhart. There was something familiar about the man, he was sure of it. Perhaps they had met before? No, that was quite impossible. There was nothing about his face that was familiar, so it must be something else…

Bruno wracked his brains for a few moments longer then gave up. He finally admitted the futility of the exercise. A fresh pot was placed in his hand just as he set his empty one down, and he carried on drinking. An hour or so later, two of Sterkel's comrades made their excuses to leave and Bruno decided to call it a day too. He got to his feet, a little unsteadily, and made tracks for the taproom door, steadfastly refusing all offers of more beer.

The cool air hit him like a slap to the face, sobering him a little. He looked around for Sterkel's mates, but they'd already gone. It didn't matter. He'd no desire to walk with them, anyway. He buttoned his coat to gird himself against the chill night, and set off at a steady pace for home. He had barely taken a dozen steps into the shadows on the far side of the market place when he heard a voice call out.

'Bruno! Hey, Bruno! Over here.' Bruno turned around. He didn't recognise the voice but assumed it was Schmidt, or Meissner, one of Sterkel's mob. What did they want now? He was in half a mind to keep walking, but his usual tolerant humour led him back toward the corner of the square.

'Now listen,' he called out. 'I've had enough. If you're away to another ale house you can count me out.' He was slurring; he'd drunk more than he realised. He looked about, but there was no sign of anybody there at all.

'Ah, Morr rot the lot of them,' he muttered. Then, as he turned to go, somebody or something hit him hard. A firm, jolting blow to the jaw knocked Bruno off his feet. He hit the hard cobblestones with a thud. But he was more surprised than hurt, and the wound was mostly to

his pride. He shook his mane of hair, trying to shift the
dizzy daemons from his head.

'Come on,' he remonstrated. 'That's not funny. If I was
sober I'd tan the hide off you.'

As he clambered back to his feet he was hit again. This
time there was no mistaking the malice in the blow. A
club smashed into his face, sending him sprawling. As
he lay on the ground he got a kick to his ribs, and then
a second. He was hauled back onto his feet. Two or three
men had a hold of him, and were dragging him further
into the shadows.

Bruno fought back with everything he had, but he
knew it was not going to be enough. The faceless attackers were at least as big and powerful as he was and they
weren't going to give up. One of the men had grabbed
him from behind, pinioning his arms.

'What do you want?' Bruno shouted at them. 'Take my
damned money, if that's it.' Another fist rammed hard
into his face. He felt blood flow down his face, and a
salty, metal taste in his mouth. Now he knew for sure.
This was no joke, no common robbery. These men
meant to kill him. Bruno lashed out in the only way he
could – with his feet. One boot caught one of his attackers a heavy blow to the groin. The man cursed
vengefully, but there were at least two others still trying
to drag Bruno away, out of sight. He had a fleeting vision
of himself lying knifed in an alleyway, or floating face
down in the canal. Bruno redoubled his efforts to break
free, knowing his life depended upon it.

The next few moments were a blur. Bruno heard one
of the men call out a warning. One of the others turned
around. He was vaguely aware of yet another figure
emerging out of the gloom. He saw the flicker of steel as
a blade was pulled, then he heard a muffled scream. The
man who'd been holding him swore then loosened his

grip. Bruno seized his chance to wrestle free, turning to land a punch into the man's face. The man staggered to one side and pushed Bruno out of the way. He turned to run. Bruno thrust out an arm and grabbed hold of his attacker by the shirt. The man fell, taking Bruno with him.

Now his attacker was sprawled on top of him, his hands wrapped around Bruno's windpipe. Bruno jabbed a punch into the man's ribs, but he couldn't shake him off or relieve the pressure against his throat. He was starting to choke.

Then, suddenly, the pressure lifted. The dead weight pinning him down was pulled away, to reveal someone else gazing down, a bloodied knife clutched in one hand. Bruno's attacker jumped back in an attempt to save himself, but the blade caught him in the neck, and ripped through his throat.

Half-stunned, Bruno looked up at his rescuer – if rescuer was what he was. A face he didn't recognise peered back at him. Bruno noticed that he had a cut running above one eye, the legacy of an older wound. The man extended a hand and pulled Bruno to his feet.

'I think,' the man said, 'it's about time we introduced ourselves properly.'

CHAPTER TWELVE
Alliance

THEY TOOK MIKHAL Kumansky, blindfolded, to the meeting place of the True Path. It was in a secret place, deep within a remote part of the city. Sightless, he was led along corridors and down narrow steps until, finally, he came to a room, where he was made to kneel. He crouched for what seemed like a very long time in the darkness; isolated, but not alone. There were others there like him, other chosen ones who were kneeling, still and quiet in the cold gloom. They were biding their time, waiting.

Waiting for what? That was still unclear. Waiting for deliverance, waiting for mercy, waiting for answers to the questions tumbling through their minds? Finally the blindfold was removed, and Mikhal could look about the room – or cellar – that he had been brought to. He had been right: he was not alone. Kneeling in identical postures around the darkened space were five or six others, dressed in identical grey robes, with cowls pulled up over their heads. We are the chosen ones, Mikhal told himself, those the True Path has chosen for redemption. Our sacrifice will be equalled by our glory. He repeated the phrase to himself, over and over again, willing himself to believe.

Over time there had been several such gatherings. To begin, he had been just part of a crowd, another faceless acolyte lost amongst the many who were drawn to the teachings of the True Path. But the disciples had looked into his soul, and they had not found Mikhal wanting. Having begun as one among hundreds he was now a chosen one, brought to kneel before the master. A process of selection was underway. That much Mikhal understood. How that selection had been made, or where it would lead, he did not know. All he knew was that, for the first time in a long while, he had a sense of purpose, a sense of belonging.

For years Mikhal had scratched feebly at the fabric of life, without being able to escape the shadows cast by his dead father, and his living, breathing, hero of a brother. But now he had brothers of a different kind, and a master who could look deep into his soul, to lay bare every fear, every weakness within. His sin would be scourged, and through his pain he would be made whole at last. They would lead him from the shadows; his sacrifice would be his glory. At last, he had the chance to make a difference. Finally, he would make his mark on history.

The master of the True Path was amongst them. As one with his brothers, Mikhal prostrated himself upon the cold stone. The preacher walked amid their ranks, laying his hand upon the head of first one disciple, then another, bestowing the gift of his touch. Mikhal felt the master's hand on his brow, and knew that he was blessed. Knew, too, that with that blessing came obligation.

He lay still, waiting for the soothing voice of certainty that – unbeknownst to Mikhal – Bruno had also heard, that day in the Ledermarkt. When at last the master spoke, it seemed as if he was addressing him alone.

'You have come from the many to become the few.' The words echoed in the room, a solemn affirmation. 'Your privilege shall be to carry the burden of redemption for all Altdorf. Through your sacrifice, the souls of the many will be redeemed.'

Mikhal pressed his face hard against the coarse paving, numb to all physical discomfort. These were the words he had been waiting all his life to hear.

'Soon you will come to know new truths,' the master continued. 'New possibilities, new paths. You will be shown the ways of the gods, and they shall be given new names in your hearing. But first we must purge the poison that lies like a sickness amongst us.'

The master paused. The silence hung like a heavy ache in the darkened room. Mikhal felt the blood flush hot in his face. The master was talking about him. It was he, Mikhal, who had brought the sickness to this place. He had tainted it with his guilt. He felt his lungs constrict, as though the air had been sucked from his body. His very being was withering under the master's knowing gaze. By the time the zealot leader spoke again, Mikhal was possessed with a longing to unburden himself, which would not be denied.

'One of you,' the master said, gravely. 'One of you harbours the sickness of sin in his thoughts. Who here must admit that sin?'

In a moment, Mikhal had scrambled to his feet, anxious lest another should steal the light of his confession. But he was alone; the other disciples had stayed kneeling, too frightened or awed to move. The master gestured to Mikhal. Just as he had that morning in the

Ledermarkt, Mikhal Kumansky stepped forward, fear and anticipation equal partners in his heart.

The master laid his hand on Mikhal's head again. Mikhal knelt at his feet, and awaited judgement.

'There is anger in you,' the master said, softly now. 'Anger against us.'

'No,' Mikhal protested, but his heart had caught the lie and spun it to a whisper on his tongue, barely audible.

'Speak it,' the master directed. 'Speak, or else it will fester like a gangrenous sore inside you. Speak.'

Mikhal could feel the tears in his eyes. 'My ship,' he blurted out. 'I pledged my ship in the service of the True Path. I did all that was asked of me. And now my ship is destroyed.' He coughed, choking on a sudden spasm of grief. 'My livelihood is destroyed.'

'And for that,' the master surmised, 'you blame your brothers of the True Path.'

Mikhal said nothing. He knelt upon the floor, shaking uncontrollably.

'Listen to me,' the master said. 'Listen to me, all of you. Here is a lesson for all who would follow the True Path.' The silence of the waiting disciples filled the room.

'You have taken the vows of sacrifice,' the master told them. 'Now you must learn that the path of sacrifice, once taken, knows no limit, no end. You speak of loss, but a time is coming when such loss will be nothing; nothing more than grains of dust, carried by the wind.'

You have shown weakness,' he said, addressing Mikhal directly. 'But you have also shown that you are ready to yield. You bend like a supple tree beneath the yoke laid upon you. That is good.' He raised Mikhal to his feet.

'The time of sacrifice is now upon you.'

* * *

THE COLD CLOTH against his face helped ease the pain a little. Bruno sucked in his breath and mumbled the umpteenth curse to the gods.

'Taal's breath,' he exclaimed. 'My head hurts.'

'Not as much as it will in the morning,' the man holding the cloth promised him. 'By dawn you'll be sporting a bruise the size of an onion. But at least you'll know you're still alive.'

'It'll make a change,' Bruno grumbled. 'It seems that everyone I have met lately wants to kill me.'

The man gave Bruno a strange look; a kind of half smile. Bruno wiped his face and looked around, taking in the room for the first time. His memory of the aftermath of the attack was mostly a blur. He remembered being helped up – by the stranger standing over him now, he supposed – and walking some distance through the harbour district until they'd reached this house. It was cold, dank, and smelt of rats – or rat's urine, at the very least. But it was a refuge, and for that he counted his blessings.

'Nice place you have here,' he muttered. He wrinkled his nose. 'Could do with a little freshening up.'

'Not my house,' the other man corrected him. 'Just one of the houses we use.'

'We?'

The other man smiled, but side stepped the question. 'As I said earlier, it's about time we introduced ourselves properly.'

Bruno sat up and offered his hand. Whoever his rescuer was, he certainly owed him his life. 'Bruno Hausmann,' he said. 'And you?'

'You can call me Nikolas,' the other man replied. 'That's how Stefan knew me.'

Bruno couldn't suppress the gasp of surprise. 'Stefan! Then you–'

'We've met,' Nikolas confirmed. The smile returned. 'You and I are already acquainted, after a fashion. Last time, I think *you* were trying to kill *me*.'

Bruno stared back in frank disbelief. He looked again at the man's face, noticing the half-healed wound just above his left eye. Gradually, realisation dawned.

'The *Karla*!' he exclaimed. 'It was you on the deck!'

'It was,' Nikolas admitted. 'And you pitched me into the dock for my troubles.'

Bruno struggled to regain his composure. 'But what in the name of Sigmar were you doing,' he demanded at last, 'lurking around at that time of night?'

Nikolas shrugged. 'I might well ask you the same question.'

'That you might,' Bruno conceded. The two men regarded each other for a few moments as the stalemate held.

'We must share a little trust,' Nikolas offered at last. 'There are things we must talk about. For the sake of all Altdorf. For the sake of the Empire itself.'

Bruno gave it some thought, then nodded. 'Perhaps you were after the same as me,' he said. 'Looking for the truth. I'm half minded to pay another visit.'

'A little late for that,' Nikolas said. 'The *Karla* was sunk, just after dusk this evening.'

'Sunk?' Bruno replied, incredulous. 'What, some kind of accident?'

'I doubt it. Someone had taken the trouble to set fire to her first.'

Bruno sat back, absorbing the news. 'What about Mikhal?' he asked at last.

'Disappeared,' Nikolas replied. 'No trace of him anywhere. We don't think he was aboard when the ship sank.'

'That "we" again,' Bruno observed. 'You're talking about the Keepers of the Flame?'

Nikolas didn't deny it. 'Like you, we want to know what the zealots may have planned,' he said. 'Like you, we have concerns, but little proof.'

Bruno frowned, perplexed. His head was throbbing too much for him to make sense of this. 'Why not simply have your men arrest them? If there's a risk, then snuff it out. That's what I'd do.'

Nikolas laughed, and shook his head. 'Not possible. Firstly, consider the times we live in. The Empire is at war. Pious fervour is considered a badge of loyalty, not treachery.'

'So our Grand Theogonist keeps telling us,' Bruno muttered.

'Which means,' Nikolas continued, 'that we could only move against the zealots with certain proof of their treachery.'

'But there is proof,' Bruno insisted. 'You and I both know that.'

'Is there? Where is your proof? Is it on board the *Karla*, at the bottom of the harbour? And who would be your witness? Mikhal Kumansky, now vanished without trace?'

'But you and your people could–'

'Listen,' Nikolas interrupted. 'Let me share at least one secret of the Keepers with you. We are not an army. There are those who serve us, formally or informally. Those we call the eyes, who watch over Altdorf. But as a force, with the power to intervene, to do as it will–' He laughed. 'Put it this way, Bruno. As far as you and I are concerned, I *am* the Keepers of the Flame.'

Bruno thought about the others he had met over the past year or more. Men who had claimed allegiance to the secret order. Men like Otto Brandauer, here in Altdorf, or Castelguerre who was now leading his men at Erengrad.

'There must be others,' he insisted. 'Men of authority who you report to.'

'There are, and I shall not name them,' Nikolas said, firmly. 'But believe me, we are few in number. We cannot act alone.'

Frustration was getting the better of Bruno. At heart he was a simple man, and liked simple answers. The idea came to him in a flash of inspiration. 'Then go to Ehrhart!' he said.

Nikolas's inscrutable features registered a momentary flicker of surprise. 'Ehrhart? Why do you mention that name?'

Bruno was about to continue, when caution held him in check. How did he know that he could trust these people? How could he be sure that Nikolas hadn't truly meant to kill him that night on board the *Karla*?'

'I meant, go to the watch,' he blustered. 'They'd surely be able to deal with this.'

'As I said, we haven't the evidence,' Nikolas countered. He tilted his head to one side and fixed Bruno with a cool, searching stare. Bruno had a sudden, uncomfortable awareness of Nikolas the interrogator, the inquisitor. Doubtless, he was good at it. 'You mentioned Ehrhart in particular. Why? Have you been to see him?'

Bruno hesitated, but he had run out of ideas. If Nikolas had really meant him harm, then surely he wouldn't be sitting here talking with him now. Besides, his head was hurting too much for any more subterfuge.

'Yes,' he said. 'I went to see him. Today, as it happens.' He waited whilst Nikolas sat, deep in private thought.

'So,' Bruno asked, 'what now?'

'Now?' Nikolas looked up. 'Now, I think you must tell me everything you told Ehrhart and everything that he told you. Then, you get some rest, while I do some thinking.'

Bruno sat back and stretched out his legs. In truth he was achingly, desperately tired. Sleep would be welcome indeed. 'Very well,' he said at last. 'There's just one other thing.'

'Name it.'

'You know about Stefan. Where's he's gone, I mean. What he's doing.'

'Of course.'

'Then,' Bruno began, tentatively, 'in return for my telling you my story, will you tell me what his mission is, and when he might return?'

Nikolas smiled a simple, disarming smile. 'Sigmar willing, he will return to Altdorf very soon,' he said. 'More than that, I cannot say. For all our sakes. Now,' he fixed Bruno with the same questioning stare. 'Does that make you trust me more, or less?'

Bruno thought about it for a moment. 'All right,' he said. 'Fairly spoken.' He started to laugh, then stopped. His face darkened.

'What is it?' Nikolas demanded. 'Tell me.'

'I was thinking of Mikhal, the last time we met, before Stefan went,' Bruno said. He glanced up at Nikolas. 'Do you remember the rains that fell so long and hard across the city?'

Nikolas raised an eyebrow. 'I should think every soul in Altdorf remembers. For more than a week I wondered if we should all be drowned.'

'There was something Mikhal said, it was like a prophecy,' Bruno went on. 'Something about the rain. Something like, "First there will be rain, then there will be fire."' He laughed, uneasily. 'And the rains are over now.'

IN THE HIDDEN world below the streets of Altdorf, the tunnellers' journey had reached its end. It had ended with the breaching of a cellar wall; brick after careful brick slowly prised from its resting place, until the gap was big enough for a mortal man to pass through. There was no celebration when the last brick crumbled away. The time for the invaders to celebrate would come later. Now it was time for the seeds of death to be sown. The bitter harvest would follow, soon enough.

The skaven squeezed its furred body through the gap that divided the netherworld from the city of men they called Altdorf. The creature elbowed the gang master aside, eager to set first foot in the place that his kin had once claimed as their own. The space exposed on the other side was cavernous, the air stale and cold. No mortal man had recently set foot here, but the skaven could still smell them. The scent of their blood filled its twitching nostrils, and its belly churned, yearning to feast anew.

'Bring light,' it growled. 'Show me this place.'

The gang master nodded, and a torch was brought up. Light flared, sending long shadows across the walls of the chamber. The skaven looked around, picking out the bales tied with canvas and twine stacked upon the floor, the barrels with their sour smell of wine, the wooden chests filled with books and icons that glittered silver and gold in the candlelight.

'Is this it?' the gang master demanded.

'This is the place,' the skaven affirmed. 'Stinking hole of man.'

'Very well.' The leader beckoned to the mutants standing in the shadows. 'Bring the casks. But carefully. Keep them away from the flame.'

Two at a time, a dozen figures squeezed through the gap in the wall into the chamber. Each pair laboured under the weight of a barrel that was about half the size of a man. The barrels were marked with the words "Imperial Quartermaster – Nuln".

'Steady,' the gang master directed. 'I want them well hidden amongst the other barrels. They mustn't be discovered before time.'

'I say do it now,' the skaven muttered. 'Do it now, then vengeance served.'

'This is about more than your petty vengeance,' the gang master replied. 'The Dark Gods shall decree when the time is right. You have no more say in this.'

The rat-like creature reared up on its hind legs, and turned to face the far wall of the chamber. The wall was decked with insignia: the oaths of men in fealty to their warrior lord, Sigmar, and to gods that they worshipped. The skaven growled, a low guttural moan that echoed throughout the chamber.

'This place insults memory of my kind,' it spat. 'Do it now, I say.'

'Keep quiet, Morr damn you,' the gang master hissed. 'Or I swear I'll still your tongue for you.'

The skaven's eyes flashed an evil yellow in the torchlight. Its jaw cracked open as it bared its teeth at the mutant. The rows of yellowed fangs were filed down to a savage sharpness. 'I rip you open from gut to stinking mouth first,' it snarled back.

The skaven began to growl louder. A steady stream of saliva spilled from its open jaws, and its eyes grew wide and wild.

'Cease the infernal noise!' the gang master commanded. The skaven made no reply, but edged a step closer, drooling. The gang master raised a hand and gave a signal. It had long been pre-arranged, and was understood at once by those at his command. Two of the gang plunged forward to seize the skaven, ready to silence it by any means.

The first was too hasty. The skaven caught him easily and snatched the hooded figure between its jaws, ripping the flesh from the mutant's body like a dog tearing meat from a bone.

The mutant was dead before he had time to scream, his dark blood spilling out in a pool on the floor of the chamber. But before the skaven could release its prey, two more mutants had fallen upon it, and then a third, wrestling it to the ground and clamping its jaws tight shut. The skaven thrashed wildly, but in vain. Sheer weight of numbers prevailed. Gradually the thrashing subsided, and the skaven lay still, pinned down by the gang. The gang master uttered a foul oath, and pulled a long-bladed knife from beneath his cloak. He knelt by the side of the trapped creature, and seized hold of a knot of fur at the base of the skaven's neck. He pulled at its head, lifting it clear of the ground.

'A shame you'll not live to see the fruit of your labours,' he whispered. 'But be consoled in this: I never intended to let you live, anyway.'

Unable to move its body, the skaven rolled one eye to gaze into the face of the gang master. It looked up at him with undiluted hatred, forcing the words through bloodied and twisted jaws

'All your kind will perish with them.'

The gang master spat in the skaven's face. 'Filthy scum.'

He plunged the knife deep, slitting its throat from top to bottom. The light faded from the creature's eyes as its head slipped down, cracking hard against the cellar floor.

The gang master checked carefully to make sure the skaven was dead. 'Clean up this mess,' he commanded. He pointed to the corpse of the mutant. 'That one too. I want the chamber left exactly as we found it – except for the offerings we leave behind. Nobody must know we've been here.' He wiped the blade clean on the coarse fur of the skaven's body, and then put the weapon away.

'Not yet, at least.'

THE SWIRLING UNDERCURRENT caught hold of the boat like a mighty hand, propelling it forward with a sudden and unexpected force. It took them out of the narrow channel and into the open water beyond. The wind started to blow in heavy gusts. Nagel glanced at the scudding clouds then stood up, balancing himself carefully against the rocking motion.

'This is our best chance,' he declared. 'If we can get the sail up we'll make real progress.'

Stefan focused on the stretch of water behind the boat. Almost an hour had passed since they had cast off, and there was no sign of pursuit from Stahlfort. Now with the tide tugging the boat through the water, he stowed his oar and went to help Nagel.

'Have they given up?' he asked. 'Is it possible?'

Nagel looked at him as though he were mad. 'You don't know Krieger,' he said, bitterly. 'He won't give up. Since the day a fugitive cost him his eye he's made it his business to make sure no one ever gets off the island. He won't give up, ever.'

Stefan glanced over his shoulder. The jagged profile of Stahlfort was still in clear view, but it was the only thing on the horizon. Perhaps the guards had run into trouble trying to launch another boat. Perhaps, he hoped, there would be no pursuit. He looked at their prisoner who sat slumped and motionless in the prow.

'Von Diehl's not such a great prize,' he said. 'There must come a point where they'll give up on him.'

Nagel laughed, his usual, bitter laugh. 'Who said this is about von Diehl?' he asked. 'We killed one of their men, didn't we? What makes you think Krieger will ever forgive us that?' Stefan loosed the knot tethering the sail to the mast and pulled the canvas free. 'Let's get this rigged,' he said, tersely.

With the canvas up, and the sail securely rigged, the boat gathered more speed. For the first time in what seemed like an age, Stefan felt he could relax, if only for a moment. The killing of the guard continued to trouble him, and he hadn't needed Nagel to remind him of it. But every hour that passed was taking them closer to Altdorf, towards the Keepers of the Flame, towards judgement for Heinrich von Diehl. He refused to believe that the sacrifices they had made would be in vain.

'What about some food?' Maier chipped in, his cheerful tone a contrast to the dour Nagel. Natalia visibly brightened at the suggestion.

'It feels like I haven't eaten for days,' she said. She looked around the interior of the boat doubtfully. 'Where are we going to find food, though? Are we going to have to fish it out of the river?'

Maier looked to Nagel. 'These boats must carry some provisions. Well, don't they?'

Nagel finished fastening the last of the ropes that secured the sail. 'They might,' he said. 'If we're in luck.' He pointed towards a wooden panel in the stern, near Stefan's feet. 'Try there,' he suggested then turned back to his work. Stefan took out his knife and prised the wooden fascia free from the bulkhead. He reached inside the space. Without food, and without horses, they wouldn't get far.

He rummaged inside the hollow space until he felt something tucked away near the back. It was a hard, flat object, wrapped in an oilskin cloth. Stefan pulled it out and laid it on the bench in front of him. He untied the string holding the package together, and opened it out. Inside were several long strips of dried meat and wafers of biscuit. None of it looked appetising, but food it undoubtedly was.

'Is that it?' Natalia asked. Without waiting for an answer she swung over to the stern of the small boat, and searched the compartment again. Her efforts were rewarded by the recovery of two more identical parcels. They unwrapped the little packages and sat contemplating their spoils.

'Enough,' Maier concluded. 'Enough for the four of us, for a few days, if we ration carefully.'

'Four?' Natalia shot Maier a quizzical look, and nodded towards the prow of the boat. 'Aren't you forgetting him?'

Heinrich von Diehl was lying in the narrow space afforded by the prow, asleep or unconscious. Every few moments he would shiver, as though suffering the early stages of a fever.

'You'd waste precious rations on him?' Nagel enquired, sourly.

'What else?' Stefan snapped back. 'If we don't keep him alive, then our whole mission has been futile.' He watched von Diehl with a growing sense of unease.

'He wasn't shaking like that a while ago,' Natalia said. 'Do you think he's ill?'

Maier looked at the prone figure. 'He doesn't look so good,' he said. 'But you can do something can't you? Some healing, I mean?'

Natalia stared back at him. 'You're talking to me?' she asked.

Maier shook his head. 'I just thought–'

Natalia pushed her face close to Maier's. 'I'm a magician, not a healer,' she said. 'There's a difference. If you need a nursemaid, you can take that job on yourself.'

'That's enough,' Stefan broke in. Natalia sat back, her face settling into a sulky pout. Maier shrugged, nonplussed. Nagel gave a brief, wry smile.

'If he's ill we'll deal with it between us,' Stefan stated. 'We all need some food. We'll share it between us, each according to their needs.' He jerked a thumb in the direction of von Diehl. 'That includes him, too.'

'What about something to drink?' Natalia demanded, tetchily. 'If all we have is biscuits and dry salt meat we'll die of thirst before we starve.'

Nagel pointed to the expanse of water flowing around them. 'The Reik is freshwater. Drink as much of it as you want.'

Maier produced a knife. 'Five rations it is then,' he announced, and began to pare the dried meat into portions. He held a strip out, and glanced at Natalia. She took the food without comment.

Stefan took two portions and moved up to the prow. Von Diehl was lying with his legs drawn up, and his arms wrapped around himself. The shivering, if anything, had got worse. He looked like a sick, old man. Stefan reached out, tentatively then stopped short. Apprehension held him back. This is for Altdorf, he reminded himself, not for him. He took hold of von Diehl's shoulder and shook him, gently at first, to try and get him to wake. Von Diehl coughed. A spasm wracked his body. He opened one bleary eye, and muttered something in a language that Stefan did not recognise.

Stefan shook him again, aware of how hard it was to bring himself to touch the other man. 'Wake up,' he commanded. 'What's wrong with you?'

Von Diehl stirred again, but this time he seemed aware of Stefan crouching over him. He gazed up at Stefan with watery eyes.

'I've been locked up in the pit of Morr for more than a year,' he said, his voice parched and hoarse. 'Forgive me if I do not have the manners of good health.'

'You need food,' Stefan told him. He held the strip of meat out tentatively, the way he might offer food to a wild beast. Von Diehl put it to his lips, and bit off a small morsel. He started to chew, staring up at Stefan all the while.

'This disgusts you, doesn't it?' he said. 'I disgust you.'

'I have no interest in you one way or the other,' Stefan replied. 'Other than getting you to Altdorf.'

Von Diehl chewed at the leathery strip, slowly, mechanically. A dribble of saliva leaked from the corner of his mouth. 'That's not true,' he said, quietly. 'Not true at all.'

'Just eat,' Stefan snapped. He turned away, and watched Natalia, as she leant from the side to cup water into her hands. The river was unusually clear, a prism of sparkling blue. Natalia lifted her hands from the river. As she gathered the water to her mouth, a shadow, dark and very large, appeared from nowhere, gliding through the aquamarine depths beneath the hull. Natalia screamed, a shrill, piercing sound, and toppled back into the boat.

'Merciful gods!' she cried out. 'What in the name of Shallya was that?'

Stefan caught a glimpse of something churning the surface of the water. But then it was gone, leaving only ripples in its wake. Silence followed, broken by the sound of Nagel's laughter.

'You fine city dwellers don't know a thing, do you?' He sat back, with his arms folded across his chest, obviously enjoying the moment. 'I warned you earlier, didn't I, about the water? About how you wouldn't want to get too close to it. What did you think?' he demanded of Natalia. 'That it was just the five of us and this boat, alone in the gods' great creation?' He snorted with derision. 'Anyway, it was only a common eel.'

'That was no eel,' Natalia retorted, anger replacing her fear. 'There are monsters lurking down there.'

Nagel turned his back to her, and leaned across the stern. He spat, slowly and deliberately, into the water. 'There's a world below us, just as there is one above. Stay clear of what you don't understand.' A dismissive laugh bubbled up his throat, but it caught and died. He sat staring over the stern, across the water beyond Stefan. Stefan saw the expression on his change, and knew at once that something was badly wrong. He turned around, and saw what Nagel had seen. It was just a speck, no more than a fleck of black against the far horizon. But the significance was not lost on him. It was enough to confirm his fears.

'We've got company,' he announced. 'Company gaining on us fast.'

CHAPTER THIRTEEN
The Black Sail

A SECOND BOAT, taller and larger than their own, had materialised beyond the stern. Over the space of a few minutes the distant shape grew steadily closer, until the superstructure of the boat and the black sail billowing from its mast were clearly visible. Propelled by the gusting wind and a full complement of oarsmen, the newcomer was closing fast. Stefan knew that his hopes of evading pursuit were lost. Now they must somehow outrun the other boat, or perish.

The oars were dropped back to the water to push the vessel on. The slender boat began to pick up speed. For a while the gap between hunter and hunted widened again, and the black sail slipped back towards the horizon. But the respite was brief. The pursuing vessel gathered a momentum of its own, first matching then swiftly surpassing the speed of Stefan's crew. The space between the boats shrank away.

Stefan looked to Natalia. They needed her magic now.

'It's beyond my power,' she muttered. 'Even if I had recovered all of my energies, it would still be beyond my power.' She stared out at the vast expanse of water. The dark form of the boat was steadily closing in. 'To stop or slow a boat that large...' She shook her head, slowly and deliberately. 'Beyond my power.'

A quiet despair began to build. All they were doing, in fact all they could do, was postpone the moment when the other boat would overhaul them. They could extend or foreshorten their fate, but they could not deny it. They could neither outrun, nor outfight their pursuers. With a full crew of armed men aboard the other boat, they would be outnumbered at least three to one. Sooner or later, they would be over-whelmed.

A tense silence fell over the boat, the only sound the surge of water around the oars. A thin, gossamer shroud of mist had settled over the river Reik. The distant shore-line blurred then disappeared in the milky haze. The outer world fell away until all that was left was the dark plinth of the water, and the two boats ploughing through it. It was a graceful, fateful dance towards death.

Soon the other boat was close enough for Stefan to make out figures on the deck, even through the mist. There were a dozen of them, maybe more. The black sail billowed full in the strong breeze blowing down the river. Emblazoned in white upon it, the insignia of the prisoner weighed down in chains, a stark reminder of their destiny.

Voices echoed like ghosts across the narrowing gap between the boats. Someone was hailing them from the prow of the pursuing vessel. It was Krieger.

'Perhaps we should give them what they want,' Natalia blurted out. 'There must be something—'

'He wants our surrender,' Nagel said, without feeling or hope. 'Outright, unconditional. He's not interested in anything else.'

Natalia glanced back at the prisoner. 'But if we offered them von Die–'

'The outcome would be exactly same,' Nagel responded, quashing all hope. 'There's no dealing with Krieger. No terms, except his terms.'

'We could try,' Natalia insisted, desperately. 'They're not interested in us. They just want him back.'

For the first time in several hours, von Diehl raised his head from the deck. He looked at the others then peered out across the expanse of water behind them. He seemed to grasp the situation. The cultist turned back, looking in turn at Natalia, and then Stefan.

'The lady fears for her life,' he murmured. Just the effort of speaking seemed to exhaust him. He spaced his words between long, laboured breaths. 'Are you – ready to sacrifice me?'

'Keep quiet,' Stefan shot back. 'Stay out of this.' He looked to Nagel, who read his question exactly. The former guard shook his head.

'With or without him, they'll still come after us.'

'Then let him pull his weight,' Maier shouted back. 'Loosen his chains, and give him an oar. Let him sweat before we all die.' Stefan took one look at von Diehl's feeble frame. He doubted whether the cultist could make even a token contribution. Were they truly going to end their days back in Stahlfort for this?

Unbidden, an idea came to him. What if they put von Diehl out of the boat? It would buy them time and speed, if nothing else. He glanced at Nagel, and saw he'd had the same idea. Stefan swore, then dismissed the thought. He redoubled his effort on the oars. He had been given a mission, and he would not relinquish it now. He would not.

Krieger stood atop the prow of the pursuing vessel, statuesque and impassive; a beast of prey waiting for his quarry to run to ground. The distance between the boats was less than thirty yards. At this rate they had five minutes, ten at most before the black sail drew level.

A shout came from Maier, who was watching the way ahead. 'The river's dividing!' he called out.

Stefan looked around. Through the thickening fog he saw a darker blur of grey: a huge spur of rock dividing the river in two.

'To the left,' Nagel screamed out. 'In the name of Ulric, steer her to the left!'

Stefan stared into the gathering gloom. The two channels looked indistinguishable. 'Why left?' he yelled.

'The falls,' Nagel shouted back 'The right leads straight over the Reikshalle Falls! We'll be cut off!'

The fork in the river rushed towards them. The black sail closed in behind. The world, and all its possibilities, was narrowing fast.

Stefan made his decision, knowing that there could be no turning back.

'Head to the right,' he called out. 'Towards the falls.'

Nagel stared at him, incredulous. 'Didn't you hear?' he yelled. 'There's no way out from there. We'll be trapped.'

'We're not going to be trapped,' Stefan replied. 'Now, steer right!' He shipped his oar and lowered it back into the water on the other side of the boat. After a moment's hesitation, Natalia and Maier followed his lead. The prow nosed towards the right. Only Nagel continued as he was, stubbornly trying to turn the boat back.

'Row with us, not against, damn you!' Stefan raged.

The black sail raced in towards them, no more than ten yards now separated the boats.

'Row!' he shouted again at Nagel. 'That's an order.'

Maier drew his sword and jabbed the point of the blade towards Nagel's chest. 'Do what he says.'

Nagel swore a vicious oath, and slammed his oar back into the swirling water. The rock face slid past on their left, as the boat entered the narrower channel.

'How long before we hit the falls?' Stefan demanded.

'A few minutes at most,' Nagel replied, a sour rage in his voice. 'You won't have long to wait.'

A giant hand seemed to take hold of the boat from below, and fling it through the water. The oars became redundant, so strong was the force of the tide that gripped them.

Stefan kept his gaze fixed on Krieger's boat. The black sail was still matching their pace, but it was no longer gaining. Stefan heard the voices from the deck, screaming at them to turn the vessel about. Stefan settled himself in the stern, and muttered a prayer.

The water started to churn violently. The little boat was being thrown from side to side on its plunge downstream. They shipped their oars and concentrated on simply holding on. The boat shuddered as its hull scraped across rock, but it kept ploughing on, rushing ever faster towards the waterfall. Stefan saw the pursuing vessel rear up in the water. He watched the frantic efforts of the crew to keep her from keeling over. The boat rolled then righted itself. The black sail started to turn, the prow nudging around until the vessel was side on to them.

'They're turning back!' Maier shouted out, delighted. 'They're giving up the chase!'

'They're not mad,' Nagel retorted. 'They'll drop anchor at the neck of the channel and wait for us to follow them out. They've caught us like a cork in a bottle.' As he stared at Stefan, incredulity formed on his features.

'We'll have to pull around soon, or the tide'll be too strong,' he warned. 'Stefan! Do you hear me?'

'I hear you,' Stefan whispered. 'But we're not turning around. There's only one way out of here. We're going on.'

Now Stefan's plan was graphically clear. Natalia crossed her hands across her breast and stammered a prayer. Even Maier turned a deathly pale.

'Get to the back of the boat,' Stefan yelled. Fear was written on the faces of each and every one of them. He imagined the same look was mirrored in his own face. Only von Diehl seemed oblivious to whatever fate now rushed towards them. He alone was calm, almost serene in the face of impending oblivion.

'Unchain him,' Stefan told Maier. 'Bring him back up to the stern.'

The black sail fell back into the mist. Krieger had called off the pursuit. They'd won a victory, of sorts. Now they would learn its price.

The waters surged and rose around the boat, battering it with a savage power. Even if they had wanted to, they could not have turned back now. The flow was too strong; it was pulling them irresistibly towards the unforgiving embrace of the Reikshalle Falls. The wooden hull was their only sanctuary, and it felt very fragile, against the vast, raging Reik. Maier shoved von Diehl towards the back of the boat. They were all equal now, before the mercy of the gods.

The boat hurtled towards a ghostly oblivion. All that was visible ahead was a wall of white. 'How much longer now?' Stefan asked.

'Four, five minutes, maybe less,' Nagel told him. All eyes were on Stefan. You led us into this, they seemed to be saying. Now lead us out. Even a lifetime of cheating death had not prepared Stefan for a moment such as this. What should they do? Cling to the boat and hope that somehow it survived the plunge down the falls intact? That seemed unlikely. The boat would probably be ripped apart, and all aboard destroyed with it. Their only chance was to try and get clear as the boat tumbled over the falls, and pray that the furious flow would somehow carry them safely to the calmer waters below. If there were rocks at the foot of the falls, then they were dead. But then, Stefan reflected, they were probably dead anyway.

'Listen,' he told them. 'Hold on till the river carries us to the edge of the falls. Then jump. Get as far from the boat as you can.'

Natalia was trembling. She stared blankly at Stefan, and shook her head. 'I'm not moving,' she shouted back at him. 'I'm staying right here.'

'Do as he says!' The command came from Nagel. 'Once we hit the falls, your only chance will be to jump.'

'I'm going to die.' Natalia said.

'One day,' Stefan agreed. 'But not today, if you do what I tell you.' He had to sound convincing. There was no room for doubt now. But, the truth was, he had no idea whether any of them would come through the next few minutes alive.

The waters roared, obliterating all other sound. They had reached the point of all unravelling. The boat shuddered, pounded by the unstoppable torrent. There seemed every chance it would be torn apart before it even reached the waterfall, but, somehow, it held together. In the last moments, each of them turned to their own private thoughts, their own gods. Not even von Diehl was immune from the spell cast by the onrushing doom. He cast his eyes down, and offered some invocation to whatever Dark Power he claimed as his own. A last prayer, a last hope.

For Stefan, there seemed to be a point, just before the boat hit the waterfall, when order was restored to the world. In the space of that stolen moment, he wondered whether he had done enough. Whether the life he had dedicated to the struggle between light and dark had made any difference. Whether the sum of his efforts had tipped the scales in any meaningful way. He thought about his father, long dead in the ground in Kislev. Would they be reunited soon, somewhere along the lost plains of Morr? He thought about Mikhal, and all those that he would leave behind in Altdorf. How would they remember him?

The boat shuddered and pitched from side to side, locked in the throes of death. They were surely at the end. Stefan looked up and saw the mist suddenly lift, raising the veil from the world. It was as if the gods were gifting them one last glimpse of existence, before the light of their souls was dimmed forever. He saw the banks rushing past, a blur of green and grey. And, directly ahead, a rage of foaming water at the very edge of the Reikshalle Falls. He turned to his companions to offer some last encouragement, but all his words were lost. The last thing he saw was Maier, sheltering Natalia in his arms. And Nagel, his back turned towards Heinrich von Diehl. Both men were staring out, blankly, into the void.

Then the river was gone, and the boat was suspended in space, with nothing but the blue of the sky above and the boiling waters far below. Stefan felt it start to fall, the prow of the boat first tilting then plunging like an arrow towards the vortex.

The moment had a strange, surreal serenity. It seemed almost inconceivable that something so pure, so perfect could harm them. Dimly, Stefan remembered his own orders. He had to get out. The boat had turned almost vertical and nothing was any longer in its place. He screamed out to Natalia, but couldn't even hear his own voice against the roar. He was alone, trapped in the screaming abyss, falling through eternity.

He pushed hard against the side of the boat, and jumped. He had no sense of whether he had jumped up, down, or to one side of the doomed craft. All points of reference had vanished. He caught a last glimpse of the boat, a dark shadow against the blur of white, tumbling towards its doom. Then it was gone. Stefan was alone, abandoned to the mercy of the furious water. There was no time for strategy, no time even to feel fear. All he could do was try to breathe and surrender his life to the mercy of Sigmar.

The Reik wrapped him in its cold, furious embrace, and hurled him down.

He fell for what seemed a very long time, plunging down through the curtain of water that rushed toward the base of the waterfall. If he was about to die as his body was torn apart on the waiting rocks, then he would know little or nothing of it. But that was no consolation to Stefan. As his body spun through the falling water, helpless as a broken doll, he realised that he was not ready for death. There were still battles to be won, and answers to be found. He would not yield to the embrace of Morr, not yet.

He hit the water at the foot of the falls, or rather the water hit him. His body smashed hard against the icy barrier of the lake, and was immediately sucked down into the depths. It felt like he was about to explode. A huge, unstoppable force was squeezing every last drop of air and life from out of his body. The power of the waterfall was unremitting and irresistible; Stefan had no choice but to go with it, and let it carry him deeper into the watery chasm below the surface of the lake. His lifetime was measured out in seconds now. A scattering of moments before the pressure pounding against his chest became too much, and the river flooded into his lungs. The centrifugal force of the waterfall spun him around as he was sucked ever deeper within it. Stefan wasted no energy fighting it. The deep would claim him now, or else it would let him go.

He felt a thunderous jolt, and his body was catapulted forward. Suddenly he was swimming free. Far above his head, through the dense curtain of water, he could see the feeble glow of the sun like a tarnished coin in the sky. He swam towards it, kicking out now with every ounce of strength he had left. The sun was life, a desperate, impossible dream of survival. He was not going to let it slip away now. He swam for what seemed an age, battling the icy currents. Then the water around him sieved from black to emerald green, and light flooded in.

His head broke the surface of the water, and he was gasping sweet, clean air. His energy was all but spent, and the treacherous water could still claim him. But the light and air gave him strength as well as hope. Stefan fought back, striking out through the water, away from the torrent tumbling from the falls towards the safety of the shore. Still the current tried to suck him back down, but gradually the force relented, and Stefan could swim freely. He flipped onto his back and floated free, scanning the surface of the pool for any sign of the others.

At first, all he could see was broken debris from the wreck. Then, one after the other, the heads of his companions bobbed up above the surface of the water. First Nagel emerged, swearing foul murder and spewing great spouts of water from his mouth. Then Natalia slipped free of the treacherous pull of the tide. A few seconds later, Maier surfaced with a bewildered grin. He looked about and saw Stefan floating in the water close by. 'Sigmar take you, you bastard,' he spluttered. 'How did you know we would make it?'

'I didn't,' Stefan replied, candidly. He tilted his head back and gazed up towards the head of the falls. Just visible along the bank to one side was a row of figures, no bigger than ants at that distance: Krieger and his men.

Stefan called across to Nagel. 'Will they try and follow?'

Nagel coughed, forcing the last of the water from his lungs. 'Would you, if you had any choice?'

'Is there any other way down?' Stefan asked him.

'Not without going the long way around,' Nagel shouted back. 'It would take them days, at the very least.'

Stefan smiled. The man who never gave up would have to get used to the taste of defeat. There was a sudden movement in the water beneath him, and Natalia broke through the surface nearby. 'Where is he?' she gasped.

'Where's who?'

'Von Diehl. He hasn't surfaced.'

Stefan looked around. There was no sign of the cultist. His first, instinctive thought was that von Diehl had somehow managed to escape from their plunge across the rapids. Stefan imagined the wretched figure hauling himself from the water onto dry land, regaining strength with every stride. All their effort, all the sacrifice would have been for nothing. The mocking laughter of the Dark Gods would ring long and loud in his ears.

Then came the sound of frenzied splashing in the water towards the centre of the pool. Now he saw the cultist. Far from making his way to freedom, von Diehl was struggling, apparently helpless, in the deeper water more than twenty feet from shore. Stefan stared for a moment, unable to take the scene. The cultist who might prove the key to the future of Altdorf was drowning. Von Diehl, the dark servant of all that was evil, *could not swim.*

In other circumstances, the absurdity of the moment would have been cause for laughter, but this was no laughing matter. To lose von Diehl like this would be barely better than having him escape. And the consequences might be just as catastrophic. Stefan plunged forward, intent on rescue. But someone had already beaten him to it. Nagel tore towards the thrashing figure of von Diehl, ploughing through the water with a muscular determination. The gods only knew where he found the strength, but he was swimming as though his own life depended upon it.

Even then, it seemed Nagel might not be in time. Twice, von Diehl's exhausted head slipped beneath the surface. The third time he did not reappear. Nagel cursed, and re-doubled his efforts, digging deep to find yet more speed. He reached the point where the cultist had submerged for the final time, and dived. For a few seconds there was nothing except a few air bubbles rising from the deep. Then, just when it seemed both were lost, Nagel burst back to the surface, gripping the spluttering cultist by the scruff of his neck.

He began to swim back towards shore, towing the bedraggled von Diehl in his wake. Natalia waded into the shallows, applauding wildly. Stefan was of a mind to join in. Had he misjudged the surly Nagel so badly? Of all them, he had proved his worth just when the need was greatest.

A few moments more, and they would have reached the shallows. Von Diehl was moaning, self-pityingly, but he was still very much alive. The hard work had been done; they had all survived the rapids, or so Stefan had assumed.

As Nagel closed upon the shore, Stefan caught sight of something else moving in the water close to the two men. He was suddenly aware of a dark shadow, a large object travelling at speed and with an evil grace. The water shimmered and rippled then, briefly, the creature broke the surface. Stefan had a glimpse of an elongated body, several times the size of a normal man, studded along its length with venomous-looking spines. Stefan shouted out a warning, and rushed forward towards Nagel and von Diehl, but it was already too late.

The waters parted in a great wave, and a monster from Stefan's darkest dreams rose up from the depths. Its scale-encrusted, thickly coiled body had the appearance of a serpent, but this was a creature many times the size of any serpent Stefan had ever seen or imagined. The beast reared out of the lake, water draining from the lethal spines. Its bulbous, misshapen head was marked with what looked like a dozen slime encrusted wounds. One by one, the wounds opened to reveal an array of eyes that burned like malevolent beacons of red-gold fire. The eyes swivelled, and fixed a pitiless gaze upon their prey – upon Nagel.

Nagel released von Diehl and thrust out an arm to fend off the mutant beast, but it was useless. The monster flexed open its jaws, exposing a double row of fangs, each the size of a sword-blade. The beast pulled back its head and fell upon Nagel. The massive jaws snapped shut around his body, dragging him down and drowning his dying screams. The waters boiled as man and monster thrashed just below the surface. Then, as suddenly as it had begun, the movement stopped and the waters settled. A scattering of bubbles rose to the surface of the pool; white foam flecked red with blood.

A transformation had come over von Diehl. All whimpering had ceased the moment that the beast had risen from the lake. From nowhere, he had somehow found the ability to swim, and to swim strongly until the water was shallow enough for him to wade the last few yards to shore. Not once, not even as Nagel screamed in agony, had von Diehl paused or looked back in the direction of the man who had saved his life. Maier pulled the cultist out of the water and tossed him, face down, on the rock-strewn shoreline.

As the first shock of what he had just witnessed faded, a pent-up fury exploded inside of Stefan. He took hold of von Diehl, and pulled him round to face him. He drew back his arm, ready to strike. 'A brave man just died on you account,' he raged. 'And all you were concerned about was saving your skin.'

Von Diehl gazed up at him, an insouciant half-smile playing around his lips.

'What do you want? Sorrow? Gratitude? Isn't that what you were offering – a chance to save my miserable skin?' He coughed, and spat out another mouthful of water. 'I didn't ask to be rescued.'

Stefan stood over the cultist, his fist tightly clenched. But he never delivered the blow. He simply turned away, filled with anger and disgust. 'Find something to tie him up with,' he told Maier. 'Make sure it's secure.'

Natalia turned from the shore, her eyes filled with tears. 'What do we do now?'

'Now?' Stefan looked around, taking in the waterfall, the slate grey cliffs, and the barren, unforgiving land beyond the river. He was wet, freezing cold, and every part of his body ached as though it had been beaten. There was only one thing they could do.

'We walk,' he said. 'We walk until we find a way out of this, or we die in the attempt.'

CHAPTER FOURTEEN
Wilderness

THEY MADE CAMP late in the day, taking what shelter they could in the sparse, spindly trees that grew between the snaking limbs of the river. Natalia worked magic of a more fundamental kind to kindle a fire from the armfuls of damp, green wood they had gathered. As they warmed themselves, and ate the food salvaged from the boat, things started to feel a little better. But their situation still wasn't promising. They'd lost the horses. Now the boat was gone, too. Both had been necessary sacrifices, but it had left them with the prospect of a long and treacherous trek on foot. Worse still, the precious documents that might have gained them entry back into Altdorf lay buried miles back to their north. To return in search of them now would mean a lengthy and probably dangerous diversion. And even if they could recover the forged identities, the time lost might mean that the papers would be out of date. Whatever they did, they faced serious problems.

Worse still, they were lost, with little sense of how far they'd come, and more to the point, how many long miles remained. Without maps, they would have to depend on the sun and stars to guide them. But all of these setbacks paled against the loss of Nagel. He might not have been much of a companion, but as a comrade he had more than proved his worth in that last, selfless act that had cost him his life. Of all of them, he had proved he could set aside his own interests for sake of the greater good. Could Stefan expect the same of Maier or Natalia? The truth was, he wasn't sure.

At least they wouldn't starve, or die of thirst for a while yet. The river water was clean, and they had saved enough food from the boat to last them three or four days. And in three or four days they would be – where? Stefan had no real idea. He gazed up into the cloudless sky. It had grown dark: the twin moons pale, floating orbs in the evening sky. With every hour the temperature fell a little more. It would be a cold night, they would have to keep the fire well tended. Stefan shivered and rubbed his hand against his sleeves to ward off the chill. He noticed Natalia looking over in his direction, and beckoned her across.

'You don't mind if I join you?' Without waiting for an answer, she settled herself down, close to his side. For a moment Stefan imagined himself putting an arm around her, and feeling the spread of warmth as her body nestled against his own. But there was a line between them that was not to be crossed, not yet at least. Natalia drew her knees up and hugged them, shivering.

'I told Karl I'll take first watch when he's ready to turn in,' she said. 'Get it over with.'

'It could be a long night,' Stefan observed. 'Is von Diehl sleeping?'

She nodded. 'Soon as he'd eaten. I don't suppose he cares much for our company.'

'The feeling's mutual,' Stefan assured her. He sat back, contemplating the night sky and waiting for the conversation to take its course. He had grown used to her being around, but it still jolted him sometimes to remember that Alexei Zucharov had been her flesh and blood. As he watched her face in the firelight, he could see the same drive and intensity that had marked Alexei from other men. What was it that drove Natalia, he wondered? What had brought her to this desolate place?

'You did the right thing,' she said, breaking the silence between them. Stefan wasn't sure what she meant. He glanced up at her, puzzled.

'You made the right decision, taking the boat over the falls,' she explained. 'It was our only hope. I see that now.'

'It was a gamble,' Stefan said, quietly. 'And I was lucky. This time we won.'

'But will the gamble be worth it?' she asked. Her gaze flicked towards the sleeping figure of Heinrich von Diehl. 'All this, just for one wretched old man?'

'Evil can take many shapes,' Stefan replied. The words carried a significance he had not fully intended. There was a brief pause.

'Perhaps,' Natalia finally agreed. 'I suppose that must be so.'

'Von Diehl's frailty doesn't make him any less dangerous,' Stefan continued. 'The gamble will be worth it. It has to be.'

Natalia nodded, uncertainly. 'Of course.' She studied Stefan in silence for a few moments. 'You're thinking about Nagel,' she said. 'Blaming yourself for his death.'

'No,' Stefan replied. 'I'm sad about his death. But I don't blame myself. There's a difference.' He spoke the words with conviction, but inside, he wasn't so sure.

'It's not something I've experienced before,' Natalia murmured. 'The death of a comrade, first hand.'

'It's something you meet all too often in our trade,' Stefan replied. 'Not that it makes it any easier.'

'You were there when Alexei died,' she said. 'That must have been… hard.'

Stefan stared into the fire. The image of Zucharov – or the grotesque monster he had become – flashed into his mind. There were many feelings associated with the moment of Alexei's death: fear, grief and elation. Relief that somehow, he, Stefan, had survived.

But he would not share that with Natalia. Would not – or could not – share it yet. There was a vulnerability, a fragility to the girl that he needed to shield. Perhaps there would be a time and a place some day to explain what really happened. But it would not be here, and it would not be now. For the moment, he would protect Natalia Zucharov from that terrible truth.

He tossed a stick into the fire and watched it burn. 'It was the hardest thing in my life,' he said to her. Natalia made no reply, but seemed to draw comfort from his words. What comfort, he wondered, would the bare truth have offered her?

Natalia shivered. 'Merciful Shallya, it's cold.' She turned and looked at Stefan, her eyes glittering in the firelight.

'Are we going to get out of here?' she asked.

'I can't promise that.' There were some things he would not protect her from. 'But if you ask me what I believe, then the answer is yes. I truly believe that we'll make it back.'

A brief, wistful smile flickered across Natalia's face. 'Then I shall believe, too. I shall return home safe from my adventure.' Her eyes sought out Maier, sitting cross-legged on the ground on the far side of the camp, a few feet from von Diehl.

'I promised I'd take first watch,' she said.

'May as well get it over,' Stefan agreed. Natalia smiled again, but there was a sadness in her eyes that she could not mask. She clambered to her feet, and brushed the dust from her clothes.

'I don't think it will ever be over,' she said. 'Not for me, it won't be.'

MAIER MADE WAY for Natalia as she came over. Natalia settled herself on the ground and took the offered blanket, nestling down deep inside of it.

'Ready for this?' Maier asked.

'Ready for what?'

'Will you be all right, keeping watch on your own?'

Natalia shot Maier a dismissive look. 'Of course.'

Maier put a hand inside his jerkin and produced a small pewter flask. 'Take this for company.'

Natalia eyed the flask. 'What is it?'

'The last of the gin,' Maier said. 'Something I salvaged from Stahlfort, before it got wasted on that vermin Dorf.'

Natalia reached out and took the flask from Maier. 'Thanks for the thought,' she said. She looked over at the lumpen huddle that was von Diehl. 'He hasn't stirred?'

'Sleeping like a babe, so far. I'll doubt he'll give you any trouble. But shout if he does.'

'Don't worry,' Natalia assured him: 'I will.'

'Two hours,' Maier reminded her. 'Two hours, then wake me. Mark it by the stars.'

'Don't worry,' Natalia said again. 'I'm not likely to forget.' She was beginning to tire of Maier's attention, kindly meant or otherwise.

'All right then,' he said, apparently satisfied. 'I'll be just over there.'

There was a few minutes of activity whilst first Maier, then Stefan, bedded down for sleep. Eventually all was still, and for the first time in a very long day, Natalia felt that she could relax – or get as near to it as was possible in the freezing Reikland night. She sat for a while appreciating the sense of solitude. Her body was exhausted, but she would have little difficulty in staying awake. Most of the nights she had talked with Stefan about Alexei, she had gone on to dream about her brother.

The dreams were not always welcome. Sometimes Alexei came to rage against his death, screaming bloody vengeance against the force that had stolen away his life. She would wake, sweating and terrified, just as Alexei was about to name his murderer. In other dreams, her brother would appear half in shadow, his face concealed. Natalia would beg him to take that final step forward into the light, but he never did. At the critical moment, just as he turned his face from the shadows towards her, she would jolt awake. Each time, it would be with a terrible sense of foreboding stirring inside of her. If staying awake for two hours postponed dreams such as those, then it was a small price to pay.

For a while she just watched von Diehl. He lay with his face turned towards her, his eyes slightly parted in the way that wild animals sometimes slept. At first she wondered if the cultist was actually awake, but by and by she grew reassured that he was sound asleep. His body rose and fell in a gentle rhythm, each exhalation of breath accompanied by a dry, wheezing sound like air expelled from a bellows. Natalia had no idea of how dangerous von Diehl truly was, or even how dangerous he was supposed to be. Not very would have been her conclusion. But she trusted the judgement of the Keepers. If they wanted von Diehl in Altdorf, then she would give her all to make sure the task was accomplished. In some, small way she would be walking in her brother's footsteps.

The pewter flask was lying on the ground at her feet. She picked it up, pulled the cork stopper out with her teeth, and took a small sip. The gin had an immediate effect, suffusing her mouth and throat with comforting warmth. But the taste was unpleasant, bitter and raw. She swilled the liquid once around her mouth and spat it out, replacing the stopper in the flask.

It was quiet. Apart from the rasping wheeze of von Diehl's breath, the only sound was the wind stirring in the trees, and the distant, urgent rush of the river. The moons and their attendant stars cast a pale, milky glow upon the land, softening the light from the dying fire. It was still bitterly cold, but for the moment Natalia felt at peace. It disturbed her to admit that it was a feeling she had grown quite unaccustomed to.

She tilted her face towards the heavens, plotting the slow passage of the stars across the sky. An hour had passed already; before long she would be rousing Maier, and trying to find some sleep of her own. Until then, it was just her watching over one enfeebled old man, alone in the wilderness. She gazed around, trying to pick out shapes and forms through the darkness. The patchwork vista of rivers and marshy land seemed to stretch out forever. She had no idea that the world could be so huge, or so lonely. When she didn't dream of Alexei, she would surely dream of returning home to Altdorf. For now, a dream was all it remained.

The cold was biting. No matter what she did to get warm, it still penetrated, chilling her to the marrow. The fire was burning low. She realised with a guilty start that she'd been neglecting it. Perhaps with more fuel it might produce a little precious heat. She looked around. The fuel they'd gathered was almost exhausted. She would have to find more to keep the fire alive. She gazed at von Diehl. Would it be safe to leave him for a few moments?

The cultist had barely stirred, other than to groan once or twice in his sleep. The chances of him waking seemed remote. Besides, it wouldn't do if the others woke to find she had let the fire die. It wouldn't take long.

Gingerly, she got to her feet, trying to make as little noise as possible. Von Diehl turned in his blanket and muttered a few incomprehensible words. His breathing resumed its slow and regular pace. It's all right, Natalia told herself. This will only take a moment.

They had pitched their camp as far above the waterline as possible, on a thin strip of bare ground in a cleft between the sparse, wispy trees. Even so, most of the wood readily to hand was too green, or too damp, and Natalia was too exhausted to use her magic to spark it to life. She pushed on a little further, treading cautiously through the dark, gathering any dry tinder she found. Every few seconds she glanced back over her shoulder, to make sure that the camp, and von Diehl, were in clear view. After five minutes she had gathered an armful of sticks and twigs, enough to keep the fire burning for about an hour. It wasn't enough, but getting more would mean straying further still from the camp.

Natalia paused. If Stefan could gamble, then so could she. She steeled herself, and pushed on into the deeper thicket of trees further ahead. She spent a minute gathering wood from the low branches and fallen debris scattered about then hurried back.

To her relief, she found everything exactly as she had left it. Von Diehl seemed to stir at her approach. His sleeping face turned towards her, and for a moment Natalia experienced the unsettling sensation of having the unconscious, half-lidded eyes staring directly at her. The cultist moaned quietly, and rolled back onto his side. Natalia breathed a sigh of relief, and resumed her position by the fire.

She wasn't aware of time passing, but the next thing she knew, Maier's hand was on her shoulder, shaking her violently. She looked up in alarm.

'What's the matter?'

Maier stared down at her in disbelief. 'The matter? What's been happening here?' Before Natalia could answer, Maier strode across to where von Diehl had been lying. Natalia saw him aim a hefty kick at the prisoner. The 'body' broke apart into fragments of stone and folds of blanket. There was no von Diehl.

Natalia sprang to her feet. A sudden, guilty panic flooded through her. She rubbed her eyes, as if willing him to reappear once more.

'It's not possible,' she protested. 'He was right there, only a moment ago.'

'It's more than possible,' Maier retorted, angrily. 'He's gone!'

Stefan was awake and on his feet. There was no need for him to ask what had happened. Maier reached out and grabbed hold of Natalia, his face contorted with anger. Stefan pulled him away, prising the two of them apart.

'Taal's breath,' he yelled. 'Pull yourselves together. Both of you.' He turned to Natalia. 'What happened? How did he get away?'

Natalia gesticulated, helplessly. 'I don't know!' she insisted. 'I swear, one moment he was there, the next–'

'It's my fault,' Maier cut in, unexpectedly. He held the gin flask out in front of Stefan. 'I shouldn't have let her have this.'

'I didn't touch the filthy stuff,' Natalia retorted, angrily. By way of response, Maier pulled the cork from the neck of the flask and tipped it upside down. A thin dribble of clear liquid poured onto the ground, no more than a few last drops.

Natalia shook her head in disbelief. 'I swear,' she said to Stefan. 'I didn't touch it. And even if I had–'

'We're wasting time,' Stefan said. He wasn't interested in whether she had drunk the gin or not. All he needed to know was where von Diehl had gone and how he had managed to get away. 'How long was he out of your sight?' he demanded.

Natalia turned away, avoiding the stare of the two men. 'I was watching him all the time,' she said. But the lie in her voice caught her out. Maier spun her round to face him. 'Tell the truth!'

Natalia pushed him away. 'The fire was going out,' she snapped. 'I had to get more wood. Did you want us all to freeze to death?'

'How long was von Diehl out of your sight?' Stefan asked again. 'How long exactly?'

'Only moments,' Natalia insisted. 'But, listen, he was still there when I got back to the camp. I swear by the goddess he was.'

Maier turned to Stefan, ignoring Natalia now. 'We'll find him,' he said. 'He can't have got far.'

Stefan nodded. 'We'll split up,' he said. 'He won't have headed back up towards the falls so he must have gone either due east, to follow the river downstream. Or else he's headed north into the wetlands.'

'I'll take the river,' Maier offered.

'Agreed,' Stefan said. 'I'll search the swamps.'

'What about me?' Natalia asked. 'Where shall I look?'

'Nowhere,' Stefan told her, curtly. 'Stay by the camp until we get back.'

'Think you can do that?' Maier asked, sarcastically. Without waiting for her answer, he pulled a branch from the fire to serve as a torch, and strode towards the river. Stefan buckled his sword about his waist, avoiding eye contact. He wasn't sure who he was more furious with – Natalia or himself.

'I'm sorry,' she said. A note of defiance crept back into her voice. 'But it wasn't my fault.'

Stefan chose a brand from the flames. 'Keep the fire going,' he instructed her. 'We'll need it to find our way back.'

He lifted his torch, and set off before Natalia could reply. The time for words was over.

HE CHOSE A path almost at random, keeping the orange flicker of the fire at his back. Maier's words – he can't have got far – were fixed in his mind. It was true: there was a limit to how far a frail man could travel in treacherous conditions like these. On the other hand, how far was far? The dark expanse of land surrounding the waterways was barren, but it wasn't without hiding places, especially for a creature possessed of as much guile and cunning as von Diehl. The chances of finding him were not that good.

Stefan held the torch low to the ground. The flames reflected in the water pooled at his feet. Danger was everywhere, at any moment the sodden earth might subside, and drag him down in the cloying embrace of the swamp. If von Diehl hadn't already escaped, then he might equally well be dead. A part of him even rejoiced at the idea. But if he was dead, then what? All of this, the sacrifice and the killing would have been for nothing.

There was no option but to press on, slowly. If he turned back now, it would be the end. There would be nothing left for them but the long journey home, to an uncertain future. More than once, he shouted out to von Diehl, in the faint hope that he might respond. The name felt like poison on his tongue as he shouted it into the night. The sound echoed across the empty expanse, but met with no answer.

By now the light of the fire was a distant speck of light against the night sky. Soon, he would have to turn back. In his heart, von Diehl was already lost, but he could not surrender to the idea, not yet. His thoughts started to wander. Could it be possible that Natalia had allowed von Diehl's escape, or, even worse, been a party to it?

For a moment he contemplated the possibility that she had somehow been touched by the same malignant power that had claimed the soul of her brother. Pray Sigmar, it could not be. Alexei Zucharov had been poisoned by Chaos in battle. In victory, he had let greed get the better of caution. When he stripped the amulet from the body of the Chaos knight, his own destruction had become inevitable. That didn't mean that Natalia was destined to follow her brother down that same, dark path. Nevertheless, the thought that she had somehow allowed their prisoner to escape gnawed at Stefan.

Just when it seemed that all was lost, he heard a voice. A single shout ringing out from west of the camp. It was Maier. Stefan turned and ran as fast as he dared towards the sound. More than once he slipped and felt the powerful suction of the marshlands trying to pull him down, but adrenaline and sheer determination carried him through.

He reached the hard flint path that ran alongside the northernmost bank of the river. Maier called out Stefan's name again. Stefan shouted back, and ran harder. Now he could see Maier's torch amidst a knot of bushes away to the right. Stefan left the path and plunged into the dense undergrowth, using his sword to scythe a path through the tangled vegetation. He burst through into the clearing, with no idea of what he was about to find.

Karl Maier was crouched close to the ground. With one hand he was holding the burning torch aloft. The other seemed at first to be pressed down inside a hole in the ground. When Stefan looked closer, he saw that just beside Maier the solid earth gave way to swamp, a treacherous quagmire the size of a small lake. Heinrich von Diehl was trapped in the quicksand. Only Maier's grip on the other man's tunic was keeping him from slipping under.

Stefan gazed at the cultist with a mixture of pity and revulsion. He remembered the ambush on the way out to Stahlfort, how the fat man had struggled uselessly against the unrelenting hunger of the swamp. Von Diehl had clearly struggled in the same way, and with the same result. His face and hair were coated in a glutinous, grey-brown slime. Only his terrified eyes, glimmering in the torchlight, betrayed the fact that Maier had hold of a living being.

Maier glanced around with his self-satisfied grin. 'Tempting, isn't it? One good push and I could send our friend right to Morr.'

'Tempting, but we need this wretch alive,' Stefan replied. 'Come on. Let's get him out of there.'

'Careful,' Maier warned. 'One slip and we'll both be in as well. Then it'll be a one-way journey for us all.'

Stefan edged forward until he was close enough to reach von Diehl. He grabbed hold of a handful of greasy, saturated cloth. As he started to pull, he felt the ground beneath him sliding away. A cloying sludge rose up over his ankles. He could feel the strength of the swamp like a ravenous mouth, sucking him down. Maier caught hold of his arm, and Stefan pulled himself clear, scrambling back until his feet found solid ground again.

'I told you,' Maier gasped. 'Careful.'

Von Diehl was steadily slipping further into the swamp. Most of his body was submerged now, only one eye and half of his mouth was clear of the choking filth. A bubble of air escaped the cultist's lips as he struggled to draw breath. Stefan edged forward again, more cautiously this time. 'We have to hurry,' he told Maier. 'He doesn't have much longer.'

He lost his grip twice before he finally got enough purchase on von Diehl's tunic. The swamp was fighting them to the last, determined to deliver von Diehl to the kingdom of Morr. But Stefan and Maier clung on. Inch by slow inch, they began to drag the cultist out.

'Keep going,' Maier urged. 'We've got him now.'

'How in Ulric's name did you find him?' Stefan asked.

'Pure chance,' Maier replied. 'I was about to head back to the camp when I heard a sound like an animal whimpering.' He laughed. 'There he was, floundering about in the swamp like a pig in a hole. The bastard wasn't so proud that he wasn't going to sing for help.'

Von Diehl's head came clear of the swamp. The cultist coughed, spewing out a lungful of filthy liquid

'Count yourself lucky,' Stefan told him. 'Another minute and you'd have been dead.' The cultist stared back at him, exhausted, his resistance utterly broken.

BACK AT THE camp, they cleaned up their prisoner as best they could, using clean water drawn from the river to wash away the filth of the swamp. Against his better judgement, Stefan gave him a wafer of the dried meat ration to chew upon. None of it seemed to make much impression on von Diehl's spirits.

'I'm freezing to death,' he complained. 'I'm soaked in freezing water and starving hungry. Why shouldn't I feel sorry for myself?'

'You should be grateful we didn't leave you to die,' Stefan told him. 'Sigmar knows, it would have been one more sin purged from the world if we had.'

Von Diehl worked the leathery strip of meat, chewing then spitting out the residue at regular intervals. 'There's no reason for me to be grateful,' he responded, between mouthfuls. 'None of what you are doing is for my benefit.'

'I know,' Stefan said, bitterly. 'You didn't ask to be rescued.'

'But you would have died if we'd left you in Stahlfort,' Natalia reminded him.

'I'm going to die anyway,' von Diehl replied. He glanced up at Stefan. 'Isn't that so?'

'We all die some time,' Stefan said. 'If we're lucky, we have the chance to repent our sins before we do.'

Von Diehl grunted, dismissively. 'Death is death,' he sneered. 'And no amount of dressing can hide its simple beauty.' He threw the remains of the meat into the fire. 'Anyway, all I want is sleep. I don't care about anything else.'

'We need more fuel for the fire,' Natalia pointed out. 'I could go and start gathering–'

'Don't bother,' Stefan told her. 'There'll be no more bedding down tonight. We're all awake now. We'll strike camp, and get moving.'

'But I need rest!' von Diehl protested.

'Then you'll welcome it all the more when it comes,' Stefan snapped back. He nodded to Maier. 'Get ready to move out. We'll keep going until daybreak, and see how far that takes us.' He took a last look around the camp. 'Every step we take towards Altdorf can only be to the good. The sooner we bid farewell to this cursed place the better.'

CHAPTER FIFTEEN
Day of the Dead

THE ASSASSINS CAME as first light broke across Altdorf, smashing a pane of glass in the student's billet to force their entry. The first to die saw precious little of his final day in the mortal world. The soft-spoken janitor, known to the students only as Max, heard the intruders breaking in, but the knowledge did him little good. He had been expecting this day, but when it finally came, there was to be no escape. The dark-robed figures trapped him in the walkway that ran outside the student dormitory, cutting off any retreat. Unable to run, the janitor fought. He fought the intruders with the strength and will of a wild beast, but his ferocity was no match for their greater numbers. Before the first of the students had stirred from sleep, Max was dead, felled by three murderous blows from a long-bladed knife.

As the janitor lay dying, Thomas van Elbst was setting out his market stall for the beginning of another day. He laid out the salted fish in rows and offered prayers for a crisp, clear Altdorf morning, and for trade to be brisk enough to clear his wares before the fish began to stink. He was bending down with his back to the street when his murderers approached. Too late, he heard the footfalls on the cobblestones. Some deeper instinct made him look round and reach for the gutting knife at his side. His fingers touched, but never closed on, the hasp. The first assassin seized him by the hair and lifted his face towards the winter sun. The other slit open his throat, as quickly and neatly as Thomas gutting his catch. It was over in moments, the only witness to the scene already drowning in his own blood.

For Jana Karsten, the end came on her way from prayers at the temple, in a quiet lane between the merchant quarter and the Konigsplatz. Just the other side of the Heimsrucke Bridge, Jana slipped from the bright sunlight into the shadows of the Furstenstrasse, and in so doing slipped from life to death. Two more assassins were waiting for her there. One clamped a tight hand across her screaming mouth, the other stabbed her through the heart. It was a death so quick it could be almost considered merciful. But there was no thought given to mercy that day.

Three deaths, all within the city walls of Altdorf, and all within minutes of each other. By the time the bells across the city had chimed eleven that morning, they were joined by six more. A student, a baker, two merchants, a humble clerk and a revered professor of sciences from the university. The dead had nothing in common except a shared oath to serve the secret order known as the Keepers of the Flame… Nothing until that fateful morning. Now grim mortality had become their common bond.

* * *

MARCUS ALBRECHT ABSORBED Ehrhart's news in stunned silence. When at last he spoke, his voice was hoarse and dry as dust. It was the voice of a broken man.

'When?' he asked, almost in a whisper. 'When did it happen?'

'We can't be sure.' Gustav Ehrhart was pacing the floor of his office. He came and stood by Albrecht's side, and rested a consoling hand on his shoulder. 'The first bodies were found at about three, this Aubentag. The others over the course of the next few days. But–' His hand tightened upon the other man's shoulder, 'it looks as though many, if not all, were killed that first day.'

Marcus Albrecht choked back a sob of grief and raw anger. The weeks that had followed their last meeting had been clouded by a growing, ill-defined sense of unease. Now, over the course of a few brutal days, Albrecht's trusted sources had been all but wiped out. The eyes and the ears of the Keepers of the Flame stopped in one bloody, orchestrated campaign.

He turned away from the window, his face bloodless and drawn, and gave voice to the one question turning endlessly in his mind.

'Why?'

Gustav Ehrhart leaned forward, and rested his heavy frame against the table. His studied expression mirrored the pain written clear upon Albrecht's face. 'I am sorry to bring you here, at this hour, to hear such brutal tidings,' he said. 'But we are being conspired against, by forces we know and understand only too well.'

Albrecht could feel the helpless rage welling up like a great storm inside him. He was consumed by thoughts of revenge for the murderous acts.

'What is their purpose?' he demanded. 'Why choose now to strike against us?' He shook his head, sorrowfully. 'I have brought this upon us,' he said. 'My reckless actions have cost loyal servants their lives.' He grasped the beaker of water in front of him, and drained it in one gulp. 'I must call a halt to this madness,' he said. 'Send word to the others of the Ten. Tell them Altdorf is not safe.'

'You must do nothing of the sort,' Ehrhart insisted. 'Can't you see? This is a test of will. The true intent behind this bloody deed is to deflect you from your greater purpose. It's precisely because Chaos fears the gathering of the Ten that they have acted now. Call a halt, and you will have played directly into their hands.'

'Altdorf is not safe,' Albrecht repeated. 'You cannot tell me otherwise.'

'It will be made safe,' Ehrhart countered.

'How so?'

'You shall have the watch, my men, at your disposal. I shall guarantee protection for the Ten, and all others who need it. ' He ran his fingers through his thick, steel-grey hair. 'By Sigmar,' he declared. 'Peter Selendorf was too proud to accept my offer of sanctuary. Don't tell me you are too?'

Albrecht sank his head in his hands. He could not shake off the notion that he was responsible for the ruin that had swept like a plague through the Keepers of the Flame. Ehrhart left Albrecht to his reflections for a few moments. A faint smile flitted across the commander's face. 'There is some crumb of comfort,' he said. 'Some better news.'

'Name it,' Albrecht said miserably.

'Word has reached the watch from the western Reik-land. News from a prison island.'

Albrecht looked up. Hope flickered briefly in his eyes. 'Stahlfort?'

Ehrhart nodded. 'If all continues to go to plan, then Kumansky will reach Altdorf in a matter of days.' He grasped the other man's hand. 'You must hold firm,' he insisted, vehemently. 'Don't turn back now, not when we are so close. So much rests upon your courage, old friend.'

Albrecht looked away, his face clouded by doubt. 'I don't know,' he said. 'Truly, I just don't know.'

'All you need do is let me protect you,' Ehrhart told him. 'I just need names, locations. The names of the Ten, for exam–'

'I cannot tell you that!' Albrecht exclaimed.

The watch commander shrugged. 'Perhaps not that,' he conceded. 'But there are others, surely, that we must shield from the bloody slaughter that the Dark Ones are intent on visiting upon us?'

'Who are you thinking of?'

'Well, Nikolas, for one,' Ehrhart replied. 'And – what was his name, that friend of Kumansky's? Bruno Haus-mann, was it? What has happened to him?'

Marcus Albrecht's eyes flicked up to look at the other man. He reached out for the beaker of water, but it was empty. He turned the cup between his fingers.

'Bruno,' he said. 'I had forgotten about him.'

As THE LAST rays of the sun fanned out across the dark-ening mass of the Reikland, they came upon it – a single, solitary building amongst the jagged ruins lying low within the folds of the circling hills. It was hidden away from the watching world, almost totally concealed.

Stefan stood on the low crest of the hill, looking down. Some time long ago there must have been a vil-lage there. The ghosts of other buildings, farms and houses, still remained: a fallen wall here, a chimney lying amidst rubble there; hollowed shells of what once was. But that was clearly long ago. No light shone now through the gathering gloom. No voices called, no animals stirred. There was no life in this place. The single, abandoned building was the only structure left standing.

'What do you think it is?' Maier asked. Stefan gazed down at the scarred, blackened walls. The building was set on two tiers, its few windows mostly on the upper level. It looked battered, but solidly built, probably the only reason it had survived so long. Under other circumstances, Stefan would barely have given the crumbling structure a second glance. But now, with cold night drawing in, the dismal place might prove to be their sanctuary. That is, if it wasn't a trap.

'Well?' he asked Maier. The other man shrugged. 'It would be shelter,' he said. 'For one night, at least.'

'Please,' Natalia implored them. 'I beg of you. I can't go on any further. I can't, Stefan.'

That was the truth for all of them, and Stefan knew it. The choice was a stark one. Bed down in the open and take their chances with the freezing temperatures, and whatever else the night might hold, or stop here, and shelter inside. There were no other options.

He thought it through. If there were anyone out there waiting to attack, then it would make little difference whether they stayed outside, or took shelter here. The solid walls would at least give them a position to defend, there was no arguing with that. That left the possibility that someone or something was lying in wait for them *inside* the building.

He started down the slope towards the dark outline of the house. 'Come on,' he said to the others. 'We're going to take a look.'

At the foot of the hill he stopped and handed his knife to Natalia. 'Stay here with von Diehl,' he said. 'Don't be afraid to use this if anything happens.'

'Don't worry,' Natalia assured him. 'I won't.'

'Let's check inside,' Stefan said to Maier. 'Keep your ears and eyes open.'

As soon as they were out of earshot, Maier muttered 'Do you think you can trust her?'

'What do you mean?'

'Well,' Maier said. 'Von Diehl's escaped once already while she was supposedly guarding him.'

'She won't let the same thing happen twice,' Stefan said. In truth, he felt less certain than he sounded, but he had made his decision. 'Let's just get the job done,' he said.

They picked his way through the rubble and shattered timbers of other broken buildings. If this had once been a village or settlement, then it had almost certainly been sacked, burnt to the ground by raiders. A shiver passed through him, carrying the recollection of his childhood home. He remembered the smoke hanging like a poisonous fog across the charred and burning houses.

The two-storey structure had largely survived whatever horrors had befallen the village. A heavy, oak door on the lower floor was still in place, and the walls were intact. Most of the windows had sturdy shutters fastened across them. The design of the building suggested an observation post or a watchtower of some sort. It had been built with defence in mind, and it looked like the defence had held, for a while. If necessary, it could be defended again. If it came to that.

Stefan stepped into the darkened interior, lifting his torch to get a better view of what lay inside. A series of interconnecting rooms led off from a large central space; all of them empty. The floors were littered, and the walls, where they were not blackened by fire, had been daubed with crude, ugly runes. The place smelled cold and lifeless, long-deserted.

He scuffed his foot through the debris at his feet, revealing a tiny figure amidst the broken stone and splinters of wood. He bent down and picked it up. It was a child's doll or puppet. The fabric was mostly rotted away and two of the limbs were missing. In those final days or hours the watchtower had become a sanctuary, a last, ultimately futile refuge place from the horror that had swept through the village. Stefan replaced the doll where he had found it, and moved on.

In one corner, a set of stone steps led to the upper floor.

'Stay here,' he told Maier. He put one foot on the bottom step and started to climb slowly towards the top. For a moment he thought he heard something move, the faintest scuffling of feet on the floor above. He paused, and listened but heard nothing but the low moaning of the wind.

Stefan climbed until his head was level with the floor above. He raised the torch. The layout more or less replicated the floor below. Everywhere lay the wreckage of a lost life. The walls were filthy and defaced. A single wooden chair, improbably intact, sat alone in the middle of the room.

Stefan lowered the torch and climbed up into the room. Instantaneously, a pair of eyes flashed out in front of him then darted away. Stefan reeled back in shock and surprise, almost losing his footing on the steps. By the time he realised it was only a rat, he had recovered his balance and his calm.

'What's happening?' Maier called from below.

'Nothing,' Stefan replied. 'Nothing at all. The place is empty.'

From a shutterless upper window he could see Natalia, standing with von Diehl. She looked up towards him, a look of hopeful expectation on her face.

'It's all right,' Stefan called down. 'We can shelter here.'

'Shallya be praised,' Natalia replied, visibly relieved. 'I was beginning to think this day would never end.'

Stefan stared at von Diehl as Natalia led him down towards the tower. He was searching for a clue, any sign that might hint at the truth behind the inscrutable mask. They had found their sanctuary, but Stefan did not feel like resting. The day might be at an end, but the long night still lay ahead of them.

BRUNO WAS PULLED from his dreams by distant sounds of hammering. Then he felt a hand shaking him insistently by the shoulder.

'Wake up,' a voice called out. 'Bruno, you must wake up!'

Bruno sat up abruptly. In his confusion, he wasn't even sure where he was. Then, as he saw Nikolas's face looking down, he remembered. The anonymous house on Klagen Strasse, its locked doors and shuttered windows. The place Nikolas had brought him to had become his temporary home, but it had lately come to feel more like a prison, with Bruno barely moving beyond the four drab rooms.

'What's happening?' he muttered, his mind still fogged by sleep. Nikolas tugged at the bedding and got Bruno onto his feet. 'We have to get out,' he said. 'Now.' As if to underline the urgency, there was the sound of glass smashing somewhere below. The noises Bruno had thought belonged to his dreams were real. Someone was breaking in.

He pulled on the rest of his clothes. 'Who is it?' he asked Nikolas. 'What do they want?'

Nikolas thrust a knife into Bruno's hand. 'I don't know who it is,' he said. 'The same people who've been making house calls all over Altdorf in the last few days,

I imagine. And they're either after me, or you, or both of us. Either way, we don't stay around to find out.'

Bruno fumbled through the gloom, to the landing. He was fully alert now, and his heart was pounding. 'I thought this place was safe.'

Nikolas shot him a dark look. 'It was,' he said, 'until now.'

A thunderous crash from the ground floor announced that the main door had given way. Nikolas turned back from the stairs. 'This way,' he said. 'There's a window at the back. We can get out over the wall and escape through the alley by the side of the house.'

'Escape? Escape where?'

'Let's worry about that later,' Nikolas advised. 'Come on.'

The window facing the alley was small, only just large enough for a single man. Bruno followed Nikolas out, compressing his bulky frame through the narrow aperture. Footsteps pounded on the wooden stairs inside the house. There wasn't much time.

The window opened out onto a sloping roof. Bruno tumbled out and immediately lost his footing on the loose, slippery tiles. He slithered helplessly down until Nikolas's steadying hand caught hold of him. For a moment the two men lay motionless, struggling to regain their breath. Nikolas put a finger to his lips, and indicated the dark strip of the alley below. Half-hidden in the shadows were two figures; men standing guard on the back of the house.

'Who are these people?' Bruno whispered again.

'They want us dead, that's all we need to know. Stay with me and be careful. We mustn't make a sound.'

Bruno followed Nikolas as he inched his way cautiously along the edge of the roof. At one end there was a wall giving access to the street below. Bruno calculated the distance; it was too far to jump. He glanced down. The surface of the wall was uneven, with missing bricks and wooden beams that jutted out at intervals. It ought to be possible to climb.

The two men were standing at the far end of the street, by the side door to the house, their attention fixed on what was happening inside. Nikolas wasted no time in climbing down from the roof and finding a foothold on the brickwork. Bruno waited until he was clear, then followed. Now they would be at their most vulnerable. If the two thugs below spotted them, they were dead men.

Nikolas was about a dozen feet from the ground when, without warning, one of the men turned back along the alley towards them. He was close enough for Bruno to get a good look at him, a vicious-looking brute, with a regimented, almost military bearing. He seemed to be getting impatient.

'I'm sick of hanging around,' Bruno heard him say. 'I'm going in to see what's happening.'

'You'll wait here,' the other man hissed. 'Those were the orders, and you'll stick to them.'

The first man stooped directly below Nikolas. Nikolas glanced up at Bruno. Bruno understood at once what he had decided to do. Nikolas leant back from his position on the wall, held firm for a moment longer, and then jumped. The man below must have heard something because he looked up, but not in time. He shouted out to his comrade, but his cry was stifled as Nikolas knocked him to the ground. In that instant, the slow, almost dream-like moment was broken. Things started to move fast. Bruno scrambled down towards the street. Nikolas and the first man were locked in a desperate struggle. The second man was racing towards them, sword at the ready.

Bruno was still probably twenty feet from the ground when he, too, decided to jump. He fell awkwardly, but the adrenaline pumping through him blotted out any pain. The first man broke free from Nikolas and spun towards Bruno. Bruno struck him hard beneath the chin, and knocked him over. The second man struck out at Bruno. The razor steel of the sword sliced through his jerkin and cut through the flesh on his arm like ripe fruit. Bruno swore, ducked down beneath a second blow, and charged his opponent head-on. The man lashed out with his sword; a wild and erratic strike that fell well wide. Bruno seized his chance, and butted the man back against the wall. He followed through with his knife. He thrust the short blade as deep as he could into the man's chest, and held it there until he was sure his opponent was dead.

The first man had regained his feet, and had Nikolas forced back against the side of the house. He was fighting back bravely, but the sheer brute force of the other man was overpowering him. Bruno dived in, leaping onto the other man's back. The man shrugged him off easily, and turned back to finish Nikolas. Bruno went in again, avoiding the flailing fists of the other man. He managed to land a thrust with his knife, which just nicked their opponent's shoulder blade. The big man lashed a fist into Nikolas's face and spun around to target Bruno.

He caught Bruno with his first blow, and knocked the knife from his grip. Soon his thick, meaty hands were around Bruno's neck, crushing the life out of him. Bruno brought his knee sharply up into the other man's groin. The attacker groaned and pulled back. Bruno cracked a punch against his jaw, then another. The man staggered, but did not fall. Just as he was about to renew his assault on Bruno, Nikolas fell upon him from behind. With the bigger man still trying to force Nikolas off, Bruno took his chance to reclaim the knife. He grasped the hilt with both hands and thrust into his opponent's face. The big man tried to fend him off, but this time he was too slow. He hit the cobblestones with a heavy thud, and did not move again.

Nikolas glanced briefly down at the bodies to satisfy himself that they were really dead. 'Let's get out before the others show up,' he said, and started to run towards the top of the alley. As they emerged into the street at the far end, he turned back to Bruno.

'We must split up,' he said. 'It'll be safer if we don't stay together. Is there somewhere you can go?'

Bruno's head was spinning. 'I think so,' he muttered.

'Then go there,' Nikolas implored him. 'Go now.' He hesitated for an instant, wrestling with a private dilemma. 'Wait, though,' he said. 'There are things you should know, in case… in case something happens to me.

'The first is that Stefan could be back in Altdorf within three or four days, gods willing. You need to look out for him, if you haven't already heard from me.' He looked around, nervously. A commotion broke out in the darkness behind them; shouts echoed from the far end of the alley.

'For Sigmar's sake man, hurry,' Bruno urged.

'The second is a name – the name of the man I serve. Marcus Albrecht. Seek him out if all else fails. Now–' He shoved Bruno away from him. 'Now go! And Sigmar speed you.'

NIKOLAS WATCHED BRUNO set off with a heavy heart. He knew that in passing the name onto Bruno he had broken one of his most solemn vows. He wasn't sure beyond all doubt that he could trust Bruno, but he

wasn't sure beyond all doubt that he could trust anybody. What he did know was that only one of them was
going to get away. If it was to be Bruno, then he had to
know. If it wasn't, then it probably no longer mattered.

He had begun running towards the more populated
streets at the heart of the city. He was well clear of the
house on Klagen Strasse when he heard footsteps keeping pace behind him. His hand went to the dagger in his
pocket, the only protection he had left. By the time
another two figures appeared, to block the street ahead,
he had been expecting it. But he wasn't expecting the
voice that called out through the darkness. The familiar
voice shouting out his name.

Nikolas experienced a momentary surge of relief, followed by a wave of sickness. This wasn't rescue. This was
the end.

CHAPTER SIXTEEN
Sanctuary

THE NIGHT HOURS crept by in a cold and eerie calm. Once the business of eating and a little conversation was finished, there was little else to do but bed down, and try to get some sleep before dawn. Once again, the night would be broken down into watches. Natalia had begged Stefan to allow her to take her share, but Stefan was reluctant to let her repeat her mistake – whatever that had been. In the end, he compromised. Natalia and Maier would share the first watch, so each would be the guardian of the other's vigilance. Stefan would take the second shift, the dead watch from the still of night until the first rays of light began to streak the sky with grey. It was a wasteful use of resources, but he was happier with it that way. If anything went wrong, he would have only himself to blame.

He slept uneasily for two or three hours, the icy cold never really releasing him from its numbing grip. When

Maier finally roused him it was almost a relief. Even asleep, he had been nagged by a restlessness which hinted at trouble not far ahead. Awake, and with his sword clenched firmly in his hand, was the nearest he would get to feeling at ease that night.

Maier's face, ghostly pale in the sallow moonlight, hovered above him. Stefan stretched and rubbed the last remnants of poor sleep from his eyes.

'Anything to report?'

'Nothing. Not a whisper from our friend. Natalia's in poor humour. She thinks you don't trust her.'

Stefan shivered. His sleep had left him feeling no less exhausted. 'What did you tell her?'

'I told her it was true,' Maier reported. 'That you didn't trust her.'

'Many thanks for that,' Stefan clambered to his feet and thrust the blanket towards Maier. 'That will help enormously.'

Natalia was gazing out from the upper floor window. Stefan laid a hand lightly on her shoulder. 'You've earned some rest,' he told her, gently. 'Get some sleep.'

Natalia did not turn. 'Is this how it's going to be now? Do I need a guard before I'm allowed to watch over him?'

'You're not being guarded,' Stefan replied, evenly.

'It feels that way.'

'Then I'm sorry,' Stefan said. 'But we haven't got a satisfactory answer for how von Diehl was able to escape.'

Natalia flicked a glance in his direction. For a moment she looked as though she would offer an explanation, then thought better of it. 'No,' she admitted. 'We haven't. But it wasn't my fault.'

'And it wasn't mine, either,' Stefan pointed out. 'Look. Let's see how the night goes, then we'll think again.'

'I didn't touch that rotgut gin,' Natalia insisted. 'And I didn't let him out of my sight. Not for more than an instant.'

'Sometimes an instant is all it takes,' Stefan replied. Natalia glared, but her anger barely masked her exhaustion. Neither was in much mood for a fight.

'Where do I sleep?' she asked, wearily.

'Wherever you like,' Stefan replied. 'Keep to the upper floor. It'll be safer here.'

Natalia cleared a space in the furthest corner of the main room. She tossed her blanket down, and stretched out.

'You can be so wrong about people,' she said. She curled up, her back towards Stefan, signalling the end of the conversation.

'You can,' Stefan murmured. 'But we all have chances to redeem ourselves.'

He sat still for a few minutes until he was sure both the others were asleep. Then he moved to the window, careful to keep one eye upon von Diehl. If Natalia's experience had taught Stefan anything, it was that he couldn't afford to let the prisoner out of his sight for a moment. He positioned himself carefully in the ragged gap in the sidewall, and leant out, cautiously.

The night was still and quiet. The moon Mannslieb and its sickly twin, Morrslieb, shone out against the black velvet sky, bathing the ghostly remnants of the settlement in a wash of silver light. Stefan scanned the horizon for any sign of movement. Nothing. Not a single fire, not the faintest flickering from a distant lamp. Other than the steady keening of the wind, the only sound was the distant roar of the river. To all intents and purposes they were alone in a vast and empty land. But as Stefan looked out into the night, he was not alone. All around him he seemed to see spirits – spirits of the living; spirits of the dead.

He thought of Bruno, the friend and comrade left behind in Altdorf, and he thought of Mikhal. In all of his travels, his brother had never seemed further away from Stefan than he did now. He gave thanks to Sigmar that Bruno would be there to protect him from whatever madness he had fallen into. To protect him, if necessary, from himself. There was no man Stefan trusted more than Bruno. Yet still he felt uneasy. He had to get home, and soon.

Not that their problems would end there. Without proper papers, getting back into the city might prove far harder than getting out, particularly with von Diehl in tow. Much would depend on the resourcefulness of his companions. Could he trust them both, beyond all doubt? Even now, he still couldn't be sure.

Inevitably, thoughts of Natalia led to her brother. Alexei was nearly four months dead, yet it felt like he had walked with Stefan every day of this long journey. Sometimes he visited Stefan in his dreams, sometimes in the quiet of waking solitude.

The last moments of Alexei Zucharov's life were scored indelibly upon Stefan's memory. Time and again, Stefan gazed upon Zucharov's horribly altered form and saw the terrible changes wrought by Chaos. His body remembered their last battle: the sheer exhaustion weighing down his limbs; the fear, yes, fear that had electrified him as their struggle reached its crisis. Never before had Stefan come so close to death. But, at the bitter end, it was not he who had died.

Again he saw the waters close above Zucharov's head. Each time a part of him expected his nemesis to rise again, but he never did. Each time he was left only with the voice in his head – the voice, not of the mutant warrior but of the man he once had been – sorrowful, reproachful. *Stefan*, the voice would whisper to him, *you have killed me.* That was how it had to end. Only one of them could ever have walked away from the madness of Sigmarsgeist. Yet there was a part of Stefan that would always hear the doubts in his mind. *You could have done more,* they told him. *You should have done more to save your friend.*

Something stirred in the darkness behind him. Stefan spun around, guiltily aware that he had allowed his concentration to wander. Von Diehl hadn't moved so much as an inch, but his eyes were wide open. He was staring directly at Stefan.

Stefan shivered, shrugging off the unsettling thought that the other man had been reading his thoughts like the pages of an open book.

'What do you want?' he demanded. 'Dawn's a long way off.'

'A long way,' von Diehl agreed. His whispered tones suggested some kind of complicity between the two men that Stefan wanted no part of. Nonetheless, he lowered his voice to reply. 'What do you want?' he repeated.

Von Diehl propped himself up on one wiry arm. 'Nothing,' he answered. 'I'm awake, you're awake, that's all. I thought that we might talk.'

'We have nothing to talk about,' Stefan replied, curtly. He started to turn back towards the window, but realised it would be foolhardy in the extreme to shift his attention from the cultist while he was awake. Reluctantly, he allowed himself to meet the other man's gaze. He saw von Diehl smile, and felt the bitter stab of a small defeat pass through him. Stefan folded his arms across his chest, ready to see out the rest of the night in silence if that was what it took.

'You hate me, don't you?' von Diehl said. There was no suggestion of hurt or malice in his tone, only a mild, cultured curiosity. Stefan knew he should ignore the bait, but the words were out of his mouth before he knew it.

'Of course I hate you,' he said. 'I hate all evil, everything that you stand for. Hate it with all my heart.'

He expected some response from von Diehl, some flaring of anger. The cultist might even be roused into attacking him. Perhaps a part of Stefan wanted that. To restore their relationship to its natural term. Good and evil: polar opposites, locked in battle. That was a relationship he could understand. Instead, there was nothing. Von Diehl regarded Stefan benignly, weighing his words as though they were two scholars locked in debate.

'Evil,' von Diehl murmured. 'Hatred. Strong words. But then you are a man of strong passions, Stefan Kumansky.' He smiled. 'I can admire that.'

'I don't want your admiration.' Stefan told him. 'And I don't seek your approval. You are my enemy, nothing more.'

Von Diehl rose to his knees. He held out his hands, as if to prove that the ropes around his wrists were still secure, then shuffled a few steps towards Stefan. Stefan's instinct was to back away, but he held his ground. He tightened his hold around his sword, ready to strike if necessary.

'I am evil,' von Diehl whispered. 'I don't deny that. I serve a master known to you as the lord of evil incarnate. But tell me this,' he glanced up at Stefan. 'How can you be so certain that yours is a better way? What is it about the destiny promised by your gods, that gives you the will to fight?'

'I'm not interested in this,' Stefan told him. He was used to meeting evil in all its guises, meeting it with his courage and his sword. But this, this probing, articulate evil, was something else. He was waiting for von Diehl to hand him some excuse to lash out. It wasn't happening.

'What is it?' von Diehl persisted. 'Truly, I want to learn. To try and understand. Poverty? Disease and suffering? Is this what you are fighting for?'

Stefan forced a laugh of bitter derision. 'I suppose your Dark Masters would offer us something better?'

'Not better, necessarily,' von Diehl countered, mildly. 'But different. A world in which change is always possible. A world in which no orthodoxy could not be challenged.'

Against his will, Stefan found himself being drawn into the dialogue. It should be simple, right against wrong. Yet he knew he was not winning the argument. 'You can dress a snake in fine livery,' he answered at last. 'But it still remains a serpent.'

Why was he even allowing von Diehl to engage with him like this? What was the cultist trying to get from him?

'If you're trying to win me to your cause, you're wasting your time,' he said. 'I will stand against you and your kind until the last breath leaves my body.'

'Of course you will,' von Diehl agreed. 'We would not have it otherwise. For we need you as much as you need us.'

A slow chill crept up through Stefan's body; deeper and colder than anything the night could offer. 'What do you mean?' he asked. He was suddenly, horribly drawn to the answer about to come.

Von Diehl had his absolute attention now, and he knew it. The cultist nodded, almost imperceptibly, acknowledging a subtle shift. 'Your whole life has been given over to your fight against evil. Your whole existence is grounded upon that struggle. Without us, you would have no further reason to exist. What would you be? You would be nothing.'

The denial caught in Stefan's throat.

'We understand that,' von Diehl continued. 'We admire it. Truly, we do. Conviction, strength, absolute determination. These are universal qualities. These are the gifts that the gods bestowed on man, before mediocrity and weakness rotted his ambition.'

'The day you and your kind are swept from the world will be the greatest day of my life,' Stefan retorted. But a flickering of doubt, poisonous and insistent, had wormed its way inside his mind. He waited for the cultist's response.

'You know that day will never come,' von Diehl answered. 'And in your heart you pray that it won't. Because that would be the day that your life lost all purpose, all meaning.'

Stefan shook his head, emphatically. But he could feel the solid ground begin to crumble beneath him as the foundations of his faith turned to sand. Could it really be possible that each quest, each battle he fought was really only to satisfy a need inside him, part of a constant struggle to fill some aching void? He tried to imagine a world without Chaos, a world in which he had put down his sword, and turned his labours to peaceful deeds. He found he could not. The page in that future life stayed blank, devoid of colour or meaning.

Then, at last, an image came to him. But not the image he was expecting. It was the face of Alexei Zucharov, or rather the hideous, tattooed face of the mutant that he had finally become. The images etched upon Zucharov's skin danced as a leering, triumphant grin spread across his face. Zucharov laughed at him.

You can never defeat us, Zucharov taunted him. *Because then you would have defeated yourself.*

Stefan stood up and brushed the ghastly visage from his mind. 'As long as the world is haunted by you and your kind, there will be need for men like me,' he said, defiantly.

Von Diehl nodded, apparently pleased to have teased this response from his captor. 'Exactly,' he said softly. 'Exactly.'

Stefan was spared the need to respond by a sound that came from outside, beyond the watchtower. He sprang to the window, sword drawn. The moons had retreated behind the covering of cloud, and he could see nothing. But something was out there, of that he was absolutely certain. Stefan's instincts took control, all doubts and thoughts of his conversation with the cultist instantly banished.

What he had heard was a footfall. A man or beast was creeping closer to the outer wall. That it – or they – had been trying to keep their presence quiet suggested that their intent was neither accidental nor innocent. In an instant, Stefan had absorbed the implications of the situation. In his mind, their sanctuary was now a fortress under siege. He glanced back inside the room, ready to wake Natalia and Maier.

Heinrich von Diehl met his gaze, his eyes bright with anticipation.

'They're here,' von Diehl said to him.

'Who's here?' Stefan snapped back. 'Your friends?' He felt a strange, paradoxical easing of the tension inside of him. The thought that it might be some kind of trap was strangely reassuring. Von Diehl's response was a slow, but definite shake of his head.

'Not my friends,' he said. 'Our enemies.'

Stefan was distracted by more sounds from outside. Now he was sure that there was more than one of them. Whatever they were. He turned, and levelled the point of his sword against von Diehl's throat.

'If you know who or what's out there, you'd better tell me now.'

The cultist spread his hands as wide as the ropes would allow. 'I have no more idea than you,' he said. 'But my surmise is they mean us no good.'

Stefan said nothing, but acknowledged that he would surmise much the same. He called out softly to Maier and Natalia, asleep at opposite ends of the room. 'Wake up,' he hissed. 'We have company.'

Maier woke instantaneously, as though his sleeping body had been anticipating the call. Natalia was slower to rouse, but when she did she sat bolt upright, her face taut and pinched. 'What is it?' she demanded. 'What's happening?'

'Keep your voices down,' Stefan urged. He pointed to the window. 'Something's moving about outside. More than one of them, I think. It sounds like they're checking the building.'

'Before moving inside,' Maier said.

'Perhaps they won't get that far,' Natalia suggested, nervously. 'Perhaps they'll decide there's nothing of interest in here, and move on.'

'I doubt it,' Stefan muttered, grimly. 'I think they've got the scent of us. I think they're waiting until they have the place surrounded. Then they'll make their move.'

'Then there's no chance of us getting out first,' Maier said. 'How many do you think there are?'

'I don't know,' Stefan said. 'If we're lucky, no more than three or four.'

'Bandits? Beastmen? What are we dealing with?'

Stefan inched his way forward, and leaned as far out of the window gap as he dared without giving his presence away. It was still pitch dark, and impossible to make out anything moving in the blackness below. But he could hear sounds of feet shuffling amongst the debris scattered around the outside of the building. Whoever was out there was slowly but steadily positioning themselves around the outside of the building, effectively sealing off any avenues of escape.

'Can they get in?' Natalia whispered.

'Not easily,' Stefan told her. 'We've barricaded the only door below. It'll take them a while to get through that. But it won't hold them indefinitely.'

A light flared below as a torch was sparked into life. The single brand flared brightly in the darkness, throwing a swathe of light across the courtyard on either side of the window. Stefan caught a fleeting glance of five or six figures, human in part, but with all the outer appearance of wild animals. They were grotesque, hybrid creatures culled from nightmares, with gnarled horns that protruded through cracked metal helmets; limbs that ended in ugly, cloven stumps decked with claws and razor-sharp fangs, and bodies covered with a patchwork of leathery hide and dry fur like the coat of pigs. If they had once been men, then they were men no longer, but some hideous fusion of man and beast.

Stefan pulled back from the window and turned to others. 'Bad news,' he said. 'Firstly, they're mutants – some kind of beastmen, perhaps. Secondly, there's at least half a dozen of them out there.'

'Half a dozen? We can deal with that,' Maier said, brightly.

'Half a dozen that I can see,' Stefan reminded him. 'If there are others lurking around the back, then it's probably more like ten.'

Maier's face fell. Natalia drew back into her corner. 'Beastmen?' she whispered, hoarsely. 'Is that bad?'

'Yes,' Stefan told her. 'It's bad.' He looked to von Diehl. The cultist had been content to watch the situation develop with a look of cool, detached interest.

'Not your friends, eh?' Stefan said, caustically. 'Well, they look like they've got the mark of mutation on them to me.'

Von Diehl simply shrugged. 'Not all the creatures of the Dark Gods are allies. I told you before,' he said. 'Outside are our enemies. They'll tear the hide from my body as gladly as they'll feast on the meat from yours.'

'He's probably right,' Maier added. 'I doubt they'll care much who they find once they're inside.'

'Is that supposed to be some kind of consolation?' Stefan asked, tersely.

'No,' Maier replied, defensively. 'I just thought–'

'Get round the other side of the building,' Stefan said. 'See how many you can see.' Maier was gone only a few moments. When he returned, his expression told the story.

'Another three, for sure. Maybe four or five in all.'

'Then we've got at least ten altogether,' Stefan reckoned.

'If we knew what they wanted,' Natalia said, keeping her voice low. 'Maybe we could bargain with them.'

Her suggestion amused von Diehl. 'The only thing we have of interest to them is the blood in our veins and the marrow in our bones,' he told her. 'They'll take that whether we barter it or not.'

Stefan knew that he was probably right. Light flared outside, and flooded the upper floor room with bright amber. Stefan looked out. The beastmen were ranged in a circle around the outer walls, a ring of fire drawn around the building by their flaming torches. The mutant creatures were in open view now, rearing up in all their ugly, awesome might. Every one of them was armed.

'I think they know we're here,' Maier said, glumly.

'Thank Sigmar this place was built from stone, not wood,' Stefan said. 'Or else they'd be burning us alive by now.'

Von Diehl chuckled. 'Didn't you know?' he said. 'Beastmen prefer their meat raw.'

'Ten against three,' Stefan muttered. He'd seen enough of the strength and sheer animal ferocity of their mutant enemies to know that their situation was desperate. Von Diehl regarded him, placidly. He lifted his arms, displaying the rope binding his wrists together.

'Ten against four would be better odds.'

'I haven't taken all leave of my senses,' Stefan said. 'We've got enough problems waiting for us out there without adding to them.'

'I'm serious,' von Diehl insisted. 'I could make the difference.'

'I'm serious, too.' He glanced in Maier's direction. 'We'll hold the lower floor. Natalia, you stay up here with him. So long as he's tied secure, he won't give you any trouble.' He nodded, encouragingly. 'We'll be all right.'

Maier followed him down the steps. 'I hope you're right,' he muttered.

'They've got to get in first,' Stefan said. 'That has to give us a chance.'

Something struck the side of the watchtower. A heavy thud, like the sound of a battering rod was rammed hard against the outer wall. There was a brief pause, then a second and third impact, each in a slightly different position.

'They're testing the strength of the walls,' Maier said. 'Looking for the weakest point.'

Stefan cast his gaze around the rooms on the lower floor. The only door in had been heavily barricaded with everything they could lay hands upon. The beastmen would get through eventually, but it would take them a while. That left the three small windows as the weakest points of defence. The shutters had been fastened, but the wood was too rotten to offer much resistance. If the attackers were going to break through anywhere, it would surely be there.

Maier had been rummaging amongst the piles of refuse scattered across the floor. He tugged at something buried deep in the debris, and pulled it clear with a cry of triumph.

'Sigmar's smiling on us, Stefan!'

Maier was holding a bow. The angled frame was bent slightly out of true but it was undoubtedly still service-able. He sieved through the debris again, and emerged moments later with a long leather pouch. The leather was dank and mould-encrusted, but the half dozen or so arrows tucked inside looked good.

'Looks like someone put up a fight before laying down their lives.' The two men shared a moment of satisfaction. The odds had shifted, just a little. Maier slotted an arrow and slowly pulled the drawstring taught, testing its strength. Next moment, there was a thunderous crack, and one of the lower windows blew apart, show-ering the room with splinters of wood.

In the half-second it took Stefan to turn around, the beastman was halfway through the breach in the wall. He had a fleeting glance of a tapered, goat-like head, forcing its way into the room. Its thin, black lips flared in a savage snarl of lust and rage.

Maier didn't hesitate. He dropped onto one knee to take aim, and let the arrow fly. The shaft shot straight and true, lodging deep in the base of the mutant's neck. The creature's eyes bulged wide, and a plume of ochre gore spewed from between its jaws. It staggered forward then slumped across the window, blocking the space with its body.

A second window burst open, the wooden shuttering shattered by a series of rapid blows from outside. Before

Maier could reload, a lithe, long-limbed creature had squeezed its sinuous body through the gaping hole and into the house. It dropped onto the floor and sprang back up in one muscular bound. Its yellow-gold eyes flicked around the room, and picked out the two human figures. It licked its lips, and sprang at Maier. Stefan caught the creature in mid-air, his sword scything through the dark-furred body. The beastman emitted a howl of rage and pain, and twisted maniacally to try and shake itself free. But its frenzied contortions only impaled it deeper upon the blade. Stefan took hold of the sword two-handed, and smashed the creature's body hard against the far wall. The beastman crumpled into a heap, its body twitching. A foul stench of entrails filled the room.

'That will give them something to think about,' Maier yelled.

'They don't do much thinking,' Stefan replied.

Seconds passed in silence. Then a strange scrabbling, scratching sound came from outside. Stefan swore. 'Ulric's blood. They're climbing the side wall. They're trying to reach the upper floor. Stay here,' he told Maier. 'I've got to get back to Natalia.'

He rushed up the steps just in time to see Natalia at the window, the knife clenched in her hand.

Stefan shouted. 'Get back from there!'

Natalia looked around in alarm. As she pulled back, a horned beastman vaulted through the unguarded window. His clawed limbs raked at Natalia. Natalia struck out, and the knife caught the beastman a glancing blow across one arm. But Natalia was off-balance; she stumbled, losing her footing on the uneven floor. Von Diehl scrambled onto his feet and scuttled towards the safety of the far corner. The beastman spared the cultist the briefest of glances, and grunted with satisfaction. It towered over Natalia, savouring an easy kill.

Stefan picked a heavy chunk of broken stone from the floor and hurled it. The rock bounced harmlessly off the creature's thick-furred hide, but at least Stefan had its attention. The beastman snarled, bared its fangs then swung across the room towards Stefan. Stefan put up his sword, and the beastman met the blade with his own. Man and mutant traded blows. The beastman looked lumbering and heavy with its oversized, horned head and ugly, angular body. But it was surprisingly agile, and able to handle sword better than most men.

Stefan fell back towards the stairwell. The beastman closed on him, near enough for Stefan to smell its rancid breath. The creature lashed at Stefan with its sword, unable to find the killing blow. Finally, in frustration, the creature pulled back, and lifted its weapon up high to aim a crushing stroke at Stefan's head.

For a moment it was vulnerable, and Stefan took full advantage. He drove his sword hard into the creature's body, burying the blade up to the hilt in its thick, leathery flesh. The beastman tottered back, but did not fall. Stefan prised his sword free, ready to strike again, but Natalia was there first. She hurled herself at the mutant creature and stabbed at it repeatedly with the short-bladed knife. The beastman tried to fend her off, but it was wounded and weakened.

Natalia drove home the knife one more time. The creature fell, steadying itself on one leg as it went down. Stefan swung his blade hard and fast, in a full arc, and cut the creature's head from its body.

An eerie silence fell across the room. Stefan and Natalia sat apart from one another. Dark liquid oozed from the carcass of the mutant between them. Von Diehl edged closer to the dead beastman, and turned it over with the toe of his boot. He stood, looking down upon the dead beastman with an almost academic interest.

'A creature of Khorne,' he murmured, and smiled. 'A fitting end for a servant of the Blood God.'

Natalia raised her head. 'Listen.' There was nothing now, only silence.

'Maybe we've got the better of them.'

'Maybe,' Stefan agreed. His body ached, and there was a nagging pain in one wrist where the beastman's sword had found its mark. He dearly wanted to believe it was over. Then he heard Maier's voice, calling out to him from below.

'Stefan!' There was no mistaking the note of alarm. Stefan got to his feet, and hurriedly wiped the crust of filth from the blade of his sword as he ran down the steps. Maier had managed to barricade the windows once more, but the look on his face told Stefan that things were anything but under control.

'What is it?' Stefan demanded. 'What's happening?'

By way of answer, Maier pointed down towards the floor with his sword. The room was filled with a rumbling sound that seemed to come from below the earth itself. As Stefan looked on, something punched through the wooden floor directly in front of him, sending a shower of debris across the room. A hole opened up, then a second, and a third.

Stefan exchanged glances with Maier, but no words were necessary. In their haste to secure the interior of the abandoned building, they'd neglected to check whether the tower could be breached through the cellar below.

The attack from above ground had been just a diversion. Now the beastmen had them trapped.

CHAPTER SEVENTEEN
Fugitive

BRUNO WAS ABOUT to give up when the door he had been hammering upon so urgently was opened, the merest crack. A stumpy figure of a man appeared in the gap, his heavily creased face lit by the waxy glow of an oil lantern. The man lifted the lantern and peered out into the alley. He saw Bruno and frowned.

'What d'you want?' he demanded. 'Knocking loud enough to raise the dead, and at this hour, too. Ain't we got a right to sleep?'

Bruno started to push his way inside, but the stocky fellow on the other side of the door held firm, his strength belying his lack of stature.

'Please, let me in,' Bruno urged. 'I need to see Franz. Franz Sterkel.'

The man behind the door shot him a look of practiced bemusement. 'No one of that name here. Never heard of him.' He went to slam the door shut, but Bruno had his foot wedged in the gap now, and he wasn't about to give up. 'Give him a message,' Bruno insisted. 'Tell him Bruno Hausmann is here to call in a favour. Tell him I'm ready for that drink.'

The doorkeeper looked Bruno up and down. He took in his bedraggled appearance and the dried blood spattered across the front of his shirt.

'Got ourselves in a bit of trouble, have we?'

'Please. Just give Franz the message.'

The man mumbled a curse. 'Not a moment's peace.' Before Bruno could stop him, he'd kicked the obstructing foot out from the doorway and slammed the heavy panel. Precious minutes passed. Bruno looked about in desperation, convinced that at any moment his pursuers would appear at the top of the street. He had his fist raised to pound on the door one final time, when without warning, it was reopened wide enough to allow him through.

'You're in luck,' the man informed him, sullenly. 'Happens there is someone of that name in tonight. Keep your voice down, though. No need to tell the whole world why you're here.'

A wave of relief flooded over Bruno as he followed the little man into the house, and the door was closed and bolted behind them. For the first time since leaving Nikolas, he felt relatively safe. Franz Sterkel wasn't the first man he would normally turn to. But, in a strange kind of way, he was one of the few people that Bruno could trust right now. Sterkel might be a criminal, a thief and even a cheat, but he wasn't in with the zealots, or with Chaos for that matter. Bruno had turned a half-blind eye to some of Sterkel's deeds in the past. Now he was hoping for something in return.

He followed the little man through a twisting maze of narrow corridors, into the belly of the house. Despite the doorkeeper's indignant insistence that the household was asleep, it soon became apparent that more than a few of those under the roof tonight were very much awake. Through cracks in doorways, Bruno glimpsed groups of men playing cards, drinking, or talking in close, conspiratorial huddles. Sterkel himself was in a room near the very top of the house. Bruno's escort approached the door, coughed loudly, and knocked, twice.

'Come,' Sterkel's voice called. The doorkeeper nodded in Bruno's direction then turned, his job done. Bruno pushed the door and stepped inside. There wasn't much in the room, but his old acquaintance clearly had all he needed to keep him comfortable. Bruno took in the half-empty bottle of brandtwein on the table by the large, unkempt bed. Sprawled across the bed was a young woman wearing a man's shirt and little else. The girl's straw-blonde hair fell in a mess of curls around her face. Bruno was very much aware that he had interrupted something. The young woman smiled at him, and folded her long legs demurely.

Sterkel was seated upon the edge of the bed, buttoning his breeches without any apparent modesty. He glanced up at Bruno and gave him a brief, frosty stare. 'This better be good, mate,' he said.

Bruno took a step further inside, suddenly feeling terribly self-conscious. There was one chair in the room; he wondered if he ought to sit upon it. Sterkel saw him hesitate, and jerked a thumb in the direction of the door. 'Later,' he said to the girl. 'Bring that sister of yours with you too.'

Bruno waited while the girl skipped from the room, then went and stood with his hands resting on the back of the chair. Sterkel eyed him up and down, seemingly enjoying his discomfort. Then he laughed, and the icy glare dissolved. 'Don't worry. There's plenty more where that came from. But this is a funny time to turn up for a drink.'

'I don't want a drink,' Bruno began. 'Or rather, that's not why I'm here.'

Franz Sterkel raised an eyebrow, as if to say, well then?

Bruno sat down, and ran his hands through his hair. 'I need somewhere to hide,' he said. 'Someone's trying to kill me.' He looked up at Sterkel. 'Actually, someone's been trying to kill me for quite a while. But now they're getting serious.'

Sterkel nodded, half-interested. 'And who would that be?' he enquired. 'Who would be so keen on having you dead, I mean?'

'I don't know,' Bruno said. 'But I do know that I'm fast running out of people I can trust.'

'Except your old mate Franz, eh?'

Bruno was desperately tired. He felt he could sleep for a very long time. He swallowed hard, digesting his credulity and his pride in one deep gulp. 'Exactly,' he said. 'Exactly.'

THE BEASTMEN POURED from the gaping hole in the floor of the building, threatening to overwhelm the defenders in moments. Maier took one down with a swift arrow, but there were plenty more coming. Stefan struck down another as it emerged from the ground, his blade cleaving deep into the thickly muscled flesh around the beastman's neck. The creature died with a horrible, screaming sound, but two more beastmen had already risen to take its place.

It was only a matter of time before Stefan and Maier were forced to retreat. Seven beastmen were now inside the watchtower. In what seemed like no time at all, the lower floor had been surrendered. In a few, disastrous

moments the odds of survival had been whittled away
to near zero. Stefan and Maier retreated, fending off the
onslaught with their blades, falling back towards the
upper level.

The cultist watched the unfolding disaster with the
same unblinking expression of serenity on his face. If he
had any fear of death, he did not show it. He held his
tethered hands up to Stefan, a further reminder of his
captivity.

'You need me,' he told Stefan calmly. 'Without my
help, we shall all die.'

A beastman rushed the stairs, trying to gain a foothold
on the upper ground. Stefan held him off, forcing the
creature back. He thrust and parried until the mutant
staggered and tumbled backwards into the others following in its wake.

'Stefan.' There was an urgency in Maier's voice now.
'He may be right. What have we got to lose? If we're
going to perish anyway, what's to be risked in freeing
von Diehl?'

Natalia looked to Stefan, her face drained of colour.
'In the name of Shallya, Stefan,' she pleaded. 'We need
all the help we can get.'

Von Diehl watched with the eyes of a hawk. He
seemed not to care whether Stefan freed him or not, but
he was coldly fascinated by the dilemma which he saw
so clearly written in Stefan's mind. To free evil to fight
evil – what sort of choice was that?

Another pair of beastmen rushed the steps. Maier fired
his bow wildly, and missed. The two creatures reached the
upper level, with four more on their heels. A battle to the
death was about to take place in the twilit gloom of the
ruined building. Stefan took one last look at his prisoner.

'Cut his ropes,' he barked at Maier. 'Give him a knife
to fight with.'

Then pandemonium broke loose. Stefan felt the cold metal kiss of a blade against his skin. He ducked down and brought up his guard. He was fighting for his life. Natalia, Maier and von Diehl all disappeared from sight. Each was on their own now, locked in a struggle to the death with an old and implacable enemy.

Natalia had asked the gods for courage, but at the moment of crisis she found only blind terror. She ran from the room, fleeing down the narrow corridor to try and find any crevice, any corner that might offer shelter from the murderous creatures. Her rational mind told her that there could be no hiding place, but that did not stop the fear from spearing through her and pushing her on. All her guile and craft was forgotten. There was, in any case, no art of magic that could work its spell upon the crude, bestial minds of the beastmen. They were beyond her reach.

In her heart Natalia wanted to fight, but she could not. She was paralysed by fear. She ran, and, when there was nowhere else to run, she cowered in the shadows like a terrified child. It was no refuge, she knew that. She had to fight, fight or die, but once she had crouched down, half-hidden in the gloom, her limbs locked, and turned to ice. She could not move.

From her hiding place, Natalia listened the sounds of violent struggle. She tried to imagine Stefan and Maier forcing the beastmen back, courage and skill overcoming vastly superior odds. But the image would not hold. All she could imagine were more and more of the half-human monsters pouring into the house, bent upon their destruction. There was nothing she could do but wait to die.

When the looming outline of a beastman filled the doorway ahead of her, it was almost a relief. The room was dark, filled with a deep, impenetrable blackness, yet

Natalia sensed at once that the beastman knew she was there. It had smelled her fear, her self-loathing. It was coming for her, coming to deliver her from her cowardice. She huddled deeper into the corner and screwed her eyes shut. Her last thoughts were of Alexei. This was not the parting tribute to her brother she had planned. In her dreams her death had been lit by glory, her soul vanquished only at a heavy cost to their enemies. The light of life would have had one last, glorious flourishing before it was snuffed out forever. Now, she would soon be joining Alexei among the immortals. But it was not meant to have been like this.

Shame and her still flickering will to live forced her to open her eyes. The knife in her grip felt like clay, cold and useless in her hand. She looked up, and saw that where there had been one beastman, there were now two. So now it was certain. There would be no escape, no rescue. Perhaps even Stefan himself was dead. Now it was her turn.

A cold, passionless detachment came over her. She saw the first beastman step aside and stare at the second creature for a moment. Even through her fear, Natalia sensed something was out of place. Somehow, things were not as they seemed. The first beastman turned its attention back towards her. It closed on her with a slow lumbering gait. The second creature was a few paces behind, clutching a knife. The blade was surely meant for her, but as Natalia looked on, she saw the mutant creature slide the blade into the flank of its comrade, twisting it home until gouts of dark blood spurted from the wound.

For a moment there was utter confusion. Natalia saw the wounded mutant stagger and topple towards her. Instinctively, she shielded her eyes and flinched away as the creature pounded down to the ground.

Natalia crouched, motionless, waiting for the blow intended for her, but it never came. When at last she lifted her head and looked up again, she saw only the slim outline of a man, a bloodied blade now in his hand. Heinrich von Diehl watched the fear written on Natalia's face turn to a look of dazed confusion. He addressed her in a tone of mannered concern.

'Are you all right?'

Natalia looked around, bewildered. The second beast-man had simply vanished. 'What happened?'

'Nothing happened,' von Diehl said, quietly. 'It will remain our secret.'

'What do you mean – our secret?'

Von Diehl put a finger to his lips. 'You won't say a word about what you saw. Nor will I, about what I saw.'

Natalia's head was spinning. 'What you saw?' she asked, weakly.

The cultist lowered his head until they were all but cheek-to-cheek. 'No one need know that your courage deserted you,' he whispered. 'Why need others learn of your dishonour?'

Natalia started to protest, but there was to be no time. Another beastman thundered into the room. It saw von Diehl and Natalia and roared with rage. This one was wounded, but no less dangerous for that. Natalia scrambled to her feet, sudden energy flowing where moments before there had only been icy fear. The paralysis had vanished, and now she was determined to make amends. She hurled herself at the beastman with a reckless fury, but the beastman had its attention fixed on von Diehl. Von Diehl circled around the beast, baiting it with the knife.

The beastman followed the blood-smeared weapon with its eyes as though entranced. Every few seconds it grabbed at the knife with its thick, cloven hand. Each time von Diehl flicked the blade away, out of the beast-man's reach. It was a game, a taunting, teasing game that he was playing with the Blood God's creature. The beast-man snarled, baring its fangs in a show of anger, but it couldn't manage to snatch the weapon from the cultist.

Natalia had the sense of being slowly lulled into a trance. Gradually the beastman's strength and rage were being sapped. Von Diehl was moving more slowly, his opponent growing increasingly soporific, until the ill-matched pair reached a point of absolute stillness. Natalia looked on, transfixed. She understood the arcane methodology of the magic being used, but the potency of the unfolding spell was well beyond her reach.

The beastman stood stock-still, a grotesque statue star-ing at von Diehl through passive, feral eyes. The wound to its face wept a steady flow of blood, but the creature seemed barely to notice. The cultist stared, approvingly, into the creature's unblinking eyes. He nodded, once, and then plunged the knife into the flesh at the base of the beastman's throat. He drove it home with such vio-lence that it lifted the heavy beast off its feet. The beastman crashed to the ground. For a few moments it lay, limbs thrashing uselessly on the blood-soaked floor. Then all was still.

Von Diehl wiped the blade of the knife carefully on his sleeve, and slipped it back into his pocket. He took Natalia by the arm, and started to lead her away.

'Come along,' he whispered to her. 'Our friends still need our help.'

'DID YOU SLEEP well?'

Bruno took the offered plate and beaker of ale, and sat down to eat. Not unusually, he was ravenous. More sur-prisingly, perhaps, he had slept well. Better than he'd slept for a good few nights now. He chewed on a hunk of bread, and took a good mouthful of the beer.

'I did, many thanks,' he reported, between mouthfuls. So engrossed was Bruno in eating that he failed to notice for a good few moments that everyone in the room – Sterkel himself and half a dozen or so of his men – was staring at him with the sort of intensity that indicated something was up. When at last the realisation dawned, Bruno set down his mug and pushed the food to one side.

'What's up?' he asked. Sterkel raised an eyebrow in mock surprise. 'Thought you were in a bit of a hurry last night.'

'I was, and I explained why,' Bruno replied. 'Someone was… is trying to kill me.'

A couple of men at the back of the room started to chuckle. Sterkel silenced them with a glare. 'Trying to kill *you*, is it?'

Now Bruno knew something was wrong. 'What is it?' he demanded of Sterkel. 'Tell me, man. What's happened?'

Sterkel reached into his pocket and pulled out a crumpled sheet of paper, a notice or poster of some kind. 'One of my lads saw them putting these up around town at dawn this morning,' he explained. 'They don't hang about, the watch. I'll grant 'em that.'

Bruno shook his head, nonplussed. 'Sorry,' he said. 'I've no idea what you're talking about.'

Sterkel lifted the paper higher so that it unfurled along its length. Bruno took a good look at it. And then he understood. The shock of realisation was cathartic. All at once Bruno saw the truth that, at the back of his mind, he had been stumbling towards for the last few days. Now, at last he made the link. The link that joined his visit to the offices of the watch, with the voice of the preacher, the day that he had followed Mikhal to the gathering in the warehouse. The link between them was one single man.

MARCUS ALBRECHT WEPT without shame. When the summons had first come, he had feared the worst. Now, standing in the windowless room beneath the guardhouse of the east watch, the tears spilled freely down his cheeks, falling upon the mutilated corpse of the man laid out before him. The body was all that remained of a dear friend whose name he would never now have reason to speak again. Only when his tears were spent did he allow the sergeant to replace the shroud across the body. In that final act, Nikolas was gone, and another cornerstone of the Keepers of the Flame had crumbled away forever.

Gustav Ehrhart dismissed his sergeant from the room, and led Albrecht to a chair where he could rest with his grief for a few moments. He laid a steadying hand on the other man's shoulder, but Albrecht would not be consoled.

'Of all the lives stolen from us these last terrible days, this is the worst.' He took a handkerchief from his breast pocket and pressed it against his eyes. 'The worst by far.' He lifted his reddened gaze towards the watch commander.

'Where did you find him?'

'Klagen Strasse. My men were on their way to stand guard. I regret they were too late.'

'But, Bruno Hausmann–' Albrecht's voice trailed off into incredulous silence. 'Are you *sure*?'

Ehrhart came and sat by his side. 'We can't be positive,' he said. 'But the facts tell a compelling tale. Nikolas was sheltering this man, Hausmann. That much we do know, yes?'

Albrecht nodded, miserably.

'When my men got to the house, they found Nikolas dead and Hausmann vanished without trace. There is no evidence to suggest anyone else was involved. And now Hausmann has gone into hiding. If he were innocent, why should he do that?' He paused whilst Albrecht absorbed the words.

'Do you think he's involved in the other deaths as well?'

'We must consider the possibility.'

'But why?' Albrecht demanded. 'And on his own? It hardly seems credible.'

'He may not be acting alone,' Ehrhart pointed out. 'He may have had help.'

Albrecht frowned. 'You're talking about the zealots?'

Ehrhart shrugged. 'Who knows? But it was you, Marcus, who first alerted me to them.' The commander coughed, and cleared his throat self-consciously. 'There is – another aspect,' he said. 'An aspect, I fear of even greater gravity.'

Albrecht's face was a crumpled mask of pain. He didn't look as though he could take any worse news.

'Hausmann is a close associate of Stefan Kumansky,' Ehrhart went on. 'In fact, you will not find any closer comrades.' Albrecht sank his head in his hands. 'The fact is,' Ehrhart continued, 'If Bruno Hausmann *is* guilty of this terrible deed, then we have to consider the possibility that Kumansky is implicated as well. Worse, we have to consider that Kumansky may have been plotting against us from the very start. After all, we know that his brother is involved with the True Path. And he, too, has disappeared.'

Marcus Albrecht slumped forward, and emitted a low moan of despair. 'Great Sigmar forgive me! I am the architect of all our ruin.'

'Don't judge yourself so harshly,' Ehrhart counselled. 'It was my urging that brought Stefan Kumansky to this business in the first place.' He squeezed the other man's hand. 'Courage, my friend. We're watching the zealots. Any move they make, I'll know about it. As for Bruno Hausmann – we'll smoke him out before too long. See here–' He opened the desk in front of him and produced a large sheet of parchment for Albrecht's inspection. Bruno's name and description were displayed in bold black letters on the sheet, together with those of another wanted man, Karl Hoche.

'My men are putting these up all across the city,' he told Albrecht. 'As you can see, Hausmann isn't the first good man to have fallen prey to the charms of evil. Nor will he be the last.' He rolled up the poster and replaced it in the drawer. 'Don't worry,' he said. 'We'll have our man before long. Just wait and see.'

Albrecht shook his head, despairingly. 'All this mayhem, all this death. And so close to the ceremony of Blessing of the Souls.' He looked up, agitated and angry. 'By Sigmar, I vow Johann Esmer has brought this calamity upon us!'

'Don't be ridiculous,' Ehrhart countered. 'And don't so much as whisper such thoughts, not in my company.'

Albrecht sunk his head in his hands. 'Sorry,' he exclaimed. 'It's the grief speaking, Gustav. The grief and the sheer rage of it all.' He glanced up. 'But the Grand Theogonist has encouraged these zealot bands, that much at least is true.'

'You wouldn't expect me to comment on that,' Ehrhart replied, guardedly. 'To do as much would be heresy. It's true the Blessing of the Souls has given the zealots a purpose and a focus. That doesn't make Esmer accountable for them.'

'Nikolas would have said much the same thing,' Albrecht said, sadly. He broke off and gazed down at the ground, sunk in despair. 'Our plans are in total disarray,' he muttered. 'Perhaps I should after all send word to the Ten. It cannot be safe for the Keepers of the Flame to come to Altdorf.'

'No! Now above all we must hold firm,' Ehrhart insisted. 'If you were to abandon the plan now, you would be playing directly into our enemy's hands.'

Albrecht nodded, despondently. 'In any event, it would probably be too late to get a message through. But about Stefan?' he asked, glumly. 'What do we do about him?'

'We can do nothing, until he reaches Altdorf,' Ehrhart replied, crisply. 'And when he does, we'll be waiting. Then we'll know the truth of things, eh?'

Marcus Albrecht looked up, and forced a rueful smile from his cracked and broken face. 'Yes,' he replied. 'It seems that we will.'

STEFAN LAUNCHED HIS sword, two-handed. The keen steel ripped through the beastman's flesh, opening a jagged wound across its flank. The creature toppled and fell, and Stefan was granted another, brief respite. The place was filled with the stink of a charnel house. Between them, Stefan and Maier had slaughtered four of the creatures, but still it was not enough. Still the beastmen kept coming. He no longer knew if Natalia and von Diehl were alive or dead. If they were dead, then their mission was good as over. But Stefan knew he must fight on. If his life were to end here, then he would be sure that it would not be cheaply bought.

He wiped a hand across his face and looked across the room, trying to pick out Maier in the gloom. His comrade was locked in combat with a beastman almost twice his own size, a gargantuan creature with twisted shards of bone protruding from its skull, and eyes that burned like crimson coals. Maier landed two clean blows on the mutant with his blade, yet made no impact at all. Then, as he tried to make space to strike again, Maier slipped, momentarily losing his footing. The beastman lashed out, swatting him like a fly with its meaty fist. Maier was sent sprawling and the sword was knocked from his grip. He was at the monster's mercy. Stefan had to distract the murderous beast, and draw its wrath onto himself.

'Over here,' he shouted out. 'Come and pit your miserable strength against me. Or are you the kind of warrior that only fights a fallen foe?'

The beastman uttered a deep growl and swung around to face him. Each of its hands held a sword heavy enough to cut a man clean in two. The beastman lifted the swords as though they were matchwood. Stefan hefted his weapon and stood ready to fend off the attack. The beastman fixed him with its glittering eyes and charged, intent on finishing him in one attack. Stefan stood his ground, but it was like fighting two creatures at once. No sooner had he parried a blow from one of the creature's swords, than the second was bearing down on him. It was an incessant, exhausting assault.

Stefan used the advantage of his greater speed to try and get behind the guard of the slower, bulkier creature. But even when his blade found its mark, it was to little effect. He was being pushed back, surrendering ground, step by step. Maier hadn't moved. Maybe the blow had only stunned him, but if things continued like this then the end for all of them was surely in sight. Then, just as it seemed things could hardly get worse, they did. With fateful timing, a second beastman, uglier and larger than even the first, lumbered into the room, effectively cutting off any prospect of retreat. Stefan redoubled his efforts to fend off the attack from two fronts, but now they would have the better of him, and he knew it. The towering beastmen closed in on him, battering down his resistance with a steady, mechanical insistence. Soon all pretence at attack had gone. All Stefan could do was defend himself until his strength gave out. He drew his sword up across his face, and prayed to the gods for deliverance. But deliverance, when it came, was from another, quite unexpected quarter.

Von Diehl appeared from nowhere. Afterwards Stefan would swear that he literally materialised between the two creatures. The beastmen hadn't seen him, or at least, didn't see him soon enough to react. Stefan registered the look of surprise and alarm on the creature's face as it saw the shaft of steel too late. Von Diehl wielded the knife with the practiced skill of the assassin. The blade flashed through the air and lodged in the first beastman's gut. The creature howled and grabbed at the knife to wrench it free, but von Diehl held firm, pressing the blade home, twisting it savagely.

The second beastman had been slow to react, but now it turned its fury on the cultist. Von Diehl moved with improbable speed, but it was not fast enough. The beastman caught him by the neck and lifted him off the ground, meaning to dash his body to pulp against the hard flint wall. For a moment, all the beastman's attention was upon von Diehl, and Stefan was forgotten. Stefan seized that precious moment. He reached for one of the fallen swords and lifted it up to waist height. He swung the blade two-handed, putting all his weight behind the blow. The sword slewed into the beastman's trunk-like leg, cleaving muscle and flesh from the bone.

The creature crashed down, still clawing at von Diehl. Stefan stepped back to deliver the decisive blow, plunging the long blade deep into the beastman's back. Bones cracked beneath the force of the heavy blade, and a plume of blood sprayed up, covering Stefan in a foul gore. Stefan was oblivious. He hauled the sword out of the beastman's body and plunged it back down, striking again and again until he was sure the creature was dead.

Stefan sank to his knees, his strength utterly spent. He had given his all, but it was not going to be enough. As he looked up, yet another beastman appeared in the doorway. Stefan knew he could not fight this one as well. He looked for Maier, for von Diehl even, but both of them were down. They had nothing left to give.

The beastman turned its gnarled head from side to side, surveying the bloody slaughter. As it took a step into the room, it was struck from behind, an arrow thudding into the creature's back. The beastman's features clouded with a dull incomprehension. It reached behind its back and plucked out half of the shaft, tossing it aside as if it were nothing but a minor irritation. As the beastman turned around it was struck again; this time the shaft passed directly through its eye. For a moment the creature stood as still as a statue, then it toppled back. The floor of the building shuddered as its body hit the ground.

Stefan looked up to see Natalia standing in the doorway. Her bow was braced, ready to loose another arrow, but there was nothing left to attack. For a few moments she and Stefan stared at each other in silence. Then, slowly, Natalia slackened the drawstring and set the bow down. Her face was bruised and bloodied, but there was a fire in her eyes that had not been there before.

'All of them are dead,' she said, to no one in particular. 'We killed them. We killed them all.'

'We did,' Stefan concurred. 'You did.' He held her steady gaze for a moment.

'He would have been proud of you,' he said.

CHAPTER EIGHTEEN
Homebound

THEY QUIT THE watchtower at dawn the next day, as the first light of the sun crept above the blanket of covering mist. Stefan knew they would be vulnerable. Any raiders lying in wait in the surrounding hills would have been able to pick them off with ease. But the hours passed, and no attack came. They had been lucky; the beastmen had been hunting alone. And now they would lie, forgotten, in the ruins.

Hunger became their greatest enemy. The rations salvaged from the boat were almost exhausted, and by the end of that day the last wafers of meat were gone. From then on they would have to survive on whatever they could take from the land: berries and a bird or two when they were quick enough to catch them. Natalia charmed a fat fish from the river, and that kept them going for a day or two more. And at least they did not lack for water to drink. But Stefan was under no illusion. They would need to find provisions soon if there was to be any hope of reaching Altdorf.

What food they gathered was divided, equally, between all four. There was no sense in making a distinction between von Diehl and the others in that respect. But the ropes were back around the cultist's wrists. With the beastmen defeated, Stefan had seen to it that the roles of captor and captive were quickly restored, to the obvious disgust of the cultist.

Little was said about the night in the house. Natalia, in particular, seemed unwilling to talk in anything but the vaguest terms about her experience. As for Stefan, he knew the difference von Diehl had made had been critical. It was even possible that, without the cultist's intervention, they would not have survived. Recognition of that truth left him deeply uncomfortable. He didn't want to think too much about it, or about anything that compromised his view that good and evil were separate and distinct, two opposite and opposing forces. He put von Diehl and the beastmen to the back of his mind, and focused instead on the task in hand: staying alive, and getting home.

They tracked steadily south and east as day followed long day. The river and its tributaries receded, and hills covered in dense forest grew up where before had been only a flat expanse of swampland. Shortly after daybreak, on the third day after leaving the watchtower, they reached the top of a steep path that led between two rocky peaks. As they crested the hill and looked down, the slate roofs and bell towers of a small town were revealed in the shade of the valley below.

Stefan stood and looked in wonderment. To see a living town again after so long in the wilderness was a treasure almost beyond belief. Food, fresh water, horses, even a bed for the night if they wanted it, and no more than an hour's journey ahead of them.

'I recognise that place,' Natalia said, excitedly. 'Unless I'm mistaken, it's Balzen. We stopped there on the way through. Do you remember?'

Stefan did remember. He remembered a warming meal, hospitality, and a people prepared to trade fairly with strangers. 'We were welcome enough there last time,' he said.

There was no excitement in Maier's voice. 'There may be a different kind of welcome this time,' he said, soberly. 'Look closer. There, in the market square.'

Stefan looked. At first he saw nothing out of the ordinary, just the same nondescript clutch of houses and outbuildings, a chapel and a market square. But around the square there was movement, spilling out along the ribbons of streets and lanes that radiated out from the hub of the town. Viewed from a distance they might have been ants, tiny, insect-like creatures crawling over Balzen. But they were not ants; they were men. The rising sun bore down on the glittering, miniature figures. There were at least two score of them, men on horseback, all clad in silver-grey armour.

'Soldiers,' Natalia whispered.

'Friends of yours?' von Diehl enquired, caustically.

Stefan swore under his breath. 'What do you think?' he asked Maier. 'Maybe it's nothing to worry about?'

'Maybe,' Maier agreed, none too convinced. 'On the other hand, they could be looking for somebody.'

'Looking for us.'

'From Stahlfort?' Natalia asked, incredulous.

Stefan exchanged glances with Maier. Maier shrugged. 'I don't know,' Maier said at last. 'It's possible. Maybe they managed to get a message from the island to the garrison at Marienburg. They could be moving to cut us off from the west, while troops from the island follow our trail in from the north.'

'Or it could just be coincidence,' Stefan offered. 'A troop movement passing through and looking for provisions just like us.'

They sat on the hilltop in silence, watching the distant milling of the soldiers.

'We could keep going,' Natalia suggested after a while. 'Maybe there'll be another town, not much further on.'

Stefan shook his head. 'There's no other town. I doubt there's another settlement within three days' march of here, whichever direction we chose. Even if there was, I seriously doubt that we'd make it.'

'So what do we do?'

'We go in,' Maier answered her. 'Or, rather, I go in.'

'Not on your own,' Stefan said firmly. 'It could be suicide.'

'The more of us ride in there, the more likely that would be,' Maier insisted. 'Look, I can be in and out before they know I'm there. If they are looking for us, then one man on his own will be less likely to attract their attention.'

Stefan had to admit that was true. But it would still be a significant risk. Perhaps it should be him that went down the hillside, not Maier. That was what his heart was telling him, but his head took the opposite view. Above all else, his job was to get Heinrich von Diehl back to Altdorf. Besides which, he could be gone for hours. He wasn't going to let the cultist out of his sight for that long.

'Well?' Maier asked.

'All right,' Stefan said eventually. 'But don't take any unnecessary risks. May Sigmar go with you, Karl.'

Maier shrugged and smiled, nonchalantly. 'All part of the job, old friend.' He stood up, fastened his sword harness securely around his waist, and set off at a steady stroll down the hill. A man without a care in the world.

Stefan watched him until he was out of sight. 'Brave man,' he murmured.

'Braver than you?' von Diehl suggested.

Stefan held down the anger boiling up inside him; he was determined not to play into the cultist's hands again.

'No, truly,' von Diehl continued. 'I'm interested. How do you rank courage in your world? Does one heroic deed stand better than another, or is it the number of notches on your sword that counts most? There must be a way of weighing bravery. Surely it matters to you?'

'What matters is that I have a few hours free of your insidious prattle,' Stefan muttered. He glanced at Natalia. 'You sit with him awhile. I've had enough.'

Von Diehl beamed a complicit smile at Natalia. 'Our leader is in poor spirits today.'

Natalia said nothing, but went to sit a few paces away. Von Diehl held his hands up to indicate he was still a prisoner. 'Sit nearer. Then we can talk.'

'What makes you think I want to talk?'

'We're much alike, you and I. Come. What harm can it do, to pass the time in conversation?'

Natalia shook her head, doubtfully. But all the same she shuffled a little closer. From the corner of her eye she could see Stefan sitting up on the hill. Every few moments his gaze would flick across towards her; keeping a careful watch. It was safe enough. She could come to no harm like this.

Von Diehl studied her for a few moments. 'Maybe you'd rather be talking to Stefan?' he asked. Natalia shook her head. 'I talk to him often enough.'

'What about?'

'Anything I choose,' Natalia replied, haughtily. 'Much of the time we talk about my brother.' As soon as the words were out, Natalia was regretting them. Too late, she realised she should not have shared this intimacy with von Diehl.

'Ah, your brother. Alexei, is that right? What happened to him?'

Now Natalia had to respond. Anything else would have been to deny Alexei's memory.

'He died,' she said, brusquely. 'Died in the struggle against your kind.'

'Ah yes.' Von Diehl nodded, as if just reminded of a mundane, insignificant detail. 'Stefan was with him that day, is that right?'

Natalia squirmed, and shifted a few inches further away. Something was making her feel deeply uneasy, but she couldn't put her finger on what it was.

'As it happens, yes. Stefan and Alexei were there together. What of it?'

Von Diehl shrugged. 'Nothing. It's just curious, that's all.'

Natalia waited for the cultist to elaborate. But von Diehl looked away, apparently more interested in the sweep of the surrounding hills.

'What, then?' Natalia pressed. 'What is it that's so curious?'

Von Diehl looked around, startled. 'Curious? Well, nothing really, I suppose. It's just that I've often seen you talk to Stefan. But he never seems to approach you.'

'What do you mean?' Natalia asked, uneasily.

'I only observe,' von Diehl murmured. 'It seems strange that Stefan was with your brother when he died. And yet it is always you who wants to talk. Never the other way around.'

'Stefan knows Alexei was dear to me,' Natalia replied. 'He wants to spare my feelings.' It seemed a good response, yet on some level she knew it did not fully address the question. A nagging doubt started to blossom inside her.

'This distresses you,' von Diehl observed. 'We should talk about something else.' He brightened. 'We should talk about your gifts.'

'What do you mean?'

'Your magic powers,' von Diehl replied. 'I've been watching you. You're very skilled. More skilled than you know.'

Natalia tried to laugh the comment off. It was disturbing, being complimented by this man who was the antithesis of everything she held dear.

'I don't know about that,' she said. 'I haven't done so much. I put a few guards to sleep inside the prison. So what? Any self-respecting magician could have done as much.'

'But that wasn't all,' von Diehl persisted, softly. 'That night in the watchtower. When the beastmen came.'

Natalia had a sudden image of the darkened room; her cringing like a frightened child in the corner. 'I don't want to talk about that,' she said.

'I saw what happened,' von Diehl said. His eyes held her in an unblinking stare. 'You lured the creatures to you. Then you destroyed them.'

'I don't know what you're talking about,' Natalia stammered. 'You're confusing me.' She remembered the first beastman towering above her. Remembered the way the second creature had materialised out of nowhere, and then, inexplicably, turned upon the first. Von Diehl had been in that picture, too. But it was like a confusing dream, blurred and incomplete in her memory. The more she tried to piece together events, the less sense it all made. But it was not she who had destroyed the beastmen. That much she did know.

Neil McIntosh

'I did nothing,' she said. 'It was nothing to do with me.'

'Wasn't it?' von Diehl regarded her, querulously. 'Perhaps you don't know what you are capable of.' He sighed, and turned to look back up the hill where Stefan sat alone, looking down. 'Do you think he likes you?'

'Who? Stefan? What do I care whether he likes me or not?'

'It matters to you,' von Diehl said. 'I can see that.' He paused, momentarily. 'But he can seem so cold towards you. He keeps you at arm's length. I wonder... could it be something to do with your brother?'

'What do you mean?' Natalia snapped. Von Diehl shook his head. 'No,' he said. 'Truly, it's not for me to say.' He sighed, thoughtfully, and closed his eyes, signalling the end of the conversation.

'Let's hope our friend Maier will return before too long,' he murmured.

BRUNO STARED BACK into the cracked pane of mirror, and saw a man that he barely recognised. Shorn of his flowing curls, and with three days' beard to mask his face, he was well on the way to achieving the necessary transformation. Enough of a transformation perhaps, to give him a chance of passing along the street without being recognised.

'Your own mother wouldn't know you,' a voice behind him said. 'And I'm not sure I would either.'

Bruno turned round. Franz Sterkel was standing behind him, yet another of the wanted posters in one hand. Over the last few days the posters had been multiplying like a plague of locusts across Altdorf. Now they'd started appearing with Bruno's likeness as well as his name upon them, hence the need to try and change his appearance.

Sterkel appraised Bruno with a long, knowing look. 'Comfortable enough, are they?' he asked at last. 'Your new lodgings, I mean?'

'Perfectly comfortable, thanks,' Bruno confirmed. He'd been moved three times in the last week, shipped across the city from one safe house to another. By this time he'd learnt to survive on the barest of comforts.

'What do you mean, anyway?' Bruno asked, 'you wouldn't know me?'

Sterkel pulled a sour grin. 'Never had you down for a murderer, boy.'

'I'm not a murderer,' Bruno replied, emphatically.

Sterkel held up the new poster for Bruno's inspection. 'That's not what it says here,' he said. 'Not what the talk is around the taverns, neither.'

Bruno gave the page a fleeting glance, and turned back to the looking glass. He hacked away another length of black hair. If he was going to do this, he might as well do it properly. 'I don't give a spit what they say in the taverns,' he told Sterkel. 'I didn't kill Nikolas. And who- ever did kill him was trying to kill me as well.' He looked up at his host, a look of concern on his face. 'You do believe me, don't you?'

Sterkel shrugged. 'Don't know if I do, don't know if I don't. It's quite a story, you got to admit. Would *you* believe *me*, if it was the other way around?'

Bruno was about to say he wouldn't believe anything a rogue like Sterkel told him, but he thought better of it. Instead, he said. 'So if you can't be sure you believe me, why are you helping me?'

Sterkel pulled his chair up closer to Bruno. His breath reeked of the sour tang of late nights, strong tobacco and cheap drink. 'Because, old mate, I don't have much time for preachers and zealots. No time for any of them.' He angled his head to one side and aimed a gobbet of spit into a bowl on the floor. 'Leeches and hypocrites, the whole ragbag bunch. I don't have much time to spare for the watch either, come to that. Given half the chance, they'd squeeze the very blood out of honest grafters like me.' He laughed, and aimed another shot into the spittoon. 'So, whether I believe you or not, it looks like your enemies are my enemies. And that's good enough for me.' He clapped Bruno on the shoulder. 'Besides,' he said. 'The odds are stacked against you, aren't they? Someone needs to even things up a bit, eh?'

Sterkel straddled a chair, leaning with his arms across the back of the frame. He was enjoying this adventure far more than Bruno.

'So let's see where we've got to,' he said. 'There's a whole bunch of religious lunatics involved in this plot against you. Not to mention half the Altdorf watch.'

'I don't know about the watch itself,' Bruno countered. 'But there's a commander of the watch, Ehrhart, who's involved somehow or other. He may be mixed up with the zealots as well.' He studied the vacuous look on his host's face. 'I have to get to him, somehow, Franz. He could be the key to everything.'

'Get to Ehrhart? Don't make me laugh, boy. You might as well try and snuggle up to the Emperor himself. No chance.' Sterkel took out a knife, and started digging at his nails. 'But we've been keeping a look out on your account,' he murmured. 'And there's another name keeps coming up, every time Ehrhart gets a look in.'

'Someone else in the watch?'

Sterkel shook his shaggy head. 'Nope. A dusty dry professor. College fella, university of Altdorf, no less. Couldn't be more respectable.' Whistling softly, he tucked the knife back in its sheath. 'Except, word is, he's mixed up in all sorts of strange stuff. Wasn't able to find out what, not yet anyway. One thing we have found out, though. He knew your friend Nikolas. In fact, Nikolas worked for him.'

'What's his name?' Bruno demanded, eagerly.

Sterkel eyed him up and down for a moment before deciding to yield the information. 'Albrecht,' he said. 'Marcus Albrecht. Mean anything to you?'

'It does,' Bruno muttered, darkly. 'Thanks, Franz,' he said. 'I owe you.'

'I know you do, old mate. I know you do.'

There was a discreet knock from outside, and the door was opened by one of Sterkel's men.

Sterkel looked up. 'Well?'

'Company of watchmen, doing the length of the street,' the man said. 'House-to-house search.'

Sterkel turned back towards Bruno. The sardonic mask slipped, and his expression became more serious. 'Whatever you've done, or not done, you've managed to upset some important people,' he said. He offered Bruno a hand, and helped him up from the chair. 'Time to move on again,' he told Bruno. 'Keep moving. That's the secret to staying alive in this world, old mate. Always keep moving.'

FOUR HOURS PASSED before Maier finally returned. He had gone down the hill towards the town with only his sword. Now he emerged from the blanket of trees covering the valley with a brace of horses led by a length of rope in each hand. Each of them had bulging sacks strung out across their broad backs. Stefan sprang down the hill towards his comrade, and helped guide the horses back to the summit.

The sacks were stuffed full of food: cheeses and fruit, and enough bread to last all four of them the better part of a week. Maier had even managed to find a few skins of wine to make the rest of the journey more palatable.

'Ulric's toil,' Stefan exclaimed. 'You've done well.'

Maier stood back, admiring his own efforts. 'I'd say I have,' he agreed. 'The horses are nothing special. But we'll manage.'

Stefan ran an approving eye over the bounty. 'I dare-say we will.' The road ahead seemed suddenly much easier. Not only would they have no worries about food, but they would be able to cover three or even four times the distance in a day than they'd been managing on foot. 'You had no problems?' he asked. Maier shrugged. 'None that a little money couldn't answer.'

Stefan stared back down the valley at the town below. The silver figures were still milling around the market square. Some looked as though they might be making ready to move out. 'What about them?' he asked. 'The soldiers? Or weren't they soldiers, after all?'

Maier cast a glance down the hill. 'Oh, they're soldiers all right,' he said, nonchalantly. 'And they're looking for us, as well.'

The words jolted Stefan out of his languid contemplation of the journey home. Natalia gasped, out loud.

'Looking for us? What happened down there? Did you speak to them?'

Maier picked an apple from one of the sacks and bit a chunk from it. 'A little,' he said. 'Actually, I told them I was looking for us too. You know. Bounty hunter. That kind of thing.'

'And they believed you?' Natalia asked, incredulous. Maier shrugged again. 'Looks like it, doesn't it? I'm here, anyway.'

'Such bravado,' von Diehl commented, dryly. 'Such daring.'

'Keep out of this,' Stefan told him, sharply. He caught hold of Maier. 'Let me make sure I've understood you right. The men down there are looking for us, and you walked right into the middle of them.'

'That's right,' Maier confirmed.

'Only a madman would do that,' Natalia said, aghast.

'That's right,' Maier said again. 'And they weren't looking for a madman. They were looking for three or four men, a woman, and an escaped prisoner. I told them I'd seen you.'

'You told them *what?*'

'I told them I'd seen you,' Maier said. 'Told them I'd seen you double back on the trail, heading due north. That's where I'd lost sight of you. Or us, depending on how you see it.' He flashed Stefan a smile, clearly pleased with his deception.

Stefan wasn't so convinced. 'By all the mighty,' he muttered. 'You've taken a risk.'

'And I got away with it,' Maier countered, bristling slightly now. 'That's all that matters.'

'What about the horses?' Natalia broke in. 'How did you explain away needing to buy the horses?'

'Who said I bought them?' Maier replied, the grin still playing around his lips. 'I only said that I acquired them.'

Von Diehl laughed out loud. 'He stole the nags from under the noses of the Imperial dunces.'

'Is that right?' Stefan demanded. 'Is that what happened?'

'Does it matter? I bribed the lad minding the horses to look the other way. What do you want me to do? Take them back? Look,' he said, his tone hardening. 'I've bought us some time. For the moment the soldiers will be looking in the wrong place. We've got horses. We've got food. Are you going to waste the opportunity?'

Stefan looked down into the valley below. A stream of riders had begun to file out of Balzen. Just as Maier had predicted, they were headed north, in the opposite direction.

Stefan took hold of the rope fastened round one of the horses, and steered the animal around. 'All right,' he said. 'Let's not wait around. Load up. Let's get moving.'

MIKHAL KUMANSKY'S OLD life was fading to become a relic of fractured memory. He had not been back to his home in more than a week. His offices and warehouses lay locked, empty and neglected. And the *Karla*, the sum of his life's work, lay forgotten at the bottom of the harbour. Back in time, Mikhal had had a brother, but somewhere he too had disappeared. Mikhal had shrugged off the trappings of that other existence as easily as a snake sheds its skin. He had not done so voluntarily, but neither had he offered any resistance. His days now were spent in a grey limbo; he had not seen the light of the sun or the sibling moons in a long time.

Mikhal was losing contact with the outside world. He was disorientated and confused. Most of the time, he did not know where he was. He assumed that others – others from that old life – must somewhere be looking for him, but the days passed and still they did not come. Every so often he would be taken, usually blindfolded, from one anonymous location to another. How often, and when, he struggled to recall. The people he met were unyielding in their commands, yet they were not exactly unkind. In his more lucid moments, Mikhal realised that his new guardians knew exactly how to control a man. The boundaries between coercion and co-operation were subtly played. The hooded ghosts who shepherded him across this twilit world understood those boundaries precisely.

Most of the time, he was not entirely alone. There were other souls on that same journey. Casual travellers with the disciples of the True Path, who now found themselves a part of a select few. A select few who – what? That was the enduring mystery. Mikhal knew that he had been chosen for a task, but he did not yet know what that task would be. What he did know was that his life now had purpose. When the task had been fulfilled, then all the pain, all the confusion and weakness would be lifted from him, and he would be made whole.

He slept a lot, more than could be normal. In his lucid moments, he considered the possibility that they were drugging him, pacifying him with potions that cast him adrift in a dreamless world for hours, or even days, at a time. Then again, at other times he felt more alive than ever before. He and his new comrades were made to exercise; they were forced to push their bodies to limits Mikhal had never thought possible. Sometimes the punishment felt unendurable, and yet he did endure. He had no choice. Gradually he was growing stronger, more robust. Ready to serve his destiny.

Day by day, as his body was prepared, so too was his mind. Those were the times when the lord of the True Path visited them. The sermons delivered in that rich, sonorous voice, were so assured, so redolent of truth and certainty. Gradually, Mikhal began to see his life in a totally different way. He now knew that there was a threat, a threat facing not only Altdorf or the Empire, but all of the Old World. It was a threat based upon a massive deception. Mikhal now understood that the world was, in fact, a mirror of what he had once believed it to be. Everything that he had held true was, in reality, false. And in apparent falsehood there was truth. The real truth was that the men who claimed to protect the Empire from evil were in fact those most intent upon destroying it.

It was a vast, terrible conspiracy, rooted deep like a cankerous sore within the Empire. Change, Mikhal learned, was the only hope of salvation now. The redeeming power of transformation was all that could save the world. It would sweep away the old and the corrupt. Like a purging tide, it would wash away the poison. Time was fast running out, but there was still enough time to wrest the Old World from the brink of annihilation. The transformation would be sudden, and it would be cathartic. He would be in the vanguard. He would join the great offering, the sacrifice to save the soul of the Empire. He would be the catalyst for events that would change the course of history forever.

CHAPTER NINETEEN
Gathering for the Feast

THE STREETS OF Altdorf had been bustling since shortly after dawn that fragile, spring day. Crowds braved the chill air gusting through the twisting streets of the old city. Johann Esmer, Grand Theogonist of all Altdorf, had decreed that today the people would come together in prayer, a gathering of many thousands in a single show of will: the Blessing of the Souls. Only a few months ago, it had sounded like a last, defiant stand before the sons of darkness fell upon the city. Now, as grim winter began to recede, some were daring to imagine it as something else: a vindication of hope, even a celebration of victory to come.

Bruno watched the passing crowds from his seat by the window of the Black Goat. Everywhere he looked he saw zealots and penitents, of all shapes and colours, drawn by the ceremony like moths to a flame. Every now and then, he would spy figures dressed in the sombre grey of the True Path, and the same thought would flash through his mind. Could it be him? Could it be Mikhal? But it never was. Bruno hadn't seen Stefan's brother in weeks, and it played heavily upon his mind that he had failed in the one thing that he had promised his friend.

He glanced around nervously, and took another sip from the cup on the table in front of him. The watch were after someone, and Bruno had to assume it was him. The militia had been scouring Altdorf with a ruthless efficiency, moving from house to house, street to street, sweeping the city from one corner to another. Thanks to Sterkel, Bruno had managed to stay one step ahead, rarely staying in the same dingy room two nights running. But he could not stay in hiding all of the time, he had his own search to conduct. Somehow, he had to find Mikhal. And, when, gods willing, Stefan finally returned, Bruno had to be ready.

The tavern door opened and two officers of the watch entered. Bruno shrank back and pressed his face to the window. This time he was in luck. The two men went straight to the bar, and ordered flagons of ale. They carried their drinks back to a table across the other side of the room. Before he sat down, one of the watchmen cast an eye about the room, sizing up the dozen or so drinkers. For a moment his gaze lighted upon Bruno, then flicked away.

Bruno released a pent up breath and took another sip of his beer. He forced himself to wait a few more moments, then got up, slowly and deliberately, and made his way to the door. Night would soon be falling, and Bruno had a rendezvous to keep.

'DISAPPEARED?' ALBRECHT SAID. 'Without trace?'

'So it would appear,' Ehrhart replied, brusquely. 'He must be getting help from somewhere.' A sudden sharpness entered his voice. 'In Sigmar's name, man, isn't there anything else you can tell me about Bruno Hausmann? Nikolas was sheltering him.'

'But Nikolas is dead,' Albrecht replied, dumbfounded. 'And by your reckoning it was Bruno who killed him.'

Ehrhart waved a hand in apology. 'Forgive me, my friend. But the moment of crisis is near. Now, above all, we must leave nothing to chance.'

'Perhaps he's in hiding with Mikhal Kumansky?' Albrecht suggested.

'Who?'

'Hausmann. We talked about how he and Stefan's brother might be involved in this together.'

'Of course,' Ehrhart muttered. 'Quite so.' But Albrecht had the distinct impression that Mikhal Kumansky barely registered as a priority for the other man.

'The Keepers of the Flame must be here when von Diehl is delivered,' Ehrhart continued. 'He won't give up his secrets freely. We'll need all the powers that the Keepers can muster to break him down.'

'They will be here,' Albrecht asserted. 'My brothers will not fail me.'

'They'd better not,' Ehrhart commented, sharply.

Marcus Albrecht looked down from the high window of the watch commander's office. The street below was lined on both sides with people, their faces turned expectantly towards the head of the causeway. As Albrecht looked on, a carriage with its complement of liveried outriders passed along the length of street. Cheers rang out from the watching crowds.

'Johann Esmer,' Albrecht remarked, sourly. 'The leader who stayed behind, sacrificing glory whilst his peers marched to war.'

'You're becoming obsessed with that man,' Ehrhart observed, without much sympathy. 'Forget about him.'

'Hard to forget, when the evidence is all around us,' Albrecht countered, gazing down at the crowds massing in the streets. 'His great festival has roused a hornets' nest in Altdorf. A pious plague we could well do without. What Altdorf needs right now is reason, not fervour.'

'Forget him,' Ehrhart said again. 'There are more important things to focus on. We must find Hausmann. He's our conspirator, not the Grand Theogonist.'

Albrecht shook his head, ruefully. 'Maybe I'm beginning to see conspirators everywhere,' he confessed. 'I'll be glad when all of this is over.'

'It will be over, soon enough,' Ehrhart said. 'I promise you, it will.'

THE PATH WOUND through the great forest. As the hours passed, the last rays of daylight began to creep in through the growing gaps in the canopy of trees. Finally, shortly before dusk, the city came into view, a scattering of spires straddling the distant plain perhaps thirty miles to the east. As Natalia gazed into the distance, a little cry of joy escaped her lips.

'Altdorf!' she exclaimed. 'Can it really be?'

'It can,' Stefan assured her. 'Another day's ride and we're there.'

It was a moment of sheer wonderment, a tantalising dream now so close to fulfilment. But although the end of the mission might be in sight, serious obstacles still remained along the way. The journey from Balzen to Altdorf had been slow and cautious. More than once they had had to endure the unwanted attention of raiders, common bandits, mostly, out to prey on any travellers foolish enough to risk the bleak hinterland of the Midden Moors. Those who chose to chance their hand against Stefan and his comrades found their luck was out. A dozen or more had paid the price of their lives, with no return for their violent endeavour.

The nearer they got to Altdorf, the less remote and more populated the trails through the hills and forests became. Now they had company on all but the smallest, most obscure paths. Amongst the travellers, journeymen and merchants that made up most of the traffic there were Imperial Guards and militia too. Avoiding the checkpoints was getting harder by the hour. The chances of getting through the city walls without being challenged looked slim. On their own, Stefan, Natalia and Maier might have passed for innocent travellers, but that still left von Diehl. They had to assume that there were forces from Altdorf looking for the cultist – for all of them, in all probability. To slip up now would be foolish beyond belief, but they had to get past the walls somehow.

Natalia eyed the distant ramparts of the city with a mixture of relief and anxiety. 'We don't have any papers, anything to give us an identity. I could try magic, I suppose. It might get us in.'

'Forget it,' Maier advised. 'There'll be witch hunters out with every patrol. Try any magic within a mile of the walls and they'll be on us in a moment.'

'We're going to have to talk our way through,' Stefan replied. 'But it's not going to be easy. Especially with him,' he added, meaning von Diehl.

Natalia gazed down upon the well-paved road across the plain to the gates of the city. 'So near and so far,' she murmured. 'There must be a way.'

'There's always a way,' Maier said, quietly.

'Any ideas?' Stefan asked.

Maier grinned. 'I'll wager I could get us in under the nose of the watchtowers,' he said. 'We'd be invisible to them.'

'Then what are we waiting for?' Natalia asked.

'Not so fast,' Maier cautioned. 'I said it could be done. I didn't say it would be easy.'

'What did you have in mind?' Stefan asked.

'Let me go on ahead. One man on his own has a better chance of getting through. Once I'm on the other side, I'll contact our people, and find a way to get the rest of you in.'

Stefan looked doubtful. 'He managed it in Balzen,' Natalia pointed out.

'Altdorf isn't like Balzen,' Stefan replied.

'I can do it,' Maier said firmly. 'It's our best chance.'

Stefan looked up at the gathering gloom above. Night was falling. The surrounding forest would give them adequate shelter and cover for a few hours if need be. 'All right,' he said at last. 'We'll stay here, out of sight, until dawn tomorrow. Karl, if you haven't returned by then–'

'Don't worry,' Maier assured him. 'By then, we'll be well on our way.'

MARCUS ALBRECHT HURRIED through the streets towards his chambers in the university of Altdorf, a worried man. There was a sense of something coming to a head in Altdorf, a rising tension that even the news about the war had failed to diffuse. Maybe it was the zealots that massed each day on the streets. Maybe it was the growing influence of the Grand Theogonist, or the imminence of the Blessing of the Souls. Meanwhile, Albrecht was running out of allies. His sources within Altdorf had been all but wiped out. Now even Nikolas was dead. The Ten had to come soon. In the meantime, he must be thankful for what friends remained, and that meant Gustav Ehrhart.

The streets were not safe, that much he now took for granted. Ever since that black day, when his people were hunted down and butchered, Marcus Albrecht had treated Altdorf as potentially hostile territory. Now he planned his routes with care. He stuck steadfastly to the busier roads, the streets that teemed with life until well into the night. Ehrhart had offered him an escort that evening, just as he had on evenings before. But Albrecht wasn't comfortable with that, either. As long as he stayed with the main thoroughfares, he would be all right.

That evening, the warren of streets approaching the university quarter was busier than normal. Albrecht battled to make headway through the crowds. The roadways were choked with processions of penitents and preachers, and with the seemingly almost equal number of vendors determined to make business from them. Albrecht cursed and pushed his way through, jammed amidst an assortment of ruddy-faced workmen and peasants, most of them doubtless with nowhere better to go than the next tavern.

He reached the edge of the Konigsplatz, where things were no easier. He began to fret. He had to deliver an address to the college in less than an hour. He was beginning to wish he had taken up Ehrhart's offer of an escort, if only to speed his way through this damnable rabble. He scanned the faces around him. Simple folk most of them; harmless in their way, but brutish and stupid, oblivious to the greater struggle being fought under their very noses. It had been always thus, Albrecht reflected, and probably always would be.

Something jogged him out of his aimless reflection. He took another look around him. More than a few of the faces looked strangely familiar. Hadn't some of them been with him from almost the moment he'd set off from Ehrhart's offices? For a moment, the thought entered his mind that the commander had decided to provide him with a covert escort. He entertained the idea for a second, then replaced it with an altogether darker explanation. A sudden jolt of panic ran through him, and he broke out in a sweat.

He started to push forward, desperate now to break through the crowd. 'Let me through,' he shouted. 'Make way there. Let me pass!'

Grudgingly, the crowds parted a little to let the grey-haired scholar through. Albrecht pushed on. He was unconcerned now with whose feet he might be trampling. All that mattered was to get clear, and reach the safety of the university a mere ten or twenty minutes away. He seemed to be making progress, then the crowds closed around him once more, hemming him in ever more tightly. Albrecht looked at their faces. The stocky ruffian with the scar across one cheek. The one-eyed creature with the grimy bundle of sacks over his shoulder. The sickly boy with the lop-sided walk. They'd been following him all the way. Others too. Now he was sure. They were coming for him.

He opened his mouth to shout for help, but quickly realised it would do no good. There were too many of them. They had him surrounded. How bitterly he was regretting not taking Ehrhart's escort, not that regrets would do him much good now. Albrecht felt beneath his cloak. The silver rapier was there, tucked out of sight where he always kept it. If they intended to kill him, then by Sigmar they'd pay a heavy price.

Then, out of the blue, the crowds parted like waves, and a shabby, dust-painted coach appeared ahead of him. For a moment Albrecht thought it meant to run him down, but at the last moment it veered to his left. The cabin door swung open and a voice from inside called out: 'Professor! Quickly! In here!'

Albrecht reeled back, uncertain which way to turn. Then the decision was taken out of his hands. Someone or something behind him pushed hard at his back, lifting him off his feet and propelling him into the carriage. The door slammed hard behind him. The carriage jolted forward.

Albrecht hauled himself off the floor of the coach. Two men stared across at him from the bench seat. One was a lean sallow-faced individual with dark, greasy hair who looked every inch the villain. The other, bearded man was more roundly built, with large, almost soft brown eyes. The expression on his face wasn't exactly hostile, but Albrecht was under no illusions. The two could slit his throat in an instant if they had a mind.

'Sit down,' the first man, the one who had hailed him in the street, directed.

Feeling suddenly very vulnerable, Albrecht did as he was told. The second man cupped his chin in his hands, and leaned forward.

'Now then,' Bruno said, quietly. 'We're going to have ourselves a little chat.'

THE HOURS SPENT waiting for Maier's return passed uneventfully, yet it seemed that neither Stefan nor Natalia were in any mood for sleep. As the night drew to an end, they were still sitting side by side and staring out into the dark heart of the forest, all the while keeping their careful watch over von Diehl. Natalia took a close look at von Diehl, as if to be absolutely sure that he was truly asleep, then moved nearer to Stefan. She stared up at the waxen orbs of the twin moons, and sighed, quietly.

'He will come back, won't he?'

'Maier?' Stefan asked. 'He'll come back. I'm sure of it.'

Their breaths curled into a single icy plume on the chill night air. 'To have come so far, only to fail. That would be unendurable,' Natalia murmured.

'We're not going to fail, not now,' Stefan assured her.

Natalia gazed out through the darkened woods, perhaps imagining Altdorf, and the life that they might each be returning to.

She glanced at Stefan, curious. 'Is there someone waiting for you? Apart from your family?'

'Not in the sense you mean.' He hesitated. 'But there was someone. Back in Kislev. In Erengrad.'

'What was their name?' she asked. 'If you don't mind.'

'Of course not,' Stefan countered quickly. 'Her name was Elena. Elena Yevschenko.'

'Is she…' Natalia began, tentatively. 'I mean, is she…'

'Dead?' Stefan shook his head. 'No. Not dead. Married.' He laughed, but without comfort or warmth. Natalia looked sympathetic.

'Sorry,' she said. 'That's too bad.'

'No, it's fine,' Stefan tried to assure her. 'It was a great thing. A noble marriage, that healed wounds dividing a whole city.'

'Even so.' Natalia's voice trailed off. She shivered, ever so slightly. For a while conversation eluded them.

'You know,' Natalia said, at length, 'he frightens me. A little.'

'Who?' Stefan asked, puzzled. 'Maier?'

Natalia laughed, uneasily, and lowered her voice. 'Von Diehl.' She put a hand upon Stefan's arm. He felt her nails pressing down upon his flesh. 'I've noticed things about him. Things I didn't mention before. He has powers. Powers that even I don't fully understand.'

'What have you seen?' Stefan asked.

'I'm not sure. Maybe it's only my imagination.'

'Go on,' Stefan said slowly. He took a long, hard look at von Diehl. Not for the first time, Stefan had the unsettling feeling that he could hear everything that was being said.

'The first time was in the prison,' Natalia said, quietly. 'Remember the fire spell? The one that made the guards think everything they touched was red hot?'

'It was good magic,' Stefan affirmed. 'We wouldn't have got out without that.'

'Except I'm not sure it was entirely my doing,' Natalia said. 'The magic was too good. I've never quite managed a spell like that before. At the time I just thought – well, I thought I'd been inspired. I thought the gods were smiling on us.'

'And perhaps they were.'

'But perhaps not. Perhaps I was just being used as a cipher, by the one wielding the real power.' She stared out into the forest. 'The night that von Diehl managed to escape, I swear that he was right there; right until the moment he disappeared. I swear that he was.'

'I believe you,' Stefan replied. And, at that moment, he did.

'Then there was the night in the tower, when the beast-men attacked.'

'Nothing to reproach yourself for there,' Stefan said. 'You showed great courage.'

'Courage?' Natalia laughed, edgily. 'I was frozen with fear. I wanted to be brave, but I couldn't move. It was like something had taken control over me. Then von Diehl appeared, out of nowhere, as if he–' She broke off in confusion.

'It was dark, and it was frightening,' Stefan said. 'Things quickly get confused in battle.'

'Maybe so,' Natalia agreed. 'But I can't shake off the feeling that–' she shook her head in puzzlement, and broke off. 'I don't know,' she said. 'He's a captive, and yet sometimes it feels like it's him that's in control, not us.'

'But he's still our prisoner. And we are taking him to Altdorf,' Stefan reminded her. 'There's no doubt about that.'

'I know,' Natalia said. 'That's why it doesn't make any real sense. You're right. It's probably all in my imagination.'

'I didn't say that.' Stefan turned and met her gaze. Her face in the moonlight looked pale and fragile, but her eyes still held that sense of strength that he had seen so often in her brother. They moved closer, then Natalia turned abruptly away.

'You've kept this to yourself for quite a while,' Stefan said at last. 'Why tell me now?'

Natalia shrugged. 'I don't know. It was like I was carrying a secret. I didn't want that, do you understand?'

Stefan nodded. 'I understand.'

'Soon, Shallya willing, we'll be back in Altdorf. If there are things to be said, then they need to be said now. I don't want to carry any secrets with me back to the city.'

Her words touched something deep inside of Stefan. What about the secret he had been carrying ever since he'd first met Natalia Zucharov? He had never thought of it as a deception before, but was laid bare as exactly that. He had fabricated a history; created a fantasy of what might have been. All this time, he had told himself that he was protecting Natalia from a brutal truth. But if they parted now, with the fantasy still intact, would he be any better than von Diehl and his kind?

The truth was that Stefan had indeed been there on the last day of Zucharov's life, but not as a comrade, nor an ally. In the end, Stefan's only purpose had been to destroy the creature that had once been Zucharov. He had sent Alexei to the gates of Morr. Who was he really protecting from that truth – Natalia or himself?

'There's something I must tell you, too,' he began. 'Something about Alexei.'

'Alexei?' He heard the surge in her voice as she answered. Natalia had built her life around her brother.

His memory had brought her to this place. But that reflection could not deflect Stefan from his purpose now. On the contrary, it only reinforced it.

'Whatever I say to you, I want you to remember your brother above all as a brave, courageous man,' Stefan said. 'He fought with a valour that I have never seen matched, nor do I ever expect that I will.'

This time Natalia answered him only with her silence. She looked away from Stefan, searching out the shimmering, fractured cusps of the twin moons through the canopy of the trees. 'I've known for weeks there was something more,' she said, finally. 'Something you were holding back. The sooner it's said, the better.'

Stefan reached out to her, but Natalia pulled away.

'Say it,' she insisted. 'Nothing I could learn from you would ever tarnish his memory.'

'Natalia,' Stefan began, 'there's no easy way to tell you this.'

'Then don't try and make it easy,' Natalia snapped. 'Mercy of Ulric, Stefan, if you want to spare me more torture, then tell me now!'

Stefan shut his eyes and lifted his head to the night sky. He asked Sigmar to gift him a way to soften this terrible truth. But nothing came. Natalia was not to be spared, and nor was he.

'Chaos claimed your brother at Erengrad,' he said, quietly. 'As Sigmar is my witness, Natalia, I pray that it were not so, but it was.'

Natalia sat stock still for a moment then started to shake her head, in confusion and disbelief. 'But you told me that Alexei died far from Erengrad, on the plains of Ostermark, miles to the west.'

'He did,' Stefan affirmed, soberly. 'Chaos marked Alexei at Erengrad. He died weeks later, in a city called

Sigmarsgeist. Never was so holy a name given so terrible a place.'

'Then–'

Stefan caught hold of Natalia, and forced her to look at him. 'He had been poisoned by Chaos. The transformation was slow, but once the poison had taken hold, it was unstoppable.'

Natalia stared back at him, picking through his words. 'You're trying to tell me that this – this *poison* killed my brother? That he died some wretched, lingering death, like a dog?'

'No!' Stefan blurted out. He was determined now that she would not mistake his meaning, nor would he mislead her any further. 'Alexei died in combat. But by that time he was no longer the man you knew as your brother.'

'I don't understand.'

'By the time of that final battle Alexei had become a mutant, a monster. All the strength once channelled for good had turned to evil. He had become a servant of Chaos.' He broke off, barely able to go on. 'I'm sorry Natalia. But Alexei died as my enemy.'

Natalia pulled away, the colour leeching from her face. Slowly but surely, she was struggling towards that dark place where realisation lay. 'You were with him when he died,' she said, slowly. 'But it was more than that, wasn't it? That final battle was with you. It was you who killed him. You killed my brother.'

'The monster that died had long ceased to be your brother,' Stefan insisted. 'His mortal body had become corrupted, transformed by something wholly, relentlessly evil.'

'You killed him,' Natalia repeated. 'You killed Alexei!'

Her voice rose to a scream, fuelled by a frenzy of grief and rage. Shocked, Stefan struggled to keep hold of her.

Finally he had to let go. Natalia began to shake, uncontrollably, but he let her be.

'There could only be one outcome,' he said. 'Either the creature that had once been your brother would die, or I would die. By then, no other ending was possible.'

'You killed Alexei,' Natalia gasped again, between her sobs. 'You killed my brother.'

'The creature... Alexei drowned,' Stefan said. 'He was sucked down beneath the waters of a whirlpool. I never saw him again.' He waited a few moments more then added. 'But it wasn't your brother that died, Natalia. Alexei's soul had quit the mortal world long before.'

Natalia did not respond. She sank down on the ground, locked inside a private world of pain. Stefan sat watching her, numb and helpless.

Something stirred on the ground a few feet away. Stefan spun around to find himself looking into von Diehl's searching eyes.

'Go back to sleep,' Stefan commanded. 'This doesn't concern you.'

Von Diehl sat up. He looked from Natalia to Stefan. 'Is this your valour, your honesty, your goodness?' he asked. 'Does your heart feel *good*, Stefan? And, if this is goodness, what face should evil wear?'

Stefan sprang to his feet, red anger flooding through him. He was stopped in his tracks by the sound of footsteps, coming swiftly along the hillside path towards them. The curtains of trees broke apart, and Karl Maier appeared in the clearing, a look of bewilderment on his face.

'Taal's breath!' he exclaimed. 'What's going on?'

Stefan turned away from von Diehl in disgust. 'Leave it,' he told Maier. 'I'll explain later.'

Maier shrugged. 'Whatever you say. But we need to get moving.'

'You've found a way into Altdorf?'

Maier nodded. 'But we have to reach the south-western gate before dusk. We need to get going.'

Briefly, Stefan's spirits rose. 'Have you made contact with the Keepers?'

'That I have,' Maier confirmed. He clapped a hand on Stefan's shoulder. 'Come on,' he urged. 'It's time to go home.'

CHAPTER TWENTY
Betrayal

THEY WERE ON the last stretch of the road back to Altdorf. They had escaped from the wilderness, survived Stahlfort and the unforgiving, bleak hinterland of the Midden Moors. Soon they would be home. But, for Stefan, any sense of celebration was lost. The final ride to the city had become a sombre procession.

'You seem to have upset our little friend,' Maier observed after a while. 'I hope it was worth it.'

'So do I,' Stefan replied. 'So do I.'

Maier probed a little further. 'Care to say what happened?'

'Not really,' Stefan answered. 'Let's focus on how we get back into Altdorf.'

Maier grinned. 'A mixture of cunning and knowledge, oiled with a little bribery, should see us through. Do you know the south-western approach to the city?'

Stefan shook his head: 'Not very well.'

'Well, a little way from the gate…' he broke off, and glanced behind Stefan, towards von Diehl, being led along in their wake. The cultist met Maier's gaze and curled his lips into the faintest of smiles.

'Perhaps we shouldn't discuss this in his earshot,' Maier suggested.

'Don't worry,' Stefan assured him. 'Where he's going he won't trouble us ever again.'

'All right. Just beyond the west gate there's another, smaller passage, used by military traffic, for armaments, provisions going to the front, that kind of thing.'

'So?'

'That's where a little oiling comes in useful. We arrive just before dusk, when the guard on the gate changes. We leave our horses and pick up a covered wagon that'll be waiting for us. They'll search it on the gate, but I've arranged for the watchmen to give it a light touch. It's the end of the shift; everybody wants to get home.'

'How much "oiling" did this cost you?'

'I don't know. I left that to Marcus Albrecht.'

'Albrecht! You've seen him, then?'

Maier nodded, firmly. 'He'll be waiting, once we're through the walls.'

'Good,' Stefan said. 'Very good.' He checked that Natalia was still keeping pace with them. He picked out her horse, a smear of grey against the blackness, twenty feet or so behind. She made no attempt to hail Stefan, nor make eye contact with him.

'I'd better tell her what's happening,' he said to Maier.

'Do you want me to talk to her?'

'No,' Stefan demurred. 'Best that I do it. Here,' he offered Maier the rope guiding von Diehl's horse. 'Look after him for a while.'

He tugged back on the reins, to slow his horse just a fraction, and waited for Natalia to catch up.

'We need to talk,' he said.

Natalia stared directly ahead. 'We've already talked.'

'We need to talk about what happens when we reach the city walls. There are instructions that all of us will need to follow carefully.'

'Then instruct me,' she said, tersely. 'I'm listening.'

Stefan repeated what Maier had told him. Natalia listened in silence, her gaze never once wavering from the road ahead. Stefan paused then drew a deep breath.

'Look,' he said. 'I know this has been hard for you–'

Her eyes flashed cold fire. 'You know nothing of how it's been for me,' she snapped. 'You know nothing of me, or my family.'

'What I need to know,' Stefan persisted, 'is that you are still loyal to this mission. That I can still rely upon you.' He pulled his horse to block the path. 'Otherwise you become a liability. And I won't tolerate that.'

Natalia stared back at him, disdainfully. 'I gave an oath, to the Keepers of the Flame, to deliver Heinrich von Diehl to Altdorf. I shall honour that oath.' She kicked in with her heels, and steered her horse around Stefan. 'Once we reach the city, my oath is discharged. So is any bond I once shared with you.'

She turned in the saddle to glance back towards him 'From then on, you may consider yourself my enemy.'

HIDDEN IN THE shadows on the far side of the street, Bruno rubbed his legs and arms to restore some warmth to his body. It felt like days since he'd been able to rest properly. He desperately needed sleep, but he had to stay watching a while yet. He had no reason to doubt Sterkel's information. If the enemy were going to make a move, it was probably going to be by night. That said, the coming night would be the third in a row that he'd kept watch on Ehrhart's mansion, so far without result.

He yawned and stretched, trying to stay alert. It had been hours since anything of interest had occurred. The three nights had yielded only one sighting, and that had proved to be a false alert. Late the previous evening, someone had arrived at Ehrhart's house. From his hiding place, Bruno had watched the gates of the house open, and a figure go inside. There wasn't much that Bruno could glean from his appearance, except that the visitor looked to be a man of about Stefan's height and build. He moved with the distinctive, supple grace of a swordsman, and for an instant, the thought raced through Bruno's mind that it might even be Stefan himself. He sat tight in the shadows – and waited.

After about an hour, the gates to the house had opened again and the same figure emerged, alone. A second glance confirmed he was not Stefan, but his identity remained a mystery. The anonymous man had made a cursory glance of the street, then turned left in front of the gates and quickly vanished in the direction of the outer city. Bruno had had to swallow his disappointment, and settle back to wait again.

A nearby chapel bell sounded. Bruno scrubbed at his face with his hand. He had been on the point of falling asleep; he might actually have done so for a few fleeting seconds. He leaned forward from his vantage point and peered at the house. As he did so, the gates swung. Bruno saw Ehrhart, with a dozen or so men, none wearing uniform, gathered on the wide driveway. He felt a pulse of excitement. This, at last, was what he had been waiting for.

The men were all armed. Bruno watched them check their weapons before concealing them beneath long, grey cloaks. The group emerged through the gates with the commander at their head, and moved off. Bruno stood up and reached inside the pocket of the heavy

woollen coat. There he found the small, hollowed out
wooden tube that Sterkel had given him. He put the
piece to his lips and blew. A single note, an innocuous
trill of birdsong, rang out across the darkening sky.

Bruno took the whistle from his mouth and waited. A
few seconds later, an answering call, and then another, a
little further down the street. The signal line was intact.
They were in business.

Bruno slid his sword from its scabbard and touched a
superstitious finger to the blade. The time for waiting
was over.

THE SENTRY-POST beside the south-western gate looked
deserted. Stefan slowed his horse and drew up beneath
the shadow of the walls. Straight ahead, recessed into
the ramparts, stood a single iron-gated doorway about
twenty feet across. It was barred, and securely pad-
locked.

Maier pulled his horse about and scanned the length
of the walls in both directions. 'Over there,' he said, indicating with a nod of his head. About fifty feet away, a
small covered wagon with two horses stood tethered
and empty. The canopy over the wagon was a dull olive
green, and bore the insignia of the watch: the sword of
Sigmar clasped by a scarlet hand.

'Delivered as promised,' Maier said.

The rig was empty, save for some sacking and dirty
straw piled in the cart at the back. Maier bundled von
Diehl unceremoniously into the wagon. Stefan made
the cultist lie down, and heaped the straw on top of
him.

'You'll stay as quiet as death,' he told him. 'If they find
you now, you can forget about any pardon, or any kind
of life for that matter. Understand me?' Von Diehl indicated by his silence that he understood, and allowed

Stefan to pile more straw over his body until he was completely covered. Maier climbed into the cab and waited for Natalia. Stefan sent the last of their horses on its way with a slap to its flank, and jumped into the back. Maier lifted the reins and steered the horses about.

The wagon bumped along the rutted track towards the gate. It was quiet; so far no one had stepped from the shadows to challenge them. So far, so good. The wagon jolted on for another thirty feet or so, and then the iron barrier ahead opened up. A soldier in livery clutching a lantern appeared behind the gated doorway. The guard strode over and held up his lantern to take a better look at Maier and Natalia.

'What's your business here?' he demanded, in a low voice.

'Name's Adler,' Maier said, and handed the guard a slip of parchment. The guard glanced briefly at the slip then waved them through.

'Hurry up,' he muttered. 'Through the gate and pull up the other side. Wait for me there.'

Maier took the wagon under a vaulted archway that ran through the core of the city walls. There he pulled up, as instructed. Stefan looked out from the rear of the wagon and watched the guard close up the gate behind them. The whole manoeuvre was over in a matter of seconds.

'Follow me,' the guard said to Maier. 'Don't say a word to anybody unless I tell you to.' He picked up the lantern and walked ahead. They reached the end of the arch, and emerged into a broad courtyard, open to the sky. Stefan released a pent up breath. He felt anticipation surge inside him. They were back inside the city. They had made it.

Or nearly. As the wagon bumped across the courtyard, Stefan heard footsteps rapidly closing in from the rear. A second uniformed guard hailed them with a warning shout. The first guard spun around. Stefan knew at once from his startled expression that this was not part of the plan.

'Wait there!' the second man called out. 'Where d'you think you're taking that?'

'To the armoury,' the first explained, hurriedly. 'There's a shipment waiting.' The second soldier approached the wagon, and circled it slowly. 'Why hasn't the wagon been searched?'

'There's no need,' the first protested. 'It's empty.'

The second man snorted, unimpressed then swung himself up over the back of the cart. Stefan's hand lay against his sword. He beseeched Sigmar he wouldn't have to risk the life of another honest man before this business was over. 'Listen,' he said, 'there's nothing in here but me and a lot of filthy straw. The stuff hasn't been changed in over a week.'

'I'm not fussed about that,' the man grunted. He pulled out a broadsword, and began plunging it randomly into the straw lying heaped around the bed of the truck. Three times he stabbed home, the blade slicing into the wooden floor of the wagon. As he was about to plunge the blade a fourth time, Natalia made an agile leap into the back of the wagon. She caught hold of the guard, and stayed his hand.

'What're you playing at?' the man demanded. 'Do you want some of this?'

Natalia held her ground, and gazed up into his face, holding his stare. 'That'll do,' she said, softly. 'We're running late as it is. If we're kept any longer it'll be you that answers for it.' Without breaking eye contact, she brought the sword down. 'If it really bothers you,' she said, 'you can search us again on the way back out.'

There was a moment's tense silence. The guard made a half-hearted stab at the straw then put the weapon away. 'Damn this for a job at this hour,' he muttered. 'Where did you say they were for?'

'The armoury,' the first man repeated, nervously.

The guard stared back at her for a few, long seconds. 'Remember the rules next time. Search the bloody wagon before you let it through.' He waved them on. 'Get out of here.'

The first guard nodded to Maier. 'Get moving,' he said, one eye still on the second man. 'Go left at the far end of the courtyard then ditch the wagon. Take the street signposted for Limberg. They'll be waiting for you there.'

Maier picked up the reins. The wagon jerked back into motion, under the watchful gaze of both guards. Maier breathed a sigh.

'That was close,' he whispered. 'Good magic.'

'It was persuasion, not magic,' Natalia responded, icily. 'I'm not so stupid as to start casting spells right under the noses of the witch hunters.'

'Either way, you saved our skins,' Stefan said. 'You did well.'

'I was doing my job,' she replied, coldly. 'And now it's finished.'

Once clear of the yard, they pulled up. Stefan hauled von Diehl from the back of the wagon. He shoved the cultist forward. 'Do as you're told, and you might live a while yet.'

'What a glorious prospect,' von Diehl replied, acidly. 'My gratitude knows no bounds.'

From close by came the sound of more troops, marching in their direction. Maier signalled to Stefan. 'We have to go.'

They worked their way along the length of a twisting alleyway, until it joined the street ahead.

'Where are Albrecht's people?' Stefan muttered.

'They'll be here,' Maier said. He scanned the street in both directions. A light flickered briefly in the shadows; a torch waved from left to right.

'That's them,' Maier said. 'Let's go.'

'Steady,' Stefan cautioned. He stepped up the pace, but kept one hand firmly on von Diehl's shoulder, and the other upon the hilt of his sword. The light flared a second time, then figures materialised out of the darkness on either side of them.

'Stefan,' said a voice he did not recognise. 'Welcome back to Altdorf. Congratulations.'

Stefan looked around. He counted six or seven figures, maybe more, their faces obscured by the hoods of their grey cloaks.

'Where's Albrecht?' he said to the nearest man.

'He couldn't come in person,' a voice from behind said. 'He's authorised us to take the prisoner back into the city.'

'We have papers,' a second voice to his left said. 'We have authority.'

'Just hand him over,' a third voice, ahead to the right. 'Your part in this is done.'

Stefan looked around, trying to identify the speakers. The light of the torch was right in his eyes now; he was blinded by the sudden glare. 'Nikolas is the only deputy that I'll surrender this man to,' he insisted. 'If he's not here, then I'll deliver the prisoner to Albrecht in person.'

'That won't be possible,' a fourth voice chimed in. Then there was the unmistakeable sound of steel being drawn. A sword glinted in the torchlight then scythed through the air. Stefan dived to his left, narrowly avoiding the blade as it flashed inches from his face. Instinctively, he released his grip on the prisoner, and drew his sword. Another blade came at him, but he managed to deflect the blow before it struck home.

'It's a trap!' he shouted to the others. 'Defend yourselves!'

Solid figures dissolved into a blur of movement, and the still of the night was punctured with the sounds of battle. Stefan lashed out with his sword, fending off blows that rained down from all sides. His attackers outnumbered him easily, but they were unprepared for Stefan's speed and agility. A grey-robed figure loomed out of the darkness and lunged at him with a dagger. Stefan stepped back, shifting his balance from right to left, and swung his blade in a rapid arc. The sword sliced through his assailant's arm, severing the hand from its wrist, and spraying the cobblestones with a red mist of blood. The would-be assassin screamed and fell back, but, before Stefan could draw breath, two more of the grey ghosts were upon him. Stefan felt the icy caress of steel as a blade sliced through the sleeve of his jerkin. A needle stab of pain, then numbness.

Stefan parried a second blow, then found space for retaliation. His sword cleaved flesh from bone as the first of them came at him, sword at shoulder height. The man toppled to the ground, only to be replaced by yet another assailant. There was no respite.

With Maier in support, there would surely be a good chance of overcoming the odds. But Maier had vanished, Natalia too. Stefan was on his own, forced back beneath an unending stream of blows. He launched his sword through the air, double-handed, and found space to strike home against a grey-hooded figure.

He had accounted for at least three of them now, but still they came. Another blade found its mark, biting into the flesh just above his thigh. He felt a warm, sticky flow seeping from the wound. He wouldn't be able to keep this up for much longer. Just in time, he saw another blade aimed towards him. Stefan swerved away from the blow, but lost his footing on the slick paving. He slipped back, and his head cracked hard against the cobblestones that were already wet with blood.

Stefan regained his feet as another hooded figure rushed towards him. Stefan cut him down easily enough, but a more formidable opponent was waiting. Stefan saw at once from the unnatural bulk and speed that it was a mutant; its once-human frame covered in a dark, leathery hide. Stefan traded blows with the creature. Time and again his sword made its mark, but to little effect. The mutant was wearing him down, draining away his precious reserves of strength. Where was Maier? Where was Natalia? Where were the Keepers of the Flame?

Stefan launched a last, desperate assault on his enemy. He beat away the mutant's sword with his own, and drove again and again at a fold of exposed flesh around the creature's throat. Blood spurted from a wound in the mutant's neck. The creature lashed wildly at Stefan but he hung on, ignoring the pain of his own wounds to press home his attack. The heavy creature howled, and fell forwards, taking Stefan down with it.

He heard voices, commands and booted feet running hard on the cobblestones. Stefan put up his sword to fend off the inevitable deluge. He struggled to get up, but his strength was gone. A sword crashed down. Somehow Stefan managed to turn the blade away, but he was just postponing the inevitable. He lowered himself into a crouching position, his back to the alley wall, ready to mount a final defence.

The hooded assailants loomed over him. Stefan offered a final prayer to the gods. More footsteps, louder, more insistent now. The grey figures seemed to freeze in the moonlight, then abruptly they turned and fled.

Dazed, Stefan leant forward on his sword, only the sturdy steel keeping him from collapsing. He could feel the blood pouring down his face. He looked around. Five or six bodies lay sprawled in the street. No sign of Maier, or Natalia, and no trace of their prisoner. Von Diehl had gone. On his knees, and fighting for breath, Stefan confronted the possibility that all of this had perhaps been for nothing.

He jerked his head around at the sound of footsteps approaching. Another clutch of men, seven or eight in total, were running hard towards him. Stefan dug deep to summon some last reserve strength. He raised his sword in one last gesture of defiance. The first man drew his weapon. This was it. Then a voice he recognised, but for an instant could not place, shouted out.

'Are you all right?'

Stefan looked up in confusion. The blurred face came into focus. Stefan shook his head, trying to shrug off the dazed fog of battle.

'Do I know you?'

'Taal's breath, I should hope you do!' The man dropped down on his knees so that his bearded face was level with Stefan's. He reached out an arm and drew it round Stefan's shoulder. 'I should hope you do, old friend.'

It took a moment, but then Stefan's joy was as profound as his relief. 'Bruno!' he exclaimed. 'Suffering Sigmar, man, you've changed.'

Bruno laughed, but mirthlessly. 'So have a lot of other things,' he said

CHAPTER TWENTY-ONE
The Blessing of the Souls

'STOP MOVING, MORR take you! Let me finish the job!'

Bruno swore again, and dabbed inexpertly at the wound with a moistened cloth. He was determined that Stefan would remain still while he patched him up. Stefan was burning for answers, but Bruno had decided the questions could wait until he was done with the cloth and water. Stefan's face and upper arms had borne the brunt of the assault, but few of the cuts were deep enough to cause serious concern. In that respect, at least, he had been lucky. Finally, Bruno satisfied himself that the wounds were clean, and free of infection. He wrung out the bloodied rag and tossed it into a pail beside the chair.

'There,' he said, with quiet satisfaction. 'Not the most beautiful of pictures, but you'll do.'

'You're not much of a painting yourself these days,' Stefan shot back, running an eye over Bruno's much-altered features. 'What's been going on?'

Bruno heaved a sigh. 'Where do I start?'

'At the beginning?' Stefan suggested. 'Maybe with where we are?'

A door in the corner of the room opened, and a wiry man with lank, shoulder-length hair entered. He stood with his legs squarely apart, surveying the two friends as though they were a catch he'd just landed. He gave Stefan a long hard stare. 'You're in my house,' he said. 'Or one of my houses anyway. It pays not to stay too long in the same place, in my line of work.' He leaned over and spat expertly into the pail.

'The name's Sterkel,' he said. 'Franz Sterkel.'

Stefan sifted through the names in his memory. 'I know the name,' he said. 'You're—'

'A rogue, a cut-throat and a thief,' Sterkel volunteered, matter-of-factly. 'I know.'

'He's also the reason that I'm still alive,' Bruno added, quietly.

'In that case I probably owe you as much myself,' Stefan said. 'I'm in your debt.'

Sterkel snorted, and ejected another bullet of phlegm. The notion of indebtedness seemed to give him cause for satisfaction. He pulled up a chair, and set it down between Stefan and Bruno. 'D'you mind?'

Bruno glanced at Stefan. 'In truth, there's not much he doesn't know already.'

Stefan shrugged. 'Let's try and piece together what we've landed ourselves in.'

Stefan's spirits had soared at the first sight of Bruno. Now, as his companion told him everything that had happened since he had been away, his mood grew sombre. The news about Mikhal, and the sinking of the *Karla* was particularly worrying. Stefan was concerned not so much about the boat's loss, but what Bruno had found on board.

'You're sure you found blackpowder in the hold?' he asked.

'I can't be sure,' Bruno said, hesitantly. 'There was no more than a sprinkling. But that's what it looked like, all right.'

'What did you do with it?'

'Well–' Bruno hesitated. 'I let the watch have it, actually. I couldn't think what Mikhal would be doing carrying such dangerous cargo on his boat.'

'Nor can I,' Stefan admitted. He lapsed into silence, reminded of the awful destructive power that he had witnessed on the battlefields of Erengrad. What if Chaos had managed to smuggle the same substance inside the very walls of Altdorf? The idea was too terrible to contemplate. But contemplate it he must, as well as the possibility that his own brother was somehow involved.

'If they have blackpowder, then we must assume they mean to use it, right here in Altdorf.'

'They?'

'Whoever has a hold over Mikhal. The zealots. What do they call themselves?'

'The True Path,' Bruno said.

Stefan pondered the information for a moment. 'We have to track them down.'

Sterkel laughed, abruptly. 'You'll be tripping over them before the day's out!'

'How so?'

'The Blessing of the Souls,' Sterkel said, spitting the words out with a sour loathing. 'The whole town's been building up to it for weeks. By noon today, every zealot, doom-merchant and penny-prophet in the city will be on the streets. If your brother's fallen in with 'em, then he'll be there, somewhere.'

Stefan weighed up their objectives. Finding Mikhal was by no means their only priority. If von Diehl was still alive then a great evil was potentially at large in the city. Then there was the ambush inside the city walls to consider.

'You saw Ehrhart with the men who attacked us?' he asked Bruno.

'I can't be sure it was Ehrhart himself,' Bruno conceded. 'But if he wasn't there in person, then they were working to his orders.'

Stefan nodded, thoughtfully. 'It certainly looks that way.'

'What about the others?' Bruno added. 'Do you think they're dead?'

Stefan looked up, and momentarily closed his eyes, trying to make sense of what happened in the brief anarchy of the assault. 'I don't know,' he said at last. 'The best hope is that they were captured with von Diehl for some purpose or other.' He paused. 'Maier's a good fighter. He wouldn't let himself be taken without good reason.'

'What about Natalia? Zucharov's sister?'

Stefan fell silent. He had managed to avoid thinking about Natalia.

'I don't know,' he said. 'Things hadn't been going so well with her.'

'Ah,' Bruno said. 'I take it you told her about Alexei?'

'I did,' Stefan said. 'She didn't take it well.'

'Never tell a woman anything,' Sterkel advised. 'Unless it helps you bed her.'

'Who were you were expecting to meet by the walls?' Bruno asked.

'One of the Keepers. A man called Marcus Albrecht.'

'Albrecht?' Bruno and Sterkel spoke the name in unison. Both men sounded surprised.

'Albrecht,' Stefan repeated. 'Maier met up with him earlier. He was supposed to be there when we handed over von Diehl.'

'How long ago was this?' Bruno asked. 'When did Maier meet with Albrecht?' Stefan calculated the time that had passed between Maier first entering the city and the ambush. 'Not more than a day and a night in all.'

Bruno looked puzzled. 'That can't be right.'

'Why not?'

Sterkel stood up, scraping his chair back on the hard stone floor. 'Come and see for yourself,' he suggested.

Stefan followed his host down a dimly lit corridor to a door secured with a sturdy iron hasp. Stefan waited whilst he released the lock.

'Behold,' Sterkel announced, as the door swung open. 'Our other guest.'

The look on Marcus Albrecht's face as Stefan entered was relief mixed in equal measure with anxiety.

'Stefan!' he exclaimed. 'Thank Sigmar.' Hope flickered briefly in his eyes. 'Have you got von Diehl?' he whispered. 'The time is fast upon us. You know what I'm talking about.' He peered over Stefan's shoulder then saw Bruno standing with Sterkel in the doorway. Slowly, he fell back to a sitting position, and sank his head into his hands.

'Is it true then? Have you, too, conspired against us?'

Stefan knelt down next to Albrecht. 'No one here is against you. Look elsewhere for your conspirators.'

Albrecht shook his grey locks forcefully. 'Is there no one I can trust any more?'

'You can trust me,' Stefan said, simply. Albrecht sat up, and looked Stefan directly in the eye. 'Where is von Diehl, then? Have you brought the cultist to suffer the examination of the Keepers?'

'I brought him to Altdorf,' Stefan said. 'But we were betrayed. Ambushed. Von Diehl was taken.'

'I see,' Albrecht responded, sourly. 'And your comrades? Nagel? Maier? Zucharov? Where are they?'

'You haven't seen or spoken to Maier?'

'Of course I haven't,' Albrecht countered, irritably. 'Where are they?'

'We lost Nagel. He's dead. Maier disappeared after the ambush. Natalia, too.'

Albrecht gave a short, contemptuous cry. 'Dead. Disappeared. All of them. Disappeared, like your brother. Or dead, like my loyal Nikolas.'

'When did you last speak to your friend Ehrhart?' Stefan demanded. Albrecht stared at Stefan blankly. Gradually he grasped Stefan's meaning.

'You think that Gustav Ehrhart is behind all of this?' He threw his head back and laughed. 'Ehrhart, a schemer and a murderer?' He broke off, and ran nervous fingers through his mane of hair. 'Ridiculous,' he said. But the confidence was fading from his voice.

'It was Ehrhart who ambushed Stefan,' Bruno told him. 'You can believe that or not, as you choose. But I know what I saw. And my money says he knows where von Diehl is, as well.'

'No,' Albrecht insisted. 'I don't believe a word of it.'

'Don't? Or won't? How much closer to the truth do you need to get?' Stefan demanded.

Sterkel put his hands together and flexed his knuckles. There was an unpleasant sound of bone cracking. 'Perhaps the professor needs a little lesson?' he suggested. Stefan turned and met him square on.

'Keep off him,' he insisted. 'I'm grateful for your help. But we'll do this my way.' Sterkel shrugged as if to say it was all much the same to him. Bruno looked doubtful. 'We don't have the luxury of time,' he reminded Stefan. 'If he can get us to Ehrhart, then…'

'Everyone knows where Ehrhart will be today,' Albrecht cut in angrily. 'He will be doing his duty to the city of Altdorf.'

'The Blessing of the Souls?'

'The same,' Albrecht affirmed. 'A guard of honour for Johann Esmer, our glorious Grand Theogonist.' His features wrinkled at the name. 'Today of all days I'll have no influence over whether you got anywhere near him or not.'

Stefan took Bruno aside, out of earshot. 'I don't suppose getting to him will be easy, but at least we know where he's going to be.'

'Wherever the Grand Theogonist is going to preside over the ceremony.'

'That's easy enough, too,' Sterkel said. 'The whole lot comes to a head at the cathedral of Sigmar.'

'Then that's where we must go.'

'And Mikhal?' Bruno asked.

Stefan hesitated. 'The True Path must be involved in the Blessing of the Souls somehow. If Mikhal's with them, then there must be a chance that he will show himself today as well.' He broke off. The image of the barrels of blackpowder flashed through his mind – were there two? Three? A dozen? 'We have to find him before its too late.'

Bruno glanced back at the forlorn figure of Albrecht. 'What about him?'

Stefan weighed up the options. Leaving Albrecht locked up would be the safest and easiest thing. But his connections to Ehrhart could prove invaluable. 'Get up,' he said to Albrecht. 'You're coming with us.'

Albrecht glowered. 'You have betrayed the Keepers of the Flame,' he muttered, darkly.

'I have betrayed no one,' Stefan replied. 'And I'll deliver Heinrich von Diehl to the Keepers yet.'

OVER THE LAST few days Mikhal had lost all sense of place and time. Piece by piece, layers of his being had been stripped away to the naked core. At that core was the belief that finally he had a purpose. The lord of the True Path had explained it all. He, Mikhal, would lead the sacrifice for the greater good of all mankind. First had come rain: torrents of sorrow rushing down upon the Empire, weakening hearts and flooding the souls of men with despair. Now would come fire. The purging fire of renewal.

Where was he? Mikhal Kumansky did not know for sure. By his reckoning, he was underground, somewhere in a web of secret tunnels that spread below the heart of the city. How long he had been there, he could not say. Sometimes it felt like hours, sometimes days. Sometimes it even felt he had been there all of his life; that he knew no life other than that now destined for him. The short, glorious life of the flame that burns brightest before it dies.

The wait had been long, an age spent sitting silently in the numbing cold and the tar-black darkness. But now the wait was over. Together with his brothers in their grey robes of piety, Mikhal climbed to his feet, ready for the final journey. They were led through yet more tunnels until they came at last to a breach in a wall that led into a larger space – a cellar or underground chamber. The air was dank and chill, scented with a faint, acidic smell that Mikhal did not immediately recognise. He stood, shivering, in the darkness, and awaited his instructions.

A figure stepped forward, out of the gloom. Mikhal offered a silent prayer that this would be the lord of the True Path, but it wasn't. The shrouded figure stood a full head taller than all the others. His body exuded a smell like the cloying soil of the grave that completely obliterated the sulphurous tang that hung on the still air. Something about him seemed barely human. Instinctively, Mikhal took a step back, but the figure beckoned him with a single, claw-like finger.

'Gather to me,' he whispered, 'and hear what shall come to pass.'

The voice was parched and dry like dust from the bed of a long-dead ocean. Mikhal shivered to hear it, but knew that he had no choice other than to obey. This was the voice of his master now.

Bricks were dislodged from the wall at the far end of the room. Gradually a recess was revealed, a hiding place, and inside it something covered over with a thick blanket of oilskin. The gaunt, whey-faced figure took hold of the covering and lifted it free. Mikhal stared at the neat stack of barrels underneath. Even in the poor light of the cellar he could discern the markings etched on the side of the casks. The words 'Imperial Armoury – Nuln' scored deep into his mind. The air filled once more with a sharp, acidic scent. This was his doing, he told himself. The real-isation filled him with a delicious horror.

'Hear me,' the voice rang out. 'One shall now be cho-sen for the greatest honour of all. The honour of being the catalyst of the great transformation.' He held an object aloft: a flint-wheel attached to a short wooden stock. Now Mikhal saw the cotton fuses protruding from each of the barrels, and understood.

'One amongst you will strike a blow that will resonate across all time.' The pale, sepulchral face scanned the faces of the disciples. 'Who shall it be?'

Mikhal's heart pounded. He was seized by a terrible fear, a freezing terror set deep in all his bones. He could neither move nor speak. But he was not required to. The question had been rhetorical. The master moved along the line; dead, black-bead eyes reading each of the faces, and came to rest in front of Mikhal Kumansky.

'It shall be you,' he said.

* * *

ALTDORF LOOKED READY to burst at the seams. Every street, from the narrowest thoroughfare to the broadest of the grand avenues, teemed with human life of all shapes and kinds. The people had taken to the streets in their thousands – students and merchants; clerks and traders; hawkers, peddlers and pot-boys; all of them converging upon a single point, the gilded spires of the cathedral of Sigmar. Some had come in hope – hope that the fires of war had finally burned themselves out, hope that they were at the dawn of a new and lasting peace. Others had come in trepidation. For them, the doomsayers had spoken true, and the war raging to the north was but the overture to a far darker age about to dawn.

Whatever their hopes or fears, all had been drawn this day towards the Blessing of the Souls. Today would be a day for prayer, and a day for feasting. A day to mark a new beginning, or else the beginning of the end.

Stefan and Bruno struggled through the milling crowds, with Marcus Albrecht wedged securely between them. Stefan no longer knew for sure whether Albrecht was ally or enemy, but right now he needed him. One way or the other, they were going to get to the truth.

Men of the watch mingled with the crowds. Some marshalled the flow of pilgrims, others simply watched. Their business might have been the Blessing of the Souls, but it was equally likely that they were on the look out. Looking for Stefan, possibly. Looking for Albrecht, probably. They were certainly looking for Bruno. More than once, they had to take refuge in an alleyway to avoid a patrol that threaded through the crowd.

Caution cost them time. Progress towards the cathedral square was slow, and laborious. But, gradually, they were getting closer to their destination, three anonymous men lost amongst the crowds. But they did not go entirely unobserved. Unseen by either Stefan or Bruno, someone else was watching as the three men crossed the intersection between Landstrasse and Grand Allee. As they turned into the avenue, towards the golden domes of the cathedral, the solitary figure slipped into the slow-moving stream of pilgrims some twenty feet behind, and followed in their wake.

THEY REACHED THE great square just as the cathedral bells struck twelve. The chimes rang out across the city, calling the people to prayer. An expectant silence fell on the crowds that massed in the square. All eyes turned to the high doors of the cathedral. A sea of bodies stood between Stefan and the cathedral steps. Many were already drunk, others simply intoxicated by the occasion itself. Months of anxious uncertainty were now being channelled into one, momentous day. For every face that was wreathed in smiles, Stefan saw another etched with anxiety, fear or pain. It was a volatile, combustible gathering, one that could easily be roused to a frenzy, an explosion of joy, or of rage.

A shadow fell across the crowd. Stefan turned his eyes skywards. The day had dawned clear and bright, an emblem of the hope born with the turning seasons. But now as he looked up, he saw storm clouds gathering above the city, damping the light. He shivered involuntarily, his body registering the sudden drop in temperature. He hoped that this was not a day for omens.

He scanned the crowd, looking for the grey robes of the True Path. If they were set upon causing some ill, then today would provide the ideal opportunity. Stefan saw plenty dressed in grey, too many. Probably half the people packed into the square were swaddled in heavy grey. The chances of picking out any of the zealots, let alone Mikhal, were slim. He would have to hope the True Path showed their hand.

He nudged Bruno. 'Come on. Let's try and get closer to the cathedral.'

'I can't see the point to this,' Albrecht complained. 'This is the last place von Diehl would be.'

'Maybe,' Stefan agreed. 'But we know we'll find Ehrhart here. And he's the one with the answers. By Sigmar, I'll swear he is.' He started to fight his way through the mass of bodies ahead of them. The atmosphere in the cathedral square was already approaching pandemonium, fear and excitement fuelling a frenzy amongst the crowd. Most of the pilgrims were oblivious to Stefan's presence, and few were minded to make way for the three men trying to pick a path through the seething mass. Stefan and Bruno stuck to their task with a dogged determination, edging slowly ever closer to the towering edifice of the cathedral.

They were still some twenty yards from the front of the crowd when the carved wooden doors started to open. A line of men clad in the red livery of Sigmar filed out, and mounted a guard across the entrance to the podium. A fanfare sounded, and a commotion broke out as a figure, decked from head to toe in purest white, stepped out onto the balcony above the cathedral steps. Johann Esmer, Grand Theogonist of all Altdorf turned towards his people.

A surge of raw anticipation rippled through the crowd, then died away as the figure in white lifted his hands to call for silence. Esmer looked oddly small and insignificant on top of the steps in front of the mighty cathedral; just one more mortal caught up in the eternal struggle between the darkness and the light.

But when the Grand Theogonist finally began to speak, it was with a confidence born of absolute authority: this was a man comfortable with the reins of governance. At that moment Stefan became convinced that it was Esmer who was the True Path's target that day.

'People of Altdorf!' The noise from the crowd ebbed away. 'People of Altdorf! Give humble thanks for the blessing of Sigmar!'

All across the great square, pilgrims began to fall to their knees in supplication. Stefan could feel the tangible presence of the Grand Theogonist amongst the crowd. All doubts, all misgivings were suddenly forgotten. Johann Esmer held the people in his hands; his was the absolute, undeniable power. Bruno kneeled and Stefan joined him. Marcus Albrecht hesitated a few moments before kneeling too. Held by the majesty of the moment, the people of Altdorf waited in silence upon the words of the Grand Theogonist.

The skies over the square darkened. Above the silence of the crowd a muted rumbling could be heard, like the distant echo of violent battle. A storm was coming. The Grand Theogonist looked up at the gathering clouds, momentarily awed by the presence of greater gods. He raised both arms high, as if to push away the oppressive clouds, and banish the storm.

'Brothers and sisters we are gathered here as one in the holy sight of almighty Sigmar.' Everything in the square was still, save the flags and pennants that fluttered in the mounting breeze.

'Long have you laboured in the dread shadow of war. You have known loss, and you have lived with grief. You have borne your sufferings with the fortitude of faith. Now all those shadows will soon be banished. Soon all your suffering will be at an end.'

A cheer went up from somewhere in the crowd, and then another. Stefan heard a woman weeping nearby, shedding tears of joyous relief. Encouraged, the Grand Theogonist warmed to his theme.

'Our great victory will be won through the courage in your own hearts, and through the wisdom and guidance of the church of almighty Sigmar. Open your souls to his blessing, my people! Give thanks for deliverance from out of the shadows!'

More cheers rang out, accompanied by shouts and a scattering of applause. The mood of the crowd, so volatile only minutes before, began to swing towards joyous celebration. Then a single voice, clear and strident, rang out from somewhere amidst the crowd.

'There should be no thanks given today. Today is the beginning of all ending!'

Countless heads, Stefan's included, turned to try and identify the speaker. From the balcony, armed guards moved into the crowd, intent on rooting out the voice of dissent. But as the guards pushed down the cathedral steps, a second voice rang out from somewhere further across the square.

'I have ridden this day from the battlefields,' the voice shouted. 'Battlefields that creep closer with every day that passes. I tell you the war is being lost!'

The words were greeted with a mixture of confusion and disbelief from the crowd. The more steadfast believers could be heard calling for the traitors to be hauled out and punished, urging their fellow pilgrims to ignore the words of heresy. But the voices of dissent were multiplying.

'I tell you, Middenheim is lost!' a third now called out. 'The enemy has turned his vengeful eyes upon us. It's not prayers of thanks we should be giving. We must pray to Morr for mercy in the next world, for we shall be granted none in this!'

Johann Esmer took a step back, visible disbelief on his face. The words were greeted with stunned silence around the square. A few spoke up; men who'd been at the front recently and knew that Middenheim had not fallen. But they sounded tentative, unconvinced and unconvincing. The heavy skies groaned as the winds began to whip across the cathedral square.

Then yet another voice, equally strident and clear, shouted out from the back of the crowd.

'We're condemned to die! I claim sanctuary in the house of Sigmar!'

Stefan looked around, again trying to see who had spoken. A figure standing a few paces to his rear looked quickly away. But Stefan did not register it; his attention was fixed on the crowds at the edge of the square. Streams of people were still pushing forward, compressing the numbers gathered before the cathedral into an ever-tighter space. Another voice cried out, claiming the same right to sanctuary. This time Stefan identified the ash-grey robes of the True Path.

'Sanctuary! I claim sanctuary within the Temple of Sigmar!'

A crack of thunder split the air. The people looked up, momentarily absorbed by this elemental distraction. Rain began to fall, dropping like heavy jewels from the pregnant clouds above the square. Daylight dimmed to a dull, unyielding grey. From out of the darkness, lightning arced across the Altdorf sky, a single jagged fork tracing a path towards the spires of the cathedral. The bolt missed the cathedral by a matter of feet and struck the wall of the adjacent Imperial barracks. A statue of Sigmar that overlooked the square exploded, showering the nearby crowd with shards of shattered stone. As the dust cleared, the screaming began. Everywhere now the voices could be heard.

'It is beginning! The Dark Lords are at the walls!'

'Sanctuary! I claim sanctuary in the temple of Sigmar!'

As the lightning forked again, a wave of sudden movement spread through the crowd, a panic-fuelled surge towards the steps of the cathedral. Hundreds now took up the cry for sanctuary. Men and women lost their footing in the rush. Children were plucked into the arms of parents or else risked being trampled underfoot. Stefan felt the crush of bodies all around him, sheer pressure pushing him forward.

'Taal's breath!' he shouted. 'They'll start a riot.'

Bruno turned side on to set his sturdy shoulders against the onward rush. He was a strong man, but even he could not hold his ground. 'There's only one place they can go,' he shouted back. 'Into the cathedral itself!'

The mood of the crowd had been utterly transformed. Hope, so fragile in its nurturing, had been shattered in a few brief moments. Johann Esmer took one look at the human wave surging towards the cathedral steps and retreated, leaving the red-liveried guard to protect the holy shrine. Two of the guardsmen tried to close the doors, but the first of the pilgrims had already reached the top of steps. More followed, rushing towards the imagined safety of the cathedral. Utterly wrong-footed, the guard were being overwhelmed.

Stefan took hold of Albrecht and pushed on. 'Come on,' he said. 'We've got to get up there before they storm the cathedral.'

Albrecht protested but there was little he could do to stop himself being carried forward. 'Are you mad?' he exclaimed. 'The temple's the last place we want to be!'

Stefan drew out his sword, and held it close down by his side. 'Maybe so,' he said, 'but people are going to die unless we do something.' He turned to Bruno. 'Keep close by Albrecht. Don't lose him.'

He fought his way through, elbowing aside the pilgrims who poured toward the steps. Dozens, maybe more, had already taken refuge in the holy shrine. Unless someone acted now, the dozens would soon become hundreds. In a sudden moment of chilling clarity, Stefan saw where the cargo of blackpowder had been bound. The pilgrims were stampeding towards their death.

With one last leap, he ascended the platform and turned to confront the ranks of angry, fearful faces massing behind him. He lifted his sword above his head, in plain view.

'Listen to me!' his words were at first lost amidst the din and confusion, but those nearest the top of the steps pulled up at the sight of the tall swordsman blocking their path.

'Listen to me,' Stefan repeated. 'There will be no war here. Middenheim has not fallen.' The thunder echoed ominously above his head. Rain began to hammer down. Stefan raised his gaze to the sky then turned back towards the tumult in the square below. 'This is a storm, nothing more,' he shouted. He had to bellow against the roaring wind with all the strength he could muster. 'Like all adversity, it will pass. It is no omen. You have nothing to fear.'

'Who are you to know?' an anonymous voice demanded.

Stefan stared out into the sea of faces, trying to find his interrogator. It could have been any one of the thousand, but at least he had their attention now.

'I'm a man who's seen more of war and ill-fortune in a few short years than many of you will know in a lifetime.' He raised the sword higher, and turned it slowly in an arc. Rain spattered the polished steel.

'I promise you that war is not coming to Altdorf,' he said. 'There is no cause for any of you to seek sanctuary.

And I promise too that I'll kill any man who tries to pass me here.' He looked down. His eyes made direct contact with those closest to him.

'Which of you will be the first?'

For a moment the threat was still potent. Possessed of the will, they could have rushed him en masse, and driven him aside. But the moment passed. One by one, the pilgrims averted their gaze and looked away. Some even tried to back off, and retreated clumsily down the steps into the thick of the crowd. That was when Stefan knew he had won. For now ar least, the tide had been stemmed.

He turned quickly to the men guarding the steps. 'Let us through,' he commanded. 'Then bar these doors, before any more of them get inside. Hurry.'

The guardsmen eyed one other, confused, uncertain what was expected of them. Stefan lifted his sword again leaving them in no doubt he was ready to use it.

'We have urgent business with the Grand Theogonist,' he snapped. 'Now, in Sigmar's name, let us pass!'

CHAPTER TWENTY-TWO
Then Will Come Fire

PERHAPS AS MANY as a hundred pilgrims had managed to
fight their way into the cathedral, enough to hide the
fanatics of the True Path as they went about their
ungodly business. If the zealots had managed to get
inside then they had to be found, and fast. But the
labyrinthine palace was a place of shadows: countless
dark places where a man could hide. The whole place
would need to be searched, from top to bottom.

Stefan, Bruno and Albrecht stepped beneath the high-
vaulted ceilings of the cathedral, to find themselves
surrounded by people in the throes of a kind of madness. Having reached their imagined sanctuary, most of
the pilgrims now had no idea what they should do.
Some prostrated themselves, wailing upon the ground,
offering prayers for salvation. Some ran babbling from
room to gilded room, awed by the majesty that few
common men were allowed to see. Others still sought to

turn ill fortune into opportunity and began a looting spree.

All of them presented an urgent and unexpected problem for the overwhelmed men of the cathedral guard. Stefan grabbed hold of one harassed-looking guardsmen as he sped past. The man spun round angrily. The insignia on his shoulders announced him as a ranking officer of the cathedral guard. He gestured at Stefan with his sword.

'You must leave at once,' he insisted. 'It is strictly forbidden to enter this place without the blessing of the Grand Theogonist.'

Calmly, Bruno locked his arm around the guardsman's wrist to relieve him of the sword. 'It's a bit late for that, don't you think?'

The guard stood facing Bruno, his eyes bulging. He had the look of an honest, simple man, dogged but limited.

'If I hadn't managed to stop the crowd on the cathedral steps, you'd have had a thousand pilgrims set loose in here by now,' Stefan told him.

The guardsman searched his ordered mind for a suitable riposte, but found none. He was out of his depth.

'Listen to me,' Stefan went on, firmly. 'There could be people inside the cathedral who mean to do serious harm. We have to find them before they do. Understand?'

The guard shook his head, a firm, instinctive gesture of denial. 'For all I know you're one of them,' he said. 'You're leaving, now.' He reached for his sword, momentarily forgetting that Bruno had already taken it.

Stefan stayed the man's hand. 'If that were so I'd hardly have risked my life to stem the flood of lunatics bent on getting in here, would I?'

The guardsman grappled with the paradox then gave up the struggle. He stared at the pandemonium all around him, bewildered and defeated.

'The first thing you have to do is round up these people and get them out of the cathedral. We can help you. Then the cathedral must be searched, every inch of it. Do you understand?'

The guard's frozen features came alive, and he nodded, vigorously. 'Good,' Stefan said. 'The final thing is that we must have an audience with the Grand Theogonist. Now.'

'That's impossible,' the guard protested. 'No one can see the Grand Theogonist without–'

'Then make it possible,' Stefan said. 'Or find someone who can.' Bruno levelled the point of the sword at the man's face. The officer nodded, glumly.

'I'll see what I can do,' he said.

'That's more like it,' Stefan said, encouragingly. 'Meanwhile, we'll see what can be done to clear up this mess.'

The guard hurried off on his assignment, leaving them in the cavernous vestibule of the cathedral.

'The sooner these people are out of here the better,' Stefan commented. He glanced at Albrecht. 'Are you with us?'

Albrecht glowered back at him. 'Do I have a choice?'

'You can stand here, and have Bruno guard you. Which is a waste of two good men. Or you can work with us, in the service of Altdorf.'

'I never served any other cause,' Albrecht replied, stiffly. He held out his hand. 'Give me a sword.' Stefan looked to Bruno, and nodded.

'Listen to me,' he said to both of them. 'No more innocent blood should be spilled this day, not on our account at least. Let's move these people out unharmed, if we can.'

Fuelled by excitement or fear, the pilgrims inside the cathedral represented a threat of sorts, but most were a danger only to themselves. Stefan waded into their midst with his sword drawn, hoping that the threat of his blade would prove to be persuasion enough. By and large, it was. Wailing pilgrims were brought to their feet and dragged off by the scruff of their neck. Would-be looters were interrupted before they could reach anything of value. Flagellants whipping themselves in pious fury beneath an effigy of Sigmar were robbed of their bloodied flails, and bundled unceremoniously towards the doors. Most of the pilgrims surrendered without much of a fight.

Gradually, the cathedral guard was regaining the upper hand. Thirty, forty and finally more than fifty men and women were counted out through the gates. At length, something resembling calm returned to the holy place. The inside of the cathedral seemed suddenly very quiet; a vast stillness disturbed only by the slow spiralling motes of dust, trapped in beams of penetrating sunlight. Stefan gazed around at the finely carved statues of Sigmar set at intervals around the walls. The carvings depicted the young God-Emperor in the thick of battle, victorious and triumphant against the hordes of Chaos. The images were overpowering; so certain, so confident. Order was being restored. It seemed impossible that the Empire could ever be defeated.

He looked round at the sound of footsteps approaching rapidly along the passageway. The officer of the guard was back.

'I'm sorry,' he said. 'But an audience with the Grand Theogonist will not be possible.' He sounded nervous, as though he had uncovered something unexpected.

'Why's that?' Bruno demanded.

The officer's face flushed a deep red. 'I cannot say.'

'Not good enough,' Stefan told him. 'The Grand Theogonist's life may be in danger. Do you want that on your conscience?'

The man started to shake. 'All I'm authorised to tell you,' he stammered, 'is that his excellence the Grand Theogonist has been taken to a temporary place of safety.'

'Taken where? By whom?'

Marcus Albrecht had been looking on in silence. Now he stepped forward to confront the guard. 'Taken by the commander of the east watch? By a man by the name of Gustav Ehrhart, perhaps?'

The officer paled and averted his gaze. His silence told them all they needed.

'Merciful Sigmar,' Albrecht muttered. 'Could I truly have been so blind?'

'What about the search of the building?' Bruno asked.

Now the officer was on firmer ground. 'Nothing so far,' he said, confidently. 'We've rounded up a few stragglers, but we'll probably just put them back out on the street. We're not done yet, but I'm confident that there's nothing untoward here.'

'It seems almost too easy,' Bruno commented. 'But at least we can concentrate on finding Ehrhart.'

'Maybe,' Stefan said. Something wasn't right. It had been far too easy. 'You're sure the search has turned up nothing?' he asked again. 'How much of the cathedral remains unchecked?'

'Only the upper chambers,' the officer told him. 'And those are well guarded. No one could have got that far without being seen. There's nothing else, except for…'

'Except for what?'

'Except for the vaults underneath the cathedral. But we've checked the locks on all the outer doors. None have been tampered with. No one's been down there in a while.'

Stefan hesitated. Something in the cathedral wasn't right. The near-riot in the square had been no accident.

The True Path had started the stampede in order to force as many people into or near to the cathedral as possible. Why? There had to be a reason. An image of the *Karla* came into his mind, the ships hold lined with the barrels of blackpowder.

'Take us down to the vaults,' he said, firmly.

'But the locks are intact,' the officer said. 'It's quite impossible to–'

'I don't care what's possible or impossible,' Stefan shot back. 'Just take us there.'

STEFAN SOON REALISED that searching the vaults would be no easy task. There were at least half a dozen passages leading off the single stairway that wound its way below stairs and off each of those passages were at least a dozen more bolted doors. The place was one vast maze of rooms and inter-connecting tunnels. It would take hours, if not days, to search them all properly. Time that they did not have.

'How many rooms are there down there?' Stefan asked.

'Thirty,' the guard replied. 'Maybe more.'

Stefan had to think quickly. There might be time to search a handful of rooms at most. He had to choose, and choose well.

'Listen,' he said to the guard. 'If I wanted to set a charge to cause some real damage to the cathedral, where would I place it?'

The guard eyed him suspiciously. Marcus Albrecht seized hold of the guard's arm. 'In the name of Sigmar, answer him man! The fate of all Altdorf may rest on your answer.'

It was enough to shock the guard into a response. 'There's one large chamber, right in the heart of the vaults,' he said at last. 'It's right under the cathedral tower. Destroy that, and Sigmar only knows what might happen.'

'Take us there,' Stefan demanded.

'But we've already checked the doors,' the man assured him. 'Not a soul has been down there in weeks.'

'Take us there,' Stefan repeated. 'Now.'

The guard led the way through a series of passages until they came to a set of iron doors leading to the largest and most central of the subterranean chambers. The likeness of the gods Taal and Ulric stared out from the face of the doors, stern guardians of the underworld.

'It was once used as a chapel,' the guard explained. 'But there's nothing of value down there now.' He stood back so Stefan could take a closer look. 'See what I mean. The seals are intact.'

Stefan looked. The doors were locked shut, and secure. Judging by the curtains of cobwebs over the entrance and the red rust coating the locks, they hadn't been opened for a while.

Time was running out. How critical might these few minutes prove when it came to tracking down Ehrhart and the Grand Theogonist? But the True Path had been targeting the cathedral, he was certain of that. There had to be something, somewhere, that they hadn't found.

At his insistence, two guardsmen set to work prising the corroded metal locks apart, releasing the studded iron doors. The doors cracked open and swung back with a dry, rasping sound. A waft of air, as stale as the grave, drifted up from the chamber below. Inside the vault, only darkness.

The officer shot Stefan a querulous glance. 'Satisfied?'

Stefan took the lamp from his hand. 'No,' he replied. 'Now we search.'

He started down the cobwebbed stairs, Bruno and Albrecht close behind. The officer followed with six of his men, more concerned with guarding them than offering any support.

Within a few minutes Stefan had reached the bottom, and was standing on level ground inside the dank, low-ceilinged chamber. It was ice-cold and utterly dark, save for the fitful flicker of the oil lamp.

It seemed the guard had been right. Stefan's gamble had revealed nothing. He was just about to turn back when he heard a faint sound: a cough, or was it dry laughter coming from one darkened corner? He spun around with the lamp. The sound had come from a figure not ten feet away from him: a grey-faced apparition with eyes like cold, glass beads set in a grey, waxen face. But it wasn't the sight of the mutant that held Stefan transfixed with horror. Nor was it the four other creatures lurking nearby. It was the mutant's human companion who stood attendant, at his side.

Even in the half-light Stefan could not mistake his brother. Mikhal stared back at Stefan, or rather, seemed to stare through him, as if trying to make out a half-glimpsed vision in the far distance. For one long moment, the two brothers faced each other like statues in a tableau.

As his eyes grew used to the light, Stefan took in the rest of the picture. He saw the flintlock held in Mikhal's outstretched hand. He saw the breach in the wall, where the tunnellers had broken through, and he saw the stack of barrels, with their insignia and their short, cotton-wad fuses. The pieces of the puzzle fell together. The truth outstripped even his worst dreams. The mutant gang master read the dismay on Stefan's face. His pallid face cracked open in a huge, yellow-fanged grin.

'Sigmar save us,' Bruno whispered in horror. 'There's enough blackpowder here to blow us to the gates of Morr.'

Slowly, Stefan reached back and handed him the lamp. He held up his hand to stop the guardsmen behind him from advancing any further. His eyes were locked on Mikhal. Mikhal returned his gaze, blank and unseeing, the flintlock clenched in his right hand, inches from the nearest fuse. The mutant leader seemed in no hurry. Indeed, Stefan had the overwhelming sense that he had wanted him to find them, to see Mikhal before the final, terrible act was played out.

'Mikhal,' Stefan said. 'It's Stefan. Your brother. You must put that thing down. Now.'

'Don't make any sudden movements,' Albrecht cautioned. 'One spark and we're all dead men!'

The mutants edged forward towards the stack of barrels, but fell back at the sight of the armed guards with their torches. Mikhal stood oblivious to all of them. He seemed to hear only one voice. The voice of his mutant master.

'Do it!' the creature now commanded him. 'Let the sacrifice begin!'

'Mikhal!' Stefan tried to keep his voice calm and measured, but inside his heart was pounding like a furious drum. 'If you set a flame to those barrels, countless people will die. Good people. Innocent people.'

He took a step forward. As if to mirror him, the mutants stole a little closer to Mikhal, and the deadly cargo.

Mikhal turned towards the barrels, with the thumb of his right hand braced against the wheel of the flintlock.

'Stop!' Stefan beseeched him. 'I swear, if I have to kill you to stop this deed, then, Sigmar save me, I shall.'

Mikhal touched the flintlock to the stub of the fuse. He paused and looked up. For the first time, his eyes made real contact with Stefan. Stefan could see the faint outline of the scar upon Mikhal's wrist, the scar made by the mutant's knife, more than fifteen long summers past. Mikhal gazed down at the faint, snaking line that creased his flesh.

'First came rain,' he mumbled. 'Now will come fire.'

Stefan ripped back the tunic covering his arm to reveal the mark that the self same weapon had made upon him. 'Mikhal, this isn't the mark of Chaos! This is what marks us *apart* from evil! It's what we've struggled for all of our lives!'

'Do it!' the mutant repeated. There was urgency in that dust-dry voice now. 'Light the flame!'

Mikhal Kumansky reached out towards the nearest of the barrels then stopped. He turned towards his brother. He smiled briefly, and a look of recognition flickered in his weary eyes. 'Stefan,' he muttered. 'Taal and Ulric, I'm so tired.'

He took a half step away from the stack of barrels, towards Stefan. As he did so, the mutant standing behind him snatched the flintlock from his hand. Stefan leapt forward to pull his brother to safety, but he was too late. The knife-blade flashed briefly in the mutant's hand before the creature buried it deep in Mikhal's side.

Mikhal fell without crying out, or even giving as much as a sigh. The expression on his face was almost peaceful. Stefan caught him as he crumpled to the ground, cushioning his body as he fell. All around them was a blur of movement now. As the mutants rushed forward, Bruno and the guardsmen fell upon them in a vengeful fury.

The gang master made one last desperate attempt to light the fuse. Sparks sprang from the flintlock, but the flame did not take. There would be no second chance. Bruno knocked the flint from the mutant's grip and drove at him with his sword. Lithe as a serpent, the mutant swerved aside from the blow, and struck back, stabbing at his heart with the already bloodied knife.

Bruno parried the blade and caught hold of the mutant's wrist as he moved to strike again. The mutant was surprisingly strong, but Bruno would prove the stronger. He slammed the hooded figure back hard against the wall of the chamber. The creature snarled with rage and lashed out, opening its guard. Bruno took his chance and threw his weight behind a savage two-handed strike. His blade tore into the mutant's body, all but cutting it in two. A foul stench flooded the vault as the mutant buckled and fell.

The rest of the mutants fought like wild beasts, but their madness was no match for the superior numbers bearing down on them now. The cathedral guard killed three outright and Albrecht claimed the other, wielding his sword with a speed and agility that belied his years. It was over in a matter of moments. There would be no inferno now.

Mikhal's grey robe was stained a deep red, a ruby bloom spreading from the wound to his belly. Stefan clung tight to his brother, numb with disbelief.

'By all that's holy,' he whispered. 'How did things ever come to this?'

Mikhal's glazed eyes rested on his brother. His words came in bursts, interspersed with sharp, painful breaths. 'I thought I'd seen the light of salvation, Stefan,' he said. 'May Sigmar forgive me for being such a fool.' He broke off, and forced a smile. His body was crippled, but a weight seemed to have lifted from his soul.

'I couldn't have… made more of a wreck of… things if I'd tried,' he gasped.

'You turned back to the light when it mattered most,' Stefan told him. 'In the end, your spirit held.'

Mikhal's eyes started to close. His breathing slowed. 'You'll have all that's left of the business.' He smiled again, ruefully. 'Sadly not the *Karla*, though.'

'I'll not have anything,' Stefan said, firmly. 'You're not for the kingdom of Morr, not for many a year yet.'

'Stefan.' it was Bruno. 'If you want to stay here with Mikhal, I'll go on with Albrecht and find Ehrhart.'

'I can't let you do that,' Stefan said. 'If Ehrhart's involved with von Diehl, then that's something I have to deal with.'

'What about Mikhal?'

Mikhal's breathing had steadied. He seemed to have rallied a little.

'How are you feeling?' Stefan asked. Mikhal forced another smile. 'Better, I swear.' He sat up, with obvious difficulty. 'You must go,' he told Stefan. 'There's nothing more you can do for me. I mean…' he winced suddenly, as a spasm of pain took him. 'You're right. I'm not for the next world yet. I'll be fine.'

Stefan hesitated. If there ever was a time when he needed to be in two places, then this was it. But he was a fighter, not a healer. There was little he could do for Mikhal that others couldn't do better.

'Should I stay with him, then?' Bruno asked.

'Wait a moment.' Stefan looked about, and found the officer of the guard. 'Is there a surgeon who can tend to him?'

The officer looked doubtful. 'This man has plotted against the Empire. By rights he should…'

Stefan didn't have time for argument. 'Look,' he interrupted. 'I need you to do what you can for him. Your master's safety is my priority now. Once that's assured, then the Grand Theogonist can pass judgement on Mikhal's deeds.'

The guard nodded, apparently content. 'We'll do what we can.'

Stefan turned to Bruno. 'I need you with me, old friend. You too,' he said to Albrecht.

He knelt down at his brother's side. 'Like you, I've started something that has to be finished,' he said. 'But I'll be back, I promise you.'

'I'll be fine,' Mikhal said.

Stefan eased his hand behind Mikhal's head. 'The cathedral guard have sent for a surgeon,' he explained. 'You'll be well on the way to recovery by the time I return.'

'Beloved brother,' Mikhal murmured. 'Do what must be done. And make sure you do return.'

'I shall,' Stefan said. 'I promise you, I shall.'

OUTSIDE, THE GREAT square was still in turmoil. The storm had eased, but the earlier panic had taken its toll. The remaining pilgrims were wandering amongst the debris of bodies and fallen masonry, searching for loved ones, or else plundering from the dazed or dead. Twenty or more had lost their lives in a few minutes of madness. The grey-robed zealots had melted away, or had been taken by the city militia. Slowly but surely, the rule of law was being restored.

As they picked their way across the carnage, Stefan was feeling increasingly uneasy, fearful, and not just for Mikhal's sake. This was a victory that had been too cheaply won.

'This isn't over yet,' he told Bruno. 'Not until we know what happened to Johann Esmer. And what happened to von Diehl and the others, for that matter.'

'Then we must find a way into the offices of the east watch,' Bruno suggested.

Albrecht shook his head. 'Esmer won't have gone there – not unless you're mistaken and Ehrhart's purpose is honest. My bet would be that the Grand Theogonist is a guest at Ehrhart's own residence.'

'I know the place,' Bruno cut in. 'It's not so far.'

Stefan held him back. 'Wait a moment,' he said. 'Let's think this through. Ehrhart will have men posted outside. We'll have to find a way in.'

'That shouldn't be difficult,' Albrecht observed. 'I suspect that Gustav will want to see me, one way or the other.'

Stefan frowned. 'That doesn't mean that we won't still have a battle on our hands, sooner or later. How well do you know your friend Sterkel?' he asked Bruno.

'Well enough.'

'Can he be trusted?'

Bruno shrugged. 'Line his pockets with silver and he's as trustworthy as anyone,' he said. 'And he's certainly got little love for Ehrhart or his people.'

'Good,' said Stefan. 'In that case, go and find Sterkel. Have him muster as many men as possible, and bring them to Ehrhart's mansion. With any luck, I'll be waiting for you at the gates – with some company.'

'And if luck is against you?'

'Then get inside, by any means possible. Don't wait for an invitation.'

FROM OUTSIDE, THE house with its high perimeter wall and solid iron gates was much like any other home in the wealthy merchant quarter of the city. Imposing, threatening, perhaps in its way, but hardly sinister. The tall, barred gates of the Ehrhart mansion lay open as the two men approached. Stefan and Albrecht slowed their pace. For a moment it seemed as though their entrance was to be no more than a stroll through the portals and into the house itself. Then, when they were just a few feet from the gates, two guards emerged, one from either side, their swords drawn.

'State your business,' the first said. 'Or else turn about.'

Albrecht drew a slim, wax-embossed scroll from inside the pocket of his coat. 'My name is Marcus Albrecht,' he said. 'This will announce me to your master. He will wish to see me at once.'

'And him?' the guard demanded, meaning Stefan.

'He is here with me,' Albrecht explained. 'On the same business.'

The guard grunted. He opened the scroll, and examined its contents, particularly the seal. He ran an eye over Albrecht, and appeared satisfied.

'Follow me,' he said, flatly.

Stefan exchanged wary glances with Albrecht. But he wasn't going to pass up a chance like this to gain entry to the house. Whatever faced them on the inside was another matter.

As they passed through the gates, other armed men wearing the uniform of the east watch appeared to escort them in. They were marched up a long, smooth-paved drive towards the house. Stefan gazed around, taking in the opulent surroundings. It was in houses like these, with their manicured lawns and their tall-plumed fountains, that great matters of state were decided. Where deals were brokered and struck, where the arguments of history were resolved. The place stank of wealth and of power.

'Hardly a house brought low by the deprivations of war,' Stefan remarked.

'Ehrhart has done well enough,' Albrecht agreed. He lowered his voice. 'But that doesn't make him a traitor.'

The main house loomed ahead, a handsome, white-painted facade fronted by marble pillars and statues of the God-Emperor Sigmar. Stefan and Albrecht were taken inside, and shown up a carpeted flight of stairs to a large reception area. There they were invited to wait. Stefan sat in a deep, upholstered chair and stared at the plaster walls with their elaborate motifs in embossed gold leaf; at the elegant portraits painted in oils. Everything spoke of refinement and of impeccable taste. It was starting to feel unreal.

After a few moments the doors to the main salon were opened and a footman appeared. He wore the livery of a man in waiting, but a polished sword hung conspicuously at his side. 'Commander Ehrhart sends his apologies for keeping you waiting,' the man announced. 'He asks if you would join him now.'

Stefan followed Albrecht towards the salon. The room was dark after the brightly lit reception. As the doors clicked closed behind them, the wick of a lamp was turned up, infusing the room with a soft amber glow.

'Ah! At last. Our visitors. Master, this is Marcus Albrecht, my old companion and associate. Stefan Kumansky, I think, you already know.'

Stefan now recognised the man who had spoken as Gustav Ehrhart. But his gaze was drawn not to the commander, but to the figure seated immediately to his right. The man that he had just addressed as 'master'.

The face was fuller, and the body sturdier and more thickly muscled. Where before the hair had been thinning and peppered with grey, now it was a sleek, glossy black. But, altered or not, there was no mistaking his identity. Heinrich von Diehl beamed at Stefan; the smile of a man greeting a long lost friend.

'You see?' he said to Ehrhart. 'I know this man. I told you he wouldn't disappoint us.'

CHAPTER TWENTY-THREE
Time of Reckoning

THE EFFECT ON Marcus Albrecht was instantaneous, and crushing. His shoulders hunched and fell, as if a great weight had fallen upon them. His face registered shock and disbelief.

This was the moment when his hopes and dreams were crushed, shattered beyond all redemption. He stared at the two men, dumbstruck. Gustav Ehrhart was savouring the moment. He chuckled, softly, and shook his mane of silver hair.

'Dear Marcus, I thought you would have guessed the truth before now. Peter Selendorf got near. Very near,' he said. 'He knew someone close to the Keepers planned to betray them. That was why I had to have him killed.' A thin, cruel smile spread across his face. 'Won't you please be seated?'

'Murdering swine,' Albrecht spat back. 'Treacherous filth.'

Stefan scanned the room. Ehrhart had it well guarded by men wearing the red insignia of the watch.

'How much did it take to buy them?' he demanded. Ehrhart waved the question away, as though it was in poor taste. 'Call it a far-sighted sense of loyalty,' he said. 'Most of the watch remain stubbornly true to our Emperor. But I have more than enough for my purposes.'

'Why you?' Stefan asked, coldly. 'Why betray every instinct of righteousness and decency you have ever known?' He looked around at the walls hung with silver and burnished gold. 'Why, when you want for nothing?'

Gustav Ehrhart shrugged, nonchalantly. 'What can I say? That I truly believe that the Old World – your world – has run its course. That the Empire has grown weak and corrupt, ripe and ready for the purge of change.'

Heinrich von Diehl purred, delightedly. 'All true.'

'All true,' Ehrhart agreed, 'but–' he laughed derisively. 'The true reason is much simpler.' He stretched, luxuriously. 'Greed, my friends. Lust for power. Chaos will sweep clean the ruins of this crumbling regime. I shall be ruler in the new order, and my power shall be absolute, unanswerable.'

'If you believe that, then you're a fool as well as a traitor,' Stefan growled. 'Chaos will grind you down for dog-meat once they're through with you. And believe me, they will be through with you.'

Von Diehl clapped his hands in delight. 'Stefan! How I've missed you. Missed your myopic vision, your tenacious scrabbling for feeble virtues of truth and valour.' His brow furrowed. 'It is a shame our reunion will be so brief. But, I promise you, it shall be worthwhile.'

'Just tell me what's happened to my people,' Stefan said. 'Or have they been murdered already?'

Von Diehl shook his head, emphatically. 'Oh no. Far from it. Mind you, I've no idea about that little trickster of yours… what was her name?'

'Natalia,' Ehrhart offered. 'Natalia Zucharov.'

'Natalia. Of course. No, I'm afraid Natalia slipped through our hands, right in the midst of our little skirmish.' Von Diehl leered at Stefan. 'I rather fear she has lost her love of you, Stefan. What could have caused such a thing?'

Stefan stared back at the cultist, cold rage in his heart.

'As for Karl Maier,' Ehrhart said. 'Shall I?'

'Please,' von Diehl affirmed.

Ehrhart went to a second door set in the far wall of the chamber, then gestured to two of the militia standing guard.

'Bring our guests here.'

The door led to a smaller, inner room, its walls covered with thick cladding. The room was lit by a single oil lamp suspended from the ceiling, and was empty save for a single, wooden-framed chair. Tied securely to the chair was Johann Esmer, Grand Theogonist of all Altdorf. Esmer's face was puffy and bruised, and a fresh wound had opened up beneath the swelling around one eye. He gazed at the newcomers with a look of a pitiful pleading.

'Stefan!' another voice called out. 'Do come in.'

Stefan turned to find himself staring at Karl Maier. Maier's face was flushed and lined with sweat. The blood smeared on his knuckles confirmed that it was he who had been delivering the beating. Maier glanced at the thickly padded walls, and flashed Stefan a cruel grin.

'He hasn't found his voice yet,' he said. 'But I'll have him singing before long.'

If the sight of Ehrhart had been the darkest moment for Albrecht, this was the point for Stefan. A crimson rage flared up inside of him. He lunged at the man, but three heavily built militia held him back. Stefan struggled ferociously, but could not break free.

'So it was all pretence,' he shouted at Maier. 'Every moment of every day, you were serving these scum.'

Maier feigned a look of surprise. 'Pretence? Not at all. Generally, our goals were one and the same. It was only at the end that our interests parted.' He shrugged. 'Sorry old fellow. At least let me commend you doing for an excellent job.'

'You disgust me,' Stefan snarled. Maier took a step back, and wiped his bloodied knuckles on his jerkin.

'Come now, Stefan,' he said. 'I was hoping you'd take it in better spirit. It's just business. Herr Ehrhart made me the better offer.' He drew out his blade, and examined it under the light of the lamp. 'We're not so different, you and I,' he reflected. 'We sell our swords for the best price we can. That's how we both live.'

Stefan would have happily spat on the other man, but his throat was as dry as dust. 'We're not alike in the least,' he responded. 'I sell my sword, if the cause is just. But you have sold your mortal soul, and long may you rot in Morr for it.'

'Don't judge Karl so harshly,' Ehrhart chided, mockingly. He gripped hold of Johann Esmer's head, skewing his face towards the light. 'Perhaps he's a little too enthusiastic about his work. But—' He knelt down so that he was eye to eye with the figure sitting bound to the chair. 'Your worthiness, if only you would tell us what we needed to know, then Karl would have no need to be so persistent.'

The Grand Theogonist stared back at him, a blank look of fear fixed in his eyes. But the fact that he hadn't given them what they wanted spoke for itself. Albrecht blanched. He looked shamed and appalled by the cruelty he'd been made to witness.

'In the name of Sigmar, let the man be,' he cried. 'Whatever you need, I'll tell you if I can. He's suffered enough.'

Ehrhart flashed a smile. 'Ah, worthy Marcus, ever helpful. But there are things which Johann Esmer alone must share with us, if our master is to convince in his new role.'

'New role?' Albrecht roared, incandescent with fury. 'What new role?'

'My new role as the Grand Theogonist of all Altdorf,' Von Diehl replied, evenly. He nodded in Stefan's direction. 'That was the true purpose for your bringing me here.'

Albrecht gave a short, bitter laugh. 'Do you think the people would be so easily fooled? You could never for a moment assume his identity.'

'I think that I can,' von Diehl demurred. His voice took on a harder, more insidious edge. 'And I believe that I shall.'

'You know,' Ehrhart chimed in, 'we should share our plans for Altdorf with you. It would be such a shame for you to die not knowing just how complicit you had both been in its demise.'

'Very shortly I shall appear before the people of Altdorf,' von Diehl announced. 'To their eyes, it will be the Grand Theogonist who stands before them. Johann Esmer will denounce the prophecies of Sigmar, scorn his works and lay bare the hollow promises of the Empire. He will sow the seeds of despair and desperation that will take root and spread like a fire through all of the city.'

'Preposterous,' Albrecht scoffed. 'Is that the sum of your grand insurrection?'

Von Diehl smiled. 'Barely the beginning. The deception may not hold for long, I grant you. But long enough for our needs, you can be assured. By then I shall have acquired the greater prize. By then we will have the Runefang.'

Stefan glanced at Albrecht. The word struck some distant resonance with him, but it had no meaning that he could immediately grasp. But Albrecht knew at once what von Diehl was talking about. His response was derisive laughter.

'The Runefang? The magical sword given to the elector count of Altdorf?' He snorted, incredulously. 'If that's your scheme then your stupidity exceeds your greed. Any fool would know the Runefang is far from Altdorf, no lesser mortal than Emperor Karl-Franz himself took it into battle. Even now he wields it upon the plains of Middenheim to serve the final annihilation of your kind.'

'Very good, Marcus,' Ehrhart murmured. 'You have studied your lore well.'

'But it isn't the Runefang of Altdorf we seek,' von Diehl continued, quietly. 'We seek its cousin, the Runefang of Solland.'

The colour drained from Albrecht's face. Contempt turned to transparent dread.

'That's right.' Von Diehl nodded in affirmation. 'The most powerful of all the twelve swords. The mighty sword that was held back, only to be used by the greatest of heroes in the direst of times.'

'It is here, somewhere in Altdorf,' Ehrhart said. 'And one way or another, we shall have it.'

'The Runefang is a force for good,' Albrecht blustered. 'It would not serve you, even if it should fall into your hands.'

'The Runefang is a force of magic,' von Diehl countered. 'And magic is an elemental force. It is amoral, it recognises both good and evil. Whoever can channel its power will reap a mighty harvest.' He paused, to let Albrecht absorb his words. 'Take my word, by the time the great Lord of Change has wrought his transformation on your sacred blade, it will do whatever we desire.'

'Altdorf will fall,' Ehrhart declared. 'It's people – already demoralised, beaten down – will be crushed like charred wheat beneath our armies' feet. And as Altdorf falls, so will the Empire. The momentum of change will be unstoppable.'

Marcus Albrecht shook his head, but now his face registered shock, not denial.

Ehrhart nodded to Johann Esmer. 'We'll leave you to your conversation. Truly, I would counsel that you choose to suffer no more. Very soon, I should remind you, there will be no honour left for you to protect.'

The guards led Stefan and Albrecht back to the main room.

'Your clumsy scheming in the cathedral came to nothing,' Stefan said, defiantly. 'What makes you think your other plans will meet with any better success?'

Ehrhart stared back, blankly. 'The cathedral was a minor part of the greater scheme. It barely matters that it was not destroyed.' He frowned. 'Once the Keepers of the Flame have gathered in Altdorf, then our great reckoning will be complete. But in that respect, Marcus, you have so far disappointed me.'

'And you shall be disappointed evermore,' Albrecht shouted back.

Ehrhart smiled, enigmatically, and glanced at von Diehl. 'We can afford to be patient a while yet, I'm sure.'

'Time enough yet,' von Diehl concurred. 'Time enough for the Keepers to first be damned, and then utterly destroyed.'

There was a knock at the outer door. A messenger stepped in. Ehrhart looked vexed at being disturbed, but as he listened to the news his expression changed. If before he had seemed self-satisfied, now he positively glowed. He muttered a few words in reply. The messenger stood to attention, waiting.

'Well,' Ehrhart declared. 'This is indeed a blessed day. It seems that we have your lost comrade as well. Our dear little magician was found wandering like a lost soul, not a stone's throw from the gates.'

'Natalia?' the name was on Stefan's lips before he could help himself. He prayed to Sigmar that it were not so, but he could see at once from the commander's demeanour that it was true. 'She has nothing to do with this, Ehrhart,' he snapped. 'Let her go free.'

'It's true we hadn't put any great store by her capture,' Ehrhart said. 'But, having fallen like a ripe fruit into our laps, it would seem churlish not to take advantage, would it not, master?'

'Indeed,' von Diehl replied.

Ehrhart clapped his hands, briskly. 'Have the man who took her bring her here.'

There wasn't long to wait. A few minutes later the doors swung open once again. A guard carrying a brightly polished crossbow walked in, leading a prisoner tethered at the end of a length of rope. Both wore cowls that covered their faces. The captive shuffled into the room like a sleepwalker. If this was Natalia, then she truly had fallen upon sorry times.

The guard brought the prisoner to a halt, and stood to attention.

Ehrhart scowled. Uncertainty clouded his features. 'This is the prisoner Zucharov? Well then, let's take a proper look at her.'

The guard took a firmer grip on the crossbow then drew back the hood from the prisoner's face. What was revealed was not Natalia, but a man, seemingly stunned or in some kind of trance. Stefan recognised him as one of the guards at the gates.

The commander's expression swung from bemusement to ire. 'Is this some kind of game?' he demanded. The guard didn't reply, but pulled back the hood covering his – or rather her – own face. Before the other guards had time to react, Natalia Zucharov had levelled the loaded bow squarely at their master.

'Make so much as a move and he'll get a taste of this first hand,' she said.

For one moment, nobody moved or spoke. The silence was broken by a cackle of laughter from von Diehl.

'Natalia Zucharov. So you've decided to join us after all. Excellent.'

'I've come for him,' she replied, shifting the nose of the crossbow in Stefan's direction. 'Nobody has the right to take his life but me. I'm owed that.'

Now Ehrhart joined in the laughter. 'You've come to kill Kumansky? Well, I'm sure that can be accommodated.' He turned towards von Diehl, but whatever he was about to say was cut short by the sounds of voices, and the clash of steel on steel. A loud commotion had broken out in the grounds below.

Now Stefan could savour having the upper hand. 'That will be Bruno,' he told Ehrhart. 'Bruno and some friends. Not the most sophisticated men apparently, but effective in a brutal kind of way.'

Ehrhart paled, his smug sense of authority suddenly under threat. He gestured to two of the men at the back of the room. 'See what's happened to the patrols,' he barked. 'Sort it out.'

Von Diehl gazed at Natalia with the same untroubled smile on his face. 'There's plenty of time,' he murmured. 'Time is, literally, endless.' He edged forward. Natalia tensed, and moved the crossbow so it was aimed somewhere between the cultist and Stefan.

'You've done well,' von Diehl told her. 'Very well, for such a modest magician.'

'My magic was good enough to get me past his guards,'

Von Diehl nodded. 'Of course. But don't get any false notion of what you are capable of.' He smiled. 'All that business in the prison and out in the wildlands. You couldn't have done any of it without me. I was steering you all the time, child.' He raised one hand, and mimed the action of lifting a string. 'Like a puppet.'

The sounds of fighting below intensified. It was getting closer. 'Put down the crossbow,' Ehrhart told Natalia. 'Drop your pathetic little toy and I might even spare your life.'

'Natalia–' Stefan called out. Natalia turned. Raw anger was etched on her face. Her finger curled around the trigger of the crossbow, then pandemonium broke loose. Stefan heard the trigger mechanism click home. Instinctively, he threw himself down. From the corner of his eye, he saw von Diehl stagger back and pull his hand in front of his face. The bolt speared through his outstretched hand, and pinned him against the wall. For the first time, Stefan heard the satisfying sound of von Diehl screaming in pure, undisguised agony.

Stefan reacted quickly, much more quickly than the bewildered guards. He jabbed his elbow into the ribs of the man behind him, winding him. Before the guard could recover, Stefan had his sword. A second man came at him, but Stefan swerved away from the lunging attack and struck back, driving the sword up through the man's belly into his chest. He ripped the blade from the dead guard's grip and tossed it towards Albrecht.

Albrecht caught the weapon in one hand and turned crisply, to take on the two nearest guards. Ehrhart's men were younger and fitter, but Albrecht's ferocity made up for what his advancing years had claimed. He lay in to them, wielding the blade in a furious assault, killing one outright and driving the other back.

Ehrhart drew his sword. He eyed both Stefan and Albrecht, and then went for the older man. In so doing, he had taken his eye off Natalia. It proved a costly mistake. This time her aim was true. The bolt struck the commander through the neck, sending a crimson plume spurting across the room. Ehrhart spun around, choking on a fountain of blood. His frozen eyes stared up at Marcus Albrecht. Albrecht spat in the face of the man that had betrayed him. 'May your soul never find rest,' he snarled.

The door crashed open behind them. Just in time, Stefan turned to confront Karl Maier, the insouciant smile still stretched across his boyish face. Stefan raised his blade, squaring up to the other swordsman. Maier mirrored his move.

'Oh, Stefan,' Maier murmured. 'It shouldn't have come to this.'

'You should have thought of that before you bartered your soul,' Stefan replied. 'Now, fight.'

Maier fought. He fought every bit as well as Stefan had expected, and then more. For once Stefan was facing an opponent both lighter and faster than himself. Maier seemed to anticipate his every move; he darted and wove between Stefan's blows, jabbing home with his own sword at each opportunity. Worse still, Maier was fresh and rested, his only exertion some casual brutality in the interrogation of his prisoner. Stefan was fighting at his very limit; fighting to stay alive. Maier sensed he had the edge, and he knew how to exploit it. He was doing exactly what Stefan would have done. Rather than expend valuable energy going for a quick kill, Maier was opting for containment, only breaking from the game of cat and mouse to counter-attack with ruthless efficiency.

Stefan was putting all his effort into trying to break down Maier's guard. But for every blow that found its mark, and grazed his opponent's flesh, or tore through the fabric of his tunic, another two would fly harmlessly wide. He was wasting precious strength and energy. Both men were tiring, but Stefan knew that he was tiring faster.

He took a step back, forced into retreat to buy time. His fighter's balance deserted him, and he stumbled. Maier's response was instantaneous and unforgiving. His sword lashed down at Stefan, aimed precisely at the exposed flesh between Stefan's shoulder and his neck. Just in time, Stefan blocked the stroke with his own blade. The impact of steel on steel sent a shock wave through his whole body, and spun him about. Maier struck out again, the sword-blade a stream of steel snaking through the air. Stefan heard a cry, a voice – his voice – shouting out in anguish and pain. Looking down, he saw a dark blush of blood deepen as it spread from his flank down the length of his body.

A grin spread across Maier's face, the hungry smile of the hunter closing upon the kill. He smashed home his sword again and again, each thunderous blow weakening Stefan a little more. Stefan thought again of Natalia. Was she still there? In the confusion of battle he had lost track of everyone else. If she was there, she had chosen not to intervene. She would be neither Stefan's salvation, nor his damnation. That destiny had fallen to Karl Maier, and he was precariously close to fulfilling it.

Stefan roused himself one final time. He stood up under the assault, and for a moment, traded blow for blow with his opponent. Maier was happy to trade; he knew the cards were stacked in his favour. Stefan felt the wall against his back. Now there was nowhere left to go. Maier stepped in, feinted to the left, and drove his sword directly at Stefan. Just for once he misjudged. His aim was only fractionally out of true, but it was enough for the blade to surge wide and wedge deep into the thick wooden beam behind him. A flicker of alarm registered on Maier's face as he read the danger. He tugged desperately on the weapon to pull it free.

It was no more than half a chance, but Stefan took it gratefully. As Maier pulled the blade clear, Stefan attacked. He drove his sword in a mighty two-handed sweep towards the middle of Maier's body. Just in time, Maier freed his sword and obstructed the blow, but the force was enough to knock him off-balance. As he reeled under the impact of the strike, Stefan went in again, channelling every last fibre of his being into one final assault. He beat aside Maier's guard, and knocked the sword from his grasp. Maier stared at Stefan, shocked, and flicked out a hand to try to reach the fallen sword. He was fast, but this time Stefan was quicker. Before Maier could reach the weapon he thrust the blade home, gouging deep into the flesh below Maier's ribs.

Maier blinked and coughed twice. A narrow dribble of blood escaped his lips. He dabbed at his flank with his hand, as if unable to quite believe he had been wounded. With one last effort he stood upright, and turned to face his conqueror. He made a sound, something between a laugh and a cry.

'Stefan,' he gasped. 'The thing is–'

Stefan didn't wait to hear what the thing was. He plunged the sword deep into Maier's belly, twisting the blade as he drove it home. Maier grunted and crashed down. Light flickered briefly in his eyes then dulled. Karl Maier was dead.

Stefan was close to collapse, every last ounce of strength surrendered. But the battle wasn't over yet.

Somehow he had to keep going. From the antechamber, the terrified eyes of the Grand Theogonist were fixed on Stefan. What Stefan had to do now was to save Johann Esmer at any cost.

As he turned to look around the room, Stefan saw Natalia. She raised the loaded crossbow and aimed it squarely at him.

'Natalia, in Sigmar's name,' Stefan cried out. Natalia stared back, unmoved.

'This belonged to my brother,' she said, calmly. 'It came from his collection of weapons. Take my word for it, I've had plenty of practice with this weapon.' Her expression hardened. 'The first bolt should have been for you, or at least the second.'

She raised the sight to her eye. 'But don't worry. There's still the third. Ironic, don't you think, that it should be a bolt from Alexei's bow that finally kills you? Ironic, and just.'

Stefan pressed down on his sword, the battered steel the only thing keeping his weary body from falling. The gap separating him from Natalia wasn't great, but, in his present state, he had no hope of getting to her before she pulled the trigger.

'Listen,' he said, fighting for breath. 'Kill me if you must, if you think that will somehow right a wrong, or make the world a better place. Kill me, and get on with it.'

Natalia frowned, and shifted the weapon in between her hands. She looked uneasy.

'But if you *truly* care about justice, about righting the great evils which afflict our world,' Stefan said, 'then you'll grant a truce. A temporary one, if you wish.' He turned towards the Grand Theogonist. 'If you have no loyalty to me, then you must have loyalty to him and to Altdorf.'

Natalia hesitated. Uncertainty clouded her features. Emotions battled inside her. She broke eye contact with Stefan, and looked away for just a moment. At that moment Stefan knew that she would not kill him. Not yet, at least. He quickly took stock of the situation. Marcus Albrecht was sprawled upon the ground, alive but exhausted. Ehrhart's men were in retreat. Those that didn't hadn't died had fled the chamber, or were trying to stave off the assault by Sterkel's men. Gustav Ehrhart lay where Natalia's dart had felled him. He was drenched in his own blood and his dead eyes stared out across eternity.

But there was now no von Diehl. No trace remained of the cultist, other than the dark, ruby stain upon one wall. That and the stub of the crossbow bolt that was still embedded in the wall. Natalia followed Stefan's gaze, and gave a cry of disbelief. 'That's not possible! He was skewered like a hog on a spit, pinned to that wall, just a moment ago.'

'Well, he's not there now,' Stefan replied. 'And whilst he's free then nothing can be considered safe.'

A look almost like pity crossed Natalia's face. But it wasn't pity. It was something harder. Disdain, a weary disgust.

'You know,' she said, 'perhaps I should envy you. So driven, so single-minded. Nothing comes before duty. Not even… not even…' she hesitated. 'Ah, what difference would it make,' she muttered. 'So be it. My debt of blood is suspended. But consider it just a postponement. A tactical decision by someone as cold and calculating as yourself.' She lowered the crossbow. 'What is it you want?'

Before Stefan could answer the doors to the main chamber burst open, and one of Ehrhart's men came in, or rather, was thrown in, his lifeless body tossed through the open doorway like a discarded doll. Four or five other men followed, heavily armed and definitely alive. Stefan didn't recognise any of them, but they certainly weren't Ehrhart's. The first sized Stefan up, and thrust out his sword, menacingly.

'Who are you?' he demanded.

'My name is Stefan Kumansky,' Stefan replied. The man said nothing then grunted. The name seemed to satisfy him. He lowered the sword a fraction.

'Now tell me something,' Stefan said. 'Is someone called Bruno Hausmann with you?' The other man grinned, revealing an uneven row of tar-blackened teeth. 'That he is,' he confirmed. 'He's still having his fill of the fun down below.'

Stefan turned to Natalia. 'Take the Grand Theogonist. Get him to safety. Marcus too. Get help for them both. Then find Bruno, Bruno Hausmann.'

'And tell him what?'

'Tell him I've gone after von Diehl. And I'm going to need his help.'

CHAPTER TWENTY-FOUR
Deliverance

ONCE HE WAS alone, Stefan gauged the extent of his wounds. Gingerly he peeled away the torn fragment of tunic to reveal a crimson gash like a gaping, painted mouth. It looked ugly, but the blood around the edge was starting to congeal: a good sign. The best thing now would be to rest, but rest was not an option.

Stefan had to find von Diehl, and quickly. The house was large, but the cultist's choices would be limited. It was unlikely that he had gone towards the fighting below, or that he had escaped the house entirely. That meant that he was almost certainly nearby, hidden in one of the rooms on the upper level. Stefan ripped a length of clean cloth from his tunic and bound it tightly around the wound. Then he took up his sword and began the search.

The top of the house was deserted save for the bodies of the dead. There was no one left but Stefan and – somewhere – Heinrich von Diehl. Stefan moved from room to room, opening every door, examining even the smallest recess. Soon he had searched every room, wihout success. But nothing could shake his conviction that the cultist was there, somewhere. Stefan closed his eyes and prayed for instinct to guide him where vision could not. He re-traced his steps along the main corridor bisecting the building.

Half way along, a nagging, insistent doubt made him stop. He was outside the door of a small antechamber. He had checked the room already, but instinct now told him to check again. He pushed open the door and stepped inside. The room had been used as a storeroom, the musty cell piled high with books, scrolls, ornaments and other bric-a-brac; the sort of things a wealthy man might put away when he had no further use for them. Stefan sifted again through the dusty piles of artefacts, checking in case any hiding place had been overlooked, but he found nothing.

He was on the point of heading back when his attention was drawn to a painting hanging on one wall. It was slightly askew, as if it had recently been jogged or moved. Stefan stepped across the piles of bundled papers to take a closer look. The painting portrayed a formal scene: Imperial dignitaries gathered for a ceremony. Paintings like it were common enough in Altdorf, in higher society. Stefan recognised the likenesses of the Emperor, Karl-Franz, and several nobles. Their regalia and the insignia on their robes announced them as the elector counts. To the left of the picture, looking out, stood the Grand Theogonist, Johann Esmer.

But when he looked closer, he saw it wasn't Esmer. The face was Esmer's, without doubt. But the eyes – the cruel, taunting eyes that appeared fixed on something none of the others could see – belonged to someone else. Stefan would have recognised those eyes anywhere – they were the eyes of Heinrich von Diehl.

He grasped the frame and lifted it off the wall. He had meant to look again at the picture, but now his attention was now held by what lay concealed behind it. It was a tiny rune or icon, no more than six inches long, recessed into the surface of the wall. It was painted in the shape of a staff, with a black, eyeless serpent coiled tightly along its length.

Stefan steeled himself and reached out his hand. His whole body was shaking. Gently, he touched his palm to the wall. The icon felt cold and faintly damp against his skin. For a moment, nothing. Then he felt a vibration, a tiny tremor run though the wall, as though somewhere, a distant engine had been set in motion. The wall shuddered, then slid back to reveal a passage to a second room. Stefan tightened his grip on his sword, and stepped through.

The second room was vast, an enormous space completely at odds with the apparent dimensions of the house. The air inside was cold and lifeless, utterly still. The space was empty, the bare walls void of even the simplest decoration. Stefan was still pondering the mystery when someone behind him spoke.

'Well done, Stefan,' the voice said. 'You have found our chapel.'

Stefan spun around. It was as though von Diehl had simply materialised from empty space.

'It was you I was looking for,' Stefan replied. 'Now I have you.'

Von Diehl stepped further into the room. He held his wounded hand beneath the folds of his cloak. He was still bleeding.

Stefan raised his sword and stepped towards the cultist. 'You're coming with me.'

'On the contrary,' von Diehl said. 'It is you who will accompany me. Or did you think that I drew you to this place for nothing?'

Before Stefan could respond, von Diehl extended his hand and screamed something in a foul, unintelligible tongue. A rod of sheer, concentrated light arced from the cultist's finger across the span of the room. The chamber filled with a blazing incandescence, and a sound like a thousand explosions detonated inside Stefan's head. He fell to the ground, clutching his hands to his face. The walls around him started to shiver and blur. Stefan watched the solid geometry of the room break apart. Shapes melted and flowed into one another like streams of a river vanishing into the blistering white void. Finally the earthen floor dissolved beneath him, and he was falling, falling from the mortal world through all eternity.

Stefan was surely hurtling towards oblivion, into the cold embrace of Morr, pitiless god of death. He screwed his eyes closed and waited for the end, the shattering impact when his body would be crushed and his soul cast loose in the perpetual twilight of the netherworld.

The end did not come. To his amazement, Stefan felt the deadly velocity easing, as if some unseen, benign force was cushioning his descent. When he finally came to rest he felt only a gentle, soothing warmth.

Stefan lay still, barely daring to breathe. Perhaps he really was dead. Perhaps this was the forgiving death of the just; a place where all ill and pain were banished. But perhaps not. As he started to move, Stefan felt a sudden stab of pain, a tangible reminder of his wounds. Confused, and utterly disorientated, he raised his head to look around.

He was lying flat upon a plinth, a broad divan set in the centre of a high-ceilinged room with white-painted walls. Thick velvet curtains were drawn across windows on the far side. He could hear the sound of human voices somewhere in the distance; hundreds, if not thousands of them. Gingerly he got up, and went to the window. As he pulled back the heavy drape, light flooded in, the warming light of the sun on a high summer's day. Stefan let the warmth soak into his body. Despite his wounds, he felt better than he had remembered in a long time.

He looked down from the window. Beneath him was the great square; crammed to every corner with crowds of people. But this was not the same fearful, restless mass that had gathered for the Blessing of the Souls. He scanned the faces below. There was no unrest here. The crowd radiated happiness, a joyous sense of content. It was as though they were waiting for something. Something profound, something wondrous.

He looked beyond the square to the rooftops. He had known the city for the greater part of his life, yet he had never seen it like this. Sunlight glimmered on the burnished domes and spires, dappling the city in golden light. Stefan breathed in deeply. The air smelled fresh, cleaner than he had ever known it. There was no sickness in this place, no disease, no sadness. As he looked into the crowd he felt a sudden surge of emotion. It was as if all the wars had finally been won; all the sorrows of the world banished. It was a victory the like of which Stefan had barely even imagined.

'Wonderful, isn't it?'

It was a woman's voice somewhere from an adjacent room. His first thought was that it might be Natalia. But the voice, though so achingly familiar, wasn't Natalia's. The woman began to sing, a gentle lilting melody, a song from a far distant place. Stefan could almost taste and smell her presence now – close, so close to him.

This must be some kind of dream. Some bizarre inversion of the nightmare Nikolas had shown him. Yet everything felt so real. The excitement racing inside him felt real, too. He walked towards the archway dividing the two rooms.

She was sitting at a table, her back towards him. Right until that moment, Stefan had tried to convince himself that it would be Natalia. But now, as he glimpsed the ash-pale hair flowing to her shoulders, and the fine, chiselled profile of her face, Stefan knew it was not. As she turned to face him, her name was already on his lips.

'Elena... *Elena*?'

She nodded once, and smiled. Her pale, cornflower eyes filled with a warmth that Stefan knew was meant for him alone. She looked impossibly beautiful, more beautiful even than Stefan had remembered her.

'It's been a long time, Stefan,' she said. 'Much too long.'

Stefan stared at her, waiting for the vision to melt away before his eyes. But it did not.

'Elena Kuragin,' he whispered. 'But you were in Erengrad... Chaos had attacked again. Has the city finally fallen?'

She laughed and shook her head softly, still smiling. 'Erengrad has not fallen. How could it? There was no war, no siege. By the way,' she added, teasingly. 'It's Elena *Yevschenko*, not Kuragin.'

Utter confusion and a desperate, longing hope battled inside Stefan. 'But I was there,' he insisted. 'I fought the Chaos army outside the walls. I was there when you pledged your hand in marriage. Are you telling me that Peter Kuragin isn't real?'

When she took his hand in hers, he did not desist. 'Peter Kuragin is real enough,' she assured him. 'Growing fat and old in Erengrad, no doubt. But we are not married. We have never even met.'

'But I was there,' Stefan insisted.

When Elena clasped his hand gently between her own, Stefan realised he had wanted this moment more than anything else he could have imagined.

'You were there,' Elena agreed. 'But the war, and my marriage to Kuragin belong to another past. This-' She looked around, towards the sound of the crowds outside, 'this is the world you could have chosen. The world you could still choose. A world without war or fear. A world where I am married-' she leant forward. 'To you, Stefan.'

Stefan began to draw her to him. Then some unbidden impulse pulled him back. Elena's face registered a sudden, amused surprise.

'What's the matter?' she asked. 'Is it really too good to be true?'

'I've been shown the future before,' Stefan said. 'A vision of horror beyond my worst imaginings. Why should this future be more real?'

A momentary pain clouded her face. 'Why can't we make it real? Isn't this what you – what *we* deserve?' She took his hand again and led him towards the window balcony.

'The people are waiting, Stefan. Waiting to acclaim their saviour, the man who led them from darkness into the light.'

'Who?'

'The Grand Theogonist, who else?'

'Johann Esmer?'

Elena laughed, freely and openly at mention of the name. 'Johann Esmer? You think that *Esmer* could have inspired such love, such devotion?' She placed her hand on his back, easing him closer. 'No, my love. In this world, Altdorf has another Grand Theogonist. His name is Stefan Kumansky.'

Stefan's head was spinning. He was giddy, his spirit overflowing with thoughts and feelings he barely understood. He steadied himself, and took a step back from the window.

'I – I am the Grand Theogonist?' he asked, dazedly.

She gripped his hand. He could feel the sharpness of her nails biting into his flesh. 'You are,' she said. 'Or you could be. If you wanted to be.'

Stefan gazed at the sea of expectant faces. 'What do they want from me?'

'They want to see a sign, a token of your dominion,' Elena told him. 'They want you to show them the Runefang of Solland.'

'The Runefang of Solland?' Stefan could hear his own voice, but now it belonged to someone else. Another Stefan, from another life. 'I don't have it,' he whispered.

'But you could find it,' Elena assured him. 'All you need is the will. Look,' she pointed down again at the waiting crowds. 'They're yours. They will do whatever you command.'

Stefan looked. A thousand possibilities, untouched and unexplored, flooded his mind. Wasn't this exactly what he had always wanted? Wasn't this the right future, the just future, not only for him, but for all of Altdorf? And if he could truly command such power, then could not darkness could be banished from the Old World for all eternity?

A stab of pain from his wound cut through him, bringing a moment of cold clarity. Stefan looked down again at the masses gathered in the great square. So many people, so many. But they were not *his* people – he belonged to them, not the reverse. He turned back to Elena.

'The gods bestow greatness,' he told her. 'Man has neither cause nor right to choose it for himself.'

The beatific smile faded from Elena's face, and something harder took its place. 'What are you frightened of?' she snapped. 'Haven't you the stomach to take what is rightfully yours?'

'I have no rights other than those gifted by almighty Sigmar,' Stefan retorted. 'To say otherwise is heresy. Even from your lips.' As he spoke, he realised that Elena too was in pain. She was clasping her left hand tight against her breast. He reached out to comfort her, but she pulled away. He looked again at her hand. It was shimmering; the flesh shivering with minute vibrations. Gradually, the skin was darkening: a patch of deep red spreading out from the centre of her palm.

'What's the matter?' Stefan demanded. 'Are you hurt?'

Elena didn't answer, but now she had no need to. Now Stefan could see the wound opening up; the raw fissure in the flesh where the crossbow bolt had passed through. When at last she spoke, the response was no longer intelligible, the voice no longer Elena's. The shimmering spread until her whole body had become a blur, a shifting, moving wave of shape and colour. Whatever was standing opposite Stefan was no longer Elena Yevschenko. But another, equally recognisable, figure was taking shape before his eyes.

Heinrich von Diehl stared at Stefan with a baleful hatred. Stefan now saw the cultist for what he truly was. A creature of darkness, the merciless emissary of the Lord of Change. Von Diehl towered over Stefan, the frail prisoner of Stahlfort transformed into a mighty, vengeful warrior. He balled his fist until the blood wept from the wound, oblivious to any pain.

'I hoped you might yet be convinced, Stefan. That you might have the wit to grasp what was being offered you. I see now I was wasting my time.'

'You were always wasting your time,' Stefan told him. 'Your foul gods shall never have their dominion.'

Von Diehl spat, contemptuously. His features settled into a sadistic grin.

'You crave another future?' he sneered. 'You shall have it.' The cultist extended one sinuous arm and unleashed a second bolt of blinding light. Stefan flinched as a wave of heat hit him, billowing up from the square below. When he looked down, he found himself staring at a scene of unimaginable horror. A wall of molten fire rolled in a wave across the square, obliterating every living thing in its path. The crowd scattered in terror, trying in vain to escape the inferno. Cries of joy became screams of anguish.

In a few terrible moments, the light of a thousand living souls was wiped out. Bodies were rendered to blistered, charred meat. The air filled with the sickening stench of burning flesh, and with the pitiful screams of the dying. The screaming was never-ending. Soon it had spread beyond the boundaries of the city, flooding across the Empire, across the whole Old World. It was the unending cry of a world locked for eternity in perpetual pain.

'Welcome to mankind's destiny, Stefan. Welcome to the realm of Chaos.'

Stefan clamped his hands to his ears to block out the sound, but the screaming was inside his head. It was everywhere.

'Stop this torture,' he thundered. 'Stop this madness!'

Von Diehl laughed and clapped his hands together. The screaming ceased, as abruptly as it had begun. A pall of black smoke drifted across the cathedral square.

When it had passed, the space below was empty; a place of dust and weeds in the midst of a dead city. The sky beyond the window thickened to a dull pewter grey. Von Diehl's body shimmered and flickered in the fading light.

'What is this?' Stefan demanded. 'Some other future that you have fabricated?'

'Which future do you want?' Von Diehl asked. 'I can show you hundreds, all of them possible. This is just the beginning. In the time to come there will be thousands, hundreds of thousands of dead. All your struggles, all your puny, futile battles will count for nothing. You are nothing, Stefan Kumansky. You can change nothing, influence nothing.'

Stefan raised up his sword and advanced on the cultist. 'I can finish what I have begun,' he asserted.

The cultist drew back his hand. Out of nowhere, a sword appeared in his grip. The cultist spat out a dark prayer. The sword began to glow with sickly, yellow-green phosphorescence. Von Diehl stepped towards Stefan, his sword sparking and crackling in his hand.

'I was hoping you would lead me to the Runefang. But it seems I will have to do it without you.' He traced a line of fire upon the ground.

'Or – how about this – perhaps I could *become* you?' He launched out with the sword. The fireblade sliced the air with improbable speed. Stefan flung himself back, the deadly blade kissing the skin of his cheek as he swerved away. Before he could respond, the cultist was on him again, his sword dripping fire as it scythed the air.

Stefan fought as though the lives of all mankind depended on the outcome. He fought with every ounce of strength left to him, with all the craft and guile he had ever learned. But with every stroke, every furious, fiery clash of steel, the cultist and his daemonic blade were growing stronger, faster, and more skilful. Von Diehl tore at Stefan with the fury and strength of a madman. The heavy blade smashed through wood and stone, leaving a trail of burning debris in its wake. Stefan threw himself from one side to the other, knowing that even one clean strike from the cultist's sword could prove fatal.

Von Diehl aimed a thunderous blow at Stefan's head. Stefan parried it away and hit back. He caught von Diehl with the flat of his blade, knocking the cultist off balance. Stefan angled his sword and drove in again, aiming below his opponent's ribs. His aim was true, but it was like striking against solid iron: the blade buckled and flexed, then sprang free. Stefan backed off, gasping for breath. Von Diehl took his sword in both hands and advanced steadily upon Stefan. His face cracked open in a mocking grin.

'Think, Stefan. If I am this powerful now, think what I will be capable of with the Runefang of Solland.'

He aimed another blow at Stefan. Stefan anticipated it and met the cultist's sword with his own. The fireblade glowed white-hot as it struck against his sword. Stefan could feel the daemonic energy flowing through his arm, poisoning him, weakening him. He broke away and launched a torrent of blows at his adversary. Nothing seemed to wound von Diehl, but the sheer energy of his attack forced the cultist into a temporary retreat.

For a moment von Diehl looked dazed; stunned by the ferocity of Stefan's defence. Then the sardonic smile returned. He stepped forward again.

'Small victories, a fleeting postponement. Enjoy them whilst you can. I can afford to wait. I can wait for all eternity, if necessary.' The sword whirled above his head then plunged down, an attack more murderous and sustained than any before. Faster and faster came the blows, each one like a hammer driven into Stefan's body. His sword was blunt and battered; the steel yielding under the inhuman assault. Stefan stumbled and fell. He thrust out his blade in a final defence and looked up to meet the inevitable, fatal blow.

Von Diehl's eyes glowed blood red, radiating an intense, undiluted evil. His angular face contorted in hatred and rage. This was it – the end. Stefan had nothing left to give. He was beaten down, broken. Before the gates of Morr swung wide, Stefan shouted out a last declaration of defiance.

'The final outcome will be the same. You can't win.'

Von Diehl's threw him a sardonic smile. 'Still you don't understand,' he murmured. 'We have already won.'

Then, to Stefan's astonishment, the cultist cast the weapon down. The fireblade flickered then dulled.

'Consider all that has happened,' he said. The patient smile played at the corners of his mouth. 'A feared servant of Chaos is set free, and smuggled to Altdorf. Loyal soldiers of the Empire are murdered.'

'Serpent's words,' Stefan shouted.

'There is a plot to destroy the cathedral of Sigmar, with barrels of blackpowder stolen from the Imperial armoury in Nuln. Witnesses will remember seeing those barrels being loaded on board a ship called the *Karla*.

'But the plotting doesn't end there. There's a plan to assassinate the Grand Theogonist himself.' He shook his head. 'Such wickedness. Such evil. But who is responsible? Whose names are linked to all these conspiracies?'

He smiled, knowingly. 'A secret order known as the Keepers of the Flame. A merchant, Mikhal Kumansky. And the final name. The common thread, that runs through it all. You, Stefan. Stefan Kumansky.'

The cold horror of the realisation that had been creeping up over Stefan now hit him with full, juddering force. From the first moment until the last, he had been the target. The eternal war against darkness, which Stefan had previously seen all around him, had suddenly become personal in a way he could never have foreseen.

'So this is about me,' he said, quietly.

'You have long been a thorn in my master's side. But for your meddling, Erengrad and perhaps all of Kislev, would have fallen long ago.'

'If it hadn't been me, it would have been someone else,' Stefan retorted. 'The will of man will always prevail. You can't destroy us.'

Von Diehl smiled. 'You are already destroyed.'

'So this is my punishment?' Stefan demanded. 'The punishment of Tzeentch?'

Von Diehl shook his head. 'Still you see good and evil as opposed and separate. But they are as intertwined as day and night. You are part of us. And we are part of you. You can no more escape us than you can escape yourself. No, Stefan. This is not your punishment.' He paused.

'This is your reward.'

Heinrich von Diehl fixed Stefan with a cold-beaded stare. 'Imagine how it will feel,' he said, softly. 'To have battled us along every step of the way. To have come so far, and to still have lost.'

He began to laugh. His laughter rolled across the open spaces of the cathedral square, a doom-laden sound like thunder cast down by the gods. The cathedral began to tremble. Fissures opened up in the floor and the walls around Stefan began to crumble and break. The darkening sky turned the colour of black lead; all light leeched away. Stefan looked about for von Diehl, but he was gone. The great square ruptured and cracked open, the walls of the city shattered and fell to dust. Everything was being destroyed – every brick, every stone. Stefan would be the last to die. The final witness to the end of all existence.

A single, piercing, human cry made Stefan look up. For a moment he thought he saw the dark curtain of cloud break apart, and the image of a man's face, half-remembered, looking down on him. Barely conscious of what he was doing, Stefan reached out with his hand. The last thing he remembered was being lifted up from the ground, and dragged from a dying world.

STEFAN DIDN'T KNOW where he was, or how long he had lain there. Gradually he drifted back into consciousness and opened his eyes. His body ached with an unimaginable pain, but at least he was alive. He was back inside the hidden room, the secret chapel where he had encountered von Diehl. The cultist and his nightmarish visions had gone, vanished without trace.

Natalia Zucharov was standing over him, the loaded crossbow in her hands. Stefan wondered if she meant to kill him. If so, he would have neither the strength nor the will to resist her. But that was not what was in Natalia's mind. Instead she took Stefan's arm and helped him to sit up.

She gazed at him with a strange, mournful look on her face. 'Where were you, Stefan? Where did you go?'

Stefan stared at her, trying to remember. 'I was in a place beyond all imagining – a place the likes of which I hope never to see again.' He struggled with the memory and the terrifying enormity of it all. 'Von Diehl called it the realm of Chaos.'

'You can thank Johann Esmer that you survived.' Stefan looked around to see Bruno enter the room.

'Esmer? The Grand Theogonist?'

'He saved your mortal soul. He brought you back to this world, Stefan. Body and soul.'

'And von Diehl?'

Bruno shrugged, helplessly. 'Gone. Dead, perhaps. But it's over, Stefan. We survived.'

Stefan tried to sit up a little further. His head pounded, and his throat was dry and burning raw. 'Yes, we have all survived. There is some comfort in that.'

There was a silence; drawn out and uncomfortable. Stefan looked at Bruno and saw the grief written in his face. 'What is it?'

Natalia spoke. 'You don't know, do you?'

'What do you mean?' Stefan demanded. 'Know what?' But he could already feel the knife inside him, the final, scouring turn of the blade.

'Stefan–' Bruno stammered. 'Natalia was at the cathedral, just after we left. The guards there told her–'

'Told her what?'

'Mikhal,' Natalia said. 'He's dead, Stefan.'

Stefan shook his head, emphatically. 'No,' he said. 'That can't be. He was recovering, he was growing stronger with every minute that passed.'

Bruno took his comrade's hands in his own. 'Mikhal saved his bravest deed for last, Stefan. He knew you wouldn't leave him if you knew how badly he'd been wounded. He would be proud to know his sacrifice wasn't in vain.'

The knife inside Stefan turned, and kept turning. Even in the darkness of the realm of Chaos, he had never thought it possible to know pain like this.

'It seems we were both destined to know the grief of losing a brother,' Natalia said. There was no hint of satisfaction in her voice. 'Whatever I once would have wished for you, Stefan, I swear I would not have wished for that.'

Stefan slumped back against the wall and closed his eyes. He had been pulled back from the brink of death, only to face a truth worse than death itself. Somewhere in the background he heard the sound of voices, and booted feet. Dozens of men were moving through the corridors of the house.

'It's the watch,' Bruno announced. 'They've taken the house.'

An instinctive reflex made Stefan ask, 'Ehrhart's men?'

'No,' Bruno replied. 'They're all either arrested or dead. These are men of the south watch. Looks like they've been sent in to take control.'

Stefan lifted his head, and managed to open his eyes a fraction. 'So be it, then,' he said. 'Now we shall all be judged.'

CHAPTER TWENTY-FIVE
Judgement: Keepers of the Flame

FOR FOURTEEN DAYS and nights, Stefan was a prisoner of the south watch. He was kept in a stinking hole in the ground, deep inside the Imperial palace of justice with no contact with the outside world. He shared his days with a pack of starving rats, and survived on a diet of gritty bread and a pail of flyspecked water. On the fifteenth day he was taken to wash, and was given clean clothes. Then, without warning or explanation, he was led from his cell and taken, under escort, to an anonymous house in the Almerstoet district. There, in a shabby room on the upper floor, Marcus Albrecht was waiting. So too was an imposing, silver-haired man whose placid features resonated with a quiet, but absolute authority. It was a face Stefan remembered only too well from better days, glorious days on the battlefields of Erengrad.

Their greeting was warm, but restrained, the greeting of old comrades, meeting in grave times. Gastez

Castelguerre held out a chair, and bid Stefan rest. Behind the welcoming smile, the strain and tension of a man shouldering a heavy burden was plain to see. Stefan sat and drank greedily from a beaker of wine. After two weeks in the care of the watch, it tasted like nectar sent down by the gods. He sat back, trying to adjust to the sudden and unexplained reversal of fortune.

'How goes the war?' Stefan said at last. Castelguerre must have ridden directly from his command at Middenheim. Right there and then, it was all Stefan could think to ask.

'Not well,' Castelguerre replied. 'Not as well as we would have the people believe, at least. The battle isn't won yet. Not by a long way.'

Marcus Albrecht had been sitting with his head down, sunk in his thoughts. He looked up at Castelguerre apprehensively.

'I sent messages to the Ten,' he said. 'To the Keepers of the Flame. Only you came, Gastez. Only you.'

Castelguerre's expression darkened. 'I intercepted your messages. I stopped the others riding on your fool's errand. Stopped them before any more damage was done.'

Albrecht's jaw dropped. He looked chastened and stunned by Castelguerre's outburst. 'I don't understand,' he mumbled.

'I think you do,' Castelguerre countered, crisply. 'What sort of risk did you think you were taking, trying to bring the Ten to Altdorf in such times?'

'Von Diehl,' Albrecht replied. 'If the Ten could have broken von Diehl, then the war could have been shortened by months, or even years.'

'So you allowed yourself to believe. Or so Ehrhart let you believe. The truth is you were used. You thought that you were clever enough to outwit Chaos on your own. You reached for glory, without thinking of the consequences.' He ran his fingers through his mane of steel-grey hair, and then rubbed the tiredness from his eyes. 'Chaos used you, Marcus. They teased out your weaknesses, and exploited them mercilessly. Only good fortune, and the deeds of some brave men, averted a catastrophe.'

He turned to Stefan. 'I'm sorry that you got involved in this. Sorry that you too have been tarred with this ignominy.'

The words stirred a sickness in the pit of Stefan's stomach. 'But it can't all have been a falsehood. I saw visions of Altdorf, saw the future as it would be if we did nothing.'

'True enough,' Castelguerre nodded. 'Without your valour, and your heroism, that vision might well have come to pass. But it is also true that when you set von Diehl free from Stahlfort, you were setting free the very forces that would make that nightmare a reality. Do you understand what I'm telling you, Stefan?'

Stefan understood only too well. He remembered what von Diehl had told him too. There was no absolute division. He had helped create that which he had tried to destroy.

Albrecht shook his head in disbelief. 'There must be some evidence,' he muttered. 'Evidence of what really happened.'

'Must there?' Castelguerre held the other man's stare for what felt like a long time. 'Von Diehl is gone. No trace of his existence remains. Ehrhart is dead. His guilt dies with him.'

After a long pause, Stefan asked, 'What now?'

'Now? Now we repair the damage, as best we can. The reputation of the Keepers of the Flame is in ruins. If and when the Ten – those that remain of them – ever meet together again, it will be a clandestine gathering, opposed by many. And mistrusted by almost all.'

'What happens to me?' Stefan asked.

Castelguerre frowned. 'I've petitioned on your behalf with the Grand Theogonist,' he said. 'You've earned his gratitude, of course, for the actions which saved Altdorf, and his life. But he has already intervened twice to spare your life.'

'Twice?'

Castelguerre nodded. 'Else you would not be here now. Esmer is a pragmatist. There are limits to his gratitude, and some things are beyond even his influence.'

'The escape from Stahlfort,' Stefan said. 'The death of the guard.'

'Exactly,' Castelguerre affirmed. 'I've managed to secure a pardon against both of your lives. Beyond that, I can promise nothing.'

Stefan looked up. 'What about Bruno?' he asked.

'Bruno at least has come out of this well,' Castelguerre said. 'Untainted with any suggestion of dishonour. The men who killed Nikolas gave themselves up to the east watch. Their tongues were easily loosened. Bruno's reputation is clear. There might even be a position for him as a commander of the watch. After all, someone will need to replace Ehrhart.'

'What about Sterkel?' Stefan asked. 'We owe much to him.'

Castelguerre looked away, as if distracted. 'Sterkel was arrested three days ago,' he said. 'His cellars were brimfull of treasure looted from Ehrhart's house. The watch had been after for him for quite some time. Now they had the perfect excuse.'

'But where's the justice in that?' Stefan protested, hotly. 'Ehrhart was a traitor, probably a thief as well.

Sterkel and his men fought like heroes. If he profited from his valour, it was no more than he deserved.'

'He broke the law,' Castelguerre said firmly, shaking his head. 'And now the law will make him pay.'

'What will happen to him?'

Castelgeurre shrugged uncomfortably. 'The custom in Altdorf is for looters to be hung, is it not? I've offered as much as I can in mitigation. He may yet live to see out his life in prison.' He glanced up at Stefan. 'The law does not recognise fairness, Stefan. I regret it will not treat you fairly either.'

'We are both to leave the city,' Albrecht told Stefan, his voice flat and dispassionate. 'Exile, apparently, is to be our destiny.' He stood up with some difficulty, and walked to the window. A pale sky, streaked with blue, was breaking over Altdorf.

'However you judge me, I did what I did believing it was right.'

'Where will you go?' Stefan asked.

'Oh, that's all arranged,' Albrecht said. 'A chair awaits me at the university of Wurtbad. I'm told it's not a bad place, in its way. A little quiet, by all accounts. A place people go to be forgotten.' He laughed; a thin, sad sound. 'A place they go to die.'

'It won't be for ever,' Castelguerre told him.

Albrecht took a step towards the door then turned. 'How long is forever?' he mused. 'None of us will ever know.'

Stefan watched as he took his leave. He knew they would never meet again. Castelguerre had remained standing. Now he gestured to Stefan to follow him. 'I want a few words with you in private,' he said. 'But first, there is someone else who wants to speak with you.'

* * *

HE FOUND NATALIA Zucharov in a small walled garden hidden away behind the house. She was dressed in the long, emerald robe of one of the colleges of magic, and her dark hair flowed loose over her shoulders. She looked both older, and more child-like, than Stefan remembered. She turned, blinking in the early morning sun, then made space on the bench for Stefan to sit down. She glanced at him, neither animosity nor warmth in her eyes, then set down her book.

'You know, ever since I was a child, I've tried to see the world as a place of perfect symmetry. Absolute good, absolute evil. A place without doubts, or questions of what is right and what is wrong.'

'I've had that same struggle,' Stefan said, quietly. 'It never felt harder than it does now.'

'Ever since Alexei was lost, that perfect world has been falling apart,' she continued. 'Now I can't ever go back to that certainty I once had.'

'Would killing me have helped you hold onto your belief?'

Natalia hesitated. 'No,' she said at last. She gathered up the folds of her robe, and nervously smoothed out the heavy tresses with her hands. 'I wanted to tell you that I have revoked my vow of vengeance. You need no longer look for me over your shoulder.'

'I'm glad of that,' Stefan began. 'At least, I think I am.' They looked at each other for a moment; so close yet still so distant. On impulse, Stefan reached out a hand towards her, but Natalia immediately backed away.

'I'll tell you something,' she added. 'When Alexei first told me about the mysterious swordsman he had been keeping company with, I had a dream – a schoolgirl's dream of marrying the valiant hero, the knight who embodied all of my muddled ideals.' She looked directly into Stefan's eyes, as if to make sure he understood her meaning. 'But that will never be,' she said, emphatically. 'A schoolgirl's dream was all it ever was.'

'Natalia–'

'No,' she insisted. 'Let me finish. I need you to under-stand. I have forgiven you for what happened. As Shallya is my witness, I have even tried to understand. But I can't forget. Not ever.'

She stood up, and pressed her book under her arm. 'We must part, now and for evermore,' she said. 'Then perhaps, in time, we can say that the wounds have healed. As much as they will ever heal.'

They stood for a few moments in the sheltered warmth of the garden, two people together and yet utterly alone.

At last Stefan said, 'What will happen to you now?'

'Now?' Natalia replied. 'Now, I carry on. Apparently I am allowed to return to my studies at the college of magic. Someone has put in a good word for me. They have convinced the collegiate that my errant behaviour should be pardoned, if not condoned. I have a future, so they tell me.'

'You will be a good magician,' Stefan told her. 'One of the very best.'

Natalia blushed, almost imperceptibly. 'I have Castelguerre to thank for that chance, I think.' She folded her hands across her breast and took a step towards the gate.

'Goodbye, Stefan. I wish I could say we'll meet again in happier times. But I know that we will not.'

She turned, without waiting for a reply, and walked away.

CASTELGUERRE RE-JOINED STEFAN shortly afterwards. They walked for a while along the narrow paths that twisted through the garden. The Bretonnian was in a solemn mood. 'What Albrecht said is true, I'm afraid, Stefan. You will have to leave the city. And I cannot say when you may be able to return.'

'I'm not sure I could have stayed, even if I had the choice. Altdorf feels empty after Mikhal's death. It's as if I've lost my home for a second time.'

The two men walked together, keeping the same gentle pace. 'Do you remember what I said to you after the battle of Erengrad?' Castelgeurre asked. 'When I asked if you would join the Keepers of the Flame? The offer is still open.'

Stefan stopped and turned to look at him, incredulous. 'After all that's happened?' he asked. 'But how could that be? You said yourself the order has been discredited, its ranks decimated.'

'The order itself, yes,' Castelguerre agreed. 'But the Keepers of the Flame is more than an order. The Keepers of the Flame is here, Stefan.' He touched a finger to his brow. 'And it is there, in your soul, and in the soul of all who continue to struggle for the light. It is a spirit, a belief. It's a thirst for justice that can never be quenched.'

He took Stefan's arm. 'I meant what I said about the war. Things are not going as well as we would have the people believe. But the tide will turn. We shall prevail, if we have men of honour and valour in our ranks. Men like you, Stefan.'

Stefan glanced at his companion. 'You're asking me to join your army at the front?'

Castelguerre nodded. 'I am.'

'How much time do I have to decide?'

'No time. You must decide here and now.'

Stefan hesitated, but only briefly. 'Then my answer is yes,' he said. 'Even after all that has happened,' he said. 'As long as I draw breath, I shall hold my sword ready to do battle for the cause.'

They had reached the end of the path. Castelguerre stood back to let Stefan pass. 'We leave at dawn tomorrow,' he told him. 'Any farewells you have must be made tonight.'

STEFAN MET WITH Bruno in the bar of the Helmsman. They sat at the corner table that they had occupied so many times in the past. They left a chair empty between them: Mikhal's place. For an hour or so they drank beer and talked, as far as possible, of old times, better times. At length, by unspoken consent, the conversation moved towards the future.

'I've heard there's a position in the watch for you, if you play your cards well,' Stefan said. Bruno raised his eyebrows, as if unable to quite grasp the idea.

'I heard as much, too,' he said. 'Imagine it. Me strutting about in uniform, my chest puffed out.' He laughed, embarrassed. 'You never know, though, I might just surprise them.' He glanced at Stefan. 'I might just say yes.' He made to sip his beer then stopped short, his mug suspended over the table.

'You're really going, aren't you?'

'Yes,' Stefan said. 'I'm really going.'

'When?'

'Tomorrow. First light.'

Bruno sipped half-heartedly at his beer then pushed it away, something weighing heavily on his mind. 'Stefan, a long time ago, I made you a promise. A promise to fight at your side, and to ride with you until the journey reached its end.'

'The journey has reached its end, old friend,' Stefan said, gently. He raised his mug, and bid Bruno drink with him. 'That journey's over. It's time for new journeys to begin. It's time to go our separate ways.'

Bruno tried to cheer up. He drained a good quantity of beer from the mug. 'Ah well, they say the war's all but done, anyway,' he said. 'I dare say you'll be turning back before you've even got there.'

'I dare say,' Stefan replied, smiling. 'I dare say I will.'

Bruno laughed and gathered up the empty mugs to fetch another round. 'We'll see them all out, won't we Stefan?'

'We'll be there right to the end,' Stefan agreed. 'You and I, and others like us. Fighters, soldiers, heroes all. We're the defenders of all that's true, you and I. We're the Keepers of the Flame.'

IT WAS RAINING by the time that Stefan left the Helmsman, a gentle but insistent rain washing the streets and alleyways of the old town clean. Stefan paused outside the tavern and looked around. Where would he go? He could go anywhere, and he could go nowhere. Finally he drew his cape up over his shoulders and set off briskly through the streets, past houses and shops he had known for half his life. As he headed north, he tried to fix it all in his mind – every brick, every facade, every passing face from the life he had known. But he knew that it was impossible. He knew that, in time, it would all begin to fade, vanishing into the distant mists of lost memory.

Everything, all of it, would pass. Nothing, in the end, would endure forever.

Coming soon from the Black Library

DARKBLADE: THE DAEMON'S CURSE

A Warhammer novel
by Dan Abnett and Mike Lee

THE SHADOWBLADE RODE the Sea of Malice with a winter gale at her back, her indigo-dyed sails of human hide stretched to their limit and the slate-gray sea hissing along her sharply-raked hull. Her druchii crew knew their trade well, gliding effortlessly along the pitching deck like hungry shades at the sibilant orders of their captain. They wore heavy robes and thick leather kheitans to keep out the icy wind, and their dark eyes glittered like onyx between folds of dark woollen scarves. They were racing before the storm with a full load of cargo chained below, but the craggy southern coastline and the mouth of the river leading to Karond Kar lay only a few miles off the bow. The wind howled hungrily in the black rigging, singing an eerie counterpoint to the muffled cries rising from the hold, and the sailors laughed in quiet, sepulchral tones, thinking back to the revels of the night before.

Malus Darkblade stood at the corsair's prow, one mailed hand resting on the ship's rail as he watched the sharp towers of the dark city rise before him. A heavy cloak of nauglir hide hung from his narrow shoulders and wisps of black hair spilled from the confines of a voluminous hood to twist and dance in the wind. The cold clawed at his face and he bared his teeth at its touch. The highborn pulled a carefully folded token from his belt and held it to his lips, breathing in its heady perfume. It smelled of blood and brine, setting his senses on edge.

This is the taste of victory, he thought, his lips twisting into a mirthless smile.

The raiding cruise had been a gamble from the outset, and he'd pushed his luck every step of the way. With only one small ship, an equally small crew and a late start hindering his efforts it wasn't enough to merely succeed; nothing short of a rousing triumph would impress his reluctant allies back at Hag Graef. So they had lingered along Bretonnia's western coast weeks after their peers had set course for home. The captain had complained bitterly about turning weather and the damnable Ulthuan Seaguard until Malus had put a knife to his throat and threatened to take command of the *Shadowblade* himself.

When a gale blew up in the dead of night off the shores of Couronne all had seemed lost, and six sailors had vanished beneath the black waves fighting to keep the wind and the sea from dashing the corsair against the rocks. But by dawn their luck had turned along with the wind; the coastal patrols had fared far worse than they, having been cast up on the rocks or blown down the long inlet towards the free city of Marienburg. In swift succession the raiders struck three villages along the coast and sacked the battered fort at Montblanc in four days of slaughter before escaping out to sea with a hold full of slaves and two chests brimming with gold and silver coin.

He would see to it that his backers were well paid for their efforts; it had been no small thing to find a highborn at the Hag willing to risk the ire of his family to lend the funds he needed for the voyage. After being stalemated for so long it was tempting to let the money flow through his hands like spilled blood, hiring assassins, tormentors and vauvalka to revenge himself on his brothers and sisters. Part of him yearned for an orgy of revenge, of torture and death and agonies that lingered beyond death. The need was sharp, like steel on the tongue, and sent a shiver of anticipation along his spine.

The darkness awaits, brothers and sisters, he thought, his eyes alight with menace. You've kept me from it far too long.

The darkly-stained deck creaked slightly and heeled a bit to starboard as the corsair settled onto a course aimed for the narrow river mouth leading to the City of Ships. Closer now, Malus could make out the tall, craggy towers of the sea gate rising on both banks of the narrow approach; a heavy iron chain stretched between them, just beneath the surface of the swift-running water. Cold mists clung to the rocky shore and the flanks of the towers, shifting and swirling before the wind.

From high in the corsair's rigging a sailor blew a hunting horn, its long, eerie wail echoing across the surface of the water. There came no reply, but Malus's skin prickled as he studied the thin arrow slits of the citadels and knew that predatory eyes were studying him in turn.

The highborn's ears caught a subtle change in the sound of the corsair's hissing wake, and faint sounds like a chorus of mournful spirits rising from the water near the hull.

He peered over the rail and his sharp eyes caught sleek, dark shapes gliding effortlessly just beneath the surface of the water. They passed in and out of view, vanishing into the icy depths as silently as ghosts, only to reappear again in the blink of an eye. As he watched, one of the figures rolled onto its back and regarded him with wide, almond-shaped eyes. Malus caught a glimpse of pale, almost luminous skin, a smooth belly and small, round breasts. Its face broke the surface with barely a ripple, water gleaming on high, sharp cheekbones and blue-tinged lips. *Aaaahhh*, it seemed to sigh, a thin, wavering sound, then it sank back into the depths, its lithe body surrounded by sinuous strands of indigo-colored hair.

'Shall I catch a fish for you, my lord?'

The highborn turned to find four cloaked figures standing just beyond sword's reach from him – proper hithuan for lieutenants and favoured retainers. The dual hilts of high-born swords rode high on their hips, and fine silversteel mail glinted in the weak afternoon light over black, grey or indigo kheitans. All of the druchii had their hoods up against the punishing, icy wind, save one. She was taller than her companions, her long, black hair woven in a multitude of long, thin braids and bound back into a corsair's topknot. Fine, white scars crisscrossed her oval face, from her high cheekbones to her pointed chin, and the tip of her right ear had been sliced away in a battle long ago. Three livid red cuts, fresh from the night's revels, ran in parallel lines down her long, pale neck, disappearing beneath the gleaming curve of a silversteel hadrilkar etched with the cold one sigil of Malus' house. As ever, there was a glint of mockery in Khetlan Silverblade's appraising stare. 'Will you have her for your plate, your rack or your bed?' Ravanna Ithil asked.

'Must I choose?'

The retainers laughed, a sound like bones rattling in a crypt. One of the hooded highborn, a druchii with sharp features and a shaven head save for a corsair topknot, arched a thin eyebrow. 'Do my lord's tastes run to beasts, now?' he hissed, drawing more cold chuckles from his companions.

The druchii woman shot her companion a sarcastic look. 'Listen to Dolthaic. He sounds jealous. Or hopeful.'

Dolthaic snarled, lashing out at the woman with the back of a mailed gauntlet that the tall raider batted easily aside.

Malus laughed along with the cruel mirth. The years of inaction had soured the spirits of his small warband, to the point where he'd begun to wonder which of them would try to assassinate him first. A season of blood and pillage had changed all that, sating their appetites for a time and promising a chance for more. 'Arleth Vann, how fares the cargo?' he asked.

'Well indeed, my lord,' spoke the third retainer, his sibilant whisper barely audible above the keening wind. The druchii's head was bald as an egg, and his face and neck were thin to the point of cadaverousness, like a man rendered down to corded muscle and bone by a long and merciless fever. His eyes were a pale yellow-gold, like those of a wolf. 'We had a small amount of spoilage on the return crossing, but no more than expected. Enough to keep the cook busy and give the survivors some meat in their stew to see them through the march to the Hag.'

The fourth retainer pulled back his hood and spat a thin stream of greenish juice over the rail. He was the very image of a druchii noble, with fine-boned features, a mane of lustrous black hair and a face that looked merciless even in repose. Like Malus, his cloak was made of nauglir hide, and his kheitan was expensive dwarf skin, tough but supple. The silversteel hadrilkar around his neck looked dull and tawdry against the fine craftsmanship of the noble's attire. 'That's still good coin lost needlessly,' Vanhir said, his rich and melodious voice all at odds with his stern demeanor. 'If we'd made port at Clar Karond, your backers would already have their investments repaid, and us besides,' he said, showing white teeth filed to fashionable points. 'The slave lords will not be pleased at the breach of custom.'

'The *Hanil Khar* is two days from now. I have no time to waste haggling with traders and flattering the whipmasters at the Tower of Slaves,' Malus hissed. 'I intend to stand in the Court of Thorns at the Hag, in the presence of my father and my... *illustrious* siblings,' he said, the words dripping with venom, 'and present the Drachau with a worthy tribute gift.' And show the court that I am a power to reckon with after all, he thought. 'We march for Hag Graef as soon as the cargo is ready to travel.'

Dolthaic frowned. 'But what of the gale? It will be a hard march to the Hag in the teeth of a winter storm–'

'We'll march through snow, ice and the Outer Darkness if we must!' Malus snapped. 'I will stand in the City of Shadow in two days' time or every one of you will answer for it.'

The retainers growled an acknowledgment. Vanhir studied Malus with narrowed eyes. 'And what then, after you've made your grand entrance and showered the Drachau with gifts? Back to the blood pits and the gambling dens?'

Dolthaic grinned like a wolf. 'After four months at sea I've got a thirst or two I wouldn't mind quenching.'

'I shall indulge myself for a time,' Malus said carefully. 'I have an image to maintain, after all. Then, I shall begin putting my new fortune to good use. There's much to be done.'

They were close enough to hear the booming of the waves against the shoreline, and the citadels of the sea gate loomed high above the *Shadowblade*, barely a mile ahead and to either side of the corsair's rakish bow. The gusting wind carried the sounds of a struggle aft. Malus looked back and saw three druchii warriors wrestling with a man-acled human slave. As the highborn watched, the slave smashed his forehead into the face of one of his captors. There was a *crunch* of cartilage and blood sprayed from the warrior's nose. The druchii staggered a half step back and raised a short-handled mace with a bubbling snarl.

'No!' Malus cried, his sharp, commanding voice carrying easily over the wind. 'Remember my oath!' The druchii warrior, blood streaming down his face and staining his bared teeth, caught the highborn's eye and lowered his weapon. Malus beckoned with a gauntleted hand. 'Bring him here.'

The slave wrenched his body violently, trying to tear free of his captors' grip. The mace-wielding druchii gave the human a shove, pushing him off his feet, and the other two warriors lunged forward, dragging the man across the deck. The four retainers slid aside to let them pass, eying the slave with cold, predatory interest.

The warriors forced the slave to his knees – even then, he rose nearly to the druchii's shoulders. He was powerfully built, with broad shoulders and lean, muscular arms beneath a torn, stained gambeson. He wore dark woollen breeches over ragged boots, and his hands were crusted with scabs and blue with cold. The man was young and bore more than one battle-scar on his face, possibly a yeoman or a Bretonnian squire. He fixed Malus with a hateful glare and began bleating something in his guttural tongue.

The highborn gave the human a disgusted look and nodded to the two warriors. 'Remove his chains,' he said, then
turned to Arleth Vann. 'Shut the beast up.'

The retainer glided across the deck, swift as a snake, and
grabbed the slave with a clawlike grip at the point where his
neck met his right shoulder. A steel-clad thumb dug into
the nerve juncture, and the slave's heated words vanished in
a sharp hiss, his whole body going taut with agony. There
was a soft rattle of metal, and the two druchii warriors
retreated, holding a set of manacles between them.

Malus smiled. 'Good. Now tell him what I have to say.'
He stepped before the slave, staring down into his pain-
filled eyes. 'Are you the one called Mathieu?'

Arleth Vann translated, almost whispering the thickly-
accented Bretonnian into the man's ear. Grunting with
pain, the slave nodded.

'Good. I have a rather amusing story to tell you, Mathieu. Yesterday, I stood at the entrance to the slaves' hold
and announced that, as a gesture of charity I would release
one of your number unharmed before we made port in
Naggaroth. Do you remember?'

A tumult of emotions flickered across the slave's eyes: hope,
fear and sadness, all tangled together. Again, he nodded.

'Good. You all talked among yourselves, and in the end
you chose a young girl. Slender and red-haired. Green eyes
like eastern jade and sweet, pale skin. You know of whom
I speak?'

Tears welled in the slave's eyes. He struggled vainly to
speak despite Arleth Vann's terrible grip.

'Of course you do,' Malus smiled. 'She was your
betrothed, after all. Yes, she told me this, Mathieu. She fell
to her knees and begged for you to go free in her place.
Because she *loved* you.' He chuckled softly, thinking back to
the scene. 'I confess, I was astonished. She said I could do
anything I wanted with her, so long as you went free. *Anything.*' He leaned close to the slave, close enough to smell
the fear-sweat staining his filthy clothes. 'So I put her to the
test.'

'Clar Karond was but a day away, and the crew deserved a reward for their labors, so I gave her to them. She entertained them for *hours*, even with their unsophisticated ways. Such screams… Surely you heard them. They were *exquisite.*'

Malus paused for a moment as Arleth Vann struggled for the right translation, though by this point the slave's eyes had glazed over, fixed on some distant point only he could see. His muscular body trembled. 'After the crew was spent they returned her to me, and I let my lieutenants take their turn.' Off to the side, Khetlyn grinned and whispered something to Dolthaic, who smiled hungrily in return. 'Again, she did not disappoint. *Such* pleasures, Mathieu. Such sweet skin. The blood sparkled across it like tiny rubies.' He held out the token in his cupped hand, unfolding it gently and reverently. 'You were a very lucky man, Mathieu. She was a gift fit for a prince. Here. I saved you her face. Would you like one last kiss before you go?'

With a shriek of perfect anguish the slave surged to his feet, but Arleth Vann lashed out with his other hand and sank his fingertips into the nerve juncture beneath the thick muscle of the human's upper right arm. The slave staggered, unmanned by blinding pain. His eyes were wide, and Malus could see the darkness there, spreading into the human's mind like a stain. The slave let out a despairing wail.

'Wait, Mathieu. Listen. You haven't heard the really amusing part yet. By the time the crew was done with her she was begging, *pleading* to be set free instead of you. She cursed your name and renounced her love for you again and again. But of course, I had my oath to consider – I said I would let a slave go *unharmed*, you see, and that hardly applied to her any more. So in the end her *love* won out, and oh, how she hated it!' Malus threw back his head and laughed. 'Enjoy your freedom, Mathieu.'

All at once Arleth Vann changed his grip on the man, seizing him by the neck and the belt of his breeches, and with surprising strength the lithe druchii picked the large man off the deck and threw him over the rail. He hit the water with a loud, flat *slap* and disappeared into the freezing depths. The druchii slid along the rail, watching intently. The wind whistled and howled, but the sighing of the mere-witches had fallen silent.

When the man surfaced, gasping for air, he was no longer alone. Two of the sea creatures clung to him, wrapping their thin, pale arms around his chest. Ebon talons sank deep, drawing blooms of crimson across the white fabric of the man's gambeson. Thick indigo strands – not rich hair, but ropy, saw-edged tentacles – wrapped around wrist and throat, sloughing off long strips of skin as they wound tightly around their victim.

Mathieu choked out a single, gulping scream before one of the mere-witches covered his open mouth with her own, then they sank beneath the surface and were lost in the *Shadowblade's* wake.

A rattling, ringing sound filled the air ahead – the citadels were lowering the great chain barring entrance to the river. Tendrils of icy sea mist, drawn by the corsair's passage, rolled in on either side of the river mouth, whirling and tangling in their wake. High atop the tower to the left, Malus could see lithe figures in dark robes and billowing scarves appear at a small cupola to observe their progress. They offered no sign of greeting, no gesture of welcome, merely watched in stony silence. As the ship cleared the river chain, one of the figures raised a horn to his lips and blew a long, wailing note, warning the City of Ships of the bloody-handed reavers heading their way.

Malus Darkblade turned back to his retainers, a slow, heartless smile spreading across his face.

'It's good to be home.'

The story continues in
DARKBLADE
THE DAEMON'S CURSE
Coming soon from The Black Library

READ TILL YOU BLEED

DO YOU HAVE THEM ALL?